Joe

To my Brother Who
has always Been There
And Supported Me

to my Little Brother
THANK you for Your Support

W.IS.E.

WORLD INTERPLANETARY
SPACE EXPLORATION

W.IS.E.

World
Interplanetary Space
Exploration

FROZEN WORLD

Daniel Gencur

Contents

This is dedicated to my wife, family, and friends who have supported me and inspired me to tell this story, as well as those friends and family who are not here to see this story published.

One

2242 A.D.

Renee

There, I was lost in deep thought about how the allure of the unknown was strong in the darkness of space. Many followed the call to sign on to the first space vessel they could find. The first ships that most people would join were the ones that would consist of short errands between planets before moving on to the big boys. Most people yearned for deep space vessels. Those that could make it to those missions had to endure years in space. Some people I heard called it a hardship; I called it a challenge. Most civilians called it an honor, being on an adventure with so many new unexplored places. Those explorers who made their way onto those missions became family. At least that's what I've come to call everyone on my ship, the Star Rider. Most crew members had been with me for more than two or more missions. Each mission lasted about three to five years before returning home. After a couple of months at home to restock the ship and do some upgrades, the ship heads back out into space.

Thinking of the planet we were investigating reminded me of home—a small planet that roamed around the sun. I was looking out of the windows, pondering my morning thoughts, when the sun shone brightly on my ship. It caused a glare, and it glistened in the light. There were several windows on the Star Rider, but I liked to look out the ones toward the front of the ship on an upper deck on the bridge.

I stared out the window and looked at my reflection. I saw a strong woman who was in her late fifties with blonde hair and was starting to have gray hair, or what others called them to be wisdom-highlights. My eyes were ice blue, and I could stare anyone down when needed. I had an athletic frame and was considered lean. My stature was five feet ten inches, and I weighed about a hundred and seventy-five pounds.

I recalled my fast-track career to Captain. I worked on any freighter that took to the skies. I was known to be a leader. My love for deep space grew with my time in the unknown depths. I remember when I couldn't wait to have my own ship, and I worked anywhere I could. I finally was able to join a crew and became their third officer. After several months of being on a mission, the second officer died in an accident on a distant planet. With that, I earned the promotion and was one step closer to my goal. Three years passed, and several others retired; thus, I was given command of the ship.

I searched far and wide to recruit some of the best in their fields. That was twenty-eight years ago, and this was my home now. No planet could give me the thrill of being in space.

After staring out the window for a few more moments, I inhaled deeply to ready myself for the trouble the day might bring. I walked toward the bridge's center and felt the worry lines crease on my forehead. I couldn't let my crew see how uneasy I was about having a team on a surface with no backup shuttle in case something were to go wrong. I needed to know why the other shuttle had yet to be repaired; our equipment needed to be top-notch. I wanted to cancel the mission due to the lack of equipment. I couldn't deter the mission because this might be the last planet we visit before returning home. No matter how bad I wanted to.

The team had been on the surface for four days and nights, and this was the rise of the fifth day. The team was due to return today, and once they were safely onboard, I could finally relax and enjoy the smooth ride toward home.

I walked around the bridge to access my commands. Located in the front of the bridge is where the pilot sits with their back toward the main bridge. They sit in front of a console and a switchboard with multiple lights and switches to command the flying vessel. In the upper right corner of the console, there was a display screen with mapped star charts. Over in the left corner was another display containing information about the ship's assessments. The two main science stations were to the left of the pilot's chair, where a few lights lit up on the consoles. Above the consoles were three different monitors, all spewing further information. It was up to the science monitor to determine the best way to interpret the data and relay it to the crew. To the right of the council were eight more displays. These were used to relay information from outside the ship, such as missions to planets or asteroids or when one needed to be on the spacewalk. When not used during missions, the screen played different areas of the ship for security purposes. My chair was in the center of the bridge. There were two small consoles to the left and right of my chair. Each one had two smaller displays that allowed me to see any information needed without leaving my post. There were other stations along the back wall of the bridge, and they were used to monitor other ship systems. To my right was the communications console manned around the clock whenever someone was outside or off the ship.

I walked toward my chair and nodded at everyone at their stations. I waited a moment for everyone to continue to work. Mostly, everybody would wait for me to release them back to their duties with a simple nod unless there was some emergency on the ship.

"Communications, have they left the surface of the planet yet?" I asked in a somber voice

The communications officer turned in his chair and replied, "According to their last transmission, they are working on loading their gear onto the shuttle. They should lift off to return to the ship in about twenty minutes. Once they lift off, they should be back onboard in about an hour."

I turned my chair toward him and asked, "What's the delay? I thought that they should be on their way back by now."

"I was told from the ground that someone left some equipment at site six."

"Who did they send to retrieve that equipment?"

"Sam and Lisa were sent in the rover with Pops driving."

"That's not a rover. That is one of the electric hot rods that Pops has been working on." I said while trying not to show my irritation.

I had a sinking suspicion that nobody left anything behind. I knew Pops had used this rover before and liked to play in it when he could. I also knew he had been working on another rover that he had hoped to take on this trip but needed more time to finish. I tried to imagine what was going on down there, and part of me wished that I could go down there and join them. I thought about calling them and yelling but decided to let it slide for now since this was the last planet they would visit before they turned for home. During the long trip home, they would spend most of their time analyzing and cataloging the samples they had collected.

Little did Pops know that I could turn on the microphone and camera on his outer space sportscar at any time. I flipped the switch on my control panel, and in seconds, a clear image of the three was in perfect view.

I could only hear the whining from the vehicle at first. I was able to see Pops, whose real name was Frederick Brutiss. Nobody actually called him that. Pops was an old-timer when it came to space travel. He had first gone into space when the first planets were just starting to be explored. He was in his early seventies, stood six foot tall, and weighed about two hundred and five pounds. His hair was completely gray. Nobody was actually sure of his age, just what the rumors were. His career on the vessel was as an explosives expert, and he loved to blow stuff up. From the passenger's side sat Sam and Lisa. Sam Hauzer was a computer hardware and electronics specialist. He was a young man in his mid-thirties. He weighed about one hundred and seventy-five pounds and stood about five foot ten inches tall with short brown hair cut as military style. Lisa was also in her mid-thirties and usually had long blonde hair back in a ponytail with brown eyes. She stood about five foot ten and weighed about one hundred and fifty pounds, a little less than me. She had what some would call an athletic build due to her rigorous training schedule. She was so beautiful that men would chase after her from time to time. Her position was as a computer programmer. Sam excelled with the electronics, but she excelled with the programming. They made a great team. Whatever the problems were, if they involved programming and electronics, then they could solve them.

"You know, we were rarely able to find a planet so similar to Earth," Lisa shouted over the rover's whining.

"Kind of reminds me of home," Sam said

"Yeah, except how the light is more yellow than home. There isn't a lot of grass. The ground was a sandy substance, with more vegetation across the surface. Overall, it's an open area," Lisa countered.

The whining sound continued until they reached their destination. The three of them climbed out, and I could see dust trying to settle around them. I could no longer see them, but they were still within hearing distance. They are all laughing.

"That was awesome! I wish we didn't have to go back so soon. This will probably be the last time we can have some fun. Most of the planets and asteroids we land on don't have a surface we could roam on," Sam said with excitement.

"That was so fun! I agree with Sam. I wish that we didn't have to go back so soon." Lisa piped in

I didn't have to see him, but Pops was grinning ear to ear and remarked, "If you think this rover is fun, you should take a ride with me on the other rover that I'm working on. That one is going to have some real power."

"I know we took this trip just to have fun, but what will we do when we return without the equipment we allegedly came out here to get?" Lisa said

Pops laughed, "I have that covered." I heard clanking around the back of the rover. "Here is the equipment that we came here to get."

They all stay out of view of the camera and laugh briefly. They finally walk into view and climb back into the rover for their return trip. While hanging on, Sam glanced down at the radio and was surprised to see the Captain on the camera.

★ ★ ★ ★ ★ ★ ★ ★ ★ ★ ★ ★ ★

Annette

I stared at the schematics of the ship. Under the belly of the vessel was a loading platform in which crew members waited for the rover to return. I usually loved to be down, waiting eagerly for the other's return. Listening to the crewmates talk about what they had accomplished on this mission. Inside of the shuttle was a cargo bay, which held the rover and the rest of the gear and samples stowed away. The bridge was small and only made for three to four crew members. Typically, there were only three on the bridge. The pilot, co-pilot, and someone to man the science and communications station. For this mission, there were two women plus me on the bridge.

I sat at the communications station quietly, reading the latest news from home. This was going to be my last mission into space. I had already made up my mind to stay on Earth and retire. I looked over toward the pilot's chair, and Kellie Bricks was kicked back and relaxing while we waited. I often observed that her long, dark hair was almost perfect. Her eyes were chocolate brown, and stood about five foot seven inches and weighed about one hundred and forty pounds. She was one of the ship's pilots and the newest member. I had heard rumors that Kellie had never dreamt of working in space, and her reason for working here now differed from most people's. The love of her life left her to explore the dark beauty of space. She discovered space's attraction and tried to follow her ex-lover's trail. Watching her work was remarkably beautiful, as she was a naturally gifted pilot. I followed her career; she had started with older freighters on short runs and worked her way up. Now, we were on the same ship.

Carla Kruft was in the co-pilot's seat. Like Kellie, she was a young, gifted pilot. Unlike Kellie, she had dreamed of going into space since she was little. She talked about it whenever she could and reminisced about her childhood whenever possible. She was slim, with blonde hair and a blue-eyed heartbreaker. She was in it for romance and adventures more than a job. I listened as she typed away on the computer, which wasn't unusual.

The tapping on the keyboard finally got my attention. I glanced over to Carla and watched her vigorously typing. On the screen, I saw a picture of a guy on one side and the words she typed on the other. I watch as Carla presses send, another picture of a guy appears on the screen, and I watch as the messages continue. Like the last one, Carla pushed send, another guy's image appeared, and Carla began the cycle repeatedly. I watched and was fascinated to see Carla go from one guy to the next. Some of the guys were dressed casually, some were dressed professionally, and others were dressed provocatively. I slowly stood up and quietly walked toward Carla, who never took her eyes off the screen. When I get near, I can't help but be intrigued by the images, and I can no longer stay quiet.

"Do you actually know all of these guys?" I asked.

Carla stopped typing and turned to me. "I know a few and have met a couple, but most of them are just men who have left me a message on my website."

I'm somewhat shocked and reply jokingly, "You have a website? Why do you have a website?"

She shrugged and replied, "I thought everyone who came here had a website. Don't you?"

I shook my head no, "I never had a reason to set one up. Why did you?"

Carla smiled wryly, "Why, Annette Armstell, for someone five foot five, has brown hair and is only in her late forties. You should have a website to connect with others. Long story short, there was a guy that I used to like back home who wanted to follow my journey. One thing led to another, and some guys found out about my page. The next thing I know, I'm popular. I have about eight hundred followers writing to me all the time. Some want to know about life out here, and others ask how to start their adventures into space. Then you have the ones that ask how to be my boy toy once I arrive back on Earth."

"Doesn't it bother you having these strangers sending you inappropriate messages?" I asked.

"Yeah, at first. Then I started really looking at the pictures. It can get your blood pumping just by looking and imagining what images could do, if you know what I mean." Carla pushed a few keys to open a file with pictures of men.

"Wow." My eyes widen as I can't help but stare at the pictures

I noticed Kellie sitting in her chair, eyes closed, and quietly resting during our conversation. She opened her eyes and looked into mine. She looked curious and leaned over to see what had stirred us up. She raised her eyebrows and smiled in approval.

I glanced over to see Kellie looking at the pictures and nodding approvingly. " It looks like the ice is melting, and Kellie approves."

Carla looked at Kellie and then commented, "She may approve of these guys, but she's not interested. You could put her in a room with all these guys, and no one would stand a chance with her."

"Are you trying to tell me that she isn't interested in men?" I asked in a low voice so Kellie couldn't overhear.

Kellie sat up, turned to them, and asked, "What makes you think that, Carla?"

"I heard about you when I was in pilot training. Most women would love to have guys chasing them. There was one pilot instructor that told me the story about you. How you broke his heart to chase after a guy who left you to go work in space. He would give you anything you wanted, but you wouldn't have it. You had your mind made up on finding that one special guy," Carla explained.

"Was the trainer handsome?" I asked, trying to diffuse the situation.

"Yes, he was, and he was rich too," Carla replied

I looked at Kellie, surprised. "You turned down a good-looking, rich guy to come out here. Are you crazy?"

Kellie shrugged and answered, "He just wasn't my type."

"What kind of person are you looking for?" I asked Kellie.

"There is more out there than just money and good looks," Kellie replied softly.

"Yeah, I heard that she is more into the intellectual type of person. In fact, that person is a member of our crew." Carla adds

"Are you serious? Please tell me who," I asked with uncontrolled excitement.

"Rumor has it, Sam," answers Carla. "He was the reason that she came out here."

"I can't believe it. I never would have thought you would ever be a couple. Besides, isn't he seeing someone else? How do you know this?" I asked in disbelief.

Kellie had a severe look on her face as Carla continued to tell her story. I wonder if there was something that Carla knew that Sam might have told her.

"As I mentioned, I heard about them in pilot training. It's a story that is passed from class to class. As far as Sam seeing someone else, I'm not really sure. I have heard some rumors about who it might be. There are a lot of rumors on a ship like ours. In fact, there are a few rumors that he got Kellie her job on the ship and that they even tried again, but it didn't work." Carla continued.

"Is any of this true, Kellie? Did Sam get you this position?" I asked

Kellie did a small, polite smile, then smirked. "Yes, it's true. We did have a relationship, and we still do. Sam helped me get the position when the ship I was piloting was decommissioned. We started to re-kindle our relationship, but because of the time that had passed, we decided to step back a while to give each other some room."

"How long were you apart before you got together on this ship?" I asked in confusion

"We were apart for about twelve years, but I know we'll be together," Kellie answered.

Carla raised her eyebrows and looked at me before saying, "I thought I heard that he was seeing Lisa."

Kellie's expression tightened as she heard the name.

I watched as Kellie's mind was churning. As though she had suspected the rumors to be true.

She bit her tongue and said, "He is only friends with her. They work together a lot, and I can see how everyone can conclude they are a couple. "

At that moment, she glanced outside, and the rover was coming back. Kellie stood up and stated, "There they are. We can finally get the rover loaded and return to the ship. I'm going down below to get the ship buttoned up once they are onboard so we can get underway as soon as possible. Let the Captain know we will be underway as soon as we secure the rover." She turned and went down the stairs to the lower deck.

Carla and I were stunned by Kellie's reaction. I could tell by the tone of her voice that she was jealous of Lisa. Something about the way she moved and the look she gave them made me feel uneasy.

"That sounds like an obsessed person to me. I would hate to be Sam with her around." Carla stated as she looked at me.

"I know what you mean. She's been in space too long. When a person gets to that point, they are scary and can be dangerous to those around them." I added

"Another rumor was that multiple complaints have been filed with the Captain. Up until now, I thought that they were just rumors. After seeing the look in her eyes and hearing her, I can see why some people have complained about her."

"If the Captain's smart, she would replace her once we return home."

I returned to my station, let Carla return to work, and prepared the ship for lift-off. I watched outside the shuttle via cameras. The crew members who had been hanging out to enjoy the planet were now returning to the shuttle while the cargo door closed and was secured. After the last crew member boarded the shuttle, the crew ramp was closed, and the shuttle was ready for takeoff.

The shuttle sat quietly in the field, ready for takeoff. The silence was broken by the engines powering up, getting louder and louder. After a few moments, the shuttle began to lift into the air. It was slow at first as it climbed higher and higher. Once the shuttle was high enough, the rear engines were engaged, and the shuttle began moving forward at an upward angle.

I watched from the cameras as the planet became smaller and smaller as it rose into the sky. The shuttle soon exited the planet's atmosphere and began the journey to rendezvous with the ship. The trip doesn't take long as their ship is soon in sight. They make a few course adjustments as they line up with the ship to land. The shuttle's forward momentum slows as it enters the ship's landing bay. Once in position, the ship slowly descended until the landing gear touched the deck.

Dust that was kicked up in the air was quickly vented. Soon, the engines go silent, and the shuttle is home. There is a pause as the landing bay doors close, and a small tow crane locks onto the shuttle and moves it to a shuttle pad. Once the shuttle is safely detached, it is raised up to the deck above where it was stored. As the shuttle was being placed into the bay, there was a pause while the area was pressurized. I glanced back toward Kellie and watched as she waited for a green light indicating that the bay was pressurized; she pushed a button to lower the crew ramp. We all watch the monitor with excitement as the crew departs the shuttle. I noticed that she watched closely as Sam and Lisa left the shuttle, walking side by side. She didn't take her eyes off them until they left the bay to head for the medical bay for the mandatory checkup after every mission.

✶✶✶✶✶✶✶✶✶✶✶✶✶

Sam

Lisa and I slowly walked toward the medical bay for our post-mission checkup. We laughed and joked about things that happened during this mission. As we approached the door to the medical bay, it opened automatically to allow us to enter. I saw other crew members from the mission already there getting checked out. One nurse directed us toward two open beds where we would wait our turn to be examined.

There were usually three nurses in total before the Doctor examined us. The first nurse took our vitals, the next was for blood drawing, and the third was for medication disbursement, including a vaccine. After we had been triaged, the Doctor would come through, close the curtains for privacy, and give us an individual checkup.

I really liked the Doctor. She was an attractive lady in her late forties with red hair and green eyes. She had a Southern charm and an anger that, when invoked, would make anyone run for cover. She was very good at her job, enjoyed the quiet, and had a suitable bedside manner regarding health concerns from working in space.

Lisa and I were still laughing at a joke I had said until something caught my eye. I looked over, and the laughing suddenly stopped as I saw Pops standing there with his head bowed. Beside him stood the Captain, and I could tell instantly that she wasn't happy.

She pushed Pops into our area and yelled, "What the hell were the three of you thinking when you drove off to have one last drive across the surface?" She paused momentarily, and the crew members sitting near us quickly approached another part of the room. "You must think that I'm stupid up here or something? I know for a fact you didn't go after any equipment."

Lisa looked at me, and I turned to look at Pops, and he just raised his eyebrows and shrugged his shoulders, trying for an omission of guilt.

"I don't know how you three thought you would get away with it. We had you on our sensors and could see you with our cameras. We saw you jumping that rover over those hills."

Lisa interrupts and says, "Actually, it was Pops that was...."

"Shut up! I don't want to hear who is to blame!" the Captain shouted as she stopped Lisa from speaking. "As far as I am concerned, you are all to blame. I ordered everyone to pack it up and return to the ship. I didn't say the three of you could go out for one last joyride." She looked at Pops and asked, "Doesn't anyone have something to say?"

Pops took a deep breath and started, "I can only say...."

"Enough!" The Captain shook her finger at Pops and continued, "I expected so much more from you. You are older than these two. I expected you to have used a little more common sense. If you had wrecked that rover, we would have been out a vital piece of equipment. Not to mention that any of you could have been hurt or even killed for some senseless joy ride. Then, I am responsible for all of you and the equipment." She turned to me and asked, "You have been unusually quiet. Do you have anything that you want to say?"

I glanced at Lisa, who was petrified, then looked at Pops, who, for once, was saddened by his actions. I looked at the Captain and asked, "Can we get a copy of the video you took of us on the surface?"

Stunned by his question, she stared back at me before she threw her hand in the air and stormed off. We all watched her storm away, mumbling and cursing as she went. When she finally cleared the medical bay, the three of us laughed. Other crew members in the medical bay looked over at us with grins on their faces.

"I can't believe that you even asked her for that. The way that she looked at you after you asked her made me think that she was going to strangle you," said Lisa as she slapped my arm.

"The Captain was only yelling at us because she had to. She had no intention of disciplining us for that. I can imagine that deep down, she probably wished that she was down there driving that rover." I shook my head and laughed

"I'm going to give some advice, Sam. So far, you have been lucky with the Captain. One of these days, you will push her too far, and luck will run out. She is going to have to really discipline you. We were lucky that she didn't suspend us. So just take my advice because I don't want to be around when your luck runs out." Pops shook his head as he prepared to leave.

"Well, Pops, that's good advice, but luck has nothing to do with it," I tell him.

Pops looked puzzled, but then he shrugged his shoulders. Lisa and I step off the beds and are just a few steps behind him as he leaves the medical bay.

✶✶✶✶✶✶✶✶✶✶✶✶✶

Renee

I returned to my quarters and headed straight for my desk chair. I'm still frustrated with Sam and his attitude. I leaned back and inhaled deeply, and all my troubles seemed to disappear.

After a few minutes of no emotional expression, I snickered at my thoughts; I asked myself, "Can I get a copy of that video? Only you, Sam, could think of something like that while getting yelled at. What am I going to do with you?"

I leaned forward in my chair and turned on the screen before me. I punched a few keys on the keyboard to bring up my messages and typed in my username and password to access them. The first item of every message I looked at was the sender. I noticed one from my daughter back home and opened it first. I skim through the message before clicking on the attachments. They were pictures of my grand-daughter, bringing a smile to my face and heart. I switched back to my mailbox and noticed one from the Central Command. I opened it next and began to divulge the information it contained. I was surprised and delighted with the news inside.

I leaned back in my chair again to ponder. I abruptly leaned forward and pressed the intercom button, "Bridge, this is the Captain."

"This is the bridge; go ahead, Captain," A male voice on the intercom replied.

"If we remain on this course and speed for the next month as planned, is there anything that needs to be looked at?" I asked

"Give us a moment, Captain," responded the bridge. After a minute or two of silence, the voice returned, "According to what we can determine, there's nothing but open space out there."

I was quiet for a moment while making my decision. I loved being in space, but sometimes, I wished we didn't have to return home. I didn't feel that way after this voyage. A new family member was back home—a granddaughter I wanted to meet. Thinking about retirement not being too far off, there were only a few missions left before stepping down. After retiring, there would be a severe adjustment period back on Earth.

"Turn the ship around and set a course for home." I exhaled a breath of relief.

"Yes, Captain, right away." The voice bellowed with enthusiasm.

Before he disconnected the communication, I heard, "Helm, you heard the Captain. Turn us around and set a course for home." There was a roar of cheering on the bridge.

I smiled as the thrill of heading home settled deep inside me. I had an excellent crew, and the company finally noticed their work. I was overly proud to have the opportunity to work with them.

Sam

The crew enjoyed their meal and chatted with friends in the mess hall. Lisa sat at my table. Like the rest of the crew on the latest mission, we enjoyed the peace and quiet. This was our first authentic meal since we had returned. Lisa and I started to discuss our relationship and what we would do when we returned home.

"Sam, have you thought about where we're going once we get back?" Lisa asked excitedly.

I nodded with a mouth full of food. In between bites, I replied. "I've really given it some thought, and I think a Pacific Island getaway would be amazing." I replied.

"I can almost imagine being there. The nice warm sand under our feet and in between our toes. The wind blowing through our hair with the sound of the ocean all around us." Lisa stated dreamily.

"That'll be a welcomed relief from the recirculated air and the squeaky fan motor of this ship."

'When we return home and look at the stars, do you think we'll ever look at them the same? After being out here, will we look at them differently than someone who stayed on Earth?" Lisa smiled and asked.

"I don't know; we might look at them differently. After all, we have been out here and set foot on a few of them." I shrugged as I continued to eat.

Lisa swallowed her bite of food and changed the subject. "Have you talked with Kellie yet?"

I swallowed my food with a gulp and set down my fork before answering, "No, I haven't. We were busy down on the planet, and she was busy shuttling between the ship and the planet. Besides, we're just friends."

Lisa nodded and said, "I'm not so sure about that. I think that she might feel a little different about you than you feel about her. You've had a relationship with her in the past, and you did get her a job on this ship. She might feel that this was your way of telling her that you were still interested. Besides, I would really feel better if I knew that you had talked to her about us." Lisa replied.

"Like I said before, that was a long time ago. We're just friends. I helped her get her job onboard this ship because they decommissioned her old ship, and we needed a pilot. I will admit that I thought we could start our relationship back up, but I quickly realized that too much time had passed, and those feelings were no longer there, and I think that she knows that."

"Well, you might not have any feelings for her and think that she has none for you, but I think you are wrong," says Lisa.

"What makes you think she still has feelings for me?" I asked curiously.

"I'm surprised you haven't noticed how she looks at you or how she happens to show up where you are."

"I didn't notice that." Surprised, I paused momentarily before continuing, "If she always shows up where I am, then where is she now?"

Motioning with her head, she replies, "She's right over your right shoulder in the corner."

Humoring her, I glanced over my right shoulder and was surprised to see Kellie in the corner. I suddenly remembered Kellie fighting with a woman after she had spoken with me. That was a long time ago, and I'm sure she is a different kind of person now.

I slowly turned back toward Lisa, "Ok, you win. I will talk to her when we turn the ship and head for home." I guess that was a safe decision because it would give me some time before I would have to face Kellie.

Before Lisa could say anything, an announcement sound came over the intercom system, and the screens around the room came to life. On the screen appeared the Captain. Everyone quieted down to listen to what she had to say. Most announcements were just announced over the intercom system. The only time that she used the video monitors was when she had something very important to say.

A few moments of quietness passed on the screen, and she did not speak to let everyone quiet down. She finally began to speak, "A short time ago, I received a message from home. Headquarters was very pleased with the work we have done. They stated they were excited and looking forward to our return home. We have exceeded their expectations. I was very proud when I read that. Being the Captain of such a fine crew has been my honor. With the declaration of this mission being a success, I have been given the option of turning this ship around and heading home early. As some of you may have noticed, the ship has begun to turn. A few moments ago, I gave the word to set a course for home. You have all done a fantastic job and deserve the early return home. That is all."

Loud cheering erupted from everyone in the mess hall, and more cheers could be heard throughout the ship. Everyone had worked long and hard on this mission, and a casual flight back was a welcomed thought for all. I couldn't believe we would be on extended leave when we got back because everyone knew that the ship was due for a refit and would be at the shipyard for at least two years.

I was smiling at Lisa, but that smile quickly disappeared when I saw the serious look on her face. I wondered what it was that I could have done in such a short amount of time.

After a few moments of silence from her and hearing people talk about what they will do when they get home, I finally ask Lisa, "What?"

She looks at me seriously and says, "I seem to recall you saying that you would talk to Kellie when the Captain announces that we are turning for home. Well, she just made the announcement."

I bowed my head and admitted, "I did say that." I looked her in the eyes and continued, "In my defense, I thought we weren't going to get that announcement for at least another month."

"Another month or not, you said that you would talk to her before we got back so that we could get married. I'm not going to stand for any excuses," Lisa replied, looking back into my eyes.

"I promise I will talk to her at the earliest possible moment,"

I started to think about the wedding planning and for a few moments decided to change the subject.

"You know, I may never be able to find out who my father is, but I wish he could be at our wedding," I told Lisa.

"Sam, you were adopted at a young age and may never get all of the answers you are looking for, especially since you work out in space." Lisa paused before asking, "Did your mother ever tell you?"

"It took me a long time to find my real mother. Now that I found her, I feel she wants to tell me, but for some reason, she doesn't want to tell me yet."

We both stood up to put our trays away. As we set our trays down for washing, we continued our discussion. We then left the mess hall and headed for my quarters.

"We have a lot of things to do before we get back," stated Lisa.

"We could always just have the Captain marry us," I said, smiling.

"Are you serious? You know that I am looking forward to the big wedding." Lisa smacked my arm.

"I know you are. I'm just kidding."

"One of these times, you are going to say something like that, and I am going to knock you on your ass."

"Yeah, well, until that day arrives, I'll keep on doing it so I can make you smile."

✶✶✶✶✶✶✶✶✶✶✶✶✶✶

Jason

I tried to assist Phil in the shuttle bay as he moved the shuttle to its storage spot. It had taken most of the shift to unload all the samples brought back from the surface. I didn't like that it was now the end of the shift for us to finally put away the shuttle.

The Captain's announcement excited everyone, and I wanted to relish the shenanigans in the mess hall.

We had been using an electric tug similar to the ones used to move aircraft on Earth. While at the controls, I let the rookie operator, Phil, talk me into letting him assist with furthering his education. He tried to rush the process, as he couldn't wait to partake in the merriment from the exciting news of returning home.

I tried to give him directions as he maneuvered the shuttle into position. I had moved hundreds of shuttles, but this was my first attempt with a larger one. Unlike most crew members, I believed in allowing others to learn new responsibilities. What if something happened and nobody knew how to operate a specific system? I was a true believer in cross-training.

When he reached a certain point, I motioned for Phil to stop the controls. After it stopped, I walked from the rear toward the front and began looking over the shuttle and the surrounding area as I approached the tug. I stopped because I noticed a welding cart that could be a problem and in the way of backing the shuttle into position. I walked around, moved the cart, and continued instructing Phil about the tug.

Phil watched my every move and, when I was within range, asked, "Why did you stop me?"

I walked around, placed one foot on the step of the tug, and answered, "I stopped you because I wanted to go over a few things,"

"Why do we need to go over this every time I park a shuttle? I already know how to park," Phil stated with an attitude.

I was getting slightly upset with Phil. "You need to put that attitude of yours in check. Most crew members don't even get a chance to park shuttles until they are certified back on Earth through a six-month training and safety course. So, you had better consider yourself lucky to be given the opportunity I'm giving you now."

"You're right, I'm sorry." Phil bowed his head and apologized.

"I've parked hundreds of shuttles, all shapes and sizes, and I'm always open to criticism. The moment you think you know everything you need to know about parking shuttles is the day you need to get out from behind that wheel." I explained to him.

"Sorry, I understand that you're trying to teach me how to do this right."

"That's Good. Now it's time to teach you the difference between this tug and the other one you have been using."

"There doesn't seem to be that many differences except for the size and power of this tug." Phil looked around, taking in the differences.

I smiled and began to point and explain the differences in more detail. "You're correct, in a sense. However, this tug is for moving the larger shuttles. The difference between a small shuttle and these larger ones is your field of vision. This tug has three telescopic cameras connected to the roll cage's rear. There is one off each side and one off the top. They can be activated individually by pressing those three buttons." I pointed to the buttons under a smooth, flat, black panel above Phil's head that ran along the top roll bar.

Phil reached up and pressed the buttons that lit up; whirring sounds erupted from each camera arm unfolding. He turned around and watched each arm extend with the cameras on them. He looked to the right and then the left before finally examining the one on top.

Phil was utterly fascinated and managed, "Wow, now that's cool."

I smiled and continued my explanation. "Yes, now these three cameras will allow you to see your clearance on the sides and top as you park the shuttle." I saw they were fully extended. "Once fully extended, you need to press these three buttons," I said, pointing to the buttons on the right side under the flat black panel.

Phil pressed the three buttons that lit up like before, and three small monitors lit up along the flat panel. Each one was hooked up to a camera.

"Huh, never guessed there were monitors in that panel," Phil said with amazement.

"Now you have eyes around the shuttle that you must pay attention to while parking. You also need to pay attention to your spotter. In this case, that's me. I've got one last thing to point out; you may think that is obvious. This shuttle's bigger, wider, and heavier. With that in mind, you need to move slower and give yourself more room to stop."

"Blah, blah, blah, I get what you're saying. You have nothing to worry about."

I stepped back and started to guide him in. I turned to walk away and heard Phil mumbling to himself. "Like, I don't know that this is a bigger ship. He acts like I am an idiot."

While going in reverse, he aligned himself to straighten up the shuttle, and I saw something was wrong. It looked like he tried to push the brakes but had to stomp on them. Finally, he came to a slow stop. I heard more muttering but couldn't make out what was being said. Something about not being able to stop and park the shuttle correctly. I watched as he switched gears and moved the shuttle backward again. He kept focus on the three cameras and me for guidance.

I used my hands to signal him to park. Every once in a while, I had to shout because there was no hand signal to convey my message. Luckily, the tugs were electrical, there was less noise, and he could hear me.

"Slow it down, Phil! Almost there!" I shouted

I watched Phil as he put the throttle down to slow his movements. He was looking at the monitors with a puzzled look. I grew suspicious but didn't say anything. There was a slight popping noise from the outside, and I guess Phil didn't hear it because he was still moving to park the shuttle.

I kept signaling him that he was getting closer to where he needed to be. The shuttle didn't slow down. I watched a look of panic cross Phil's face as he was pumping the brakes to stop. The shuttle wasn't obeying the command. He looked around frantically for a way to stop the tug. I continued to cross my wrists for him to stop, but he again couldn't. My heart raced with adrenaline because I needed to help him but didn't know how. I watched in an almost slow motion as Phil slammed into the bulkhead, and a loud thud erupted. I watched as Phil was thrown forward from the collision, and he hit the steering wheel. He slammed back into the seat from whiplash, and I could see he was in pain.

I was in utter shock from what I had just watched helplessly. I walked toward him to see what had happened and climbed into the cab. I reached over, opened a panel, and hit the emergency stop button.

"I tried to stop, but there were no brakes, and I had an electrical malfunction," Phil said while struggling for breath.

I just saw someone who could help take Phil to the sick bay.

"Kara!" I shouted

She saw that I was helping Phil and hurried over to help out.

"What happened?" She asked

"I'll tell you about it on the way," Phil answered for me.

"I can take him; you should really take a closer look at the tug so nobody gets hurt," Kara stated

I handed Phil over to her and headed back toward the tug. As I inched closer, I slipped on a substance on the floor but managed to regain my footing. I stooped to investigate and noticed it was brake fluid from the tug. I climbed back into the tug, reset the kill switch, and started it back up. I switched into reverse and moved the shuttle away from the bulkhead. I knew the brakes were out, so I used the emergency kill switch to stop it.

I climbed down and walked toward the rear to assess the damage. I was already trying to come up with a reasonably good explanation for Lexey and the Captain. I touched the shuttle to try to assess any more damage. There were a few places where the bulkhead was split at the seams, exposing conduits and more electrical components. I turned around and looked at the shuttle. The rear engines were damaged, and a tear in the hull was visible.

"Lexey and the Captain are going to be pissed when they see this." I looked around before talking to myself out loud, "At least it isn't a fuel line damaged. We can deal with this tomorrow."

Two

We Have A Problem

★ ★ ★ ★ ★ ★ ★ ★ ★ ★ ★ ★

Lexey

I had just taken a sip of coffee and enjoyed the warmth of the hot beverage. I stared at the liquid in my cup, hoping to see someone else in my reflection. Instead, I saw one of the youngest Chief Engineers covered with a light coating of engine grime. She was about one hundred and forty pounds and had long hair and hazel eyes. I had a strong aptitude for engineering, and everybody made fun of me for being the Captain's pet. Still, I was given the opportunity of a lifetime and wouldn't disappoint her. My thoughts trailed off onto my responsibilities, which included keeping the shuttles working and everything onboard running.

I was in the engineering area speaking with Jason about the shuttle updates. I relied on him to keep me informed on day-to-day tasks. He was just about to end his shift when he found me. He looked nervous, continued looking at his tablet, and reported, "We finally completed repairs on shuttle one. It's still in the repair station, and we plan on moving it into its proper storage area in the morning. Shuttle two still needs some very extensive repairs. We might be back home before it's fully completed,"

I tipped my head back, closed my eyes, and sighed. "If I had my way, that pilot wouldn't fly again. I can't believe anyone could tear up a ship like that. She better hope she never crosses my path because I will give her a piece of my mind."

"I don't think you have to worry about that. The crew members that were on the shuttle sustained cuts, bruises, and minor smoke inhalation. The pilot sustained severe burns over eighty percent of her body as well as scorcher lungs. The cockpit was on fire, and with circuit panels popping and exploding along with thick smoke and heat, it was a miracle she made it back. She saved the crew that she was transporting. I heard this morning she was losing the fight. They don't expect her to survive much longer."

"Yeah, she's a true hero." I was quiet for a moment and felt guilty about criticizing her. After an awkward silence, I asked, "What about shuttle three?"

"We have a little bit of a problem there," Jason replied

"What problem? It just got back from the surface." I locked eyes with him.

"Well, we unloaded everything without any issues. The problem came when we moved it. I let Phil move it, and I spotted him, and he kind of backed the shuttle into a bulkhead." Jason stated.

"What? How do you kind of back into a bulkhead? I mean, how can you not see a bulkhead? Was somebody daydreaming?" I asked, shocked.

"No one was daydreaming. An electrical malfunction of the tug caused it to accelerate, and the brakes failed. It wasn't his fault. He's in the medical bay with a couple of broken ribs from the impact."

I was sad to hear that Phil was injured. With the given details, I calculated he was injured badly.

"How bad's the damage?" I asked to distract myself.

"The bulkhead's dented pretty badly, and we'll need to replace several plates. I couldn't see any damage to the conduits, but we will know more when we remove some of the panels. The shuttle did take some damage. I saw some plates that buckled, and I believe the hull breach will need to be repaired. There are engine mounts that need to be replaced, and some conduits are bent as well." Jason reported

"That means we are back down to one working shuttle again. I hope the Captain doesn't want to make any stops on the way home. Did you check inside the shuttle to see if there was any damage in the engine compartment?"

I watched Jason mull some information over before answering, "Yup, from what I could see, the damage was mostly to the exterior,"

"Ok, in the morning, I want that shuttle moved to the repair area, and shuttle one moved to its storage spot. Then, I want repairs to that shuttle and the bulkhead. I also want someone to review the failed tug and determine what happened. When they finish, I want them to review all the other tugs. I don't want this happening again."

I said my goodbyes and headed to my quarters for some much-needed rest. I walked down the corridor and loved that this was usually a quieter time for the ship. The night shift was smaller and more tight-knit, and they normally readied the vessel for the daytime.

The lights throughout the ship were dimmed to ensure the crew felt like it was night. I recalled a study that found that dimming the lights at night during deep space travel helped the crew adjust to living in space for long periods. There were only dimmed lights in the corridors along the deck, which provided just enough light to allow for movement without bumping into anything.

✴✴✴✴✴✴✴✴✴✴✴✴✴✴

Sam

I was in my quarters with Lisa, fast asleep on my chest with my arms wrapped around her. The Captain allowed a monitor in my area that rotated the ship's security. I had just woken up briefly to noises from the monitor and was about to roll over.

The monitor showed the shuttle bay, and the night crew gathered to take a break. This was normal, but they normally made a bunch of noise. I heard more raucous tonight with bits and pieces about heading home.

"I'm so excited to have worked with all of you. You know the tradition: once the Captain announces we're going home, you must introduce yourselves. I, Rick, am finishing my third mission and in charge of you," Rick said, garbled through the monitor.

"Hi, I'm Sue. I served on several other ships before I was hired as a repair technician on this one."

"Yo, I'm Jeff. I just transferred from the day shift,"

"I'm Edward, the electrical engineer who struggles with normal decision-making."

"You all know I'm Anna, and I am the propulsion engineer,"

"Ok, everyone, we have an easy night ahead of us. According to the swing shift's report, we have a malfunctioning tug to look at. They decided to hold off moving shuttle one, and we will make some room in repair bay two for shuttle three. It would appear that it was damaged while being parked." Rick stopped

I tried to drown out the noise from the monitor.

"What? It wasn't me," Jeff started and then added, "Just because I had one small mishap doesn't mean that all of the mishaps are because of me. Besides, I barely scratched it."

"Barely scratched it? As I recall, you hit it so hard that you buckled one of the hull plates." Anna said as everyone chuckled.

"Who spilled some fuel or cleaning solution?" Edward shouted.

"I've smelled that since we came on duty. If I find out which swing shift idiot did that and didn't clean it up, I'm going to kick their ass. That smell is giving me a headache." Sue said

"When we find out who did it, we will bring them to you so you can kick their ass. Personally, I would love to see you kick someone's ass," remarked Jeff

There was a loud popping sound.

"I guess that someone's broom fell over," commented Sue.

"That may be, but as we turn for home, our crewmate and friend Edward has something he wants to say."

"As you all know, I have a wonderful woman waiting for me back home. A couple of months after we left, I discovered she was pregnant, and I would be a Father. You also know I have a beautiful baby daughter waiting at home to finally meet her Daddy. I missed seeing her birth, first tooth, and her first steps because I'm out here. So, we have been talking back and forth, and I have decided that when we get back, I won't be returning. I'm going to stay home and marry my woman and raise my child."

Anna remarked, "I think that's wonderful, and you'll make a great father!"

Jeff added, "You'll have a lot of great stories to tell your child about what you have seen out here."

The noise had finally faded away, and I could slowly drift back into sleep. It had been a long day for both Lisa and me, and we would have a lot of work to do on the long journey home.

Suddenly, the lights switched on, and an alarm sounded, breaking the silence. Lisa moved slightly and mumbled, "What is it now?"

Still half asleep, I replied, "Oh, it's just the fire alarm."

There was a short moment of silence before we both jumped awake. We looked at one another and simultaneously said, "Fire!"

We both launched from the bed at a moment's notice, adrenaline pumping through my veins. I watched the monitor; smoke coming from the engineering bay. A fire on a ship in space could be catastrophic if it is not put out quickly. I watched Rick as he made quick, jerking movements. He looked to his left and then his right. He began to assess the situation and looked around him, trying to see where the smoke was coming from.

Just thinking about the word smoke filled me instantly with panic. Rick rounded the corner, and a glow came from the area he entered.

"We have a fire!" Rick shouted, "Grab some fire extinguishers and get over here! Sue, hit the fire suppression system! Let's knock this thing out before it gets out of hand!"

It was too late; I watched the glow go from a smoke to an erupted full blaze.

"Let's get to the bridge as quickly as possible," I said as I stepped out of my quarters. I finished getting dressed, and Lisa was a few steps behind me, hopping on one foot while putting on her other boot. When we entered the corridor, the entire crew ran in both directions.

An announcement was made across the ship: "We have a fire in the shuttle bay, section three alpha. Fire teams one and three respond. Teams two and four on stand-by. Repeat: We have a fire in the shuttle bay, section three alpha. Fire teams one and three respond. Teams two and four are on standby."

Shortly after the announcement, we approached the ladders to the other decks; I heard a voice behind me that shouted, "Make a hole! Coming through!"

More of the crew moved out of the way, and Lisa and I turned to see several others in firefighting gear running toward us. I watched them grab hold of the ladder and slide down to make their way to the fire.

Renee

I stepped onto the bridge and startled the six night workers. From down the hall, I could hear them talking about home-cooked food from their hometowns.

"Report!" I shouted as I walked onto the bridge.

"We have a reported fire in the shuttle bay in section three alpha. Fire teams one and three have been dispatched to the shuttle bay. Teams two and four are standing by for orders." Willy turned and reported.

Lisa punched some buttons, and the cameras in the shuttle bay came to life on the main screen. I studied each screen briefly, assessing the best course of action. I knew every inch of my ship and took the situation seriously; a fire was nothing to joke about.

"Sam, pull the schematics for that section of the ship and the surrounding areas," I said as I walked toward him.

He pulled the data as requested, and I studied the areas. Sam attempted to study the same information as I did but needed clarification.

"What are you looking at, Captain?" Sam asked.

Without looking at him, I barked out my orders. "Willy, send team two in to help one and three. Then, I want team four to go into fuel storage to ensure the temperature stays down. Activate teams five and six. Send team five to the deck above the fire and team six to the deck below."

"Yes, Captain," responded Willy.

I turned my attention to Sam and Lisa and focused on their skills. "Why isn't the fire suppression system working?"

They both shook their heads and shrugged, not knowing the answers.

"Get me Lexey on the intercom."

"Yes, Captain, this is Lexey"

"Lexey, what's wrong with the fire suppression system?" I asked.

"There must be a shortage in the electrical system. We can't seem to get it activated. We are trying to track it down and fix it, but all our efforts have failed," Lexey's voice responded.

"I'm lending Sam and Lisa's help from the bridge. Coordinate with them and see if you three can't figure it out. The clock is ticking on fighting this fire." I said through the intercom to Lexey.

I watched the fire on the main screen: "Contact engineering and tell them to shut down the air circulation system. That will shut off the fire's food source. Willy, contact the teams and let them know what we're doing; it's going to get really hot, really fast."

I watched the fire grow around the rear and inside the shuttle. This was a nightmare situation for any Captain. Some Captains bragged about never having a fire during their career. I wished I was going to be one of them.

Pride swelled through me as I watched my crew work efficiently during this crisis. We trained for situations in case they happened, and those sessions paid off. I looked around the bridge, and the same efficiency was performed at a top level, coordinating between stations. I looked back at the screen just in time as I saw a bright flash, and several crew members were thrown back. The crew worked in unison to pull the injured out of harm's way, and others stepped in to take their place.

"Captain, I'm showing the temperatures in the fuel room are rising. We are reaching critical levels," Sue reported

"Turn on the air in that section to help cool it down," I said

"Sorry, Captain, we can't. You ordered the air circulation shut off. It's on the same circuit as the one near the shuttle," Sue replied

I took a deep breath, taking in all the information I had been given. "Tell team four to use water to cool the bulkheads. Do whatever it takes to keep that room cooled. Keep me updated on the temperature in that section."

I turned my attention back to Sam and Lisa. I overheard them talking in gibberish and hoped they had devised a way to fix the suppression system. I watched Sam run his finger along lines on his screen, tracing a path, while Lisa typed away, writing code for a program.

"If we could reroute the power system," Lisa said to herself.

I still heard Lexey's voice, which meant they were all trying to fix the issue. I had faith that the three could solve any problem on this ship. They were the best in their fields. I began to think of how to safely get everybody off the ship if the fire couldn't be contained. Two of the three shuttles were down; not everybody would make it off if we needed to head down that path.

"Lexey, isn't section twenty-two twelve alpha bravo six the bulkhead that runs behind the shuttle that is on fire?" Sam questioned Lexey through the intercom.

"Yes, I believe that's correct. I was told that the bulkhead had been damaged when the shuttle hit it."

"I think it's fair to guess that this is where our breakpoint is," said Sam, tracing other power routes before settling on one. "Do you have anyone near junction forty-one delta?"

"Yes, I do. What do you have in mind?" asked Lexey.

"If they get to panel sixty-five tango three and open it, they will see a circuit board rack. Pull out number six, which I believe will be dead. Then take the board from three and put that one in six," explained Sam.

"Isn't that a different kind of control board? I thought they weren't compatible," inquired Lexey.

"Technically, there is a difference, but with a little bit of reprogramming from Lisa. We can make it work. It will probably overload the board, but we can worry about repairing them later,"

"Ok, my guy made the switch. now what?"

"Give me a second," replied Sam.

I watched as he looked over at Lisa and nodded. She punched a few things into her computer and said something inaudible in the chaos.

"Lexey, I need you to reset the circuit for the fire suppression system in that area, and you should get a green light," Sam said as he wiped his forehead. He switched screens to the one for the fire suppression system. There were tons of red dots blinking. I watched and hoped that this worked for all our sakes. Slowly, each red light turned green.

I turned my attention from Sam and Lisa back to my monitors. The crew fighting the fire in the shuttle bay was slowly losing ground despite their best efforts. Every hose available was being used to fight this blaze. Whenever one flame was put out, another would shoot out and reignite the previous one.

I listened to the conversations from my crew, and their hope was slowly dying.

"We're losing this, and I don't want to die out here in space," one of the firefighters said.

"We're not going to die. We're going to fight this fire and go home," responded another.

"We need a miracle if we are going to beat this fire," remarked the first.

The fire suppression came to life as if it had been planned, and hundreds of gallons of fluids began to flow atop the fire. This helped put all the exterior fires out at once, leaving them with the task of putting out the fire inside the shuttle.

"You asked for a miracle. Let's get in that shuttle and put this fire out."

On the bridge, everyone continued to work hard, waiting for the signal to abandon ship or the signal that the danger was over. There was minimal conversation among the crew as everyone waited patiently. I paced back and forth, and my boots clicking on the floor made the only noise.

The silent torment was broken as a very exhausted voice came over the intercom, "Bridge, this is shuttle bay. The fire is out. Everything is under control,"

Cheers erupted from everyone on the bridge. I checked all the monitors but only saw smoke.

"This is the bridge, we acknowledge. Great job. Tell everyone down there they did a great job." I replied.

I dropped down into my chair, relieved that it was over. I told Willy, "Tell engineering to turn the air circulation back on and vent the smoke."

"Attention crew, Stand down from emergency stations. The fire is out." I said as I pressed a button to announce to the crew.

I listened to the shouts of joy from the monitors. I dreaded the next part: investigating how the fire started and assessing the damage to the ship.

Lisa looked at Sam and commented, "That was a good call, Sam. I would never have thought about moving that board. I always thought that those two boards weren't interchangeable. How did you know that it would work?"

Sam took a deep breath and responded, "It was a desperate move. A couple of months ago, I had to rebuild that board. Some of the circuits that I replaced were higher than the specifications. I had a feeling that it might work, but I really wasn't sure. I took a chance because I could fix the board, but if the ship blew up, I couldn't fix that."

"I want the two of you to work with Lexey to see if you can figure out how this happened and what systems might have been affected. I'm going to stop by the medical bay and see how many were hurt. I expect to get a report from you when I get down there." I said to Sam and Lisa.

Sam and Lisa get up from their stations and leave the bridge to join Lexey. I looked around the bridge before exiting to head to the medical bay.

Everyone was still working hard to recover. They coordinated with other crew members on system checks and cleanup efforts.

I made my way through the corridor to the medical bay, occasionally stopping to answer questions from a few crew members. I stopped by a window to look into space and thought about how close we had come to losing the ship.

Stepping into the medical bay, I was surprised to see how many crew members were getting treatment. I walked throughout the room, looking around to see the worst of the injuries. The patient beds were full with bandaged crew members resting. For those that didn't get a bed, they sat on the floor with an oxygen tank, waiting for further treatment. Some coughed from the smoke inhalation, and some moaned in pain from burns sustained.

I finally found the physician, Doctor Paula Dimefeld. I always loved how Paula never sugarcoated someone's diagnosis. She had been my ship's physician for as long as I could remember.

"How bad is it, Doctor?" I asked her after locating her in between patients.

"I suppose that it could have been worse. We have eighteen that have a minor case of smoke inhalation, some minor burns, about eight cases of second and third-degree burns, and several that have a combination of these and are going to be in here for a while," she replied.

"Did we lose anyone?" I asked while looking around at the worn-out faces of my crew.

"I am afraid we did. We lost one to smoke inhalation and two due to injuries from a small explosion. Another suffered severe third-degree burns. Everything we could do for him has already been done, but I don't think he will survive."

"The one thing I hate the most is writing those letters to go back home telling their loved ones they died. I never really know what to say to them."

"This time, you can tell them that they died as heroes. These crew members died trying to save their fellow crew members and their ship." Paula said as she placed her hand on my shoulder.

I looked over at her and slowly smiled. The thought of them being remembered as heroes brought warmth to my heart. Most of the time Captain's had to write about their crew being casualties in a stupid accident.

✷✷✷✷✷✷✷✷✷✷✷✷✷

Sam

Lisa and I arrived in the shuttle bay looking for Lexey. We needed to figure out what happened before the Captain arrived for her report. The smell of freshly burnt wires was in the air; the sulfur stuck to my lungs like a thickly coated blanket.

Other crew members cleaned up the water that lay on the floor. Some measured debris and documented everything on-site for their reports.

We saw her coming out of the shuttle, holding something in her hands.

Lexey noticed us and said, "That was a good call you made, Sam. I'm glad you know all the electrical systems as well as you do."

"It was just a desperate move. I wasn't even positive that it would work," I answered.

"It helped you save the ship. Did the Captain send the two of you down to help?" she asked.

"Yeah," Lisa replied

"Great, we can use your help."

She held up a piece of broken fuel line and handed it over so I could examine it.

"I found this busted fuel line in the shuttle. I'm pretty sure it broke when they hit the bulkhead. This was the fuel for the fire, but I just haven't been able to determine if the ignition source was outside the shuttle or inside. From my judgment, the source of the ignition is either electrical or washed away when they put out the fire. I need the two of you to determine if it was electrical while we continue to sift through the debris."

Lisa and I moved to the shuttle's rear and examined the bulkhead's damage.

"Whoever came up with the name for a wall in space to be called a bulkhead is an idiot," Lisa mumbled.

I laughed at her but kept working. Lexey moved to a workbench where debris was collected. I focused on the bulkhead while Lisa noticed the shuttle's rear.

It had been some time since we arrived, and I noticed something. I asked an engineer to remove the panel to get a better look. The three of us squatted down to get a better look.

The Captain tried to be quiet as she entered, but she accidentally kicked a piece of debris, and the sudden noise made us all jump. We quickly stood up to face her.

"This was all caused by a random set of variables. It was reported to me a few hours before the fire that a crew member lost control of a tug because of a malfunction and backed the shuttle into the bulkhead. The crew member was injured in the impact. When the shuttle was moved forward, there didn't appear to be any need for immediate concern. Apparently, we were wrong. There was damage to a fuel line that probably started slow and unnoticed but got worse. That fuel leaked out of the shuttle and spread across the deck. Sam discovered a lower plate was damaged, and the fuel leaked under it. Inside the bulkhead was an electrical line busted by the impact." Lexey said

"I can guess the rest. A spark from the electrical line that ignited the fuel and then we know what happened. Who were the crew members that backed the shuttle into the bulkhead?"

"Jason was the senior crew member, and Phil was the tug driver," responded Lexey.

The Captain bowed her head and said, "It looks as though they gave everything to fix their mistake."

"Are you saying they're dead? I thought Phil was in the medical bay." Lexey asked.

"It would appear he left the medical bay when the alarm was sounded. He died of smoke inhalation. Jason and another crew member died from their injuries, and we have one more who is badly burned and not expected to make it. How long before we know if this fire will affect any other system?"

"We'll have the plates off that bulkhead by early morning. Then we will know if anything else has been affected." Lexey replied as she examined the bulkhead.

"Keep me informed and use whoever you think you need to get the job done," stated the Captain, and then she turned and walked away.

Lisa turned to Lexey and said, "If you need our help, let us know. We're going to try to get a few hours of sleep. I would suggest you try to get some, too. It's going to be a long day tomorrow."

"I appreciate your offer of help. I have to get these guys started tearing the plates off this bulkhead. That will take a couple of hours, and I will try to get some sleep while they work on that."

"Ok, everyone, we have a lot of work ahead of us. First, we need to get this shuttle moved over to the far side of the shuttle bay so that it is out of our way. Next, we need this bulkhead section opened up from top to bottom and eight feet in both directions. I'm going to go and get some rest. When I get back here, I expect to see this opened up or for you to be very close to having it opened up." Lexey's voice concluded.

Lisa and I walked away and started to head back to my quarters. We heard Lexey's voice start strong, then slowly get softer the farther we got.

After a few hours of sleep, Lisa and I slowly moved around and tried to wake up. I had dragged my feet to the shower and was just finishing as Lisa was getting ready to take hers. I sat on the edge of the bed, ready to fall back asleep, when the intercom buzzed.

"This is Sam."

"Sam, this is Lexey. I need you to come down here. We have the plates off, and some strange lines are going through here that we can't identify. I want to see if you can help us," stated Lexey.

"I'll be down there in about fifteen minutes after I stop by the mess hall to get a cup of coffee," I said.

"I could really use one of those. Would you be willing to bring me one as well? I would really appreciate it," Lexey said.

"Sure. I'll see you in a bit."

I walked away from the intercom and back to the bathroom entrance.

"Lexey needs me to look at something. I'll meet up with you on the bridge later," I shouted over the shower noise.

Lisa poked her head out of the shower and kissed me before I left. On my way to the shuttle bay, I stopped at the mess hall to pick up two coffees. I let my mind drift to how happy I was being with Lisa. Lexey also popped into my thoughts. If I hadn't gotten together with Lisa, I might have ended up with Lexey instead. They were both my type, but Kellie, on the other hand, was putting a strain on my relationship. I noticed she was still attracted to me, and I didn't want to hurt her feelings, but I would need to talk with her and set some boundaries. Lisa thinks Kellie is obsessed with me, but I haven't seen that behavior.

I noticed the ship had finally settled down, and the morning shift was about to start their shift. Many members I passed looked exhausted after their night of terror. I entered the shuttle bay and noticed the burnt shuttle had been moved. I also saw that the bulkhead was opened, the work lights were on, and the conduits and piping were exposed. As I approached, I saw the fire had burned a lot of the wiring and would require a few days to repair.

Lexey spotted me and almost ran forward, her arms outstretched for the coffee.

"You are such a lifesaver! I really need that."

I handed it over, and she took a big swig.

"I can see your people have been really busy down here. It would appear to me that you have everything under control. What did you need my help with?"

She took another big drink and picked up her pad before setting it down. "We spent the last couple of hours examining damaged lines in this bulkhead. We were able to identify every one except two bundles that were damaged. I know what they are, but they are not on the schematics. Can you look at them and tell me what you think?"

"Sure. Where are the ones that you want me to look at?" I asked her.

"They run into those two junction boxes at the top of that ladder to your left. Several circuit boards are in there, and I figured you know this ship's circuit boards better than anyone else."

I walked over, climbed the ladder, and opened up one. I first noticed the condition of the box when I reached in and removed a circuit board. I looked it over for a few minutes, then put it back. I couldn't help it, but I was puzzled, and I'm pretty sure it showed on my face. I opened the next one, again did the same thing, and examined another board. I put it back, then slowly climbed down the ladder and walked back toward Lexey.

"Those are not supposed to be there," I told her, pointing to the junction boxes.

"That's what I was thinking."

"You realize one of those junction boxes is supposed to be three bulkheads to the right and one deck up, and the other one is supposed to be at the repair area of the shuttle bay?" I asked her.

"I knew they weren't supposed to be where they are now. What systems are supposed to run through those junction boxes?" Lexey asked.

"One of those regulates our navigation and propulsion system. The other one also works with the navigational sensor to give us our position in space,"

Lexey shook her head and then suddenly stopped. She looked at me and asked, "If those were damaged by the fire, do you think we could be off course?"

I momentarily pondered the thought and replied, "If they were damaged by the fire and threw us off course, then we wouldn't be that far off in such a short time."

"That's good to know," remarked Lexey.

"However," I began with a bit of concern in my voice, "those boards were supposed to be replaced a long time ago because they are known to fail and to cause other components in line with them to fail. It's obvious that they didn't get replaced since they weren't where they were supposed to be."

"So, what you're saying is they could have already failed, and the fire may have been a good thing because it told us there was a problem with navigation," Lexey stated.

"Good possibility,"

"I'll be in engineering going over the navigational systems,"

"I'll be on the bridge running a navigational system diagnostic. I'll call you if I find anything,"

We both hurried off in different directions but with the same purpose. We were on a mission to discover if we were still on course for home. A longtime superstition was that those who go into space on a ship off course for too long may never find their way home. I didn't want to test it out to personally discover the truth.

★★★★★★★★★★★★

Renee

On the bridge, the conversation was about the fire and those injured and killed. I sat in my chair at the center of the bridge, listening to the discussions and watching everyone. I could see a conversation going on at the science station, and another was going on at the communication station. One thing that stood out was that Kellie sat at the pilot's station, and no one was talking to her. She rarely had anyone talking to her, but she always watched what Sam and Lisa were doing.

I was drawn to my right as I saw Sam hurry onto the bridge and sit down quickly. He punched buttons, and information was displayed on multiple screens. It was unusual for Sam to come on the bridge like this, and I wondered what he was up to. I slowly got up and began to walk over to where he was. I watched him run diagnostics on several systems. I was about to say something when he pushed the intercom button.

"Lexey, can you check relay twenty-two in the navigation system? I'm not getting anything from it up here," stated Sam.

"Give me one second, Sam," replied Lexey. There was a pause before she returned and said, "That relay was blown, so I replaced it. You should see something now."

"The system is starting to come back online," stated Sam.

"I'm starting to see stuff here too and...." she stopped mid-sentence and then continued, "Sam, I think you need to see these readings on the engine output. From the information given, we have been in a turn since shortly after we turned back for home."

"According to what I am seeing up here, I must agree with you,"

"I'm on my way up there," stated Lexey.

"What are you concerned about, Sam?" I asked him.

Sam hadn't noticed me standing and was a little surprised. He continued to work as he replied, "We found two junction boxes in the bulkhead where the fire was but weren't supposed to be there. These junctions are part of our navigation system. The fire did not cause the damage but made us aware of this problem. We are off course."

"How far are we off course?" I asked, hiding my concern.

Sam pushed some buttons, and a star chart appeared on the screen. Two lines on the screen veer away from each other. Sam pointed at one of them and said, "This is where we are at, and this is where we should be."

"We need to turn now. Are the systems working again?" I said with shock.

"Yes, the systems are working again, but I think you might want to see this," Sam replied, pointing to a blinking dot on the screen.

"What is that?" I asked while looking at the dot.

"It's why we are out here, Captain. There is no record of this planet on any of our charts. It is an unidentified planet," Sam looked at me with an excited look in his eyes and continued, "The fire and the loss of our friends have everyone down. There is nothing to pick their spirits up more than finding an unidentified planet."

"We can always mark it and send someone back to check it out," I said.

"Based on what I can see here, this planet has an unusual orbit around that distant sun. I suspect it's at the apex of this end of the orbit and will probably be out of our reach by the time they send someone out here. By my calculations, it will probably be 50 to 60 years before it is back in a position where we can visit it. I know many people who would love to go down there, and it would be a real shot in the arm to boost people's spirits after what has just happened. We should at least go into orbit and take some readings. This can give us something to do while we complete the repairs and test the systems."

I looked at Sam, who seemed as though he would explode if they didn't go to check out the planet. Looking around at the crew, I saw they could use a diversion. "Well, I don't know, Sam. Everyone was looking forward to going home early." I said, teasing him.

"Captain, you know how everyone loves it when we find something that no one else has," Sam pleaded. "Besides, it's only twenty-eight hours away. We can study it from orbit for a day or so and then head home. It will give us more time to run tests and complete repairs. We will still be home early."

"Ok, Sam, we'll go take a look. Just remember, this is a quick look from orbit. We'll spend a day or two there, and then we're heading home," I said out loud for everyone to hear.

"What's going on?" asked Lexey when she arrived on the bridge.

"Sam found a planet to explore and thinks it might be a good morale booster after that fire last night," I told her as I walked away.

"So I hear that you found a planet. Only you could fall off course and find a new planet." Lexey said.

"We are only twenty-eight hours away, and the visit, combined with our being off course, will only cost us a week. While in orbit, we can fix the navigation system," Sam says while staring at the screen.

Lexey looked at the screen, which still showed where we should be and where we were. From my chair, I looked at Sam and saw him staring at the screen, making his point with Lexey. She shook her head as though she lost a battle and then headed back off the bridge. It appeared as if Sam had won their battle, and he was right. The crew was busy and excited about finding a new planet. The news had even made them forget about the fire.

Three

Let's Take A Look

Sam

It's been almost thirty hours since we discovered the planet, and Lisa and I were getting ready for our shift. I sat in my chair on one side of the room, putting on my boots, while Lisa buttoned her shirt.

"Sam, I know things have been a little crazy, but have you had a chance to talk with Kellie?

"With us fighting the fire and then finding the planet, I just haven't had a chance," I told her.

She picked up one of her boots and was putting it on, steadying herself for balance. "There's something weird about her. I almost feel that she's plotting to get rid of me. I wish you would talk to her."

"I know it bothers you. I will try to talk with her today. I don't think it's going to make much difference."

I finished tying my boots and stood and stretched, contemplating the best way to approach Kellie.

"I know, I'm just saying knowing you had spoken to her and explained that it's over would be a huge relief,"

44

I leaned over and kissed her. "I'll see if I can find her before our shift and talk with her."

I left our quarters to find Kellie, thinking the best place would be her quarters. I headed off in that direction. Along the way, several thoughts bombarded my brain. I'm pretty sure she didn't have feelings toward me anymore. We were friends now, but on the other hand, if she did have feelings, it would be a more complicated conversation. After all, getting her the job on the same ship may not have been a good idea.

The ship's intercom system broke my concentration, and I stopped to listen.

"Sam, please report to the bridge. Sam, report to the bridge please,"

I changed directions and headed toward the bridge as requested. I thought it was funny how every time I went to speak with Kellie, something always came up. I always used that as an excuse then I realized it was true. I shut the intrusive thoughts away and entered the bridge.

The Captain was chatting with Kellie, who was in the pilot seat. I realized that I wouldn't have the privacy needed to tell Kellie. I smiled and approached the Captain as she was in a cheerful mood.

"I'm glad you're here. We've arrived at your mystery planet, and I thought you would want to be here," the Captain said

"You bet I do."

The Captain and Kellie both smiled at my enthusiasm. I walked toward one of the science stations and immediately sat down to start scanning the planet. Most of the time, we're out here visiting planets and stars that are already mapped but not visited. It's rare to find something nobody has seen or knew about. Although it was by accident, I discovered it; this was my planet. I knew it could take days to map it out, and they may not find anything interesting.

I sat at my station, pushing buttons and checking the monitors as the data came in. So far, nothing of interest. The planet was covered in ice. I wasn't surprised since we were a considerable distance from the nearest sun, and this planet was adrift in space and appeared to have an unusual orbit.

Hope flooded me as I watched the screens, looking for anything interesting. So far, the planet has an atmosphere that appears to be breathable but cold and thin. By my calculations, it once may have been inhabited but is now frozen.

Hours passed, and the data didn't change much. Kellie made a course change after each orbit, giving us a new area to map. From the corner of my eye, I could tell she kept tabs on my movements.

This process was repeated over and over as the day went on. More mapping of the planet and finding the same thing every time. I started to feel slightly depressed.

The Captain strolled over and said, "Why don't you take a break. You've been at it all day. So far, we have only seen one big planet of ice."

"I was really hoping we might find something interesting here," I said as I leaned back in my chair.

"You know that this was always a possibility. Sometimes we find something, and sometimes we don't. On the bright side, you found a planet,"

"True, I still wish we could have found something. It would really boost the spirits of the crew,"

"It may not have been exactly what you hoped for, but just finding this planet has greatly impacted the crew."

A beeping sound that made me turn back to the monitors. The Captain paused as she watched and asked, "Did you find something?"

"I think so. It is on the edge of our scan," I said, pointing to the monitor. "If we move fifteen degrees to port, then I'll be able to get a better reading," I explained as I pushed more buttons.

"What do you think you have?" the Captain asked.

"I'm not really sure. There's a temperature difference in that area. There may be something interesting, and we should check it out."

I watched as she scanned the monitors and contemplated the best action. She was not impulsive; after a moment of silence, she turned to Kellie and said, "Change course fifteen degrees to port."

"Yes, Captain," she responded as she punched in our new course.

The Captain turned back and smiled. "Let's see what's there."

I watched another image on the monitor, and as it changed, I pushed different buttons to get more readings. I listed off the data as it came in live from the equipment. "That's strange, there's definitely a temperature difference. The entirety of the planet is covered in ice except for this one crater. The temperature is warmer here for some reason. The crater's about twelve miles across and descends about two and a half miles down. There must be some kind of underground heat source here. There is," I stopped suddenly from spewing information from multiple screens.

The computer beeped, indicating it had found something. I zoomed into the image using multiple buttons and monitors at my station. Once zoomed, the computer began to identify what was there. The crew was working quietly, trying to hear what was happening. I turned to the Captain with a toothy grin.

"What do you think is down there?" The Captain asked.

"I think ships. I have the computer trying to identify them as we speak,"

The bridge suddenly became quiet enough that you could hear a pin drop. The Captain's reaction was one of surprise, and she looked stunned before she could respond. She watched the readout and waited for the data to be interpreted. My blood suddenly ran cold.

"Was the computer able to identify the ships?" She asked.

I couldn't answer at first and almost stuttered on my own words. "Yes. This one at the top of the crater is eighty-six percent covered in ice and has been identified as the Nightingale that was reported lost while searching for the Discovery. This ship down in the crater is sitting at an angle of twenty degrees. It appeared the ground gave out under the landing struts on one side. It was probably caused by the weight of the ship. That ship has been identified as the Discovery." I said, pointing at the monitors.

It was now her turn to look as pale as a ghost. I could never have imagined that out of everything we could have found, it was the Discovery. This was the ship I had always talked about for years, and it was right in front of me. Located on an ice planet in the middle of nowhere. The strange thing was the ships were sitting on the only place on the planet not covered in ice.

Thinking back to every article I read, numerous ships were dispatched to search for the Discovery. The Nightingale was a medical ship out here, like a mobile hospital. Some ships would stop by for an idle chat and other company business and supplies. Rumor was that they had been searching for the Discovery and had never heard from them again. We all watched, waiting for the Captain's decision on whether we would be breaking orbit, going home, or heading down and investigating. I hoped she said the latter as my heart pounded with adrenaline from the anticipation.

"Are you sure about your identification?" she asked me.

I pulled the silhouetted image of a ship, and we looked down at it, which showed the topside view. On another screen, I did the same thing to compare the differences.

"We can identify each ship by its silhouette due to the databases built for search and rescue. The ships of the same class are unique depending on what they were to be used for. Our ship has an observation dome on the top, which means that the placement of our communications dish and antennas differs from other ships of our class. This is something that is not unique to ships of our era. They have been doing this for decades. This is the basic design of the class ship that the Discovery is." I pointed to the screen on the right and continued, "This is the silhouette of the Discovery. You can see the placement of the antennas here, the extra cluster of antennas here, and the addition to the engineering section here to accommodate the larger engines," now pointing to the main screen. "This is the scan we just made; you can see all those identification markers," I pleaded.

She examined the images for a moment, took a deep breath, and asked, "Do you know what the status of our shuttles is?"

"Shuttle one is ready to go, and shuttle two is being repaired. Shuttle three was burned badly and is a total loss," I responded.

"How long will it take to finish the repairs on shuttle two?"

"Lexey said it would be a week or longer before finishing it. She wasn't even sure of that because there still is a lot of work to be done before it will be ready to fly again."

"I don't like the idea of going down there without a second shuttle on standby. I don't think I can make you guys wait another week or more," She paused momentarily, "I'm going to put Mike in charge of this mission. I want you to go along since you are our expert on the Discovery. So, find Mike and have him report to me. I want to talk to him before sending anyone down there."

"Yes, Captain," I said excitedly and rushed to find him.

★★★★★★★★★★★★★★

Kellie

The Captain shook her head and smiled an almost motherly smile as Sam ran to find Mike.

"I think that's the most excited I've seen him in a very long time," I said to her as I walked up behind the Captain.

She looked over her shoulder to see who had spoken and regained her composure before responding. "Yes, it is. You'd think he was about to have a baby or something,"

"After this mission, we may finally get some peace and quiet. Not having to listen to any more stories about his great-great-grandfather," I remarked to the Captain.

"That's true. I'm sure any number of the crew would be happy if that happened. However, this could backfire and give him more to talk about," remarked the Captain.

I paused momentarily and almost didn't say anything until she was about to walk away. "I guess I didn't think about it that way. I had always imagined that he would stop telling stories once he had found the ship. I wonder how happy that will make those crew members that have to listen to his stories all over again?"

"I don't know. You can tell me when you return from the surface," she responded.

I was shocked and thought maybe I didn't hear her right. I was hoping I could go to be with Sam. I had already been on a mission recently, and it wasn't my turn due to the rotation.

"What? You want me to go on this mission?" I asked, bewildered.

"We're down to our last shuttle, and I need one of my best pilots at the helm to get them there and back. After all, you're not the only one I'm drafting for this mission. I know it's not your turn in the rotation, but it's my call."

It had been a long time since I felt this excitement. You can go on hundreds of landing missions, but the first one to an undiscovered world is the one you always remember the most. I knew I was a good pilot and earned the right to go on these types of missions. I could only imagine that the Captain wished she could go on this mission, but due to the regulations, it's forbidden. The Captain cannot leave their ship except in an emergency.

"Thank you, Captain. I won't let you down, I promise." I said to her.

"I know you won't. Go get ready for the mission."

I hurried off the bridge and headed for my quarters to change clothes. Once satisfied with my new attire, I headed to the shuttle bay. I needed to begin prepping the shuttle for departure. I couldn't count the numerous times I had flown a multitude of shuttles since I learned to fly. I was slightly nervous because this one was much bigger than the others I had flown.

The ship normally carried six shuttle crafts: two large, two medium, and two small. The large shuttles were mainly used to transport large equipment but could also transport crew if needed. The medium crafts were used for small equipment and crew. The small ones were for quick, short missions with a small crew.

The only one they had that was operational was the large craft. One of the medium-sized ships had been left on Earth for a complete overhaul. That ship wasn't prepared when they were ready to depart from Earth, so we left it behind. There were supposed to be two more shuttles, but they needed to be picked up from base once we returned to Earth. The large craft we were using had completed its session of tuneups and repairs. It had been down for a few weeks and had just finished before the fire.

When I arrived at the shuttle, I set my gear down by the open hatch and began a visual inspection of the shuttle's exterior.

Slowly, I walked around looking for cracks, damage, leaking fluids, and open panels. Some systems were only accessible from outside the ship; because of this, some panels could be opened up to reveal controls for monitoring those systems while repairs took place. On occasion, someone would forget to close these panels.

I had read a report of a pilot who did not perform an inspection before the flight, and the results were catastrophic.

While in flight, the exposed system failed, and the steel panel door broke off and smashed into another part of the ship, causing more damage and debris. A chain reaction occurred that eventually led to the destruction and loss of everyone on the shuttle. I couldn't help but wonder if the pilot hadn't been in such a hurry, the accident may never have occurred.

Something always nagged at the back of my mind to ensure I never let that happen on my watch. Most pilots wanted shuttles designed to access everything from inside the ship. Since shuttles were stored on a hangar deck in a pressurized environment, it was decided that access from outside would be necessary for maintenance purposes. As a pilot, I didn't agree with the decision, nor did many of my fellow pilots.

I continued my inspection by looking at the landing gear, checking for leaks and obstructions in the engines, and inspecting the ship. I made my way around the ship clockwise, ending where I had started. I picked up my gear and climbed the stairs into the open hatch. This hatch was near the ship's rear and allowed access to the cargo area. Walking through the cargo area, I looked around at the space we had to store equipment. This area was two decks high, and a catwalk was around the cargo area at the upper deck level. Mounted to the wall to the left side of the hatch in the front of the cargo area was a ladder that led up to the catwalk. From the catwalk, you could also access the command deck.

I reached a hatch at the front of the cargo bay, which was already open. I walked into an area meant for crew members and looked around. In front of me, there were enough seats to comfortably seat two dozen passengers. Looking to my left, there were four bunks used by tired or injured crew. To my right was a set of lockers for each passenger, allowing them to store their gear. The command deck, which was above the passenger area, was my primary location during this mission.

I made my way to the stairs and over to the command deck. This held a small section of monitors and control systems where I could watch everything on the ship. We had a heavy equipment crane in the cargo area, which was controlled from here.

The front was the pilot's and co-pilot's seats and the controls to fly this ship. I stored my gear in a locker behind the pilot's seat and then climbed into my assigned seat. Before doing anything, I looked at the switches, gauges, buttons, and displays. In front of me were windows like on an old jet aircraft. I looked out the window and down at the hangar deck, thinking how tiny things could look from this high up.

Returning my attention to my ship, I began my preflight check. I pushed buttons and flipped switches, allowing the ship to come alive. Panels of more buttons and switches started to light up, the monitors came to life displaying information, and below, the lights in the passenger and cargo areas lit up, too. I smiled as I brought this once quiet shuttle to life.

Renee

I stood on the deck hangar and watched each crew member selected for the mission arrive. They individually carried the gear that would be necessary for their travels. Some that entered the hangar deck were quiet, while others laughed and joked.

I selected Lexey as one of the people for this mission, and she entered alone, carrying her gear and a case with some tools in it. She paused her trek and looked at the ship and others as they walked past her. I noticed a look of uneasiness on her face rather than her normal joyful one. She seemed to be looking around as though she was never to come back aboard.

The thought of how uneasy a few of my crew were made me on edge. Maybe it was the thought of them finding these two ships that had been missing for decades. I watched her square her shoulders and then walk onto the shuttle.

Sam and Lisa met outside the hangar and entered together. Other members of the selected team continued to arrive.

Mike and I stepped onto the hanger deck while discussing some of the mission's aspects. I have always admired Mike Kirthall. He had been with the ship for several missions into deep space. He was about six feet one inch tall, bald, weighed about two hundred sixty-five pounds, and was fifty-two years old.

This was not the first time I had called upon him to lead a landing mission. However, this one was different from the rest. With the other missions, he was sent to do site surveys and mineral extraction or oversee the progress of several teams. This time, he would go down to the surface to document and catalog what happened to the Discovery and her crew. He was to solve the mystery of what happened many years ago. If there was time, they would go to the crater rim and figure out why the Nightingale also became stranded.

"I don't want you to take any unnecessary risks down there. If anything goes wrong, we don't have any easy way to get down there and get you some help." I said as I pulled him aside.

"You worry too much. We're going down with a smaller and lighter ship than the ones there now. Besides, our equipment's much more advanced than that of the past. There is nothing down there that can hurt us. After all, this is a dead, frozen world," he replied.

"I'm sure the Discovery had similar thoughts when they decided to land on that planet or the Nightingale when they landed on the rim of the crater. I hope you thought about that and picked a good landing site," I stated.

"After seeing our scans, I think I'll set down near the Discovery. I considered putting it down near the Nightingale, but it's mostly already under the ice. Not to mention, it's a long haul down to the Discovery. I figure the Discovery might have landed on an underground cavern, and the ship's weight caused it to collapse. Before we land, we will check the readings to ensure we land on solid ground."

"Let's hope nothing goes wrong. It would be at least a week or more before the other shuttle might be ready for a rescue. Normally, I might consider taking the ship down, but this ship is too big and heavy. I refuse to put my ship and the entire crew in danger,"

"I don't foresee any real danger unless you count Sam," he said with a chuckle.

Puzzled, I asked, "Why would Sam pose any danger?"

Mike threw his hands in the air and smiled, saying to forget the joke, and then stated, "We've been hearing him tell stories about his great great grandfather and that ship for years now. I would bet he knows more about that ship than any historian. hell, I would even bet he memorized every switch, button, and circuit on that ship."

"That's exactly why I am sending him with you. I don't think there is any way I could keep him on this ship. Is that going to be a problem?"

"The problem isn't his knowledge. In fact, that will be the most valuable information I will have at my disposal. The problem I see is once I get him onto that ship, I will have one hell of a time trying to get him off. He has been so obsessed with it over the years that I don't think he will want to leave it," Mike stated.

"I see how that might become a problem, but that's why I picked you to be in charge of this landing mission." I paused and hesitated before continuing, "There are many people on this ship I could have put in charge of this mission, but I chose you. Sam doesn't listen to a lot of people. He likes to do his own thing. I've noticed he does listen to you. He respects you. That's why I think if he does get lost in that ship and doesn't want to come back, you will be able to talk and make him listen to reason,"

"Does he know?" asked Mike.

"I haven't told him," I replied with a slight grin.

A look of shock crossed his face with his eyebrows raised.

Mike and I both knew that Sam was adopted and was told his adopted father had died when he was very young. His adopted mother raised him but never remarried. Personally, I thought this was the reason Sam was so hard to keep under control.

"I don't know why he would listen to me, but I'll do my best to keep him under control," Mike said.

I extended my hand to shake his, and he returned the gesture.

"Good luck, Mike. I'll see you when you get back."

I watched as Mike picked up his gear and began to walk toward the shuttle. I watched before I ran back to the bridge to hear everything happening inside the shuttle. Mike had just approached the shuttle's entry hatch when he noticed something. He set his gear down and walked over to investigate. As he got closer to the cargo loading platform, he saw Pops. He watched as he loaded case after case onto the platform. Pops had his back to him as he loaded another case onto the platform.

"Hey Pops! Do you really think we will need all of that stuff? After all, we're just going down to look at that old ship and see if we can figure out what happened."

"It's standard procedure, or at least should be, to bring weapons with us on all landing missions. That way, we will be ready if we encounter hostile aliens. After all, we have no idea what happened down there and why they never left. We should always be prepared for anything," responded Pops.

Mike laughed, "I've been on over a hundred landing missions, and I'm sure you have probably been ten times the number I have. In all of this time, have you ever once seen an alien?"

"Just because we have never seen an alien doesn't mean they are not there. Trust me, the moment you let your guard down, you're going to be glad that I brought them along,"

"Then tell me why you are bringing those explosives along?"

Pops loaded the last case onto the platform, stepped back, looked up while giving the thumbs-up, and shouted, "Ok, take her up!"

Mike looked up to see Sam at the controls, helping Pops load his gear. Sam pushed a few buttons, and the platform rose into the shuttle's belly. "Mike," he turned to look at him while he continued, "It would appear some of our rockhounds want to get some samples from this planet while we are down there."

"I'm sorry, but I cannot permit you to set off any kind of explosives near our landing site,"

"They already had this discussion with the Captain. It was decided they would work along one of the lower slopes furthest away from where we land. We will eliminate any chance of doing anything to this shuttle," stated Pops.

Mike shook his head and smiled, "I don't think they really know just how far they will have to haul all that gear. We're going to be near the center of that crater. Walking it without all of the gear they are going to need is going to take a couple of hours at best. Not to mention, the air will be a little on the thin and cold side down there. Did any of them stop to think about that?"

"Actually, yes, they did. That's why I will take them in the rover," replied Pops.

"A rover won't do you much good down there. The wheels aren't made for the kind of terrain we will encounter. Those rovers require the sun and are really underpowered."

"That's why we won't be taking any of the Mark 10's. We will be taking a Mark 2 instead,"

"Are you kidding me? Those things are antiques. They were known to be unreliable and break down. They were only good for about two hours of use, and then you had to plug them in for twenty-four hours before you could use them again. Where in the world would you dig up a relic like that? The last one that I saw was on display in a museum."

"I bought one at an auction several years back. This is no ordinary Mark 2. This is a Mark 2BX. I made a few modifications and tweaks to it."

"What kind of modifications and tweaks could you make to it? It was a poor design that didn't work out, so they scrapped that model and completely redesigned it from the ground up. What does the BX stand for?" asks Mike.

"The BX stands for Brutiss Experimental. Out of all of the models of rovers, this one had the best body and frame. When they made this one, they thought of it like an Earth vehicle. Let me show you." He walked over and pulled back the cover from his rover. He stepped toward it and slowly began to walk around it, looking closely at what was there.

"You have made more than just a few modifications. This doesn't look anything like the one that I saw in a museum."

"True. The original model had a shorter wheelbase and could only seat two. I stretched the frame and body to seat four and doubled the cargo capacity, including a place to store the explosives I might be carrying. I put foam-filled knobby tires on it for better traction. I put a completely new suspension on it for a smoother ride. I used the latest battery and electric motor technology and a few modifications to power it. This rover can do up to sixty miles per hour and hold a charge for seventy-two hours before you need to recharge it. The rest of the modifications are mostly just for show. The paint job, seats, gauges, lights, and safety cage are extras."

"When did you find time to do all of this? This rover looks great."

"I've been working on it in my spare time since we left Earth. I had hoped to finish it sooner than I did. I wanted to try her out before we headed home, but I had a few setbacks. I thought I would have to wait until our next trip to try it. When we decided to go down on this planet, it seemed the right time to test her out." Pops pointed to the far end of the hanger deck and continued, "I had converted a small area over there behind those storage containers as a work area. I only got this rover running a couple of days ago. I expect this one to run better than my other one."

"You did a great job, Pops. I can't wait to see how well it works,"

Behind him, the platform lowered back down for the next equipment load. Mike watched as Pops climbed into the rover and started it up. He carefully drove it onto the platform and stopped. Staying inside the rover, he gave Sam the thumbs up, and the platform began to rise again.

"See you onboard."

Mike stood there and watched as Pops and his rover disappeared into the belly of the shuttle. He shook his head and returned to where his gear was set down. He picked it up and made his way onto the shuttle.

Soon, everyone was onboard, the hatch was sealed, and the steps to the shuttle hatch were retracted. The shuttle sat in place to be lowered to the launch bay. As soon as everyone was clear, a warning sound was heard, and yellow warning lights flashed as the shuttle was lowered to the launch bay.

Four

Ready To Go

Kellie

It seemed our technology had only advanced so far, and the shuttles were transported to the launch bay via elevator. Once locked in place, large doors would close to seal us off from the main ship. This was standard practice during takeoffs and landings.

I sat in the pilot's seat, waiting for clearance from the bridge to depart. I had already completed the necessary checks for takeoff, so I decided to sit back in my chair to relax and enjoy the silence.

I didn't get much relaxation time as a voice came over the radio.

"Shuttle one, stand-by while we decompress the launch bay."

I jumped due to being startled by the voice, adjusted my headset, and responded. "This is shuttle one standing by."

I looked through the windows from my spot and noticed the doors were closed. I turned my attention toward the front as the tug moved us into position. The standard procedure was to wait until we were in the position and the outer doors were opening before the engines could be started. My adrenaline began to rush as I waited for the doors to fully open. I watched them patiently and every so often averted my gaze to the digital readouts showing me the pressure outside the ship. As the pressure dropped, warning lights blinked to indicate we were now in motion.

When I watched a crack of light slowly seep between the doors, I began to flip switches, and the engines began to whir, coming to life. I checked the doors to ensure they were open, and a voice came over the headset.

"Shuttle one, you are clear for departure. Good luck."

"Roger that, we'll see you when we get back," I said.

I slowly reached over and increased the shuttle's power, and it began to move forward like an aircraft leaving the airport back on Earth. As we passed through the doors and out into space, I flicked my wrist with a slight movement and turned us away from the mothership.

Once we faced the correct way to our mission, I pushed a few buttons, and the rear engines fired up and propelled us forward toward the unknown planet.

Unfortunately, the flight between the mother ship and the new planet was short. I maneuvered the shuttle into high orbit and held position.

"This is shuttle one; we have achieved high orbit around the planet. Request a comm check; how do you read?" I asked through my headset.

"Shuttle one, we are reading you loud and clear."

"Roger that. We are doing a final systems check and awaiting approval before descending. Should be complete in twenty minutes," I replied.

"Roger, shuttle one. Stand-by for final approval to descend."

"Roger that. Shuttle one standing by."

This was the point I usually didn't like: the computer automatically performed the final systems check. The computer would transmit a completed systems report to the mothership, and then clearance would be given to proceed. The whole procedure was routine but was also boring. The only time I got to do anything was when the computer located something wrong, which rarely happened. I sat back and waited in silence when I heard a noise. I turned to see who it was when Sam poked his head through the hatch.

"Hi, Sam. I thought you would be down below telling one story after another, considering," I said, smiling at him.

"No, it's pretty quiet down there. I'm not sure what to say." He looked at the planet and walked forward to sit in the co-pilot seat. He looked back at me and continued, "I always knew this day would come."

"Why is that?" I asked.

"Some call it dumb luck, but I call it destiny finding the Discovery,"

"What's the odds you would be on the ship that found it?"

Sam shook his head and replied, "I know the odds were no one would ever find it. Space is a big place, and I think we just found the proverbial needle in a haystack."

"How do you feel about actually finding it?"

"I'm excited that I was the one who located it, let alone being one of the people going down and exploring,"

I looked closely at him for a moment, then asked again, "How do you really feel about the mission?"

"What do you mean? I just told you."

"You told me what you thought I wanted to hear. I want to hear what you're really thinking and feeling."

He looked at the planet through the window and then back at me. After a short silence, he explained, "I was excited; now we are out here, I have an uneasy feeling. Two ships went down on this planet and were never heard from again. They never got off as much as a distress call. Looking at the planet, they seemed to have found one strange place on a planet of ice. I'm curious about what happened there, but I'm scared too."

"I don't think you have anything to worry about. I think you are getting caught up in the story of the Discovery. This planet may have looked entirely different when they landed here decades ago. You're probably afraid that the mystery will be over once we return. Once it is over, you may not have the stories to tell about that ship anymore."

"I understand what you're saying, and you might be right. I can't help this feeling of danger. Like it's a warning from my great-great-grandfather." He trailed off from his thoughts, and we sat in silence briefly before continuing. "Actually, Kellie, that's not why I came up here.

We've known each other for a long time. hell, there was a time when we were rarely seen apart. In fact, there was a time when we couldn't keep our hands off each other. That was before we got the space bug.

I smiled and stared at him; my heart rate quickened at the thought of where this conversation was going. It was just him and me alone, and deep down, I knew the rumors about him dating someone else weren't true. There was still a burning desire between us, and I could feel it; this was why he talked me into joining this crew. So we could be together. At first, he tried to fan the flames, but many years existed between our romance. When I first joined, I asked him to give me more time to adjust to the position and learn to work alongside him.

I saw this as payback and a chance to play hard to get before letting him back in. The chase didn't last as long as I'd hoped. He soon stopped chasing, and now it was as though we were old drinking buddies. When he left to go to space, he gave no notice he was leaving. I had awoken one day and found a note. He broke my heart, but I still cared for him no matter how much it hurt.

It was six months after he left before hearing anything. I guess by the time he would have thought I was over him and onto someone new, except when his letter arrived, the burning flame that I felt for him relit, and the need for him was strong. I became a pilot because I wanted to know what drew him away from me. After being out here for so long, I knew why he had first left and ventured off. I hoped having a common interest in space would bring us closer together. We continued to write over the years. Every so often, we would run into one another.

Piloting was a task at first rather than something enjoyable. I soon discovered I had the knack for maneuvering space crafts in the deep, dark unknown. When I first joined this crew, all I could think about was how good it would be together again. Rumors upon the ship said he still held a place in his heart for me. Sometimes, it broke my heart when others would tell me to give up and move on. Thinking about it, I've had several offers from other guys on the crew, but I turned them all away. I had concluded that if he didn't show anything by the time we had returned to Earth, I would retire from this crew. I thought about saying something but decided to be patient. This discussion could be the tipping point, and we could be back together again.

I suddenly pulled myself from my feelings and concentrated on the conversation.

"I remember those times, Sam. We had a lot of fun back then." I remarked with excitement.

"Yes, we did." He smiled, and then his expression changed. "During our time of staying in touch and since you came aboard the ship, there is something we never talked about: the day I left you and went into space."

This wasn't where I thought the conversation was going, but I decided to go along. "I never thought we needed to talk about it. You had a chance to chase your dream and went after it." I said.

He nodded and said, "That's just one of the reasons I came out here. Leaving you back then was not an easy decision. I know it hurt you when I left, even if you won't admit it. It took me a long time to get the courage to write to you. I didn't know what to say. I wasn't even sure you would write back to me."

"Of course, I would write you back. I may have been hurt, but I always knew why you came out here,"

"You knew one reason I came out here, but there were others. We were young, and I was afraid of commitment. In all truth, I was running away from you." He sighed and hung his head slightly.

I was surprised by what I just heard. I never thought I would have heard this from him. My heart began racing at the thought of what was coming. I knew there were rumors about him seeing someone else, but I hoped they weren't true. We were supposed to get back together. I imagined we had not talked much lately because he was deciding how to commit to me. I wanted to jump out of my seat and into his arms but restrained myself. After all, I didn't want to seem too eager to be with him.

"I never knew you felt that way. I'm sorry if I made you feel like I was pushing you into anything. What's your feelings today?" I asked nervously.

"Well, today, I am older and wiser than I was back then. When I wrote to you, and you replied, I was ecstatic to hear from you. All I could think about were the good times we had. I knew my stay in space would be away for long periods. All I could do was to write to you."

I listened, as this was it. This was finally the moment I had been waiting for.

"I was surprised when I heard you went into space,"

"I had to find out for myself what drew you out here. Was this more important than our relationship?" I asked, motioning to the ship and outer space.

He looked out the window and answered. "The urge to come here is powerful, and staying is like an addiction. Some can suppress it, but I'm not one of them. I had to see it for myself," He turned back, looked directly into my eyes, and continued, "When I found out that you needed a new ship, I thought this was my chance to make up for walking out on you. The day you came onboard, I thought here's my chance, but you wanted to play hard to get. That's when I realized you can't go back in time no matter how much you think you want to."

The blush and smile that had risen to my face slowly disappeared as I realized where this conversation was going. I've known him for a long time and knew his thoughts would sometimes drift before getting back on track. I had hoped this was one of those times.

"What do you mean, Sam?" I asked cautiously.

He took a moment to collect himself before continuing, "What I mean is I realized the feelings we once had, and I thought I still had, are gone. They changed over time. I still care about you, and I always will, but I just don't have those same feelings I used to,"

My smile turned into a blank stare. This wasn't what was supposed to happen. I couldn't believe what he just said to me. My heart felt like it had stopped beating, and I was paralyzed. What was I supposed to do for the remainder of the trip home? We were supposed to get back together, and now there wasn't a chance in hell. I listened to his every word carefully so the anger built inside wouldn't boil over.

"You might have heard a rumor that I have been seeing someone else. Well, it's true, I am. I wasn't looking for anyone, but it just happened. In fact, she was the one that found me. We tried to be discreet because I wanted to talk to you before you heard it from someone else, and I know waiting would have made it more awkward. We had something in the past, and I thought that seeing the two of us together on the ship may make you feel uncomfortable,"

My mind raced as the rage boiled to the top, and I tried to stuff it back down deep inside me. How could someone do this to me? Just about everyone onboard knew we had been an item in the past. Most people saw how I felt about him every time he was near. Was he really so ignorant? I had left home and made a career in space to be with him. I couldn't believe it, as I'd had several opportunities to be with others. I declined them all so we could have a chance together again. I thought that with us being on the same ship, it would rekindle our relationship. After all, where could he run to? The real question was who he ran to. Was it Lisa?

"I'm truly happy for you. I've had my eye on a guy on the ship for a while. We've gone on a couple of dates. I've heard rumors that you were seeing someone, but I didn't know who? I wish the best of luck to both of you." I replied, spewing my web of lies.

I couldn't let him know that he had hurt me again. What I really wanted to do was yell and scream at him. How could he not see what I had done for him? I hoped his new girlfriend dropped dead; I hoped to find her and push her out of an airlock. Too many angry thoughts passed through me, but I managed to smile and make him believe my lies.

This entire situation was becoming awkward. I was looking for a way out when suddenly a voice came over the radio.

"Shuttle one, your systems check has been completed, and you have been cleared to descend at your discretion."

"Roger that, preparing for the descent," I said as I put my headset back on and flipped a few more switches. "You better get below and strap in. It could get a little bumpy from here."

He left without another word, and I returned to the task at hand. I strapped in my harness before addressing the crew.

"May I have your attention, please? We have been cleared for descent to the planet's surface. I need everyone to strap in. We will begin our descent in one minute."

✳ ✳ ✳ ✳ ✳ ✳ ✳ ✳ ✳ ✳ ✳ ✳ ✳ ✳ ✳

Mike

I watched as Sam made his way down the stairs, came back, sat with Lisa, and strapped in.

"Where have you been?" Lisa leaned over and asked him.

"I was on the upper deck to have *the talk* with Kellie," he responded

"When you say you went up and had *the talk*, you really mean you had *the talk*. You mean the conversation you have been putting off repeatedly for one reason or another. That would be the conversation that caused us to have an argument earlier today." she said in a surprised tone.

"Yes," responded Sam with a sigh.

"How did things go?" Lisa questioned.

"I think it went pretty well. She had heard a rumor about the two of us, so it hadn't been that big of a shock. We talked about it. Well, actually, I did most of the talking; she didn't say much. She did wish us the best and told me she was seeing someone."

She gave him a kiss but held a look of contentment. I took this as my cue to leave and headed up the stairs to see Kellie.

On the command deck, Kellie was preparing to land the shuttle and received readouts about our landing site from the equipment. I watched as she looked over the data and double-checked a few things.

"How's the landing site looking?" I asked her.

"It's strange. The floor of the crater is solid except for one spot. Under the landing gear on one side of the Discovery, there are a few tunnels below the surface. Everywhere else is solid. I think it's strange that a tunnel rose just below the surface, ran the ship's length, then descended again." she paused and pointed to a spot on the screen. "I think this is the best place to land. I don't see any tunnels or caverns."

"You're the pilot, so I'll leave the flying to you," I said as I returned to my seat.

"Wait! You don't have to go. You can stay here and watch. After all, no one is in the co-pilot's seat, and the view from up here is spectacular. It's the best seat in the house. You'll always remember the view."

"What the heck? I'll ride up here." I hesitated briefly, then climbed into the co-pilot's seat and strapped in.

Kellie smiled and said, "Good choice. You're not going to regret your decision."

"I may be regretting it already,"

"Here we go." Kellie laughed.

She moved the controls forward a little, and the shuttle began to move toward the planet's surface. I gripped tightly onto the armrests of the seat, for I was afraid of crashing.

Being down below when we descended to a planet, all I had to deal with was the time it took to land because there were only a few windows, and I never sat near them. Up here, I could watch the ground approach. I knew this was a bad decision.

She continued her steep descent until we were several hundred meters above the surface and leveled out. I started to relax and realized that watching my fears might have been the best thing for me. I looked out the windows in awe at the sight before me. We were flying over one sheet of white glistening ice as far as the eye could see.

"There she is, Mike. It's directly ahead of us. That mound in front of us on the crater's edge is not a mound. That's the Nightingale. She is heavily buried in ice and snow."

I watched as we passed over the Nightingale. If it wasn't for the fact that the front of the ship extended a little over the rim of the crater, it would have been impossible to have even known that under this mound was a spaceship. As we passed the rim, the ground below descended. It only took a moment before I saw what we all came for. Almost below us was the Discovery, which no one had heard from in eighty-six years.

Kellie began a wide circling pattern around the ship as she slowly descended. This allowed me to look over the Discovery and the surrounding area. The ship looked decent except for one side, where the ground had given, and the landing pods were now partially buried in a trench. I expected to see hull breaches, but as far as I could tell, nothing was wrong with the ship except the landing gear being stuck. A ship of this era was designed with strong engines. With the nearest help so far away, they were outfitted with their own machine shop to manufacture any part that they might need. The landing gear was designed to break away with explosive bolts in case something like this ever happened. As we circled around, I saw no sign they had ever made an attempt to lift-off.

Several possibilities ran through my head as I looked at the monitor Kellie used for continuous scanning. It displayed above and below the surface for constant monitoring. I switched angles to get a better view while Kellie controlled the ship.

Kellie popped open the landing gear, and a muffled sound could be heard as the machine obeyed her command.

"Stand-by for landing," she announced as she maneuvered the ship to face the Discovery.

The ship settled down in the crater near the Discovery, right where we wanted it to be. The engines kicked up dust clouds, so Kellie switched them off and put the shuttle into stand-by mode.

"That was a great landing; I barely felt our touchdown. I think you picked the best possible landing site. It's definitely better than the one I had chosen," I told her with a toothy grin as I looked at her. "What's wrong?" I asked

She stared out the window at the alien landscape and replied, "This place is really creepy looking. I can't tell what it is, but something is definitely wrong."

"Kellie, you're letting your imagination run rampant. There's nothing to fear here. It's a dead, frozen wasteland,"

"Did you notice the underground tunnels when we came in?"

"Sure. A bunch of random tunnels were probably made from some underground water source or volcanic activity. Nothing special or unique about them,"

"I think you should take another look." She pushed a few buttons and showed me a replay of the scans she had taken as we descended. "These tunnels look like they were intentionally dug. They are too uniform in size to be considered random. These look like someone intentionally created a network of tunnels. They remind me of something, but I just can't remember,"

"It could be that some space pirates mined this planet for years or even decades. They could have been handing down the location from one generation to the next, or it could have been from a past civilization that no longer lives here." I said, looking at the screen.

"That's a possibility, but try to explain this. Why is there one tunnel coming up from a deep location just short of the front of the ship, turning sharp and running directly under the landing gear, turning sharp again after passing the ship's rear and descending back down to the tunnel?" asked Kellie.

"Maybe that was their route to the surface to offload whatever it was they were mining, and the Discovery just landed on their tunnel,"

"If it was just one of the landing gear, I might buy that idea. But I find that hard to believe when it's the entire port side landing gear. Besides, if that was how they brought the stuff to the surface, anyone could have looked out a window and seen it so that they could avoid it," Kellie replied, shaking her head.

"This is your first trip down to a planet but you can't jump to conclusions. You have spent far too much time with Sam. You're actually starting to sound like him. The only way to know what happened is to go over and see what we find."

"No matter what you say, I still feel bad about this place. Be careful out there,"

"We will. I want you to stay with the shuttle for now and run a complete system check. I need you to ensure this shuttle will be ready to take us out when we're ready to leave," I said, smiling at her.

"Are we staying the night, or do you plan to leave by sundown?" she inquired.

"I want to be out of here by sundown, if you can call it that, since there is very little light here," I looked at my watch to calculate the time before continuing, "eight hours and ten minutes from now. Done here or not, I don't want to spend the night here on the surface. I have a feeling that it's going to be much colder once we lose any light. I want this ship ready for lift-off when we get back,"

"I'll have the ship prepped and ready to go at all times," she said with a look of disappointment.

I got up from the co-pilot's seat and returned to the crew. Some were moving to stretch, and others were already checking their gear or craning to look out the windows at the newly discovered planet.

I looked around at the crew's excitement. They looked to me for the next step. Usually, we would set up camp somewhere or work off of the shuttle. From there, we would gather air, rock, and water samples, if applicable. This was different from any other. This time, we were here to solve a mystery—to find out what happened to these ships and their crews.

I made my way to the passenger area's center when I was stopped by Pops.

"Hey Mike, the rock hounds have asked me when I could use my rover to take them out to the edge of this crater so they could run some experiments, and I can blow some things up for them. Since you're in charge, I thought I would ask you," he asked as he grabbed my arm.

"Do you think your blasting will cause any danger to the ship?"

"Not a chance. We're going to be on the far side of the crater,"

"It would be nice to figure out why this crater differs from the rest of the planet. We can get them up there soon, but you must pull double duty."

"What do you mean double duty?" Pops asked with a quizzical look.

"First thing, you'll have to run a team out to the edge and drop them off. While they are setting up, you need to get back here, pick up another team, and take them as high up the crater as possible. I'm sending a team up to investigate the Nightingale. We are under a time crunch of about eight hours. I want to be back on the ship and ready for lift-off before it gets dark,"

"If I didn't have my own rover, I would tell you what you are asking was impossible, but I think I can get it done," stated Pops proudly.

"May I have your attention, please?" I shouted at everyone. "I need everyone to settle down. We have about eight hours to get a lot of things done, so I have decided to split everyone into teams. Pops will lead a team out to the crater's edge to do some experiments, and then he will come back and take another team as far up the crater as possible. That team will be led by Wanda, and they will investigate the Nightingale. The remaining two teams will investigate the Discovery. I will lead one team to examine the exterior, and Sam will lead the other, who will find a way to investigate the ship's interior. They will try to restore power if possible, so take the right equipment."

Sam looked surprised to hear he had been put in charge of a team. He smiled proudly as he acknowledged the position.

Pops tapped me on the shoulder and asked quietly, "Are you sure Sam is the best person to lead a team?"

"I can't think of anyone better for the job. He knows that ship better than anyone. I think he will find the quickest way into it, and I would even bet he could tell you where every conduit and circuit is. He is perfect for this assignment." I said.

"I guess you're right,"

"Now everyone needs to remember to wear your arctic gear out there. It's frigid, especially for those on their way to the Nightingale. Take your oxygen masks and use them if necessary. We have recorded temperatures of minus thirty degrees or better up there. I don't want to guess what the temperature inside the ship will be. If you can, retrieve the main computer's hard drive. That should have all the information, including the Captain's log. You need to take a small generator for those going inside the Discovery. I'm not sure you will be able to get any power. I hope the small generator will supply adequate power to at least be able to activate the emergency lights. Remember to take your flashlights and radios. Pops will drop off his team and then return for the Nightingale team. Now, everyone has to be extra careful out there. We don't want anyone to have an accident this close to going home. Now let's get to work, people," I told everyone.

Everyone acted quickly and began to suit up for the cold. Checking their flashlights and inspecting the equipment. They each completed individual radio checks with Kellie as they put their radio headset on.

I followed Pops to the cargo hold and watched him prepare the rover and check his explosives. His first team approached the rover carrying some cases of equipment. Behind them was the Nightingale team. and they were helping everyone else since they would be the last to leave the shuttle.

After several minutes, the teams were ready to depart. Pops maneuvered his rover into place on the cargo lift. With the rest of his team already inside the rover, he signaled for the lift to be lowered. There were two short blasts of a warning horn, some yellow caution lights flashed, and the lift descended to the ground below. By the wall near the lift, there is a hatch with two lights; one is yellow, and the other is green. The rest of the team made their way toward the hatch. The person first in line pushed a button beside the hatch and waited. A yellow light flashed, and then a green light signaled that a set of stairs had been lowered and fully extended to reach the ground. The hatch opened, and the crew began descending the stairs onto the surface.

It's hard to tell who is who in their arctic gear. They were all wearing their insulated boots, yellow arctic jumpsuits, parkas, and gloves, and they had masks to cover their faces and goggles to protect their eyes. They each had a backpack with the gear they thought they would need. One member from each team carried the medical kit. These suits were designed to protect us from the cold and leave no skin unprotected. Only by looking at the names sewn onto their jackets could anyone know who they stood next to. The arctic suits were good at keeping the cold away from the skin, but they still had to breathe the air.

Sam and I were the last two members of the two Discovery teams down the stairs. Sam stopped as we approached the bottom and pointed off into the distance.

"You thought I was excited to get out here? Looks like Pops was just as excited about getting down here as I was."

"He's been itching to go somewhere and try out his modified rover. He finished it after we left that last planet. He thought it would be a long time before he got to test it out. When he found out we were going to land, he just had to bring it along to try it out."

"Knowing Pops, I'm sure he's having a blast."

I smiled and nodded in agreement. I raised my arms and shouted, "Team two over here with me!"

"Team three over here with me!" Sam raised his arm and shouted.

One member of Sam's team stepped up close to him. Although they were all in the same type and color of arctic gear, I'm sure it was Lisa. I didn't hear their conversation, so I brought my attention back to my team, and we split up to make our way to the Discovery.

I allowed Sam to lead, and my team followed him toward our mark. I could tell from his pace that he was getting anxious. Over the decades since it had disappeared, there have been many theories about what happened to it. They were about to find out and put all of those theories to rest.

Five

The Investigation

★ ★ ★ ★ ★ ★ ★ ★ ★ ★ ★ ★ ★

Mike

Dreading the following conversation that needed to be completed, I pulled my tablet out and contacted Pops. From inside the rover, he appeared on the screen. "What's your status up there?" I asked

"We unloaded the equipment, and I gave them some instructions. I let them know when I'll be back to blow things up. I should be returning to the shuttle to pick up the other team," Pops responded through the screen.

Before getting another word in, I watched Pops climb out of the rover. I could still hear him even though he was out of range from the camera.

"Jason, I want you guys to set up the gear. Depending on how far up the crater I can get team four, I should be back in forty-five minutes or so. I expect a few spots to be picked for blasting and drilling for core samples. Do you think you can get it done?" Pops asked.

"No problem. I'll have Mary and Eric setup and run the drill, and Linda and Pat go collect samples and look for sites to blast. We'll have it all up and running before you get back."

"Sounds like a plan," replied Pops as he climbed back into the rover.

He put the rover into gear, and I could tell he stomped on the accelerator. I heard the tires spin. Once the rover took hold and began to move forward, he cut the wheel hard to the left, causing the back end to swing around. Even though Pops wore a mask, I knew there was one big smile.

When we arrived at the Discovery, I shut off the tablet. Everyone stopped underneath the old ship. I didn't realize she was this massive; everyone looked up in awe at the sheer size of the old ship. The engines on the ship's belly were massive compared to modern ships. We looked at this ship just like people in the past would look at a huge airplane and wonder how something that big could fly.

I leaned over to Sam and asked, "Well, now that you are here, what do you think?"

"That is one big son of a bitch." Sam replied as he took a deep breath.

"I thought you knew everything about this ship?" I asked surprisingly.

"Contrary to belief, there's more information about the mission and the crew than the ship. In fact, there's a lot of debate about the class and size of it. The shots of the exterior are from an artist's drawings. There aren't any that have something in the picture that can give you an idea of the true size. It all depends on what picture you're looking at, which determines the exterior configuration. Some interior pictures have survived, but there are many unanswered questions. I've read everything about the ship, and I can tell you it hasn't prepared me for actually being here." He paused for a moment and then pointed toward the belly of the ship. "Do you see that right there? It's the aft access ramp. Unlike today's cargo lifts, they would deploy a ramp and carry or pull things into the ship. It looks as if their access ramp has taken some damage."

"Could it have been damaged when the ground gave way?"

"Maybe, but it would have had to have been down then. Something doesn't make sense,"

"What's that?"

Sam gestured with his hands while he explained. "It was standard procedure back then to send a few people out to inspect the landing gear and where they landed. The first thing they would do was secure the entirety of the ship into full shutdown mode." Pointing ahead, he continued, "They brought drilling equipment down, so it is fair to assume they planned to drill for core samples. Also, assuming the ships were down, they felt safe. They lowered the ramp to inspect the landing gear but decided to save themselves an extra trip and bring the drilling equipment down. The ground gave way during or after the inspection, and the access ramp is damaged."

I nodded, following his thought process. "I agree with that logic, and it seems to fit what we can see. I don't understand what you think is strange?"

"The strange part is the access ramp. Why did they take it back up without repairing it first? It would have been much easier to have repaired it while it was down. They can't go back into space with damage unless they did an emergency patch from the inside, but I don't know why they would do that."

"What do you mean by an emergency patch?"

"Today, when we get hit by a micro-meteor, we have foam we spray into the hole to seal it; back then, they didn't have that. If something happened, they would get some steel and weld it shut. They would have welded several steel plates over the hole on something like this. With the foam we use, we can easily remove it without any further damage. Back then, to repair, you had to remove the plate, which required a cutting torch or a grinder. The problem is that this method creates more damage. Not to mention it's used in an emergency situation in space in case of a hull breach." stated Sam.

"Guys, you two are missing the most obvious possible reason." Lisa pointed to the ground. "Maybe they were trying to stop something out here from getting in."

The crew stared at her in disbelief, including myself. Her explanation disturbed me; there were no reports of alien encounters to date. I hoped she was reading too much into it and was wrong.

She glanced around and noticed everyone staring at her. "This place was probably a lot different when they landed here compared to today."

★★★★★★★★★★★★★★

Pops

I slowly made my way up the crater with team four as my passengers. I tried to look ahead as the rover moved side to side for anything that could be used as a pathway. I was stuck in my thoughts about how well the rover performed when we suddenly reached the highest peak it could take us. I found a spot where the rover was almost level and shut it down. Looking down at the crater wall, I was impressed; it managed to make it farther up than I had initially thought. The nose of the Nightingale loomed overhead as I looked up the crater wall.

"That's it, Wanda. This is as high as I can take you. Your team will walk the rest of the way. When you're ready to come back down, either descend on your own or call me."

"We'll be alright. Going down is a lot easier than going up. This ride saved us a lot of time." Wanda replied

We both laughed as the team climbed out of the rover and grabbed their backpacks with their equipment. They put on their climbing gear, each waiting for Wanda's signal. She signaled them and began to climb the rest of the way to the top. I shuddered at the thought of how cold it would be for them. Even wearing the arctic suit, I felt the temperature change with each breath. I started the rover and looked at the air temperature gauge, which read minus twenty-one. I was only two-thirds of the way up the wall of the crater. I could only imagine the temperature once they reached the top. I began the trip back down and soon forgot about them. The only thing between me and my team was open terrain. I decided to open up the throttle and have some fun on my way back. Turning left and right, I kicked up the dust and ice bits, and the rover responded like a precision vehicle. When I hit the bumps and hills, I occasionally went airborne. I laughed the whole time and completely forgot I was in an alien world.

✳✳✳✳✳✳✳✳✳✳✳✳✳✳

Sam

Both teams examined the exterior of the Discovery, trying to find a way in. Something caught my eye, and I stepped back and looked off in the distance, only to see a small moving cloud of dust. Curious, I tried to figure out what it was, and I reached into my backpack and pulled out a pair of binoculars. I quickly focused and chuckled at what I saw.

I lowered the binoculars and shouted, "Hey Mike, come here for a minute."

"What do you have, Sam?"

He approached me as I lowered the binoculars and handed them to him while pointing to the distant dust cloud. "Check out Pops."

Mike looked through the binoculars and laughed, "He's just having a little fun. I have to admit he's one crazy son of a gun."

"Crazy is an understatement. He's out of his mind,"

"I don't know if I would go as far as to say he is out of his mind. I just hope he doesn't kill himself," remarked Mike.

"Doesn't kill himself?" I was shocked. "Are you kidding me, or have you forgotten that he is carrying enough explosives in his toolbox on that rover to kill everyone down here?"

Mike quickly lowered the binoculars and looked at me. He had forgotten about the explosives, and he was pretty sure Pops had, too.

Pops was always known for bringing more explosives than needed. When asked why, he always said he never knew what he would get into that day and always wanted to come prepared. Most would say he was crazy and irresponsible for always bringing that much.

"That son of a bitch is out of his mind," stated Mike with anger in his voice.

"I couldn't have said it better myself, Mike."

I watched Mike get on the radio, "This is team two leader to team one leader." He paused and then repeated, "This is team two leader to team one leader." He paused again to wait for a response. "Come on, Pops, answer me. I can see you from where I'm at."

Mike pulled out his tablet and turned the rover camera on, and we could see Pops. He was having the time of his life. He didn't have a care in the world. You could hear Mike call out from the radio, and a look of disappointment crossed his face. He slowly became aware of the voice on the radio.

"Hey Mike, you have really got to try this rover of mine. This thing turned out awesome and is loads of fun," he said through the radio.

"I can see that from here. It looks like you're having a lot of fun,"

"How do I look from over there?" he asked.

"Everything looks great. Except for one detail you forgot about,"

"Oh yeah, and what detail might that be?"

"You have the potential for blowing us up. Have you forgotten you're carrying a load of explosives?"

Pops looked over his shoulder to the back, then returned his eyes to what was in front of him. His laughter stopped, and he began to slow the rover down. He took a deep breath, and you could see the realization of what could have happened all over his face.

"Sorry, I forgot. I'll be more careful," replied Pops.

Mike shook his head, looked at me, and said, "He's just excited to have a chance to take it out and play. To tell you the truth, I would have done the same if I were in his position. I just can't believe that he forgot about the explosives."

"I don't know about you, but having fun can make me forget everything else. I completely understand his actions. If I had been driving, I never would have heard your call over the music. I..." a voice cried out before I could finish.

"Hey guys! Over Here! I found a way onto the ship!" Lisa shouted from behind us.

We both turned around and saw her standing by one of the landing pods, now resting on the ground. We walked toward her as she waved us to hurry up. The closer we got, the more I saw a breach in the hull. It could be seen from a few angles. I stepped inside, pulled my flashlight, and moved it around, taking in my surroundings. Upon glancing around, Lisa tapped me on the shoulder and pointed to a partially open door.

"Good job, Lisa. Gather up the rest of the team and have them rally here. Once everyone is here, we'll enter the ship through the hatch you found." I said to her,

She hurried outside to gather the team.

Mike walked up and said, "I think she's crazy about you."

"Well, I'm crazy about her, too," I replied.

"I thought you and Kellie were a couple. What happened there?" Mike asked, looking shocked.

"We were a couple before I came onboard, and I must admit I thought for a while there was a chance for us to rekindle when she became a member of our crew. It wasn't in the stars, and now we are friends."

"I don't know. I think Kellie still has a place in her heart for you. Everyone can see the way she looks at you. I think she will freak out when she finds out about the two of you."

"Actually, I already talked to her, and she seemed ok with it. I don't think it will bother her much,"

"How long were you with Kellie?"

"Before I came into space, we were together for about two and a half years. That was five or six years ago, though. We stayed in touch, but nothing happened,"

"How long have you and Lisa been together?"

"It's been about four or five months now. We decided to keep things quiet until we had given our relationship a chance and I could talk to Kellie."

"You talked to Kellie on the way down here, didn't you?" He watched with half-squinted eyes.

I nodded yes.

"That explains why she acted weird when I got onto the flight deck. I think there's something you should know. It's about Kellie and one of your team members, Lexey."

"What about them?" I asked, puzzled.

"You should know...," he started.

Lisa returned with the rest of the team.

"We'll finish this talk later," Mike said before he changed the subject. "What's the plan once you get inside?"

"This hatch should put us on the lower deck somewhere in the cargo area. We'll go up to the mid-deck and back to engineering. With a little luck and Lexey's help, I hope to restore some power to the ship. After that, we'll split into two groups. My group will explore the upper deck while the other explores the mid-deck. About that time, your team should be done examining the exterior and can join us by the cargo area," I stated.

"Sounds like a plan. Good luck, and we'll see you inside. I'll let you know when my team joins you."

Mike left the pod, and I signaled my team to make their way to the partially open hatch. As they approached, I noticed some impact damage, as though something had rammed it. The closer I got, I could see there was damage to the hinges. Usually, the hinges are in a straight vertical line, but these weren't. It almost looked as if something very heavy had hung onto the door, and once it was open, it caused the hinges to twist. When I approached the hatch, I reached out and tried to open it. I figured it was jammed, and it was. It was only open about six inches, but it gave us enough room to grab hold of. Some of the team grabbed the hatch and tried to pull it open. A few team members looked around to see if they could find anything to pry it open.

I stood back to catch my breath for a moment. I watched their effort for a few moments and was about to move in to offer my help. I felt a tap on my shoulder and turned around to see Lisa. She motioned with her head for me to follow her. I followed her as she led me away from the others, and then she stopped and turned around to face me.

"Take a look at this." She shines her flashlight at the wall.

I looked at the wall where her flashlight beam was shining. There were dents, scratches, and black cone-shaped burn marks all over the wall. I recognized it immediately; as weapons fire, it made those marks.

My expression changed to a blank stare, trying to decipher what could have happened and why the marks were on the wall.

"What the hell happened here, Sam?" she asked.

"I don't know," I said as I sighed. I turned toward her and continued, "For years, I wanted to find this ship and solve the mystery of what happened here. When we found her, I wanted to get down here. I thought figuring out why the ground gave out under the landing gear would be easy. I figured we would rule that as just an unstable surface. The Nightingale up on the ridge, we could say that it was just too cold up there for them. It would be just a poorly chosen landing site. We are starting to get into this ship, and we find a hatch that looks like it has been hit by a missile and you find this. Obviously, the result of weapons fire. By the looks of it, they were shooting at something. All I can hope is that whatever they were shooting at was either killed or that it has long since died. I have a horrible feeling about this ship." I looked around, looking for something to explain this feeling, and said, "I want to get in there and get this done so we can get back to our shuttle and get off this frozen rock."

"I'm not sure if I want to know what we will find inside this ship," remarked Lisa.

✳✳✳✳✳✳✳✳✳✳✳✳✳✳
Wanda

I was with team four on top of the crater ridge; we had just finished clearing the ice away from the access hatch and tried to open it. We brought torches to melt the ice to gain faster access. Two team members moved the hatch release lever once the ice cleared enough for us to open. After some struggle they managed to get it unlocked. They struggled as it slowly began to open. Finally, it opened, and those who tried were out of breath. They all looked relieved that the door was open. If the hatch wasn't going to open, our only option would have been to cut a hole into the ship.

As the team lead, I was the first to step forward and use my flashlight beam to look around inside the ship. The only thing I could see was the inside of this airlock. I cautiously entered the ship, followed by the rest of the team. With each step I took, the ice cracked from under my weight. It echoed from my teammates' steps as well. I thought opening the airlock's inner hatch would be difficult. I noticed it was slightly ajar as I approached it. Grabbing the handle, I pushed with my shoulder, and it opened relatively easily. I stepped into a large room, and soon, the others joined my flashlight beam as each one stepped out of the airlock. The light reflected back at us, almost like shining a light on a mirror. The walls, the controls, and everything around were covered with a thin layer of ice. It was almost as if someone had put up a glass wall around everything like they do in a museum to keep people from touching them.

"This is amazing," remarked Bart as he looked around.

I turned around and asked him, "What's so amazing about this?"

"These ships, I read about them in the history books. I even saw one in a museum once. Back then, the engines were bulky and took up a good portion of the ship. In the first generation of deep space ships, fifty to sixty-five percent of the ships were cargo, fuel, or engines. The early ships had little room for anything like a sick bay or their own quarters. There could be as many as six people sharing a room. The engines got smaller as time passed, and living space became more important. Soon, they realized nothing could have been done without a severe accident in space. So, that is when they began to think about these ships. They were known as the third generation of ships. They couldn't solve a few problems with the third generation of ships, which was still due to the engines. So, that program was put on hold. The fourth generation of ships solved many problems, but not all. So, they immediately began work on a new design based on the fourth-generation engines. That, of course, brought on the fifth generation of ships, and these ships were the first to be built with them. The Discovery down there had, I believe, the fourth-generation engines. The engines were still too big to be used for shuttles. It wasn't until the seventh or eighth generation of engines that using shuttles became practical. Until then, the ships had to land on a planet to do any kind of rescue mission. This ship was special, and they built four of these ships and kept them in a constant rotation. One would be fueling and stocking up at Earth, the second would be on its way to deep space, the third would be in deep space, and the fourth would return home. The theory was that with this constant rotation, everyone should be near one of them," explained Bart.

"Nice history lesson, but I don't see what makes this ship so special."

"With the space the new engines created, they put in a state-of-the-art medical facility. They have equipment on here to handle any kind of emergency that might come along. They had a good-sized cargo area where they stored and distributed supplies. They were also known for having the best cooks in space. They even say this ship should have a movie theater in it.

Most importantly, this was the first ship with the new engines. Ships came from all over to visit her when she was out here. Until they went to look for the Discovery, this crew always found any missing ships and rendered aid. She went to look for the Discovery and was never heard from again," stated Bart

"I didn't know you were some kind of history buff. I'm surprised you and Sam don't sit down and exchange stories," I remarked.

"No way," he replies quickly. "Sam knows everything about two ships, the one we are part of and the Discovery down there. However, I am more interested in the history of space travel. I read about ships that did things first. Like the first ship to break a speed record, the first ship of their class, and the first ship with each new generation of engines. Now, this ship interests me. She was the first in her class to type and the first with this class of engines. It's true that we have medical ships today, but this was the first, and it's not like the ones we have today that all work out of spaceports. We built those places for us to go for supplies, entertainment, and medical needs. The medical ships that we have now are mainly search and rescue ships and trauma centers. They transport you back to the spaceport where the real hospital is. Back then, these ships had to do all of that. They had to entertain, supply, and provide medical assistance. Just think about what it would have been like to have been on a ship like this," Bart said excitedly.

While looking around the room, I noticed the others couldn't help but hear what Bart had been saying.

"Be careful, Wanda. You might have trouble getting him off this ship. It sounds like he's in love," Dawn said.

It was a good thing we were all wearing arctic suits with masks because there was no way I could stand there and not smile. As team leader, I was expected to show some restraint. The other team members didn't express as much restraint, and they all started to snicker and chuckle.

Bart looked around and replied, "I can't help it if I am passionate about history. You don't get to touch a piece of history like this every day. I'll admit I am a bit excited."

"Passionate, you say? I think that is an understatement. Would you like the rest of us to leave so that the two of you can be alone?" Berry said as he could not miss an opportunity to express his opinion.

Before Bart could respond to that remark, Rick reached into his bag, pulled out a small hand towel, tossed it to him, and said, "Here, Bart, I think you might need this; I think you're getting a little too excited. You'll need it to clean up the mess."

After that, no one could hold back from laughing, including me. There was nothing more he could do but stand there and keep his mouth shut. The laughing and joking continued for a few more minutes before I finally decided they had picked on him long enough.

"Ok, everyone, let's settle down. We still have to explore this ship. Since Bart seems to be an expert on this ship, I want Nancy and Rick to join him and explore the upper decks. The rest of us will search these lower decks. If anyone finds log books or evidence of what happened here, collect or document it. We will meet back here in an hour to compare notes."

Six

It Starts

Pat

An explosion caused rock and dirt to rain down near the blasting site. As the falling rocks diminished, we peeked from behind a mound to check out the damage.

Pops giggled, and I watched as Mary and Eric rolled their eyes and shook their heads in disbelief. The two of them walked off toward the drill near the rover.

"Thanks a lot, Pops. Pretty sure you just blew the samples halfway across the planet." Linda said.

"Hey, Pops, don't you think you used just a little too much explosives?" I added.

Pops nodded in agreement but still laughed. "I might have used just a little bit more than necessary, but considering all the ice around us. I thought the ground would have been a lot harder. After all, the drill had to go through hard rock. You guys chipped away to make blast holes. How was I supposed to know the ground was soft?"

"Pops, you're hopeless," Linda said.

"What? I didn't mean to do it," he replied.

I left the hiding spot and walked with Pops and Jason close behind.

"Pops, I think it's safe to say you love your job too much."

"Yes, I do. Where else can you get paid to blow stuff up and not get arrested?"

Everybody laughed as we continued to walk to the crater's edge, which had just been blasted away. We all looked down at the hole about twenty feet across and nine feet deep. Linda was one step ahead of me and had already set a ladder on one of the side's edges. We made our way over to the ladder and made it down.

Pops peered around and was surprised by his handiwork. "The blast crater should not have been this large for solid rock, which I thought I was blasting. This could have happened only if the surface was just a thin layer of hard rock, and everything under was very loose dirt. I don't understand how the difference could be significant just a hundred yards away. Previously, you drilled five feet and hit nothing but rock."

I began climbing down the ladder first and stopped halfway before adding. "Do you still think you didn't use too much explosives?"

"Maybe just a little too much," Pops said, pinching the air.

"If this is a little too much," added Linda, laughing, "I have to be around to see when you use way too much."

Pops busted up laughing, and I could hear him as he walked away with Jason. They were both out of sight, thus leaving Linda and me to do the dirty work. I squatted to take a handful of dirt and investigate the substance. It was loose and yet moist. I looked behind me and saw the dirt was packed down from my footsteps.

"Find anything interesting?" she asked, coming up behind me.

"I don't know. The soil is unusual. It's a lot like potting soil for plants—loose and moist yet packed together," I said as I closed my hand over the dirt.

Linda pointed at the hole's rim and said, "That layer of rock must have kept the moisture in the soil so it didn't freeze."

"Look at that over there!"

The dirt wall had collapsed, and it looked like an air pocket. Carefully, we inched closer and used our flashlights to light the way toward the underground tunnel. The blast caved in one wall on the side of the tunnel, exposing it.

"This must be one of those tunnels we heard about," remarked Linda as she looked around.

"That is so sweet!" I responded. "Look at the walls. They are dirt, rock, or just solid rock. Do you think this could be an old extinct lava tube?"

"I don't know, but I suggest we go ahead and check it out,"

We both slowly continued to enter the tunnel. It was a lot larger than I thought it would be. The both of us could comfortably stand without stooping.

As I investigated, the beam from my flashlight went from left to right. I asked Linda, "Which way would you like to go?"

She looked both ways several times and answered, "I say we go left. We can see a good distance down the tunnel to the right, but there is a curve to the left, and we can't see beyond it."

I motioned for her to lead the way, and we descended the tunnel toward the curve. We paused momentarily to investigate the tunnel and looked around in great detail before continuing. Shortly after rounding the corner, Linda screamed. I looked into the eyes of several creatures. Even in the dark, I could tell it was huge. The only way I could see anything from the creatures was from the beam of the flashlights. I hesitated at the thought of using the flashlight as a weapon as I needed it to see, but my fight or flight reflex kicked in. I looked at Linda's flashlight flailing around and the sound of her hitting the creature. I instinctively did the same, but nothing happened.

I watched as one of the creatures reached out and swung its giant paw with extended claws at Linda, and she never stood a chance. The creature sliced her open, and her intestines dropped from her body.

Fear froze me in my place as I watched a second strike sever her head from her body. I turned around and tried to run, but something sharp hit my leg, and I fell to the ground. I rolled over and swung my flashlight in any direction I could, but it was knocked from my hands. Attempting to roll back over and army crawl away, something grabbed my legs and dragged me backward into the tunnel. I dared to look away from the tunnel's depths and watched as the flashlight thrown around the corner we had ventured down began to fade. It was all happening so fast, but I concentrated on that flashlight and saw blood trickling down the lens. I felt a sharp pain in my back before it all went dark.

★★★★★★★★★★★★★★

Jason

Pops was checking on the drill's progress. I watched as he looked over the rig and then inspected the computer. We all knew the computer could only tell us so much. If he needed any additional information, Pops would need to communicate with the drillers.

"How is the drilling going?" I asked Mary.

"We're not doing too bad. We drilled the first hole over there," she said, pointing to a spot about twenty feet away. "We went down about five feet and hit nothing but solid rock. With this one, we started the same way for about two feet, then hit pockets of loose dirt. Almost five feet now, and we are in another layer of solid rock. After this one, we plan to move fifty yards further out."

"This is one of the strangest planets I've ever been on. Over there, it is solid rock; here is a mix, and not to mention where we blasted is a small layer of rock and then loose dirt. This is all interesting stuff, but it still doesn't answer the questions that brought us here. Why is this crater not covered in ice like the rest of the planet?"

The drill suddenly dropped the last foot and a half, and Mary and Eric shut it down quickly. I watched as they completed a quick check of the equipment to ensure it was not a mechanical issue. After they completed their check, both walked toward the computer and verified the readings to determine what had just happened.

"I don't know what just happened, but I can tell you it's not a mechanical problem. The equipment checks out, and the computer says that we were looking good," Eric said as he looked at Pops.

"The only thing I can think of is we hit some kind of air or gas pocket," Mary added.

"Well, whatever it is, we'll have to pull the drill out and see how deep it goes. Do you think it might be one of those underground tunnels?" Pops asked.

Both Eric and Mary looked at each other and shrugged their shoulders.

"We looked at all the scans we made before leaving the ship. We picked this spot because there were no tunnels here. In fact, there are very few that are even near the surface. Since this is a dead, frozen planet, there is no way that a tunnel could have been made here since we left the ship," replied Eric.

"So, considering our scans are not perfect, it has to be some sort of air or gas pocket. If it was a tunnel, we could have seen that easily. A pocket of some sort would have shown up as a dark mass, and we could have mistaken it for a rock," Mary said.

"Alright, let's pull the drill out and see what we have," I said to them.

They moved back toward the drill and began to work on removing it.

"Run over to the blast site and get Linda and Pat. Since they have had a chance to look at things below the surface, maybe they can help us figure out what we have here." Pops said to me.

I walked into the distance to get the others while Pops helped Mary and Eric. The blast site really wasn't that far from where we were. A protrusion from the wall of the crater prevented us from having a direct line of sight with each part of the team. As I walked around the protrusion, I could see the blast site and noticed no one up top. I figured they must be in the hole taking samples.

"Pat, Linda," I shouted as I approached the hole.

I expected them to answer or pop out of the hole to see what was up, but no response or movement was detected. I reached the hole's edge and peered into it to get a better look but saw nothing.

"Where the hell can they be?" I mumbled to myself. I looked around and saw a glimmer of light. "Is that a cave or a tunnel? Whatever that is, they must be inside and can't hear me. I guess I will have to go down there and get them." I continued talking to myself.

I decided to climb down the ladder and investigate the situation. I strained my eyes from the significant light fluctuation. I began to walk to the far side of the hole where I thought I had seen the light. The closer I got, the more I could tell there was a hole in the tunnel wall. I stepped through the hole, flicked on my flashlight, and adjusted my eyesight to just the beam's light. I moved the beam right and couldn't see anything, then moved it to the left and noticed a bend in the tunnel. I saw another flashlight beam on the tunnel's floor.

"That's strange," I said aloud.

Many thoughts raced through my head about why the flashlight would be on the ground, and I decided one of them must have set it down and forgotten about it. After all, there were two of them, and both of them had flashlights. Maybe one was holding the light while the other collected samples.

Slowly, I walked toward the light. A sudden uneasy feeling began to come over me.

"Linda! Pat! Can you hear me?" I yelled out.

No response, only silence. I stopped at the flashlight and squatted down to take a closer look. The lens was broken, and it had dents like it had been used as a weapon. I saw blood on the handle, and as I continued my examination, a deep, long, emanating growl came from ahead of me. Slowly, I looked toward the noise and saw something so vile it made my heart race, and cold chills ran down my spine. Glowing eyes looked at me from a few hundred yards in the tunnel. I stood petrified as they got larger and closer as the creature came toward me. A sudden thought pierced my being, and I knew I didn't want to be around when whatever was on the other end of the tunnel got to me.

I leaped to my feet, ran faster than I had ever done in my entire life, and headed toward the tunnel entrance. I was just a few feet short of the exit when something tripped me, and I hit the ground, sliding on my stomach. The flashlight hit the ground, broke my grip, and tumbled a few feet before me. In one swift motion, I rolled over, got myself into a sitting position, and backpedaled to get away. I tried to reach for my flashlight to use it as a weapon. I watched as the glowing eyes were just a few feet from me. It opened its mouth, and an eerie, deep growl was released. I continued to backpedal while trying to reach around for my dropped flashlight. I never took my eyes off the creature. I couldn't believe the glow from the flashlight had lured me here and was the only thing that allowed me to see the silhouette of the bulking figure.

Finally, I took hold of my flashlight and immediately swung at the creature, hoping it would scare it off. A dull thud was the only sound the flashlight made as it hit its tough exterior. The attack didn't have the effect I had hoped for. Instead of scaring it, I was enraged. It moved so fast I didn't see what had happened, only felt the excruciating pain as it bit my calf about midway with my foot inside its mouth. It felt like razors pierced my skin, and I shrieked in pain. I didn't know if anyone could hear me, but I continued yelling even though I could feel the blood pooling around the wounds. I repeatedly hit the creature with my flashlight, hoping it would release me. The creature picked me up by my leg, which was still in its mouth, and threw me against the ceiling like a rag doll. As I began to fall, the creature bit me harder, severing my leg. I hit the ground so hard it knocked the wind from me, and I let go of my only useless weapon, the flashlight.

Stunned by the pain, I felt blood trickle down my face and heard the crunching of bones. I knew what happened to the other crews that had landed here so long ago and were never heard from again. My crewmates and I were now added to that list of never being heard from again. My only hope was that the others could figure it out before they, too, suffered the same fate. Consciousness slowly drifted in and out, and I felt the creature bite my other leg. It dragged me deeper into the tunnel, leaving small pools of blood and a banged-up flashlight behind me.

★★★★★★★★★★★★★★

Pops

Mary, Eric, and I finally finished withdrawing the drill from the ground. A foul odor made us turn our heads while we slid the drilling rig out of the way. We each took several steps back, fanning our hands in front of our faces as though we could swat away the odor.

"I've smelled some nasty stuff in my years, but damn, this is the worst thing I've ever smelled. Did you get this smell when you drilled the last hole?" I asked.

"No, there wasn't a smell from the last hole. We must have hit a gas pocket." Eric shook his head while he covered his mouth with his hands.

"I'm glad we have these arctic masks on. They can filter out some of the smell. I would hate to guess what it would smell like without them." Mary added, covering her mouth.

I followed their lead and covered my mouth as I inched slowly toward the hole we drilled. Eric and Mary looked at each other and decided to keep their distance. Knowing I would never see anything through that tiny hole, I focused on the drill. Immediately, I noticed something on the bottom of it.

"Look at the drill! There's some organic matter on it. You must have hit something else down there, and whatever it was had to be alive and not frozen," I said.

"Knowing our luck, we hit the alien equivalent of a cesspool," commented Eric.

"Whatever it is, I think we need to find the others. That way no one will have to stay near that stench too long." I said as I looked toward the rest of the site. "Jason should have been back with the others by now. "Why don't the two of you go investigate. It will be an excuse to get some fresh air."

"Yeah, we'll let them be the first to go in and examine the organic matter and enjoy the smell since they weren't here to get the first blast of it like we did," remarked Mary as she began to walk off.

We all laughed, and I watched as Mary and Eric headed off to get the others. I got into my rover, moved it away from the pungent smell, and waited for the others to return.

★★★★★★★★★★★★★

Jeff

I watched as Mike stood on the edge of a completely collapsed trench where the landing gear rested. In between each landing pods were small bridges made from the land where the ground had not collapsed. I looked up at the gear pods and down in the trench at the landing gear. They were massive in size to support the weight of a ship this size. Upon examination, they were surprisingly in pretty good shape, considering what had happened. If we could get the engines working, maybe we could get the ship off the planet. The biggest concern would have been the rock and debris that had buried the landing pads. I checked back into the pods situation and quickly made a side note about putting charges in the right place and detached the landing pads in case of an emergency.

"Hey Mike, what are you thinking?" I asked as I walked up behind him.

"The damage to the outside of the ship isn't that bad. I'm sure they had plenty of fuel to power the engines and pull themselves clear. Even in a worse-case situation, they could have blown the gear on the side and repaired it on the way home or even when they got home. I can't figure out why they didn't?" Mike turned around and responded.

"From the outside, we can't find any answers; let's hope Sam has better luck on the inside. There has to be an answer somewhere,"

"Yeah, maybe. I can't shake this uneasy feeling about this planet. When we were on the ship looking down, it seemed like a good idea to come down and investigate. Now we're here and can see this stuff with our own eyes. I'm beginning to think it was a terrible idea to come down here," Mike said as he looked around the planet.

"I think you're getting a little paranoid. You no doubt want to get this done and over with so we can go home. Personally, I could really use a nice long vacation after this mission. After all, there's nothing to be scared of. We are the only living creatures on this planet," I stated.

"How can you be sure? How can you say that we are the only living beings out here in space?" Mike turned and looked me straight in the eyes.

"Listen, Mike, I'm not saying that we are the only living beings in the universe. We have been traveling the stars for nearly a hundred years, and no one has ever encountered an alien life form. No one has so much as seen an alien bug or artifact."

"Doesn't mean they aren't out there or weren't out there. I mean, just take a look around us. This ship here," Mike said while gesturing his hand toward the ship, "was designed to land on planets. They were equipped with the best kind of ground-penetrating radar that was available. Using it when you land is standard procedure. The same regulations from then are still in effect today, and our radar is a lot more advanced,"

He took my arm, walked to the edge of the collapsed trench, and pointed.

See that trench? Any good pilot would never put their ship down on unstable ground like that. I want you to think this one over. For the sake of argument, let's say that the radar was down, and they had decided to land anyway. What are the odds that a ship of this size with six landing gear managed to place three of them directly over an underground tunnel? What are the odds the tunnel would be straight and long enough to allow all three to break through?"

I briefly thought about what he said while looking down at the trench and then responded, "I would say the odds are pretty slim."

"Are you kidding me? Slim doesn't even cover it. The odds are more like a billion to one. When we took the readings from space, we had no theory of why the other tunnels in this area were deep except this one. For some reason, a tunnel comes up from the deep just before the forward landing gear, goes directly beneath the landing gear, and then returns to the deep just after the aft landing gear." He pointed to the different areas where the tunnel hadn't collapsed and continued, "Just look at the areas where the tunnel didn't collapse. The tunnel is layered like one tunnel on top of the other and just wide enough for the landing pads to fall through."

"What are you trying to say, Mike?"

"Remember, this is a guess, but let's assume there were aliens here when the Discovery landed. Maybe there were some kind of alien smugglers that dug tunnels underground to hide their goods. Maybe it was dumb luck that they landed on the tunnels, or it collapsed over time. I don't know, but just think about the what-ifs."

"So you're saying aliens dug these tunnels," I said as I began to understand his theory, even though it was hard to believe.

"Exactly. What else do you think made these tunnels? Maybe they are even still here watching us and waiting for their chance to kill us. Now, keep in mind that this is just a theory." Mike looked at me with wide eyes through his arctic goggles.

"It may be a theory, but it does support all of the facts we can see here," I remarked.

Mike looked at me for a moment without blinking. I didn't see Sarah standing behind me, being quiet as a mouse. She suddenly touched my shoulder, and I jumped and backed away from the touch. My heart pounded, and my breathing became uneven and heavy from the near heart attack from the scare.

"Sarah, you asshole, you scared the hell out of me! Don't you ever sneak up on me like that again!" I yelled.

"Mike is great at making up stories to scare people. This was one of his better stories; you fell for it hook, line, and sinker." Sarah said.

I watched Sarah and Mike high-five each other and laugh from a scare well done.

Pointing at the two of them, I said, "I'm going to get the two of you back for this, just wait and see. I will not forget this." I turned and walked off in the direction of the forward landing gear. As I walked off, I could still hear them talking.

"I've heard you tell many stories over the years, and I have to say this was one of your best stories yet. I really don't know how you do it. You can look around and make stuff up without even cracking a smile." Sarah said.

"It's a gift. If you really want to see something, you should come and see me play poker. That's when holding a straight face is really important. Besides, having the mask on makes telling a believable story even easier." Mike said.

"You know Mike, you almost had me believing you. If I didn't already know what you were planning to do," Sarah said.

"Sarah, you have been a good friend to me and have been my silent partner in so many practical jokes over the years. You know me so well that I don't think I could ever get away with playing a joke on you."

"What do you really think happened here?" Sarah asked.

"I don't know, Sarah, but I'm sure it didn't have anything to do with aliens. Those were probably lava tubes that made their way to the surface and broke through the rock along this trench. For all we know, this trench might have only collapsed a year or two ago. It may not even have anything to do with why this ship never returned home. I don't think there is a whole lot more we will be able to tell from out here. The answers will be in the repair and the Captain's logs."

"Well, no matter if we find out what happened or not, we will at least be getting a footnote in the history books as the ship that found the Discovery and the Nightingale," remarked Sarah.

"You're right, but they should give us more than a footnote. Maybe they should at least give us a paragraph or two. I think we're through here, so why don't you go and gather up the team and have them meet here." Mike said laughingly.

Sarah walked off to gather the team, and I was lost thinking about what had really happened. Continuing my walk, I eventually went down in the trench by the forward landing gear; I decided to take a closer look at the tunnel. What Mike said still ran through my mind. I turned on my flashlight and walked inside. After about five feet, something caught my eye. The beam from my flashlight quickly settled on a piece of cloth. I squatted to pick it up and dust it off. After I shook it a few times, I shined the light onto it and realized it was the uniform patch from a member of the Discovery. It had been torn away with some of the uniform still attached, and it looked like blood was stained.

Something touched my shoulder, and I shrugged it off and continued to examine the patch.

"Go away, Sarah! I'm not going to fall for another one of your pranks," I said as I looked at the patch and saw how the material had been ripped.

Something touched my shoulder again. This time, I was angry about the interruption. I stood up and spun around.

"That's enough, Sarah. You have really got to stop..." I stopped mid-sentence as I looked to see the glowing eyes of a creature. Dropping the patch, I turned and ran out of fear. I soon realized I was going deeper into the tunnel. I had gotten about another fifteen feet before something hit me, sending me flying through the air and hitting a tunnel wall. I slumped to the floor and began to pick myself up. I saw something coming toward me, and in one swift move, I saw the creature slash at my throat.

✳✳✳✳✳✳✳✳✳✳✳✳✳

Lisa

Sam and I made our way down one of the corridors toward the bridge with only our flashlights to light the way. We discovered we needed to walk carefully as the ship sat at an angle. We stopped suddenly as the ship's interior lights came on. We looked around as if the light was something foreign to us, and I turned to look at Sam, puzzled, only to find him with the same expression.

Sam reached for his radio and set the frequency before speaking, "Lexey, how did you manage to regain power?"

"I wish I could take all the credit, Sam, but I can't. It looks like they finished many of the ship repairs before they disappeared. All it took was a jump from our portable generator; she is up and running. We have lights, life support, and even heat. We will soon be able to get out of these damn arctic suits." Lexey said through the radio.

"That's great news, Lexey. Have you found any bodies yet?" Sam asked.

"No. It is like a ghost town down here. There are signs that many of the repairs were completed, but no sign of anyone. There is one strange thing I have noticed," stated Lexey.

"Yes?" asked Sam.

"There were a lot of modifications made from down here. Normally, an old ship like this would need a minimum of six crew members to fly it. Someone made a lot of mods so one person would be able to fly it. Some of these were completely unheard of back when this ship was flying. Others were still just theoretical and had never been tested. Whoever did this knew this ship and a great deal more. When you get to the bridge, I bet you will see a lot of mods as well," stated Lexey.

Sam looked at me and said, "At least we know someone lived for a while." He turned to the radio and asked, "How long before it will be warm enough to take these suits off?"

"It's going to be several hours before the temperature is high enough to get rid of the suits. In the meantime, watch out for possible falling ice as we thaw out this old tub,"

"Lexey, what is the status of the engines?" asked Sam.

"I don't know yet. I haven't taken a look at them. It's the next thing on my agenda. I'll call you and let you know."

"The Bridge is just a short distance ahead, and I think we should check it out," I said.

Sam looked in my direction and noticed something on the door behind me.

"You go ahead. I'm going to check out these quarters." He nodded to the one behind me. I turned to see us standing in front of the Captain's quarters. I realized what this meant to him, so I decided that going to the ship's bridge could wait.

I motioned for him to proceed and said, "I think we should check this out first. If we are going to find any answers to what happened here, this would be the most likely place to go."

Sam smiled as he stepped past me and tried to open the door. It was a little tricky because we could see it was partially blocked from the inside. The hinges were bent as though something had repeatedly hit the door. Back then, wood on a ship was unheard of, so the doors were steel hatches. We entered the room; Sam examined the door and the stuff behind it that partially blocked it.

Once he was satisfied, we went to investigate the Captain's desk. The desk was set off into the corner on the left side of the room. Above the desk to the left and in front of where you would sit were book-shelves filled with various books. Next to the desk was a locker.

I looked at all the books but didn't recognize some, so I asked, "What are these books, Sam?"

"Which ones are you asking about?" he asked.

I pointed to the ones in the middle of the shelf that I had been look-ing at, "These ones right here without anything written on the spine."

"Those are the Captain's logs. There is one for each of his space missions."

I didn't respond, but knew there was a puzzled look upon my face.

"Today, a Captain is trained and required to keep a computer record of the daily events on the ship. Back in the day, they were told to keep computer records down to just the facts of the day. The old school Captains, like my great-great grandfather, would keep a written record of their time in space. This was a place where they could write down their feelings and thoughts and describe what happened. It almost made you feel like you were there with them. It was so much better than just the cold facts. Today, our ships have a much higher storage capacity, so the Captain can record more now. However, the art of a descriptive log has been lost in time."

I nodded in acknowledgment and stepped away to take a better look at the room. At the same time, Sam continued to rustle around at the desk, looking for something. Surprised by the condition of the room, I expected to see some things strewn about, but this place was a real mess. Trash was all over the floor, and food wrappers, cans, and bottles were scattered all over the room. I figured something was missing as I got to the corner opposite the desk. When I moved some trash, I saw holes where something was once secured.

The Captain's quarters were the largest on the ship. They usually consisted of a work area with a desk, a sleeping area, a sitting area, a private bathroom, and a large closet. Sam was in the work area, and I figured that I was standing in the sleeping area. Still facing the wall, I looked to my left and saw a large window to look out into space. I assumed that must have been his sitting area, but the furniture was also gone from there. I looked to my right and noticed something I missed when we entered the room.

The room had an 'L' shape to it. When I looked, I could see something wasn't right. I made my way to the other side of the room, where I found a wall of furniture. Some had been from this room, but most had come from other crew quarters. I could see other crew members' names stenciled on some of the pieces. The furniture was stacked tight from the floor to the ceiling. Through the cracks, I could see a lot of light coming from the other side. I took a few steps back and examined the furniture wall to find a way past it. After looking it over, I noticed one piece seemed a little out of place in the lower right corner of this wall. It was a locker that was left standing upright and with the handles facing out. The other lockers in the pile were all on their sides and had the backs facing out.

I walked over to the locker, opened it, and was surprised to see that it looked like an ordinary empty locker. I thought something was wrong, so I took a step back. There wasn't any other way to the other side. I knew something was over there. I just needed to find a way to get to it. There were scrapes inside the locker, but this wasn't unusual. I had a sudden idea, so I entered the locker and closed the door. With the bright light on the other side of the locker, I could now see how it was latched. There was a simple old-fashioned gate latch on the other side of the back of the locker. I pulled off one of my gloves, reached for my pocket knife, and opened it to one of the longer blades. I stuck it into the crack made just below what I thought was the latch and drew the knife upward. My hunch was correct as the back panel released and swung open.

Immediately, I shaded my eyes from the bright lights on the side of the wall. I allowed my eyes to adjust from darkness to light and then walked around to investigate. On this side of the wall were the bathroom and the closet. There was even more trash than the other side, but most of it had been pushed into one of the corners. I walked into the bathroom and looked around. It was a mess, but it didn't really surprise me, considering the condition of the rest of the room. The vents and access panels had been welded shut as though someone tried very hard to keep something out. I was about to exit the bathroom when I saw what might have been bloody bandages mixed in with the trash.

I left them alone, decided to move to the closet, and looked around. A mattress to block the light was in the entrance, and another was on the floor for sleep. You could see where a person had slept was a slew of weapons and ammunition. In the arsenal were books, flashlights, cups, and plates. This whole area struck me as strange. A small portable stove was just outside the closet and on this side of the wall. I noticed there was a locker just above the stove on both sides. I stared at this for a while and decided these lockers looked like they were placed there for a purpose. I walked over and opened one of them, which was filled with canned food. I opened the other to find it filled with bottled water and medical supplies.

I stepped back into the middle of the area and looked around. It looked like a homeless camp for a survivalist. I was feeling very uneasy and decided to return to the other side. After I stepped out of the locker, I closed it behind me and walked around the corner to where Sam was. I discovered he was still searching fervently through the items on the desk.

"It's not here," he said as I approached.

Curious, I asked, "What's not here?"

"The last logbook—the one that would have all his entries about what happened here—is missing. I already collected the others."

"I might know where that one is. I know you have been concentrating on the desk area since we got in here, but I think there is something that you should see first." I said carefully, taking him by the arm. "Do you see anything missing?" I asked him.

"This place is a mess. Wait a minute. Where's the furniture?" he asked.

"I'm glad you asked." I walked him around the corner and gestured with my free hand at the wall of furniture.

Surprised by what he sees, he asks, "What the hell happened here?"

"Welcome to the world of the weird. The place where your vision of a normal world is about to take a turn toward the land of the strange and bizarre, a place where for every one question that you answer, three more questions take its place. If you follow me, we will begin your journey." I walked over to the locker, opened the front doors, and said, "Now, if you will, kindly follow me inside."

Sam stopped and asked, "Why are we climbing into a locker?"

"This is not just any locker," I got out my knife and unlatched the back panel. Covering my eyes, I opened and stepped through, saying, "This is a doorway to another part of the room."

Sam quickly covered his eyes from the bright lights and asked, "What is with the bright lights?"

"No idea. For some reason, he wanted it very, very bright back here. Come on over to this side. Once you get past the doorway, it's not so bad."

Sam stepped through, taking in every detail as I did, and pointed to the brighter light caused by the addition of lights hanging around the area.

"This area is just like a homeless man's survival camp. It has its own bathroom over there, its own trash dump in that corner, a stove by the wall, and two lockers full of supplies such as food, water, and medicine.

For the main attraction, we have the sleeping arrangements. I think you will find your missing log book there, and I think it's something you should check out."

Sam looked at me and then at everything around them. He walked over to the closet and peeked in. I watched as he moved the mattress from the doorway, and his face brightened as he found the Captain's log. His whole demeanor changed as though he just found the holy grail.

"You were right when you said it was really strange here. Let's go back to the main room. It's a little too strange and too bright in here for me." he said.

Why do you think he did that?" I asked as we exited and returned to the main area.

"Something must have scared him really bad. I hope he wrote down the answers," said Sam, waving the logbook.

He set the book on the desk, moved over to the window, and looked at this strange planet. He removed his goggles, mask, and gloves and took a deep breath; I did the same but began to cough.

"The air is a little stale, but you'll get used to it," he said

I coughed for a moment or two as I got used to the air. I reached into one of my pockets, pulled out some water, took a drink, and then put it away. I walked over and joined him at the window. Outside, it wasn't very bright. It was like an overcast day at noon. There was just enough light to see things without a flashlight, but not bright enough that you needed sunglasses.

I saw a plume of dust rise from over the ridge in front of me and commented, "Looks like Pops must have just set off one of his charges."

"What do you mean?" Sam asked as I pulled him from his deep thoughts.

I pointed to the rising plume of dust from behind the ridge, saying, "Right there, Sam. That plume of dust must have come from one of his charges."

Sam's eyes got huge as he realized that something was wrong. He pointed at two different points, saying, "Pops is over there to the left.

The shuttle is just over that ridge." He grabbed his radio and keyed it while shouting, "Kellie, come in!" He paused, "Kellie, come in! This is urgent!" There was no response. He keyed the radio again, "Mike, are you listening?"

"I'm here, Sam. What's going on?" Mike asked.

"Something happened over at the shuttle. I think the ground is about to give way, and I can't reach Kellie on the radio," Sam said.

"Sam, that's not possible. The radar showed that it was all solid ground. I was there when we landed, Sam. There were no tunnels where we landed," stated Mike.

"Mike, I'm telling you that the ground under our shuttle is about to collapse. We just saw a plume of dust rise from where the shuttle is. You need to get over there as soon as possible," yelled Sam.

"Sam, don't you think you may be getting a little paranoid? Just because the ground gave way under the Discovery doesn't mean it will give way under ours," said Mike.

"Mike, you are going to just have to trust me. I'm not paranoid. There is something in here I really need to show you, but right now, my concern is the shuttle. If I'm right and the ground gives way underneath the shuttle and gets seriously damaged, we may be stranded here for a long time before we get rescued. Remember, no rescue shuttle is available onboard our ship," Sam pointed out.

There was a short pause before Mike's voice sounded over the radio. "Ok, your point is understood. We'll meet you at the shuttle. I hope we find out you're wrong when we get there."

"So do I, Mike. We'll meet you at the shuttle. In the meantime, I'll continue to try to reach Kellie,"

Sam tried to reach her several more times but was met with silence each time. He looked out the window again and tried to reach her, but there was still no reply.

Seven

Something Is Wrong

✳ ✳ ✳ ✳ ✳ ✳ ✳ ✳ ✳ ✳ ✳ ✳ ✳ ✳

Lexey

Cara and I approached the bridge to give an updated status report. Along the way, we saw Sam and Lisa coming from the Captain's quarters. I noticed both still had their arctic coats on but were unzipped and weren't wearing their gloves. They were in the process of putting their masks and gloves back on as they headed our way. I signaled Cara to flatten herself against the bulkhead on the high side of the corridor so we wouldn't be in the way when they ran by.

As they got closer, I overheard him yelling and holding onto his radio, "Kellie, this is Sam. Do you copy over?" He paused and waited for an answer before he repeated himself.

"I wonder what is going on that has them in such a hurry?" Cara asked after the two of them zoomed by.

"I don't know. I've known Sam for a long time, and he doesn't get worked up like that for nothing. The last time I saw him like that, the situation was dire." I thought about the ship's layout for a moment, then asked. "Didn't we see a medical bay on the schematics one deck down?"

Cara nodded and replied, "Yeah, I think we did. Why, what do you think is happening?"

"I'm not sure yet, but if Sam's getting worked up, we can expect bad news. I know I'm just an engineer and not a medic, but I think it would be good for you to get the medical bay ready."

"Why bother? Anyone seriously injured can be loaded back onto the shuttle and transported back to the ship,"

"Under normal circumstances, I would agree, but these aren't normal circumstances. I've felt bad since we set foot on this ship and noticed I'm not the only one. People have been scouring the ship for a while now, and nobody has reported finding a body. I've gone over everything in engineering, and the crew had completed what would have been considered minor repairs. I can't find a single reason this ship couldn't leave this planet, yet here it sits."

"Maybe the crew abandoned the ship and went up to the Nightingale,"

Cara and I walked toward a ladder leading to a lower deck when I asked. "Why abandon a functional ship? If they did go up to the Nightingale, why didn't that ship take off? From the reports given, all I'm saying is that hatch doors are welded shut, and vents with plates are welded over them."

"It sounds like they were trying to keep something out, but there is no such thing as aliens. That's what they told us when we came out here."

"No such thing as aliens that we know of. Whatever it was, it must have scared them. Besides, you heard Sam as he ran by. He called for Kellie at the shuttle. We don't fly without her; if she is injured, we will need to treat her here. I'm hoping I am wrong, and there is no one injured, but we should be ready just in case,"

We headed into the medical bay, and I began to tell some stories about Sam and me from the past. Sam could be a pain sometimes, but I admired his problem-solving capabilities. He always came up with a solution that nobody else could. Deep down, there was a slight regret as I let the past relationship with Kellie and the loud music he enjoyed playing get in the way of a possible relationship. He may not openly admit it, but I believed he had feelings for Kellie. The way he called out her name as he ran past made it sound like they were more than friends. Drifting back from my thoughts, we finally arrived at the medical bay and looked around at the mess left behind. I followed Cara's lead to get the bay up and running.

★★★★★★★★★★★★★★★

Wanda

Dawn and I walked inside the Nightingale and began our investigation. Dawn stopped in front of a set of double hatch doors. Back in the day, when this ship style was built, there were concerns about decompression. It was decided every door would have hatches so they would never lose the ship. Now we use automatic pressure doors to seal off sections of the ship, so not all doors need to be hatches. This double hatch caught my eye as the configuration was unusual, even for a more modern-day ship. Dawn reached out and opened one of the hatches, flicked her light on inside, and shined it around the room.

"Well, I'll be damned," Dawn said.

I was about to open another door when I decided to turn around and walk toward her instead and asked, "Did you find something?"

"Yeah, it's a theater. I thought Bart wasn't kidding when he said this ship had one. I never heard of any ship ever having one," Dawn replied.

"Are you serious?"

"Yeah. Come here and take a look for yourself," answered Dawn.

I pulled open the other door and used my flashlight to light the room. Inside, it had a big screen at one end and enough theater seating to hold about eighty to one hundred people. The floor was slanted at an angle to give everyone a good view, just like in the movie theaters back home.

"This is incredible. It would be great on our ship, and I've never been on a ship with a movie theater. The ones they have at the spaceports are too sterile. I bet this would make you feel like you're back home. Wonder why these are not standard on today's ships?" I remarked.

"If this ship wasn't frozen like a big block of ice, I bet she could still fly and be in service today," said Dawn.

"You're probably right, of course; it would take about a couple of months to chisel this ship out of the ice. Then, it would take a couple of months to thaw, and only then would we be able to see if she could fly."

I thought momentarily while we looked around the room before continuing, "Dawn, the only thing missing is a swimming pool. Of course, today, it would be a skating rink."

Our laughter was cut short by an excited voice that cut through the radio, "Wanda, I've located the bridge and found something that I think you should see."

"What did you find, Berry?" I replied as I grabbed my radio.

"I insist you come here and take a look," Berry's voice sounded through the radio.

"Come on, spit it out. What did you find?" I shook my head, still smiling with Dawn.

A long pause before he said in a serious voice. "I found a body."

The expression fell off both of us as we stared at each other momentarily. I slowly raised the radio to my mouth again and asked for confirmation. "Did you say a body?"

"Correct, I found the body of one male sitting in the pilot's seat."

"We're on our way," I stated.

We quickly descended the corridor, approaching a ramp leading up from the left side. We followed it to the top and found ourselves in an open room. To the left was a large conference room. In front of it was the Captain's workroom, and finally, to our right was the entrance to the bridge. We turned and walked onto the bridge, and as we entered, I saw Berry standing by the pilot's seat. He looked up and motioned for us to join him. As we approached the chair, I saw a man frozen in time. His uniform was dirty, tattered, and torn. It was easy to see a large gash in his abdominal area, and it appeared a large quantity of blood soaked into the surrounding clothing. Dawn was one of the ship medics and began to examine the wound as best she could.

"That's an honorable crew member. He was injured and alone, and he chose to die at his post," remarked Berry.

"Well, that would mean a bit more if he was actually from this ship." I pointed as I peered over the body, pointing at his sleeve, "Check out the patch on the uniform. He's from the Discovery."

"What is a crew member from the Discovery doing up here on this ship?" questioned Berry.

A sudden realization hit me. I rubbed the frost and dirt off the name patch to confirm what I suspected.

"I know who this is. It's Captain Hauzer of the Discovery." I said to both of them.

"What is he doing here?" asked Berry.

"I'm not sure. So far, he is the only body we have found, and he shouldn't even be here. The computers on this ship are never going to give us any answers. Back in the day, when this ship was in service, some of the Captain's kept a written record of their missions. Let's hope this was one of them. Berry, go check the Captain's work area and see if he kept a logbook of some sort."

Berry nodded and left to do as he was instructed. I turned around and looked out the window to check the light, knowing this planet had a short daily cycle. When we landed, it would have been considered dawn; by my calculations, it was now into the afternoon. Soon, dusk would be here, darker and colder than it already was. We needed to finish up soon and begin to make our way down the crater to rejoin the others.

I turned my attention back to Dawn and asked, "What do you make of the wound?"

"It's hard to be sure because the body is frozen, so I can't be positive about what caused the wound. I just want you to know that everything I am about to say is complete conjecture," replied Dawn.

"Continue, please."

"First, I thought he might have been caught on some piece of metal somewhere or got in a knife fight with another crew member. I then noticed the tears above and below the wound. So I ripped back the uniform and noticed this." She pointed to smaller cuts above and below the wound, parallel to the primary wound.

"So, what do you think made the wound?" I asked.

"I know this will sound strange, but give me a chance to explain. When I saw the three wounds, I thought of claw marks, but these were big. So I tried to think about what else could have done this, and my mind is blank." She used her hand and demonstrated. "Most animals' claws are not at the same length. When you look at your hand, all your fingers are different lengths, with one being the longest. That is the same with the marking made from the wound on him. When the animal swiped, the longest claw made the deep gouge, and the two neighboring claws dug parallel to the primary wound, creating the pattern we see here."

"How big do you think this creature was?"

"Hard to say. Based on the wounds I see, I would guess the main claw was about an inch at its base and probably three to four inches long. The other two claws would be a little smaller, and that could make the paw about five to eight inches across. The claws would have been very sharp and strong because they cut cleanly through one of his ribs. The creature that made this would have to be bigger than a bear. Now, keep in mind that this is only conjecture."

"Unfortunately, your assessment of the facts does sound plausible. We always knew one day we would find aliens. We just hoped the first ones we encountered would be friendly," I stated.

Berry entered the bridge waving a book in the air. He said, "I found it! I found the Captain's logbook, and the Captain was a she and not a he."

He handed the book over to me and used his flashlight to shine light onto the pages. Dawn mimicked him and used her flashlight to light up the other side of the book. I thumbed through it, looking for the last entries created. Upon skimming, I found the mention of the Discovery and began there.

"Here we go," I began. "Here is the entry ordering the Nightingale to begin searching for the Discovery, and they give the last known coordinates and heading. Amazingly, this ship has never found this planet. Those coordinates are nowhere near where we are today. For the next three days, they came up empty. On the fourth day, they came across this uncharted planet, and the Captain ordered it to be searched. She had a feeling that they may have had to set down on this strange planet. They scanned the planet, and after eighteen hours, they located the Discovery on the surface. Seeing that the ground gave way under the ship's weight, she decided to land up here just to be safe. Fifteen members of her crew were sent down. That was half of the crew from the ship. Three and a half hours after they left, she said that she got some strange radio traffic and then lost touch with her crew. They tried for hours with no response. After weighing all options, she ordered the rest of the crew to be armed and decided to take them down to find out and investigate what happened. That was the last entry she made."

"It appeared she never returned to make any new entries," remarked Berry.

"That still doesn't explain what he is doing here. Just look at him. He has a bandaged arm and torn clothes, he has that big open wound that was his apparent cause of death, and he looks like he hasn't shaved or bathed in a week. If he wasn't a block of ice, I bet he would also have smelled a bit ripe." Dawn said as she pointed at the Captain, frozen in time.

"I must admit that he does look like he had a rough time before he died. My guess would be that the Captain of this ship left an entry in her log showing that all of her crew went down there. I'm willing to bet he made a similar entry in his logbook telling why he came here," I concluded.

"Take a look at this, Wanda. What do you think that they are doing down there?" Berry asked as he looked out the window.

I walked to the window and looked outside with both of them. I saw something going on but couldn't make out the commotion due to being so high up. I reached into my pack, pulled out binoculars, and looked closer. I zoomed in on the shuttle and saw a plume of dust rise from behind it. I quickly looked at the drill site and saw Pops getting something out of his rover. I looked back at the Discovery and could see one team running from the Discovery toward the shuttle. I watched as five crew members ran forward, and two trailed behind them about fifty yards. I knew we would all be stranded if something happened to the shuttle."I think we better get the others and start heading down before it gets too late," I told them.

"I think the others might be waiting for us by the airlock where we came," Berry said.

"Do you think we should call Pop for a ride down?" Dawn asked.

"No, we'll hike down. Once we make it past the dropoff location, the rest of the trip should be easier, and it'll get warmer as we go down."

"I don't know if I would call zero warm or not," commented Berry.

"It's a hell of a lot warmer than thirty below," stated Dawn as she left the bridge.

"Point taken," responded Berry as he followed us out.

We rounded the last corner and entered the room we started in by the airlock. The rest of the team was waiting on us. I looked at Bart and asked, "Did you find anything worth mentioning?"

"The hospital area was interesting, but we found no one onboard. How about you?" he replied.

"We found the theater you mentioned," answered Dawn.

"That's fantastic! I would love to see that." Bart said excitedly.

"I'm afraid we don't have the time to go back. We are running out of daylight and need to meet up with the other teams below," I stated.

I saw the disappointment on all my team members' faces but saw the understanding of our time restraint. We all filed out of the ship and tied a rope between us for safety reasons so the rest of the team could catch them if one person fell. We made our way down from the steepest part and were now at where we were dropped off. Due to the thin air and the climb's difficulty, I called for a break before we continued. The climb from here on out would be easier since the degree of incline decreased as we climbed, making it easier as we went. I decided it would be best if we stayed tethered together until we got closer to the bottom. Our line order was with me at the lead, and then Dawn, Berry, Bart, Nancy, and Rick brought the rear. After we rested for a moment, I signaled them to continue down the rocky area. I thought I heard an odd noise and signaled everyone to stop and be quiet.

I listened intently for a few seconds, slowly turned to Dawn, and asked, "Do you hear something?"

Dawn listened quietly for a couple of seconds and responded, "Maybe? I can hear something, but I don't know what it is. It sounds like it's coming from behind us." She turned and asked Rick. "Do you hear anything back there?"

He looked around, then the ground he was standing on, and responded, "I'm not sure what it is, but I think I'm standing on top of it."

Before anyone could react, the ground disappeared under Rick. He suddenly dropped, screaming and scrambling for solid ground, then disappeared. Everyone watched with a look of shock as the rope between him and Nancy became tight, and she was pulled off her feet and dragged toward the hole. Quickly, each one of us was pulled off our feet and headed toward the hole. Bart and Berry swung themselves around, grabbed the rope, and tried to plant their feet and stop the chain reaction, but had little effect. Dawn and I were being dragged along like rag dolls. I looked back and saw a boulder that I had passed moments ago. I rolled to my left, putting me on the opposite side as everyone else. My movement caused the rope to get wedged under the rock and act like a break. Everyone stopped with Nancy dangling over the edge. She looked down and screamed and tried to pull herself up but couldn't because the rope that connected her to Rick was still pulling on her. I was still pulling against the rock to stop anyone else from falling in; Bart and Berry were still pulling hard and trying to get her out. Dawn was lying on her back, unable to move because she was being pulled from both sides like a link in a chain. Growls came from the hole, and the rope below Nancy broke. The sudden change caused Bart and Berry to fall backward after yanking Nancy out of the hole.

"There's glowing eyes down there!" Nancy said, still freaked out.

She threw her hands into the air and tried to run away, but before anyone could react, another hole formed, and Nancy fell into it.

The rope began to pull again, and Berry and Bart quickly turned around and slid across the ground again. I hurried to maneuver around the rock to use it as a brake again. Dawn, who was hurting for the first time, closed her eyes in anticipation of the rope being pulled again. The pulling suddenly stopped, and Bart pulled on the rope, and no one was on the other end. Growling sounds echoed from both holes, and we unanimously decided to run. Another hole appeared before us, and I tried to stop in time to catch my balance on the edge. I looked into the hole and saw the glowing eyes Nancy had screamed about.

★★★★★★★★★★★★★

Mike

My team and I came over the ridge and could now see the shuttle. I was surprised because the shuttle was still there and on solid ground. My team paused to catch their breath and put on their oxygen masks for a quick breath of air. I turned back and saw Sam and Lisa still running toward me. In my mind, I thought about how much time Sam just caused us to lose by running back to the shuttle. The only part of this that concerned me was Kellie not answering our calls.

Knowing I was close enough for her to hear me, I pulled out my radio and tried to get her to answer. "Kellie, this is Mike. Do you copy over?" I waited for a response and tried again, "Kellie, this is Mike. Do you copy over?" I continued several more times.

Sam finally caught up and looked down at the shuttle. His face said precisely what he thought; he expected to find the shuttle half-buried. I bet my thoughts mirrored his about where the plume of dust came from.

"Has she responded yet? Sam asked me.

"She probably decided to nap while waiting for us to return," I said.

"Maybe, but I think we should check to make sure. If nothing else, we could double-check to ensure the shuttle is still on solid ground. After all, that is our ride off of this rock, and I wouldn't want anything to happen to it. Would you?" asked Sam.

I thought about it for a few minutes before agreeing with him. I've had weird feelings about this place since I saw the trench the Discovery had fallen into. Since I was actually the mission leader, I couldn't let it show this place scared the hell out of me. If I had my way, we would be on our way back to the mother ship a long time ago. Since I was ordered to investigate, that's what I'm going to do.

"Ok, if it puts you at ease, we will go on board and take a reading," I told Sam. I walked toward the shuttle, and the others followed. The good thing about working in arctic suits on this mission was that no one could see how scared or worried I really was. In fact, going on-board and taking another reading would not only make Sam feel more relaxed but would also make me feel more relaxed.

As we arrived at the shuttle, I led them up the crew ramp into the ship. The crew seemed glad to be back somewhere warm. Once inside, they removed their gloves, masks, and goggles and opened their coats. Sam, Lisa, and I headed out of the cargo area and into the passenger area. When we entered, it was easy to see one of the seats was reclined, and Kellie was asleep.

The three of us stood over her before I finally said something, "See, Sam, you got all worked up over nothing. The ship is still here, and our pilot is taking a nap. I don't know why I let you get me all worked up when there is nothing to worry about."

"Mike, I'm telling you, from up in the Discovery, we saw a plume of dust rise into the air from somewhere over here. I can't say exactly where it came from, but it sure looked like it came from here. At least it looked that way from where I was. Just ask Lisa; she saw it, too. In fact, she thought it was Pops setting off some explosives, except I told her it was in the wrong place for it to have been Pops. I swear this is where I thought it came from," explained Sam.

I asked Lisa, "Did you see it too?"

"Yes! I did. A plume of dust went up into the air from somewhere near this shuttle. We couldn't see the shuttle from where we were, but it definitely came from this area," replied Lisa.

"So the two of you believe you saw something out here, but you don't know where or what it was. Am I correct?" I asked.

"Yes, Mike," answered Sam.

Pointing at Lisa, I said. "Lisa, why don't you stay here and wake up sleeping beauty and see if she knows anything." Then I pointed at Sam and said, "You get to come with me upstairs to look at the instruments and take a new reading about what we are sitting on."

We went upstairs onto the flight deck, and Sam scrolled through the sensor readings from the station behind the pilot's sea. The readings had not stopped recording data since we landed, and I peeked over his shoulder to look at the data, too. Sam pulled up the exterior video around the time he saw the dust plume. It wasn't until he pulled up the aft cam that he saw it.

"There, Mike. It was about a hundred yards aft of the ship. What do you think that it could be?" Sam said as he pointed to the screen.

"I have no idea." I sighed.

"Could it be like Old Faithful on Earth, but because the water is frozen, it blows out dust instead of water?" asked Sam.

"If it was there when we landed, it would have shown up in our scans. This planet was so quiet you could have heard a mouse fart." I thought about what I had seen before I decided what to do. "Sam, why don't you pull up the seismic readings since we landed?"

Sam pulled up the readings as requested, pointed at the screen, and said. "This is the point when we were landing."

The screen showed a large number of spikes that indicated the vibrations caused by the engines as we landed. I pointed to the part where the spikes are getting smaller and said, "This would have to be the part where the engines shut down."

We watched as the line was flat for a few seconds, and then some more vibrations appeared. Sam pointed to them and said, "This must be where we unloaded equipment and crew."

We watched as the vibrations stopped for a while and then came back again. I pointed to it and said, "That must be the point where Pops came back to pick up Wanda's team and then drove off."

"Ok, then, that accounts for the crew leaving. This thing should have shown nothing until we came back here a short time ago."

We both watched the monitor, and it did as I expected it to, and it showed nothing happened since we left the ship. Sam pushed a button to speed up the viewing so we could get through it faster. The flat line continued for about forty-five minutes after Pops made his pick-up. Then, it changed to show some ground movement. It was hardly noticeable initially, but it became more steady and rhythmic. Sam slowed the displayed images down to get a better look.

"What do you make of that?" Sam asked as he looked up at me.

"I'm not sure, but it seems to be pretty steady, which is unusual by itself. Things that naturally occur rarely stay as steady as that. They usually have several spikes in them," I said.

We watched as the screen displayed the graph faster than in real-time. There was a sudden sharp spike, and then the line went flat again. After about five minutes, the vibrations started again at a steady pace.

"Do you think the spike we saw could have been Pops setting off one of his explosives?" asked Sam.

"It resembled a typical explosion followed by all of the little spikes from the falling debris. That doesn't explain why the vibrations stopped and started back up after a few minutes. Move it ahead, and let's see how long the vibration lasted,"

We watched until Sam and Lisa saw the plume of dust.

"Did you see that? It ended when we saw the plume of dust. After that, it's calm again," remarked Sam.

"That could mean it was just a buildup of pressure until gasses under the surface were released. When the gas broke through, it had such force that it blew the dust into the air," I answered.

"True, but it still doesn't explain why it stopped after what we think was Pops setting off an explosive,"

I thought about it and realized I couldn't find any reason why it would stop. As much as I wanted to believe everything that happened to the Discovery and what was happening now was just some sort of natural occurrence, I started to believe the only other possibility was there was some sort of outside influence making all of this happen. No one had ever seen aliens, but I couldn't rule out the possibility they existed. The fact that this planet was mainly just one big ball of rock and ice made me wonder how anything could survive here?

"Let's go and take a new reading and see what's under us," I said.

We returned to the ground-penetrating radar to do a wide scan around and under the ship. The computer only took a moment to reset and begin the scans. Sam and I watched as the images appeared on the screen. My eyes got really big as I took in the information displayed in front of me.

"Those tunnels weren't there when we landed," I said as I pointed to the screen.

The images showed what was under the front of the ship. I imme-diately knew we were in real trouble. I pushed Sam out of the way, jumped into the co-pilot's seat, and began to flip switches frantically.

"What's going on?" Sam asked me.

I pointed to the dark image on the screen, "We're sitting on an open underground cavern." I said, and when I looked over, I saw Sam was confused. "It's like sitting on an empty eggshell. It won't be long before the shell collapses. I need you to get below and get everyone strapped in. We must move the ship, pick everyone up, and get the hell out of here." He turned and headed down below as I shouted, "Kellie, get your ass up here right now! We have to take off immediately!" As I continued to flip switches, the engines began to power up.

Kellie was almost to her seat when the inevitable happened. The ground under the front of the ship gave way. Kellie was thrown for-ward, losing her balance, and hit her head. Sam was thrown backward and tumbled toward the pilot's seat and the controls. I was thrown face-first into the panels in front of me. Next, the ground gave way under the ship's rear, and Kellie tumbled down the stairs.

"Is Kellie ok?" I shouted to Sam.

"I don't know, she ended up at the bottom of the stairs and looks unconscious, and she's bleeding from her head," Sam said as he slid across the flight deck and grabbed the handrail, keeping him from tumbling down the stairs. I was thrown back hard into my seat and almost out of it since I wasn't strapped in. The ship dropped below and leveled out.

Circuits popped, sparks flew as many panels shorted out from the sudden jolts. There were many sounds of the crew as they cried out from the pain of their injuries. Objects continued to fall from the storage areas and could be heard throughout the ship. Smoke started to fill the cabin from the shorted-out electronics. The lights that still worked flickered, and the emergency lights came on, but the smoke reflected most of their light. The sounds of metal bending and breaking echoed throughout the ship.

Loose dirt fell onto the ship in different places as the ship settled on the bottom, burying two-thirds of the shuttle below the surface. Next to me, dirt poured through a hole from the broken glass and piled on the pilot's seat. Circuits randomly popped from different parts of the ship, and conduits and supports now hung down from where they used to be. Most screens that once displayed information were now blank, busted, or static.

Eight

Stranded

Those who were the first to regain their senses moved to help their fellow crewmates. I was one of those people who was also one of the nurses on the ship and the one selected to go on this mission. I was one of the lucky ones, or so I thought. Luckily, I had been seated when this happened and was only slightly shaken up from the drop. I moved from person to person, checking on their condition. Some needed a little reassurance, while others needed a little more care. Finally, I reached Lisa, who was still sitting on the deck. She stared at a minor support beam that had broken loose and swung down in front of her like a pendulum stuck in the locker just inches from her.

"Are you alright Lisa?" I inquired softly.

Lisa turned to look at me and answered, "I'm just a little bit bruised and sore, but I'll be alright. I've had hangovers that felt worse than this."

I pointed at the beam stuck in the locker and commented, "Looks like you had a close call there."

"A little too close if you ask me. Just give me a moment, and I'll be fine,"

"I've known a lot of people like you. They get hurt and claim that they are fine. Later, they end up in sick bay or worse. Let me give you a look over."

I saw Lisa was in no shape to argue with me. I could tell by how she looked around that things might be slightly fuzzy. I looked at her eyes and checked for head injuries and for concussion. As I got closer to Lisa's ribs, she cringed from pain. I carefully lifted the shirt to expose a large bruise on her left side. I gave it a quick exam before gently pulling the shirt back down.

"How bad is it?" She asked with tear-brimmed eyes.

"Well, it doesn't look like you have any internal injuries, but you do have some badly bruised and possibly cracked ribs. Try not to do anything that would irritate it. If it bothers you too much, come find me, and I will wrap them up until we get back to the ship so we can take an x-ray," I stated.

"Joan, we need you over here!" Markus shouted from the bottom of the staircase.

I looked over my shoulder toward the stairs, then back at Lisa, stood up to leave, and said, "Just sit here and relax until your head clears. I'll come back in a little bit and check on you."

As I walked away, I watched Lisa struggle to get herself back on her feet. I know it was excruciatingly painful for her to move. I hesitated to help her because I didn't want to hurt her pride. I knew I couldn't stop her. I watched as she finally got to her feet, although I'm sure her head was still spinning from being tossed around. She went to the computer council and immediately saw her frustration, knowing it was a lost cause. I saw some lights on the panel blink, but the rest were dead. The monitor was busted, and some smoke was coming from the side. I watched as she reached down and opened a side panel, and some of the circuits popped. It took her a moment longer to respond, and I could tell the head pounding, and the sore ribs made it hard for her to focus. I watched as she looked around and proceeded into the cargo bay through the hatch.

I made my way to the bottom of the stairs and found Kellie unconscious and bleeding from her head. I checked her for other injuries, and aside from some bruises one would expect from a fall, I could find nothing else wrong. I reached into the first aid kit that was nearby, pulled out some gauze and alcohol, and cleaned the wound.

"That's not as bad as it first looked," I said as I put the bandage on.

"Are you sure she's alright? She took one heck of a tumble down those stairs," Markus stated.

"I can't be one hundred percent sure without getting some x-rays, but I think she will be alright. She will be sore for a few days from all the bruising. I think she has a mild concussion, and that is my biggest concern. I don't think she will have any problem, but I would feel more confident if I could run some tests," I replied.

"What do you think happened to us?" he asked.

"I would be guessing, but I think the ground gave way under the ship."

"Do you think we will be able to get the shuttle out so we can return to the ship?" Markus asked.

I looked around the shuttle. Wires, conduits, and support struts were hanging down everywhere. Debris was strewn all over the deck, and the ship continued to creak due to the stress of the ship's current position. I knew there was no way this shuttle would ever fly again. Like the ocean vessels of the past that were about to make their way to the bottom of the ocean, witnesses would always report hearing the creaking and moaning of the ship before it would disappear beneath the waves and make its way to its final resting place. They used to call it death moans. This ship was dying, and like the ocean vessels of the past, it was making its final cry out before it would go silent forever.

"I'm afraid this shuttle is going nowhere. It's too far gone for us to fix. Besides, we don't have the resources to do any repairs." I answered.

"The Captain will send down another shuttle to come and get us, right?" asked Markus.

"I'm afraid this was the only functioning shuttle we had," I stated.

"But I saw other shuttles on the hangar deck," he remarked.

"There were two other shuttles that you saw on the hangar deck. One of them was burned the other day, and the other was badly damaged on another mission. It needs to be completely rewired and rebuilt. It will probably be weeks, if not months, before it will be completed and ready for space."

"We're going to die down here," he said silently.

I placed my hand on his shoulder, looked him straight in the eyes, and said, "You listen to me, Markus; I know this is your first mission out into space, but you should never give up hope. This is why they have you undergo all that training on Earth before you can come out here. We have some of the brightest people with us on the surface. If there is a way to get back, they will figure out how to do it."

"How are we going to get out of here if there are no working shuttles on the ship?" he asked.

"I don't know, but I'm sure someone onboard does. It may be Kellie here who knows. So keep an eye on her while I go up on the flight deck and see if anyone is injured there."

He nodded and watched me as I climbed the stairs to the flight deck. I paused to quietly watch Mike and Sam work on some systems as I reached the top. Sam was on his back working on the electronics under the panels while Mike flipped switches and pushed buttons. They had already examined other panels because circuit boards were scattered around the deck.

"Panel A12 isn't responding. I show we have some juice running through panel B7. Does that give us anything?" Mike asked.

"No, that board only works with the onboard security system. Do we have any juice going through panels A6 and C3?" asked Sam.

Mike quickly looked and answered, "It looks like we have some juice on both of them. What will that give us?"

"Well, the boards used there are similar to those in the communications system," Sam said, pulling out the boards and looking at them in the dim light of his flashlight. With a few modifications and tapping into the power running through them, we just might be able to get a signal out."

Sam pulled each board and adjusted it before he reached in, removed the old burnt boards, and tossed them onto the deck beside him. He put the replacement boards in and made temporary connections for the power.

"I hope this works," Mike stated.

"I do, too," He gave it one last look before he said, "Ok, Mike, give it a shot."

"Here we go," Mike replied,

He flipped a switch, and one of the boards immediately blew out. Sam quickly turned his head and protected his face from the sparks with his hand. After a few moments, the sparks stopped falling, and Sam looked back up inside and removed another board. He slipped back out and examined the board using his flashlight. Mike squatted down to see how bad it was.

Sam shook his head and said, "I should have known better."

"What's the problem?" Mike asked.

"I can't believe I didn't see it. All the little lights on these panels are flashing because residual electrical impulses are still in the system," Sam explained.

"Can we fix it to get out of here?" asked Mike.

"We could weld plates over the windows that broke. We could repair the structural damage that we have. We could even salvage what we would need off of the Discovery. If the engines are damaged, then all of this," he holds up the board and tosses it sliding across the deck and finishes, "would be a complete waste of our time."

Mike watched the board slide across the deck and stopped at my feet. Sam turned and looked at what Mike was looking at. He saw me standing there holding a first aid kit. I bent down, picked up the board, and walked toward them.

Mike asks, "How long have you been standing there?"

"Long enough to know things are worse than most people realize."

"How is everyone doing down there?" Sam asked.

I handed him the board and squatted in front of him to examine him while Mike got up and sat in one of the seats.

"Well, Kellie is unconscious with a deep gash to her forehead. She may have a mild concussion. We may know more once she wakes up. Lisa has some badly bruised, if not broken, ribs. We have young Markus down there who is terrified that we are going to die here. Aside from that, we have some sprains, a few possible breaks, and many bruises." I finished looking at Sam and asked, "How do you feel?"

"I feel like I just went ten rounds with the heavyweight champ. Besides, I'm doing pretty well. Mike is the one bleeding," responded Sam.

"What do you call that?" I asked while I pointed to his hand.

"I didn't even know that I cut myself," Sam said, surprised, as he looked down at his left hand and saw it was bleeding.

I took his hand and cleaned the wound before I applied the bandage. After I finished, he looked at his bandaged hand, clenching and unclenching. I stood up and moved over so Mike could have his turn at being looked over. There was a small cut on his forehead, and it didn't take long for me to clean and dress it.

"So what do we do now?" I asked Mike.

"First order of business is to find out just how badly we are really damaged so we can see if we can fix it," stated Mike.

"It's a total washout," stated Lisa as she reached the top of the stairs.

Sam smiled and walked over to give her a big hug. As he did, she cringed from the pain, and he stepped back. She put one hand on her ribs, and he placed his arm around her and helped her to a seat.

"I'm sorry. Joan told us about your ribs, and I just forgot. I'm just glad to see you're alright," Sam said as he bent down and kissed her. Mike and I looked at each other, surprised.

"What do you mean by a total washout?" Mike asked Lisa.

"I was just looking at the engines, and they were shot. We have fuel leaks, most of the pressure lines have burst, and most of the engine support struts have collapsed. We have nothing onboard to lift those engines and get them back in alignment."

"Without those engines, this ship is completely dead," Sam said.

Mike leaned back in the seat. Pretty sure this wasn't what he had in mind when coming down here. There wasn't really anything to do except abandon this shuttle.

"How are we going to get out of this shuttle? I heard some of the crew have tried to open the hatch, but dirt and rock from the outside are blocking it," I asked.

Mike shrugged and said, "We're going to have to find a torch and cut our way through the hull."

"That really won't be necessary," Sam said.

"Why not? Do you know some magical way of getting out of here that I am unaware of?" asked Mike.

"There is nothing magical about it. This ship has more exits than most people are aware of. You know about the three entry hatches on the port side, the cargo lift, and the cargo area stairs. The rest of them are concealed and only for emergency escape. There is one in the passenger area deck that will drop you down to the ground, and that won't work since we are buried. There is one on the flight deck just behind the pilot's seat."

Mike and I looked but didn't see the hatch. Sam smiled and continued, "I know you are wondering where it could be? If you remove that panel, you'll see the escape hatch." He walked over and exposed the hatch. He set down the panel and continued, "There are two opposite the ones on the port side. Finally, there are two topside emergency hatches, and these are the ones that I think we should use."

"Let me guess, they are hidden as well?" remarked Mike.

"Correct. Both are located in the cargo area off of the upper catwalk. One is at this end, just outside the hatch to the flight deck, and the other is outside the hatch to engineering. The ladder to the hatch is hidden behind some panels, just like this one. At the bottom of the ladder is the panel to activate the explosive bolts and open those hatches," explained Sam.

"Why has no one ever heard of these emergency hatches?" asked Mike.

"Nobody really wanted anyone to know that the designers were a bit paranoid. When they first tested these shuttles, if even the smallest thing happened, they would blow a hatch or even accidentally blow one of them. That's why they had the hatches concealed. The funny thing was no one had the nerve to remove them either. How safe would you feel knowing there were three main exits and six emergency exits? I'm sure you wouldn't feel very confident about the flying vessel," remarked Sam.

"I suppose you're right. If I got on a ship with many emergency exits, I'd think the designers and engineers had no faith in their ship and how well it would fly," Mike said.

"They actually tried to think ahead when they built this thing. They didn't know what might happen, so they wanted to ensure we had a way out. They intended to build a ship so we could survive in it and not a steel coffin. After all, we are out here alone. We can't just get on the phone and dial 911 and expect rescue to arrive in minutes. I, for one, am glad they put all these extra exits in."

Mike dropped his head and said, "Having an escape hatch is good, but what's the use? There is no shuttle available to come down and save us. So we have nowhere to go and no one to rescue us. We can't even let anyone know we need rescuing."

"That may not be completely true. Before we left the Discovery, Lexey had restored some of the internal power and life support. Based on the reports I was given, there is a strong possibility we could get that ship running well enough to get back to our ship," Sam said as he smiled.

I could see in his expression that Mike believed that if the Discovery could be put back into space, they would all have a fighting chance to survive. "How sure are you that we will be able to make it happen?"

"Most people would say we are crazy for trying, but I never listen to them anyway. With Lexey in engineering, Kellie as our pilot, Lisa working on the computers, me on the electronics, and the rest of the crew there for support, I think we have a very good chance at getting that ship back into space," stated Sam.

"What do you plan to do about the port side landing gear?" I asked.

"Actually, I was thinking about detaching it from the ship," replied Sam.

"How do you plan to do that?" asked Lisa.

"Some explosives at the moment of lift-off," answered Sam.

It appeared to us that this was not just a plan that Sam had thought about immediately. This was a well-thought-out plan that would have taken some time to come up with. We knew Sam would have eventually suggested taking the Discovery back with them, and if the shuttle hadn't been damaged, he would have been turned down. Now, since the shuttle was damaged and was unable to get us off the planet's surface, this was our only hope if we had any plans of getting off of this planet.

"How do you know the engines will work?" inquired Mike.

"I don't, but I can guess they were functional when they landed and could easily be made functional again. Six stations must be manned to get a ship of its era into space. That means that they need a minimum of at least six crew members to fly that ship. Three are in engineering, and the other three are on the bridge. According to Lexey, someone made some modifications in engineering to reroute those three stations to some other location, presumably the bridge. Lisa and I never made it to the bridge to confirm. I know rerouting control from engineering to the bridge would take a lot of time and effort. I don't know about you, but I wouldn't waste my time on the modifications unless I knew the engines were functional."

"Why would someone do all that work and never leave? There were twenty-five crew members onboard. What happened to them?" Mike asked.

"I was hoping the Captain's log book would give us some clues about what happened. If I was to guess, most of the crew was either incapacitated or dead," suggested Sam.

The silence on the deck was ear-piercing.

"One other thing, we haven't been able to find any bodies. We did find a few odd things we think you should see." Lisa added.

"What kind of things do you want to show me?" Mike asked.

Sam and Lisa looked at each other in silent conversation as though they wanted to tell me something, but they seemed unable to describe it in words.

"It's hard to explain. If we say what we think happened, you will think we're crazy. So we should show you instead." Lisa said.

"I agree with Lisa," Sam said.

"On that note, I'm going below to check on the others," I stated

✶✶✶✶✶✶✶✶✶✶✶✶✶✶

Mike

The ship groaned from the weight of the rock and dirt around us. I looked around, expecting the dirt to come pouring in. I stood up and, for a moment, felt a little dizzy, but it quickly passed. "Let's gather everything we can salvage and return to the Discovery. It looks like you get an extended stay on your great grandfather's ship."

Sam smiled as we went to the lower deck to inform everyone about our decision. I saw some of the crew starting to move around while others were helping those who needed help. I looked around at their faces and saw that some were scared. For some of the crew, this was their first mission, and they couldn't wait to return and tell their friends all about their adventures in space. Those who had been in space before knew sometimes things went wrong and needed to stay calm to work out the problem. I turned to look at Kellie, who still had not regained consciousness.

Sam leaned in close to me so the others could not hear and said, "We have a lot of scared people here. None of them expected this when they signed up with us. Do you have any idea what you are going to say to them?"

"No, I was never trained to deal with a situation like this," I replied.

"I don't think anyone is trained for a situation like this. If you sound like you know what you are doing, they'll listen," Sam suggested.

"I guess you're right. It really isn't what you say but how you say it." I took a deep breath, turned to the crew, and said, "Ok, everyone, listen up. We're not sure why the ground gave way under the shuttle. Unfortunately, strange things can happen out here on these alien worlds. Due to the ground collapsing, most exits have been blocked." Mumbling sounded throughout the passengers. I let it die down before I continued, "However, I have been informed there are two escape hatches on the top of this shuttle that we're going to use to get out of here and back to the surface."

"If we can't stay here, where will we go?" Markus asked.

"The Discovery. Lexey has managed to restore some power and life support." I said.

Markus was one of the crew members on their first mission. He continued to ask the questions some were afraid to ask.

"Have you told the Captain what has happened down here? Is she going to send a rescue shuttle to come and get us?"

I looked at Lisa, Joan, and Sam before I turned back to Markus and said, "Yes, I have informed our Captain of our situation."

I watched as Sam and Lisa slowly turned and looked at me with slanted eyes showing their distaste for the lie. I watched Joan look at the newer crew members to see how they reacted to the information. All three knew the communications system was knocked out, and I never made such a call. They tried not to show a surprised look in front of their crew.

"As you know, when we left, the other shuttle was undergoing some major repairs. The Captain has ordered all personnel on the ship to work around the clock to get it launched as soon as possible. However, the soonest they can be here for us is about six days. We think we can get the Discovery repaired and ready for lift-off before then."

"Why are we going to try to get that old relic ready? Why don't we just wait it out?" asked Lou.

Thinking on my feet, I answered. We could wait for them to come and get us if we wanted to. We might even make it till they get here. There is one thing I'm sure of: we never planned to be down here long. I don't think we will have enough food and water to last until then. Not to mention, the other shuttle might be ready in six days or possibly longer. There is no guarantee that they will be ready by then. It was only an estimate that they gave me. It may take them longer than expected, and we would like to be prepared. I would prefer to have a plan ready in case of complications. Besides, it allows us to work with and document that old ship, making the time go by a little faster until we are rescued. If we return to Earth with that ship and turn it over to a museum, we will forever have a place in history. Are there any other questions?" I looked around and saw that no one was ready to ask anything more; some were actually smiling. I continued, "Ok then, I want everyone to look around for anything useful. Collect everything you can; we will take an inventory when we arrive. I need someone to find a stretcher and an arctic suit for Kellie; we'll treat her injuries when we get there."

A crew member opened the locker, got the suit out for Kellie, and handed it to Joan. With Lisa's help, they put the suit on Kellie. Others were going through the lockers, stuffing their backpacks with anything they could find and filling any duffle bags they came across. Eventually, someone returned with a stretcher for Kellie and helped load her up. Joan and Lisa strapped her in tight, knowing we would have to hand her up a ladder to get her off of the shuttle.

We moved inside the cargo area, up on the catwalk. Sam showed me which panels to remove to reveal the ladder and the controls by the engineering hatch and then proceeded to the other side near the flight deck hatch. Each side had three panels to be removed. Each panel was three feet wide and three feet tall. Unlike the rest of the wall, which was made of steel, these panels were made of lightweight aluminum, making it look like steel but easier to remove.

With everyone suited back up to go outside, Sam looked over to me, and we both opened the control panel and pressed the button. There were two quick thuds as the explosive bolts went off and ejected both hatches away from the openings, leaving behind a puff of smoke. Sam and I climbed the ladders and stepped out onto the shuttle's top.

The top of the shuttle was a little higher than the edge. The ground between the edge and the ship sunk down and would make it impossible to cross. We walked the edges to find a place for all of us to cross. Sam spotted where the ground seemed to make a bridge of dirt for us. He tapped me on the shoulder, and we walked over to check it out. Sam crossed successfully without running into any loose dirt.

He returned, and we began our walk back to the openings. Sam commented, "You know you lied to everyone when you said you talked to the Captain."

"Let's just call it a small omission. Everyone needs hope and something to believe in. As you said, if I sound confident, they will believe me if they think what I'm saying is true. As long as they think a rescue is coming, they'll be calmer," I stated.

"You do realize if it takes us more than six days to get the Discovery off of the ground, they'll realize you were lying,"

"Maybe they will, and maybe they won't. I just hope they realized I did it for them,"

Sam suddenly stopped, and I took a few more steps before I realized he had done so. I turned around to see what he was doing. It was as if Sam was looking for something but couldn't see it. I looked around, too, trying to see if I could figure out what Sam was looking at. After a few moments, I turned back around, and Sam looked off in the direction Pops went. Then, I turned in the direction of the Nightingale.

I couldn't figure out what he had calculated, and I was never good at waiting games, so I asked. "What is it you're looking for? We have people waiting on us to tell them if it is alright to come up."

Sam looked around, slightly paranoid, and took a deep breath before he answered. "Have you had any weird feelings about this place since we've been here? There were moments while we were outside, and I had the distinct feeling we were being watched. In fact, I just had one a few moments ago."

"Sam, I think you're letting your mind get the better of you. This place is really creepy, and I'm sure it could make anyone's mind play tricks on them."

"Is it really my mind? Since we arrived, we've found strange things that are hard to explain. For instance, why is this crater not frozen? Why did the crews of the Nightingale and the Discovery disappear? Both crews were no strangers to space. Why did the ground give way under the landing gear of the Discovery? For that matter, why did it give way under our shuttle? You said it yourself; you were here and saw that we were landing on solid ground, and yet when we returned, it was hollow. Can you explain any of this?"

"Maybe we are just having a string of bad luck. I'm sure there is a reason for all of this, but I don't know what it is yet."

"I have an idea. I'm just having a hard time making myself believe it. Besides what I mentioned earlier, we found a few other things. That hatch in the pod we used to get onboard the Discovery looked like something had run into it and bent it. Now, bending one of those hatches takes a lot of force. Lisa showed me where she found blast marks from weapons fire. Then there is the strangest part; we haven't found a single body on the ship so far. What we found in the Captain's quarters was strange and hard to describe." He reached into his coat pocket, pulled out a folded handkerchief, and, as he opened it up, said, "I found this on his desk."

I watched as he unfolded the handkerchief to reveal an alien claw. I picked it up to look at it and asked, "What is it?"

"According to the notes with it, the Captain said it was an alien claw. It is extremely hard and very sharp. If they were to swipe their claws at you, they would cut through you like a hot knife through butter." Sam said as I returned the claw to the handkerchief.

"Are you suggesting there are aliens on this planet?" I asked.

"That would explain a great deal of what has happened here. I know most people don't believe in aliens since we have never seen any in all the time we have been in space. To tell you the truth, we may have encountered aliens before, but no one survived to tell anyone. Other ships could be buried deep in the ice from encountering them when they came here before us. Since this place was frozen and those ships landed long ago, the aliens would have died off, too. At least, I thought that until the ground collapsed beneath the shuttle," explained Sam.

Reluctantly, I said, "If you had said this before we left the ship, I would have said that you're off your rocker. However, as much as I don't want to believe we are dealing with aliens, I've had the same feelings. I find it the only possibility to explain any of this. Do you have any suggestions?"

A short silence before we both come up with the solution at the same time and say at the same time, "Pops' weapons stash,"

"Let's hope Pops brought along the good stuff if we encounter them." Sam paused briefly before adding, "We'll need to recall the other two teams and get them back to the Discovery."

"They should be on their way back soon. Once we get everyone to the surface, we will give them a call and let them know they are to meet us at the Discovery."

We returned to the hatch openings and climbed back into the ship. Once down, I gave the orders for those on Sam's side to get Kellie and themselves topside. The rest of the crew and I entered the cargo area to get Pops' weapons. We grabbed as many weapons and explosives as we could carry, and then we made our way out of the ship. Once on top, I saw Sam and his group were already on solid ground, waiting for the rest of the crew. We soon joined them and began the trip back to the Discovery.

Pops

I opened my eyes and looked at the drill, but no one could be seen. I glanced at the clock on the dash and then back toward the blast crater. I looked back at the clock and toward the blast crater again. Finally, I turned and reached for my radio, which sat next to me but stopped just short of grabbing it. Instead, I pulled myself out of the rover and took a couple of steps before stopping myself and returning to the rover.

As I returned, I mumbled, "They should have been back by now. I guess they want to play games. Well, I'll show them a game they won't soon forget." I opened the box in the back of the rover and removed what looked like a space-aged version of the pump action shotgun that fired explosive charges. I attached a power pack and pumped the weapon just like a shotgun to chamber the next round.

I walked off toward the blast crater, ready to scare and yell at the rest of the team. As I walked around the outcropping of rocks, I expected to find my team sitting there laughing, but no one was topside. I walked over to the edge, figuring they must be there since they weren't topside. I saw no one there either. Troubled by the fact they weren't anywhere to be seen, I called out their names, but no one answered. I looked around the crater and saw the faint glow of a flashlight coming from the tunnel inside the crater. I made my way down and quickly moved into the tunnel. I was about to grab my flashlight from my waist but suddenly stopped when I noticed what appeared to be drag marks by the entrance. Instead, I turned on the light mounted to my weapon and moved in cautiously. I squatted to look closer at the marks like a hunter tracking its wounded prey. My heart raced, and my adrenaline pumped the further I traveled into the tunnel. I stopped to investigate each item that caught my attention. I saw goggles, gloves, flashlights, and boots. On a few of them, I found traces of blood, and I identified each item as belonging to my missing crewmates. I no longer felt they were trying to play some practical joke on me and make me mad.

I heard the once-quiet radio come alive from the rover. "This is team two to team one. Do you copy? Over." There was a pause, "Come on Pops, answer me!" With my radio at the rover, I was unable to answer, and it went silent again. I lifted my firearm and aimed at the glowing eyes at the other end of the tunnel. 'Bam! Bam! Bam!

Nine

Something Is Among Us

✶✶✶✶✶✶✶✶✶✶✶✶✶

Mike

As soon as I put the radio away, the sounds of gunshots echoed, making it sound as though it was right beside me.

"Sounds like Pops is having a little fun with his explosives," Markus said as he looked toward the original sound.

"You're right, Markus. He probably is." I said as I nodded in agreement.

I leaned away from the group and toward Sam and quietly said, "That wasn't the sound of explosives."

"I know it sounded more like an explosive charge Pops uses with his space weapons. I wonder if Pops came face to face with one of our aliens?" Sam replied quietly so the others wouldn't hear him.

"Let's hope he survives his encounter. We could use his help getting off this rock," I stated.

Sam nodded in agreement and discontinued our conversation as we continued toward the Discovery. Our trek across the frozen tundra was much different this time than when we first arrived due to the extra weight of the equipment and supplies we scavenged from our shuttle.

Some carried the stretcher that held Kellie, and others were limping from other injuries. Lisa, Sam, and I continually looked around, surveying the landscape as we returned to the Discovery.

✶✶✶✶✶✶✶✶✶✶✶✶✶✶

Lexey

Sweat beaded along my hairline as I worked harder than I had in a long time. Dave and I had a rhythmic working atmosphere as we continued repairs inside the Discovery. I made it a personal mission to ensure I worked just as hard as if assigned to this ship.

We repaired a power panel while Cara stayed distracted and continued to look out the window.

"What do you think happened here all those years ago?" Cara asked.

"I'm not sure, and even though we're here now, I don't think we will ever know," I said without disrupting my work.

"Why are you doing all of these repairs? Do you realize that in a couple of hours, we will make our way back to the shuttle?" Cara said as she scratched her head.

I stopped momentarily and looked at her nervous posture. "When I'm nervous, or something is bothering me, I bury myself in my work. So I don't have time to think about whatever made me uncomfortable."

"That makes sense. One thing that really has me baffled is where the bodies are. Between the two ships, quite a bit of remains are missing." Cara stated.

"That is exactly why I'm trying to keep busy. It's the facts that scare the hell out of me."

Cara smiled tightly and went to look back out the window.

"Guys! Come look!" she shouted.

Due to the distress in her voice, I hurried over to the window. Dave hurried over and looked over my shoulder to see out the window. Down below, I watched other crew members approaching the ship. I saw someone on a stretcher, and many of them were walking with a significant limp. They looked like battle-hardened soldiers coming from the battlefield.

"We better meet them at the hatch. It looks like they are going to need our help." I said to both of them.

I led our little parade down the corridor when Cara suddenly asked. "It's good you decided we would need the sick bay ready. How did you know we would need it?"

"After you have been out here a while, you get to know your crewmates better, you can get a feel for the urgency of a situation,"

"What gave you that feeling this time?" asked Dave.

"Sam did. Since I've known him, I've only seen him move quickly just once before now. We had a shuttle accident, and ten people were hurt. I figured that to get him to move like that, there would be a strong possibility that someone would be hurt."

"You like him, don't you?" asked Cara.

"I guess a little. We have been working together for a long time and are friends. Why do you ask?" I replied, taken slightly aback.

"Rumor on the ship was that he and Kellie were no longer an item. That would make him a single man," stated Cara.

"I don't think that he would be interested in me. We're always arguing about something."

"Besides, I heard a rumor he's dating Lisa," added Dave.

"Dave," Cara began.

"What?" responded Dave.

"Shut up," Cara ordered.

We discontinued our conversation, went down to the hatch, and waited for the others. The room we waited in was cold because the hatch wouldn't close all the way; thus, the cold air of the planet leaked in. Luckily, we didn't have to wait long as the hatch opened, and the crew carrying Kellie was the first to go through. Joan was next, followed by the others. Cara rushed to check on Kellie. I looked around as the crew took off their goggles and masks. I saw bruises and cuts among the least bit of injuries.

"What the hell happened out there?" I asked as I stopped one of the crew.

Before he could answer, Sam answered from behind me. "The ground gave way under the shuttle, and everyone got tossed around a bit."

"Give me a couple of minutes, and I will gather up my gear and start the repairs," I responded.

"Don't bother Lexey. The shuttle is almost completely buried, and all the systems are shot and beyond repair," Sam said.

"The good news was Mike was able to get a message off to the Captain, and they are going to send down a rescue shuttle in six days," Markus said as he walked past me.

"Six days?" I asked Mike quietly, with a look of surprise on my face.

Mike pleaded with his eyes as if saying, 'Please agree with me.' "Yes, Lexey, six days," answered Mike.

I understood the look and nodded in agreement but was concerned. I didn't understand his madness for telling the crew that tidbit of information. Still, I did understand there must be a reason why. I didn't say anything about it and decided to ask him later when no one else was around.

"We got the sick bay ready while you were gone. We should get Kellie and the others there to tend to their wounds. There is a good supply of medical kits there." Cara spoke over everyone so Joan could hear her.

Kellie was carried off to the sick bay, and the other injured crewmates followed.

"I want everyone who can carry the equipment to the mess hall. We need to take a full inventory of what we could salvage." Mike ordered.

After the remaining crew left, Sam, Mike, Lisa, and I were there, and we decided to walk over to the next compartment for warmth.

I was the first to speak up. "Mike, you know the other shuttle is far from being ready. At least six weeks of work are left on it, not six days. Why did you tell them that?"

"We have an unusual situation here, and it was the only thing I could think of to calm them down. We brought a lot of rookies like Markus with us, having never been through any kind of real urgent situation; they could get scared quickly. According to Sam, you almost have this ship ready for space. How long?"

Surprised by his request, I answered, "Well, I'm not really sure how I was able to get main power and life support functioning. I never took a good look at propulsion or navigation. Someone's done a lot of modifications to those systems, and I'm going to need some time to figure them out, let alone see if the systems will even function after all this time."

"So how long?" asked Mike.

"With only a few people helping me, it may take three to five days. If I can get some help from the other teams, I might be able to get it done in a day or two. I won't guarantee anything depending on how many people I get to work with." I stated.

"You're the top priority. Take whatever people you need. Right now, this ship is our lifeboat. I want this ship ready to fly as soon as possible," ordered Mike.

I sensed something he wasn't telling me, but I reluctantly left. I glanced at Sam on my way out; he was staring at the ground, not making eye contact. It wasn't like him to be closed off. Usually, he's the one looking at you. I knew there was something they weren't telling, and Sam knew what it was.

Mike

After she left, Sam approached me and said, "Why didn't you tell her we lost contact with the other two teams? The rest of the crew must know that we're not alone."

"I didn't tell her because we don't know what happened to them. They could be having radio trouble," I replied.

"Radio trouble? I could understand losing contact with one team but not two. How do you explain losing contact with two teams that are nowhere near each other?"

"It could be that the team at the top of the crater might be too high. The other team could have turned their radio off. After all, they are messing around with explosives. As far as it goes about aliens on this planet with us, I still have trouble believing there are aliens. Why haven't we seen one by now?"

"Maybe they live underground and don't want to engage with us and say hi. Hell, I don't know why we have never seen aliens before. If aliens are on this planet, they're not very happy we're here," stated Sam.

"Other than the claw you have, do you have any other proof that there are aliens on this planet? I'm not going to our crewmates and tell them evil aliens are trying to kill us. So far, this is just an unfortunate string of bad luck. Until I have definite proof there are aliens out there, I don't want to say anything. I realize the explanation of aliens would explain what's happening. If I said something, it would be a ship full of scared and paranoid people. Do you have anything else to convince me?" I replied.

"I think after you see what we found in the Captain's quarters, you might think twice about whether or not we are dealing with aliens," Lisa stated.

Once inside the Captain's quarters, the first impression I had was there were looters once onboard, and they stole everything. Lisa showed me the barricade that had been built, and I noticed everything had been tightly fit together. There was something that both of them had missed. Some of the metal furniture had been welded together to provide extra support.

"I wonder why anyone would build a wall of furniture?" I asked as I scratched my head.

"The other side raises even more questions. I'm going to skim through the log book while Lisa shows you the other side." Sam said.

I stood there, surprised by the wall of furniture, but I watched as Lisa walked over to the locker entrance. She opened the door and stepped inside. I quizzically looked in to see what she was doing. She faced me as she opened the back of the locker. The sudden surge of bright light shone through the opening. I quickly turned my head and raised my arm to block the light. I turned around to shield my eyes because it was like a camera flash going off. Spots danced before my eyes, and it took a few minutes for me to see clearly again.

Lisa stepped backward from the locker, protecting her eyes, and said, "I'm sorry about that. I should have warned you about the bright lights."

"What the hell is with the bright lights back there?" I asked, still trying to adjust my eyesight.

"We have no idea right now why he did that. For whatever reason, he brought extra lights back there, along with a portable generator, food and water, and a closet made up to be sleeping quarters," Lisa said.

"That sounds more like a survival shelter. They would have called it a panic room if it had been built by design, but I've never heard of one on a space vessel. Show me what you found." I said to her.

Lisa led me through the locker and over to the other side. This time, I shaded my eyes as I entered, giving time to adjust to the sudden increase in light. She showed me where they found the food and water, medical supplies, a pile of used bandages, and the sleeping area.

"Over there is where we found the logbook," she said.

I looked at everything in great detail before concluding that this was the first time anyone had returned here since its creator. After looking around for about half an hour, I motioned for us to return to the other side. I was hoping Sam had found some answers.

As we walked up behind Sam, he turned around and asked me, "What did you think of that?"

"That's the strangest thing I've ever seen. It gives more questions than it answers. I hoped you had more luck?" I asked him.

"Actually, according to the log, I think there's something we should check out. Follow me, and I'll explain along the way," he replied.

"Does that logbook explain that room back there?" I asked with hesitation.

"Yes, and if you follow me, I'll explain everything," Sam said as he put the logbook in his backpack.

"Am I going to like this new information?" I asked as I followed them out of the room.

"No, this logbook talks about alien creatures that live underground and come out at night. They killed his crew and that of the Nightingale." Sam stopped and waited for a response.

I just gave him a blank stare and replied, "I know you're thinking that I'm being hard-headed about all of this alien stuff and that I don't believe in them. After the strange things I have seen so far, I'm open-minded. Don't think that I believe in aliens; it means I am listening to all possibilities, no matter how far-fetched."

"Fair enough, but I think you will be a believer once I show you." We continued down the corridor while Sam continued. "The Captain built that room as a place to hide. You see, these creatures come out mainly at night. He did say there were instances where they appeared during the day but only in the shadows. Since the creatures live underground, they are susceptible to light. Bright light will actually blind them. He installed extra lights because he saw where they would attack a single light to get darkness. That's why he put the lights high and low in there."

"If he figured out such a good defense against these creatures, where is he?"

"If you give me a minute, I will tell you about that as well."

I heaved a sigh as Sam looked over at me. I watched as Lisa had a silly smile on her face, and I finally nodded for him to agree. "When the Captain figured out that he was the only survivor of his crew, he studied the creatures. Soon, he learned he could leave his safe area for a few hours each day. He went out and welded plates over their entry points, but they always seemed to find a way in and get to him. He began to modify the ship so one person could fly it. Now, these are all things we can see and have been asking questions about."

He stopped at a floor hatch to the cargo area and opened it, and I saw lights were on down there. He poked his head inside and did a quick look around. There were numerous places where there was little to no light. Since this was a storage area, lots of lighting was of little concern. He climbed down with Lisa, and I followed him into the cargo area. Sam took out his flashlight and began to check out the container numbers.

"What exactly are we looking for?" Lisa asked as she, too, took out her flashlight.

"We're looking for container 61897. It should be one of the larger ones," stated Sam.

"What else does that log tell you about what happened here?" I inquired while assisting in the search.

"After a while, his day became routine. Gets up, eats, seals entry points, and makes modifications, then returns to his safe room. One day, when he was on his way back in the early evening, he happened to look out of the window. He saw them in the late evening carrying flashlights. He was ecstatic to see a rescue party arrive, knowing he had to warn them about the creatures. Before he could do anything, the creatures got to the rescue party."

"That must have really upset him that he couldn't do anything," remarked Lisa.

"He was devastated by this. He had no idea this was only half of the crew of the Nightingale. He couldn't sleep that night thinking about those unsuspecting crew members. He woke up early, made coffee, went to the window, and looked out. He was surprised to see more people coming down the wall of the crater. He wouldn't let the same fate happen to them as the other team met. He grabbed his weapon and gear and went to help them before they knew they would need help. Unfortunately, the creatures had already begun attacking the rest of the crew. He could only save the Captain and bring her back to his safe spot. She was badly wounded, and he tried to tend to her wounds. That is where the used bandages came from," explained Sam.

"Are you trying to tell us that these creatures are smart enough that they ambushed the crew of the Nightingale?" I asked, surprised.

"That is not exactly the way that it went down. You see, the Captain figured out that the creatures do have some limitations. What you might first mistake for intelligence is actually just instinct. He found they could be killed with his weapons and were sensitive to light. Specifically, any bright white light. Any soft white light and dying flashlights will have minimal effect on them. He also discovered they don't like the extreme cold. That means that they are limited to the lower part of this crater. If they go up too high, they will freeze," reported Sam as he continued his search.

I started to laugh. "Now that's funny. We have a creature that lives on an ice planet that can't handle the cold weather because they will freeze. Now I know he was getting a little punchy toward the end."

Sam stopped as his flashlight shone on the number 61897, and he smiled. "So you think he was going a little crazy? Come over here, and let me show you something."

"What's in it?" I asked as Lisa and I joined him.

"Before the creatures managed to kill the last of his crew, they managed to kill one and put it here in hopes of taking it back to Earth," Sam said.

Sam unlocked the container and then pulled it open. Inside was one of the creatures, as Sam had said. The hide of the creature was tough and dry. There were what looked like spikes coming from the hide. We assumed these were used for protection and to move through the underground dirt. Its teeth were still razor sharp, and its eyes would glow when we shone our lights on them. It lay there with its face looking back at them. Even in death, they were still scary, and even after all this time, it smelled terrible.

I stepped back in shock. My heart raced as I exclaimed, "Holy shit! Is that real?"

Sam responded, "According to the logbook, it is. I think they were the first humans to ever see an alien."

I looked closely and noticed there was a single claw missing.

"I guess that's where your claw came from," I said.

"This creature took the lives of four of his crew before they managed to kill it. I guess they took the claw as a reminder," Sam remarked.

The cargo bay was very quiet as we stared at the ugly creature. The sound of weapons fire suddenly broke the silence. Three shots rang out from behind us and echoed throughout the cargo area. Startled by the sudden weapons fire, Sam, Lisa, and I dropped to the deck. We turned to look where the shots were fired from and saw a crewmate standing there with his arctic gear on and wearing a set of goggles that weren't standard issue. The crewmate lowered his weapon, pulled back his hood, and raised his goggles. After recognizing who it was, we got up from the deck and rushed to him.

Sam approached him, shook his hand, and said, "It's great to see you, Pops. I know you like to make a big entrance and everything, but damn you, Pops. Did you have to scare the shit out of us?"

"It's better I scare you rather than it scares you," remarked Pops.

"What, that creature? It couldn't hurt us. It has been dead for almost a hundred years." Sam said as he pointed to the crate.

Pops leaned forward to look inside the container before he answered, "I wasn't referring to that corpse that you were looking at. I was referring to that creature there."

Upon shining his flashlight between two other containers which were behind us, we saw a corpse that was freshly killed by Pops. Our eyes widened as we realized this other creature was only about ten feet from striking us. Lisa approached Sam and took his hand while they stared at the creature.

"I don't think I have to tell you how happy we are that you came along when you did. How did you find out about these creatures?" I asked.

"It started when I blasted that area along the crater edge. Linda and Pat worked there while the rest of us worked on the drilling rig. I couldn't reach them, so I sent Jason to get them, and when he didn't return, I sent Eric and Mary. After a while, no one returned, so I decided to find them myself. I thought they were playing a joke on me. When I got to the crater, I didn't see anyone. There was a tunnel we accidentally opened, and I saw a light. As I entered, I found things that belonged to them, like their flashlights, gloves, and boots. That's when they came after me. One of them ran around a corner like a raging bull. I fired a couple of shots and dropped it in its path. I turned and made a run for the exit when another appeared in front of me. So I dropped that one with a couple of shots and got out of that tunnel. I know there were probably a dozen of those things coming toward me. I think that I probably leaped out of that crater. I was so scared that I ran as fast as possible to the rover and took off for the shuttle. Boy, was I surprised when I got there and saw that it was mostly buried. What happened to it?"

"I guess the aliens didn't want us to leave. They hallowed out the ground underneath the shuttle, and we fell through," I answered.

"Did anyone get hurt?" asked Pops.

"There are many bruises and cuts, maybe a few broken bones. The most serious injury is that Kellie is unconscious. What about the rest of your team?" I asked.

"I don't think any of them made it. Those damn creatures killed them." Pops answered.

"I'm sorry, Pops. What did you do when you got to the shuttle?" asked Sam.

"I went aboard to see if anyone was there. Thankfully, everyone was gone. I was surprised to find my weapons locker was about two-thirds empty. I loaded up everything I could. This was the only place I could think of where you would go. I'm guessing you brought the rest of the weapons aboard this ship." I nodded in acknowledgment. "Good. I think we are going to need them."

"I think we're going to need to identify where those creatures might be out there and where they can get onboard this ship and close it off. Does anyone know how long before we are out of daylight?" I said.

"When I arrived, it was starting to get darker. According to my watch, we were scheduled to meet at the shuttle ten minutes ago. That would mean we have about an hour and twenty minutes before nightfall. After that, we are in the dark," answered Pops.

"The Captain should be able to see that we are in trouble from orbit, right?" I asked Sam.

"Not exactly. The camera they would use to see us is working, but it doesn't have great resolution. Meaning that unless they fly past at just the right angle, they won't see us with that camera. They would usually rely on the camera from the rover or one of the portable ones we set up or carry, relaying those signals through the shuttle. As we all know, the shuttle is dead."

"How long before anyone reported us as missing to the Captain?" I asked.

"Well, that is hard to say exactly as well. We are due to lift off from here in about two hours, but we're allowed to stay an extra two to four hours longer. It would take about two hours to return to the ship, meaning it would be about six to ten hours before they missed us. However, I think someone would try to reach out to us long before then," explained Sam.

I took a deep breath and said, "I think we should get out of here and gather up our crew. We must bring them up to speed on what is happening here. From my count, my team and Sam's team are onboard, making Pops all that is left of his team. That puts the count at five dead. Has anyone heard from Wanda's team?"

Everyone shook their heads no. From all of our training before going into space, this was a situation they never anticipated. They should have trained them for the situation at hand. I hated losing someone due to an accident. It was accepted by most that we normally lost four or five people a year among the entire fleet. I had already lost five on this one mission, and there was no way to know how many more would die. For that matter, I wondered if we could even get off of this planet alive.

"We need to gather the weapons and personnel in the mess hall to take a head count and inventory of what we have to fight with," Sam suggested.

"Since you're the expert on this ship, Sam, is there anything we could use as weapons?"

I watched as Sam mentally calculated for a moment before he answered, "When this ship was in service, it had missions similar to ours today and was equipped the same way we are. It would have some basic weapons, some explosives, and drilling equipment. The weapons would be obsolete, the drilling equipment may not work, and the explosives would probably be unstable after all this time."

"Sam, why don't you and Pops go collect the weapons he brought with him. Lisa and I will see what they might have left on the ship. Where would they keep this stuff?"

"The forward cargo hold," Sam said as he pointed in the direction to go.

I signaled a silent thank you and started walking toward the cargo hold with Lisa in tow.

"Wait a minute, Mike; you might need this," Pops yelled as he tossed me a weapon.

"Thanks. I hope I don't have to use it, but I'm glad I have it." I said as I caught the weapon.

We continued on our way to get the weapons and complete our tasks before it got dark. Once dark, the temperature will drop, and the only light available will be that on the ship. The fate of the remaining crew is unknown, and I hoped they would come here first rather than go to the shuttle.

Ten

There Is A Problem

Renee

I walked onto the bridge and glanced around to ensure business was as usual. The pilot was at their post, making minor corrections here and there to keep us in a stable orbit. Others gathered data from the planet at their assigned stations. I didn't disturb anybody; I casually walked over, sat down, and looked around at the displays I could see clearly. I could see the displays the pilot used, and above my chair were more, which I used to stay informed of the ship's status. Upon my usual confirmation checks, everything appeared normal. I noticed one crew member was genuinely perplexed by the information in front of him.

"Hey George, have you heard from our people on the surface?" He didn't respond to my question, so I stood up and began to walk toward him, trying to get his attention. "Hey, George." Still no response. "George!" I yelled.

"Sorry, Captain. What can I do for you?" he asked, jumping from his seat.

"Have we heard from our people on the surface?" I asked somberly.

"No, but they aren't expected to check in for a couple of hours yet," he replied.

"When I looked over here a few minutes ago, you looked as though something was amiss. Is something wrong that I should know about?" I asked him.

He hesitated but finally decided to punch a few buttons, pulling up an earlier image that the radar had processed.

"This is a radar image that we took after they landed. You can see there's the Nightingale, and there's the Discovery, and there's the shuttle." He said as he pointed to the screen. He changed the image and continued, "Here is a radar shot we took a couple of hours after they landed. Everything is the same except for this little blip over here, which we think is the rover Pops took down."

"The information you've given me appears normal. Where is the problem?" I asked him.

"This one was taken on the orbit before last. Everything is the same except for the shuttle. That image changed." he said as he changed the image again.

"Why did the image change?"

"We're not sure. First, we thought it might have been a system glitch. After all, we've had a series of them lately. So we checked on things in between orbits. On the last orbit, we retook radar images and pictures. Unfortunately, we weren't orbiting at the right angle to get any pictures of the shuttle. We're still getting weird feedback about where the shuttle should be. There must be interference, or something's happened to the shuttle. I tried reaching out to them, but I got no response. Since we can't get the camera to rotate, we must change our orbit path and angle the ship to point the camera in the right direction. If we're going to do that, we have to do it during this orbit while we still have some light. By the time we return, they will be in total darkness, and the camera will be useless."

"Relay the course corrections to the pilot. I want pictures of what's going on. I don't like the idea of our people being down there and out of touch. Get in touch with engineering and get an update on the status of the other shuttle. I want that report immediately. How long will it be before we pass over the crater?"

The pilot punched in the course corrections and checked and read some information on her display monitor before responding, "We should be able to get our picture from over the crater in about twenty minutes."

I nodded my confirmation and walked back to my seat. Although lack of communication from the ground teams wasn't uncommon, I had a bad feeling about this mission. I probably wouldn't have felt so bad if the planet hadn't brought the type of questions that this one did. After seeing the images from the last two radar passes, my intuition told me something was happening. We knew before they left that the other shuttle would not be available if they ran into trouble. If they were in trouble, I would have to decide whether to take the entire ship down to the surface. The only place I land would be on the ice on the crater's rim like the Nightingale. In all the years I have been in command, there has only been one time I had to make that call. After witnessing the pictures from the Discovery, I didn't think it would be safe or possible to land my ship on the surface. I'd had this dreadful feeling I would need to make the hardest decision in my career, and it was beginning to look like I was right.

✶✶✶✶✶✶✶✶✶✶✶✶✶✶

Sam

Pops and I gathered the weapons from the rover, and it was apparent we would need to make a few trips. We wanted to ensure one of us could cover the other in case another creature decided to attack us during our trips. As we loaded up, Pops stopped and looked in the distance. I noticed he had stopped gathering weapons and looked in the same direction.

"What is it?" I asked him.

"I've got this funny feeling, but I'm not entirely sure yet. I thought I saw something, but the shadows on this planet can really play tricks on your mind," responded Pops.

"I don't see anything," I said as I strained to see off into the distance.

Pops reached into the rover, retrieved a pair of night goggles, and looked again in the direction as before.

"Get down, Sam!" he ordered.

I dropped the handful of weapons in my arms and prepared a weapon to shoot as we crouched behind the rover. My heart raced with adrenaline as Pops took another look.

"Are they the creatures?"

"I see something approaching us in a single file line. I can make out four images, but I don't think they saw us. Call Mike on the radio,"

"Mike, this is Sam. Do you copy?" I said on my radio.

"Yeah, Sam, what do you need?" Mike's voice came through the radio.

"Pops has spotted four images slowly approaching the ship. We're going to need some help out here," I said.

"We're on our way," Mike said with urgency.

"They're on their way. I still can't see anything. Which way are they coming from?" I asked as I continued to strain my eyes, looking out into the distance.

"They will be coming from over there," Pops said as he pointed in the direction.

A sudden idea popped into my mind.

"Are these high-intensity white lights on the rover?" I asked suddenly as the thought bombarded my mind.

"Of course they are. I wanted the brightest lights I could get because you never know when you'll need them. Why?"

"I need you to turn the rover so that the lights will face in the direction they are coming from, but don't turn on the lights yet."

"I can do that, but I don't see how that is going to help," he said as he got into the rover to move it.

"The creatures are very sensitive to light. When they get close, we will turn on the lights and open fire," I explained.

Pops didn't argue. Just sneakily moved the rover into place. Mike and Lisa came out of the ship for backup and approached when Pops returned from moving the rover.

"Where are they at?" asked Mike, loading his weapon.

I pointed and said, "Pops said they should be coming from over there."

"How far away are they?" Mike asked Pops.

"They just went behind that rock formation in the shadows. They will be popping out at any moment," he replied.

"Are you sure these are some of these creatures?" asked Mike.

"No, I can't completely determine what is approaching even with these goggles. All I can say for sure is something is approaching. Considering that we thought this planet was uninhabited, I would rather be cautious than dead," Pops answered.

"Ok. When you see all of them out in the open, turn on the lights, and then I want no one to shoot unless I give the order. Is that understood by everyone?" ordered Mike.

Mike looked around at everyone, and we all nodded in agreement. All of us crouched behind the rover with weapons ready. As the darkness continued to settle, the shadows from the ship and the rock formations around us made it difficult to see. The temperature continued to drop with no wind, and the surface began to take on a very eerie appearance. Close by, a low guttural growling sound came from the shadows. The hair on the nape of my neck stood on end, and I watched Pop become the hunter as he watched the figures one by one. Slowly, the figures stepped out from behind the rocks and into the open. Pops quickly handed me his goggles, and I understood the silent command. He wanted me to confirm that even in the low light, making it difficult to see that they were creatures. I tapped him on the arm to confirm and held up my fist, telling him in a silent command to hold. Besides these creatures, what else could live on this planet? As the last figure emerged, I signaled for Pops to flip on the lights.

Mike immediately recognized the shadow creatures and stood up, shouting, "Hold your fire! Hold your fire! It's our other team."

In unison, we breathed a sigh of relief and exited from our crouched positions. We lowered our weapons one by one while still being careful in case the creatures were stalking our group. Everyone was concentrating on the other team when I thought I saw one of the creatures dart back into the shadows. I tried to squint and look since it was only a few feet away but saw nothing.

"Are we glad to see you! We thought all of you were dead. Why didn't you answer our calls on the radio?" Mike said as he walked to the team.

"We had a little trouble on the way down, and we lost a few crewmembers and damaged the radios. We have to get off this planet. We're not alone here," Wanda replied with fear.

"Yes, we know. They are creatures that live underground." Mike responded calmly.

"Why are we standing here? Let's get back to the shuttle and get off this planet." Wanda said.

"Well, there has been a little incident, and the shuttle was totaled. Right now," he pointed to the Discovery, "this ship is going to be our home for now."

She looked up at the Discovery, then back at Mike, and asked, "Are you saying that we are stranded here on this planet with these creatures?"

"Yes and no. Things are a little complicated. I suggest that we get the gear off the rover and get inside before losing all of the light out here. Once inside, I will bring you up to speed on what happened and our plans to return to our ship."

We all grabbed some of the gear and headed back to the ship. Pops was the last one by the rover, so he turned off the lights to save its battery life. Each person looked around as they walked toward the ship, looking for any unusual movement in the shadows. We walked close together as they entered the ship. Out in the dark, we could hear growling and other strange noises.

✶✶✶✶✶✶✶✶✶✶✶✶✶✶

Renee

I got up from my chair and watched Geroge look over the pictures, then walked over to where he sat. I looked over his shoulder, keeping quiet. Most of the pictures were dark, and George was working with the image settings so we could see more detail. Although some of the details were easier to see, the adjustment obscured some of the other details. The pictures were taken in rapid succession as we orbited over the crater.

After watching silently, I finally asked, "What do you have, George?"

George was startled by my sudden appearance.

"This is strange; I thought the pictures would answer some of the questions, but it's raised more." He said, startled but pointing at the pictures, continued, "Since our last radar scans, the rovers moved. It's now by the Discovery, and that ship shows signs of power. Now you remember, we were getting what we thought was distortion where the shuttle was. This is the best I can do to clear up the picture, and as you can see, that wasn't a distortion of where the shuttle was." I looked closely at the picture as he continued, "The reason for the clutter is the shuttle has dropped below the surface, and there isn't much left for the radar to pick up."

"How did they fall beneath the surface? Didn't they pick a spot that was supposed to be solid?" I asked.

"We reviewed the readings numerous times to determine the best place to land. According to the readings, we could get solid ground for hundreds of feet," answered George.

"Can you explain how the shuttle is below ground level and half buried?"

I watched the answer churn inside his head as he processed my question for a moment before he responded, "I have no explanation for what is going on down there."

"What is the status of the other shuttle?"

"I'm afraid it hasn't changed. Engineering said if we got everyone on the ship to pitch in with round-the-clock shifts, maybe they could get it ready in a week. That would be if everything goes right and there are no problems," he replied.

"Damnit! If both shuttles were operational, we wouldn't have this problem. The one time we decide to take a chance, things go totally wrong." I said, feeling frustrated.

"We could still take this ship down and retrieve our crew members," suggested George.

"Absolutely not. I can't take the chance of stranding this ship on the surface. So far, two big ships and a shuttle have gone down and haven't made it back. In case you forgot, that's our shuttle down there, and it's a lot smaller and lighter than us."

"If we can't get down there to help them, then what are we going to do?" asked George.

"We will wait for them to contact us and get a situation report. I can't authorize a rescue mission even if we had another shuttle. All we can do is hope they can hold out until we get the other shuttle operational or think of something we haven't."

"Do you really think there is anything we could do to help them?" George asked, concerned.

"I don't know, but I refuse to just leave them. If we have to, we'll stay here until some additional help arrives." As I turned to walk away, I mumbled, "Damn, I wish we knew exactly what was going on down there."

I walked back to my chair, sat down, and looked up at the monitors, paying close attention to the time. If I did issue a message for help, it might be days before anyone would receive the call and even several more days before someone might respond. This was a situation no one ever wanted to think about. As Captain, this was turning into my worst nightmare. I was cut off from the crew and could see there was trouble down on the surface. There was nothing I could do, and I second-guessed my decision to send some of my crew down to the surface. Wondering if anyone was hurt or trapped on the shuttle when it fell through the ground.

The crater has fallen into the dark, and now I would have to sit and wait for daylight to return so we might get better pictures of the surface. The radio the crew would use to report was onboard the shuttle. The only radio left for them to use would be onboard the Discovery. Now, waiting would be the hardest part. Sam was brilliant regarding electronics, and I only hoped he could get the communications working. The biggest thing on my mind was the frigid temperatures on the surface.

★★★★★★★★★★★★★★

Mike

The crew gathered in the mess hall to get a headcount and be brought up to speed on the current situation. All of the weapons were laid out on the table for accessible inventory. The last of the crew gathered around the table. I looked around at the faces of the crew, and some were banged up pretty bad from the shuttle accident. Others looked tired and worn out. They already thought the battle had been lost from the expressions on their faces. Most had already heard about what happened to Pop and Wanda's team.

"Has anyone seen Jeff?" I asked.

Everyone shook their heads no.

"Not since he stormed off after your argument on the surface," Sarah said.

"That makes eight missing and presumed dead. We'll have to be much more careful from now on," I commented.

"Do you know what's going on?" asked Dave.

"We haven't put all the pieces together yet, but we know we aren't alone. There are creatures here which move in the shadows on the surface and underground in tunnels." I watched their reactions and waited for the news to sink in.

Everyone looked at each other with shock. Sam's face was one of amusement, as I told you. The survivors of the attacks showed anger and sadness for the members they had lost. As I continued looking around, I was saddened by their loss and hoped we would not lose anymore. Deep down, I felt this was far from being over. Twenty-five crew members came down, and eight were dead.

"Where are we getting our information on these creatures?" Bev asked as she broke the silence.

"The ship's Captain was the last survivor, and he recorded his observations in the logbook. He documented that bright white lights would cause them to retreat into the shadows. They can see in the dark and retreat back underground during the day, which gave him the ability to move around during the day. He also noted that they appeared to dislike the extreme cold and are limited to the lower half of the crater, where it's warmer." Sam explained.

Wanda observed the others while she listened to the information given to her. She turned her head quickly and looked at Sam after his last statement as if she wanted to say something but remained quiet. I noticed her response and her decision to remain quiet. I made a mental note to ask her about that as soon as possible.

"Why don't we just wait till morning, go up the crater, use the Nightingale, and get out of here? It has to be in much better shape than this ship." Lou suggested.

"We can't. With the exception of the bow of that ship, it's frozen in ice. Inside, there's a coating on most of the control panels, and half of the compartments are frozen shut. We would freeze to death before we ever got the life support systems up and running, let alone the time it would take to get the engines working again. At least here, we have heat, air, and a working life support system," Wanda answered.

"What do these things look like?" asked Cara.

"They are kind of like what you might get if you cross a porcupine and a wild boar, and according to firsthand experience by Wanda's team and Pops, they can range in size from a rhino to a full-grown elephant. You'll know when you see one because their eyes glow, they're ugly, and your first instinct may be to piss your pants." Sam paused briefly before he asked, "We have a couple of dead ones down in the cargo hold if anyone wants to take a look."

Cara's eyes got huge. She got quiet and shook her head no.

"These creatures are very aggressive. They had already killed eight of our fellow crewmates, and one almost got Sam, Lisa, and me down in the cargo hold. If it wasn't for Pops showing up armed when he did, we might not be here. From now on, no one will go anywhere alone. If you must go anywhere for any reason, you must take a radio, a weapon, and one of your crewmates. You need to ensure someone knows where you are going at all times. The fact that one of them got onboard and almost got us in the cargo hold means they have found a way to get in. Don't go anywhere that is not well-lit." I turned to Lexey and asked, "Can we spare the power to turn on all available lighting on this ship?"

"Internal power is no problem. I was able to restore power with only a few repairs. We can turn on every light onboard and any functioning exterior light, which wouldn't affect our power supply. It's the engines that I'll need a little more time working with. There were a lot of modifications made, which I'm still trying to figure out."

"Don't take too long. I don't know about the rest of you, but I am ready to leave this planet." I asked Joan, "What is Kellie's condition?"

"Aside from many bumps and bruises and what I'm sure will be a nasty headache, she should be fine. In fact, I'm sure that she should be back on her feet in a couple of hours," she answers.

"That's great because we need her to fly us out of here." I turned back to the rest of the crew and continued, "On the table in front of you are all our weapons. Everyone should take a weapon or two and always keep it with them. For those of you who have never handled a weapon before, please see Pops; he will teach you. Are there any questions?"

"Have you been able to contact our ship to let them know about our situation down here?" Berry finally spoke up.

I took a deep breath and looked over at Sam as if I was asking him to take this question. Sam looked down at the weapons on the table and didn't notice me looking at him. Everyone else noticed I looked at Sam, and they all turned to him for the answer, but Sam was off in his own thoughts. Lisa gave him a nudge, turned to look at her, and then noticed everyone was looking at him.

I spoke up and repeated, "Berry, and I'm sure others here would like to know if we got a message off to our ship letting them know of our situation."

"Well...umm. As you know, the radios we carry are for use on the surface and don't have the power to communicate with our ship in orbit. The radio we had to communicate with our ship was on the shuttle. We tried to send out a signal, but all of the systems on the shuttle took a beating when the shuttle went down, and I think we were able to get a signal. We were unable to confirm because it couldn't be received. We believe we can get the radio on this ship working really soon, and we will make two-way contact with our ship and advise them of our situation at that time."

"Wait a minute. I thought that Mike said he made contact with our Captain, and they were sending down a rescue shuttle in six days," stated Markus with a bit of confusion.

I spoke up, "At the time, it seemed the right thing to say. The six-day time frame was based on what we knew about the repairs before leaving. I'm sure the Captain has everyone she can work on the shuttle. I, personally, don't like being tied to just one option. This ship is our other option."

"Why change your story now?" asked Markus, surprised.

"I'm telling you now because the situation has changed. We know about those creatures, and we have lost some crew members. All we can do now is wait for the other shuttle to be fixed or get this ship ready to fly and go home. We will need everyone's help to get this ship ready," I explained.

"What makes you think this ship will fly?" asked Lou.

I shrugged and answered, "I don't know, but I know this is all we have to work with. From what Sam, Lisa, and Lexey have told me, they think it was ready before the last survivor died. I think we can finish what they started, and I believe our Captain isn't going to risk our ship by landing it here. She saw what happened to this ship, and after she saw what happened to the shuttle, she won't take the risk."

"Do you think they know anything is wrong down here?" asked Cara.

"If they followed standard procedure, they would have taken radar images as they passed over on each orbit. Even with radar, the image of the shuttle would have changed dramatically. The Captain would have wanted pictures taken of this crater. Due to some damage to our camera turret, they would have had to make a course correction to take the pictures. I guess they already saw the radar images and have concluded something was wrong. Even if they haven't realized, we are now overdue for checking in."

"We're screwed. We're all going to die. If these creatures don't kill us, we'll starve to death." stated Markus.

"We should be out of here long before we reach the point of starving to death," stated Lexey.

"I don't see how it's possible. Our shuttle was destroyed, and our ship's other shuttle is down for major repairs. What are we going to do? Fly this ship into space?" he said while chuckling.

He looked at Lexey, Sam, and me. We looked back at him with a straight-face and didn't say a word. He stopped chuckling and re-marked, "Are you kidding? This ship has been stranded for decades. It would take weeks, if not months, to get this ship ready for space."

"Actually, This ship is in pretty good shape. We should be ready to lift-off by sunrise if everyone works together."

"In case no one has noticed, we are sitting at an angle. How do you plan to get the landing gear free?" asked Lou.

"We will use explosives to detach the buried landing struts and lift-off," answered Pops.

"We could go on asking questions and venting our doubts, but it will get us nowhere. I know everyone here is scared, and I am scared too," Lisa said. We already lost some of our crewmates, and things might seem a little bleak, but we need to pull together if we're going to get out of this."

"She's right. This ship sustained some damage when the ground gave out underneath the landing gear. Most of the repairs were completed by the crew before they disappeared." I stated.

"If the creatures got them, what will stop them from getting us?" asked Lou.

"I don't think the crew from this ship was aware of the creatures until it was too late. Unfortunately, we lost eight people before we were completely aware of them. Now we have an advantage the crew of this ship didn't. We have the Captain's logbook describing everything he observed about the creatures. I need everyone to take at least one of these weapons, and after that, we'll divide into teams and get this ship ready for flight. Wanda, Markus, Sarah, and Dave will join Lexey in engineering. Sam, Lisa, Bart, and Lou will go to the bridge, and Pops, Bev, Dawn, and Berry will join me in fixing a few things in the corridors and setting the charges on the landing gear. Joan and Cara, you need to look after Kellie. Once she comes around, call engineering and have them send a team to get Cara. Then, you and Kellie will join the team on the bridge. The sooner we get to the repairs, the sooner we can get off this planet."

With that, the crew selected their weapons from the table. Some knew exactly which ones they wanted and how they worked, while others were oblivious to how to use a weapon. Those who were unsure about the weapons talked with Pops. A few of the crew, who were already familiar with the weapons, came to Pops for suggestions, and he asked them to choose a different weapon.

I watched the crew as they checked their chosen weapons, signaling for Sam and Lisa to join me but to remain quiet. My focus was on Wanda, and I noticed during the discussion that she wanted to say something but chose to be quiet. I watched as she stepped away and glanced in my direction. I motioned for her to join me, and she walked over to me, confused.

"Did you need me, Mike?"

"During our discussion, I noticed you wanted to say something but held back when we mentioned the creatures couldn't handle the cold. What was it?" I asked.

"I don't know how important it is, but we did find a body onboard the Nightingale. He was frozen in the pilot's seat," she replied.

"Why didn't you say something?"

"After all that has happened, I didn't think it was crucial." she shrugged.

"It was Captain Hauzer, wasn't it?" asked Sam.

Wanda and I both turned to him. Wanda replied, "Yes. How did you know?"

"The last entry in his logbook was that he would make a run for the Nightingale. If he made it to the Nightingale, why didn't he leave?" Sam questioned.

"I'm sorry, but he had a severe gash in his side. I think he bled out once he got onboard. I think he got that fatal wound from up there and not down here." Wanda said.

"Why would you say that?" asked Lisa.

"Based on how difficult it was for us to climb down, there's no way he could have done it wounded. Everyone knows that climbing up is a lot harder than climbing down. Besides, with a wound, he would have passed out in about twenty or thirty minutes from the blood loss. That would have put him at the top of the crater when he was attacked," Wanda said.

"Are you saying these creatures can go into the cold?" I asked.

Lisa and Sam looked at each other as if they were speaking telepathically. Sam turned to me and remarked, "Now it makes sense."

"What makes sense?" I asked, confused.

"Why does this crater have no ice, and how do the creatures survive on this planet? We thought this was a frozen planet, but actually, it isn't completely frozen. In fact, this planet may have been a lot like Earth at one time. I guess it once orbited a sun, but for some unknown reason, it fell out of orbit and into a unique one. As it moved farther from its sun, the surface began to freeze. I mean, this planet does have an atmosphere," Sam explained.

"I see where you are going with this. As the planet froze on the surface, the animal and plant life began to die off. They had to adapt to the changes going on around them. It's not unusual for more than one species to adapt and survive." Lisa chimed in.

"Exactly, we assume one species lived in the frozen mountain tops and migrated down as the temperature dropped and became the dominant species on the surface. They would live in the ice and the upper layers of the planet. The creatures we have down here in this crater may have once lived closer to the surface and were forced to go deeper to stay close to the warmer planet's core. Since this is the biggest and deepest crater on the planet, it's closest to the core, so it's not covered in ice. They must have dug tunnels close to the surface, which allowed the surface in this crater to be clear of ice. Other craters may only have thin layers of ice on them." Sam said.

I shook my head, trying to understand all the information that was just given to me, and waved my hand, signaling for them to stop. "Let me see if I understand what you're suggesting. You think one species of creature lives on the surface, and another lives in the lower part of the planet. How do they survive besides hunting us?"

"I would suspect both species used to hunt animals on the surface, but because of the changes with the planet and with the fact that their prey was dying off, they had to hunt something else. Since the creatures down here used to be closer to the surface, tunnels probably lead deeper into the planet as they try to stay closer to the warmth. I can only guess the other creatures found those tunnels and eventually found the creatures down here. My guess is they hunt each other. One species can only go up so far, and the other can only come down so far." Sam tilted his head in deep thought.

"So if they are hunting each other, why are they hunting us?" asked Wanda.

"It might be that we are like whatever species they used to hunt. In fact, they may have been humanoid. In comparison, the creatures would be like hamburgers, and we would be like prime rib," remarked Lisa.

"Just wonderful. This is what I always wanted to do: go to some unknown planet and become a steak dinner for some alien. This is not what I signed up for," I stated.

I turned and walked away to gather my team while mumbling. I overheard Sam and Wanda continue to converse about the creatures. I watched Lexey gather her team and leave for the engine room while briefing them on what she had seen, what she had done, and what she wanted them to do. I watched Wanda leave Sam and join up with Lexey. Bart and Lou join Sam and Lisa and head for the bridge.

★★★★★★★★★★★★★

Sam

Bart talked about the history of the two ships as we made our way to the bridge. There were a few dark places, and we shined our flashlights over the darkened spots before passing. As we approached our destination, more of the ship's interior lights came to life. Thankfully, this indicated that Lexey and her team made it to engineering and were working in full swing.

I wasn't sure what to expect when we got to the bridge. The last time Lisa and I headed that way, we had gotten sidetracked at the Captain's quarters. I knew there had been modifications in engineering, so I figured there would probably be some modifications to the bridge. Over the years, I studied everything I could on this ship, including the layout, but seeing the blueprint and being here were two different things. I also knew the design hadn't changed much over the years, and this ship was state-of-the-art in its time.

As we walked past the Captain's quarters, I turned to look, but Lisa nudged me to keep going. I smiled at her but kept pressing forward to our destination.

I was the first to enter the bridge and stopped just inside to look around and take it all in. The others entered and lined up beside me to see what we had to work with. It was evident that someone was rerouting some of the controls to the pilot's station. Some of the floor plates had been opened or removed, cables were coming out of the panels on the floor, and others were coming from panels above that station. Some monitors hung from the support beams above the station, and a panel or two had been added to the original control panel.

Looking around, I thought it would have been easier to get this ship operational if there hadn't been so many modifications done. I remembered that a ship of this type required several people to operate. On this ship, there are two stations on the bridge and one in engineering. The technology was more advanced on a ship like the Nightingale, and that ship was set up with all of the controls on the bridge. That ship could be flown by a single pilot but was set up for two pilots to operate. Looking at the modifications, I realized someone had tried to make it possible for a single person to fly this ship.

I took a deep breath and said, "Alright, everybody, we're going to have to figure out what these modifications are, or we're never going to get off the ground."

I heard mumbles as they spread out and began tracing the modifications. I began checking out the cables coming out of the floor panels. Lisa sat at one of the stations and started investigating the computers. Bart and Lou begin their examinations of the pilot's station.

I looked around and saw others doing their work. I remembered reading the Captain's logbook, where he had worked for weeks making these mods. I wondered what it must have felt like to be here alone. His crew was dead, and he was doing everything that he could to survive.

Eleven

Getting The Ship Ready

✱✱✱✱✱✱✱✱✱✱✱✱✱

Mike

My team and I approached a hatch on the ship's port side. I opened a panel on the wall, and inside were four switches; each one had two lights above it. Currently, the lights were red and illuminated each switch. I reached in and flipped each one separately. The lights above the switches changed from red to green, signaling that the lights were on.

"Alright, everyone. It's going to be cold in there. So zip up and have your weapons ready. We don't want any uninvited visitors," I said.

The team did as instructed, and I looked around and ensured everyone was ready before opening the hatch. Once satisfied, I unlatched the hatch and placed one hand on the handle; before opening the door, I looked to my team to signal them to be ready. With my weapon in my other hand, I pushed open the door, and the cold air hit me in the face. We held our flashlights in one hand and aimed our weapons into the landing pod. I was the first to make a move into the pod. With my heart racing, I slowly moved forward, followed by the others, each looking in different directions.

Even though the inside of the pod was well-lit, I figured out the cold air entered from the opening of the landing gear. I continued to glance around to survey my surroundings. Metal catwalks were on each of the deck levels. There were two hatches that led into this pod; one was located on the upper deck, and the other one that we used was on the lower deck. The catwalks were used to service the landing gear and had platforms that folded out to be closer. The team spread out while Pops and Berry climbed the ladder to one of the upper decks. After a bit of hesitation, I followed them, leaving Bev and Dawn on the lower deck.

As I reached the mid-deck catwalk, I walked over to Pops, who was studying the landing gear, and asked, "Do you have a plan for where you're going to place the explosives?"

Pops looked at me and then back at the landing gear before he answered. "I thought about placing the charges on the three major joints. That should allow us to separate, and the gear should fall out the bottom without damage to the ship."

I looked up at the joints Pops planned to set the charges on, then down at the opening. After looking around, I asked, "How do you plan to set off the charges in all three pods?"

He pointed to a junction box on the wall above the upper deck hatch, which I hadn't noticed. I tried not to show it, but I was confused about the plan.

"On these older ships, there are two switches on the bridge for the landing struts: one to raise the gear and the other to lower it. Both are routed through that junction box. What I plan to do is wire the explosives into that junction box so that as we lift off, we flip the switch, and it will detonate the explosives on this side. At the same time, the gear retracts on the other side of the ship," Pops said.

"I thought you were going to wire in a remote detonator,"

"It will be a remote detonator," Pops said as he raised his eyebrows.

"I thought it was going to be one of those handheld detonators," I said, chuckling.

"Wiring it directly is our best option with a ship of this size and everything inside that could interfere with the signal," Pops said proudly.

He turned and walked over to Berry, and I overheard them discussing the plan. I looked around the pod to check on my people. I glanced down at Bev and Dawn and saw they were having a serious conversation. They continuously checked their surroundings in case one of the creatures showed up. On cue, Bev looked up and realized I was looking down at them. She waved and signaled for me to join them. Confused and concerned, I made my way down the ladder, and while I walked to them, I glanced at Berry and Pops to ensure they were placing the charges.

"What's the problem?" I asked.

"I was talking with Dawn about what they discovered on the Nightingale and what happened on the way down the crater. When they found the Captain of this ship, he was on the bridge, and all of the hatches were closed. So far, he has been the only body found. We assume after a few creatures disappeared, they would retreat to a safe place. They would retreat inside this ship." Bev said.

"That's an interesting theory, although I fail to see what you're getting at?" I asked.

"Other than the Captain, we haven't found a single body. As I understand it, you found hatches closed, and some were welded closed. With the exception of the damaged hatch that we used to get onboard, there appears to be no way onto this ship, yet there are no bodies." Dawn repeated

"I heard one of the creatures almost got you down in the cargo hold," remarked Bev.

"Yeah, if it wasn't for Pops coming along, we would have been their next meal," I replied.

"If the hatch is the only way in, how did that creature get in the ship?" asked Bev.

I stared at Bev while I thought about what they had said. Dawn added, "The crew of this ship knew everything there is to know about it, and they couldn't keep them out. That only means the creatures found a way in they didn't think of and we don't know about. We will be looking for the obvious entry points, but what about the ones we don't know about or haven't thought about?"

I stared at them while I thought about what they had said. Situations like this were something that they never trained us for. We were not the military but scientists, miners, and explorers. Pops was the closest thing they had to someone with military training. This was supposed to be a simple mission. We were supposed to come down, collect samples and data, and return to the ship. Now, there were eight dead, and everyone was looking to me for answers, and I didn't have any.

After a few more moments, I took out my radio to make a call. "Lexey, this is Mike. Can you hear me?"

"Yeah, Mike, what do you need?" she replied.

"What is your status there?" I asked.

"It is slow going in some parts, and in others, we are way ahead of schedule, but I think we'll be ready on time and possibly ahead of schedule," she responded.

"That's good to hear," I replied. "Does the computer on this ship have a set of schematics in it?"

"I don't know. Give me a second to check." There was a pause. "The computer has detailed schematics of the entire ship. Is there anything you're looking for?"

"I want you to go over those schematics and see if there is any other way into this ship besides going through one of the hatches like we do. If you find anything, contact me immediately."

"Ok, Mike, I'll let you know if I find anything," she answered.

I looked up to see Pops and Berry finishing rigging the struts. I glanced around the pod, wondering if we were being watched. There were a lot of open areas and only two ways out. This was not a place I wanted to face down one of these creatures. There were only two more pods we had to rig up. So far, we have been lucky not to run into any creatures, and we hope this luck continues. Pops and Berry made their way back down to join the others.

"That's one down and two to go, Mike," stated Pops.

"I wish that it was the last one. I want to get out of here and get back inside." I said, looking around nervously.

We briefly headed back inside to warm up and then returned for the second pod, which was in the middle of the ship near the cargo bay. I knew the lighting was worse down there, and I wasn't looking forward to going back to the place where I was almost killed. I didn't want to think about it, but how did that creature get on the ship in the first place? It was a question that hadn't even crossed my mind until now. My only thought was one of delight as Pops had shown up when he did.

✶✶✶✶✶✶✶✶✶✶✶✶✶✶

Sam

I sat on the floor in front of several open floor plates on the bridge. I had studied the specs on this ship for years, but being here was very different from reading the specs. Onboard my ship, I was considered a genius, but here, I felt like I was going back to school. Lisa walked quietly up beside me and sat down. I concentrated on my work and didn't notice her sitting down at first.

"How are things coming along?" she asked.

"I feel like I'm learning this for the first time."

"I know what you mean. This ship uses a computer language that hasn't been used in decades. Have you made any progress?"

"I think I've figured out most of this stuff. It looked like he was able to make most of the connections before abandoning the ship. There are three connections here that I still need to figure out. How did you do with the computers?"

"That looks like the one thing he did finish. The monitor he hung on the left was for engineering control, and the one on the right was for navigation control. It can all be controlled from that keypad he added to the pilot's station," she replied.

"It's amazing how he modified this ship to resemble modern ships," I said in amazement.

Lisa hesitated momentarily before finally asking, "Do you think we'll make it out of here alive?"

I looked away from her gaze and averted my own down toward the deck. After a few moments of thought, I was able to look back at her and say, "I really don't know. I would like to think so. I read most of the Captain's log book. They thought they were safe on the ship but discovered they were wrong. Somehow, the creatures still got onboard. The Captain could never figure out how. Although the crew didn't make it, the Captain survived for months. We have more information on these creatures and better weapons than they did. So I think we have a good chance at coming through this alive."

She forced a small smile even though I could tell she felt scared. A noise came from the hatch that led to the bridge. We were both startled, and everyone quickly grabbed their weapons, pointed at the hatch, and waited. Two figures appeared in the shadows of the hatch, and all of us watched as they entered the light. I sighed with relief as I realized it was Kellie and Joan.

"Wait! Wait! Don't shoot! It is just the two of us!" shouted Joan with her hands extended out in front of her.

I watched to ensure everyone lowered their weapon to see that it was two of their crewmates. With the loss of some of our own and being told we were not alone on this planet, everyone was a little jumpy. I stood up, put away my weapon, and approached Kellie.

I stepped toward Kellie but stopped short. I was glad to see her back on her feet, and I knew we would need her if we were going to get off this rock.

"It is good to see you back on your feet. How do you feel?" I asked aloud.

"Except for this incredible headache, I'm doing fine considering what has happened. Joan has given me a quick overview of what happened and what we plan to do since I was knocked out." She said as she put her hand up to her temple.

"We're depending on your skills as a pilot to fly this ship. You can fly this ship, right?"

"This ship may be old, but the entire principle on every ship is the same. I should be able to fly this with no problem. As a matter of fact, I..." She said with a smile that suddenly disappeared.

"You what?" I asked as I tried to figure out what she was looking at.

She blindly walked past me toward the pilot's station. She stopped at the seat she would be sitting in and looked up at the monitors and all the cables hanging with them. Then she looked down at the modifications on the controls before looking down at the deck and the loose cabling. Her eyes followed the cables to where they disappeared below the deck plates.

She finally looked back at me and said, "I may have been a little premature in my last statement. With the pilot's station's condition, I'm unsure if I can get this ship to fly. What the hell did you guys do to the controls?"

"We didn't do any of this; we are working to figure out what has been done here. After the Captain lost all of his crew, he modified the ship so he could fly it and control the entire ship from your seat. We decided it would be easier to figure out what he did rather than figure out how to put everything back. You always said you wanted to find a ship that would challenge your skills as a pilot. Well, here it is." I said, chuckling.

I gestured with my hands toward her station, and she looked toward it. Lisa started to laugh, and Kellie turned quickly and gave her a look as if to say *don't say a word.* Lisa stopped laughing but still smiled and looked back at her as if to say *I don't care what you think.* She turned back to the controls and started to figure out what changes had been made.

✶✶✶✶✶✶✶✶✶✶✶✶✶

Lexey

As Mike had requested, I was going through the computer and looking at the schematics of the ship. I traced different routes in and out of the ship with my finger. As I went from one route to the next and from one screen to the next, it wasn't long before I noticed something. I continued to look to see if what I thought I saw was true or not.

"What are you looking for?" Wanda asked as she walked up behind me.

"You startled me!" I said with my heart pounding.

"I'm sorry about that. You were deep in thought about something. I tried not to startle you," she said apologetically.

"That's alright. Was there something you needed me for?" I replied.

"No. The repairs are done, and we have a few more things to figure out. We should finish up on time as you expected. Actually, I was wondering what you were doing over here."

"Mike called earlier and was concerned this ship may not be as secure as we think. He wanted me to look for ways into the ship other than the normal hatches." I said as I took a deep breath.

"Did you find anything?"

"I think I did. Do you remember how they thought the creatures were acting on instinct?"

"Sure. They told us that the creatures were acting on a survival instinct. Why?"

"I'm not so sure it was instinct. I think they saw a way in and brought the ship down so they could get in."

"Are you saying the creatures saw something that the original crew of this ship never saw or figured out?" asked Wanda.

"They may have seen it but felt it would be impossible for the creatures to use it," I said, shrugging.

"Where do you think they are coming in?" Wanda asked blankly.

"Right here on each pod. I almost missed it when I was looking for entry points. On each pod, there is an exhaust vent. Normally, it would be suicidal to crawl in there, or at least it would be for us. When they brought the port side down, they brought the vents closer to them. Those ports are only used when landing the ship. Normally, that wouldn't be a threat, but if they broke through at this point," I said, pointing to a junction along the exhaust port conduit. "If they broke through here, they could get into the ventilation system or various crawl spaces. If they did, they could go anywhere on the ship."

"Is there any way we could verify your theory?"

"The port aft landing pod is closest to the ground and could be the main entry point. Mike and his team should either be there now or soon. We could have them check it out."

"Do you think it's wise for us to go looking for them or at least where they might get into the ship?"

I shook my head while I reached for my radio. "I don't know if it's a wise thing, but we do need to know if it's where they could get in. If they can, we need to seal it off pronto," I speak into my radio, "Mike, I think I found something."

"What did you find?" asked Mike over the radio.

"There is a possibility they could get in through the exhaust ports located on each pod. Where are you right now?"

"We just finished wiring in the explosives in the port aft pod," he answered.

"That's good. To see if they are getting in, you will need to get someone up there to see if they broke through the conduit just past the main bulkhead. They should be able to shine their light down the conduit to see if this is the place."

"How do we get into the conduit?"

"If you look under the catwalk, you'll see a large exhaust conduit. You'll see a ladder on the wall about twenty feet from the interior bulkhead. At the top of the ladder is a small maintenance hatch. On the inside of the hatch is a small fold-down step and handhold for them to use to get there," I explained.

"Thanks, Lexey. We'll check it out. What is your situation in engineering?"

I grinned at Wanda before responding, "We have a few things to finish here, and then we'll be done."

"Good. When you finish up, get your team up to the bridge. We'll check out that conduit and then meet you there."

Wanda and I looked at each other as I set down my radio and shared a moment of silence.

"Do you think that they will find anything?" Wanda finally asked.

"Part of me hopes they do so we can seal it off, and the other part hopes they don't," I answered her.

"What if it is, and there is one of them in that conduit?"

"Then I just told Mike to send someone to their death,"

"All of the repairs are finished. The rest of the team is cleaning up now." Cara said as she walked up to us.

"We're supposed to meet on the bridge," I replied to her.

"I'll pass the word to the rest of the team," Cara said.

Wanda and I watched her walk off to tell the rest of the team. I picked up my radio, and we headed for the ladder while listening for Mike to say something on the radio to let them know what they found.

Twelve

Uninvited Guests

✶✶✶✶✶✶✶✶✶✶✶✶✶✶

Mike

I looked around to check where everyone from the group was. Pops and I were inside the pod on the catwalk while I watched Dawn climb the ladder to join us. Down below, I could see Berry and Bev as they gathered the last of their gear so they could soon join us.

I walked to the railing and shouted, "Bev, Berry. I need one of you to climb up that ladder on the wall over there. When you get to the top, I need you to open the maintenance hatch and take a look inside. I need to know if there is a breach on the other side of this bulkhead. I also need you to make sure there is nothing in there. If you see anything, shoot first. Whoever stays on the deck will cover the other one, and we will cover you from here."

Berry casually glanced at me and then down at the deck. He dropped his gear, reluctantly took out his flashlight, and checked his weapon. He looked at Bev, who was readying her weapon. She looked back and nodded.

I watched Berry approach Bev and say, "He's got my back? Who's he kidding? He's up there where it is safe in case something happens.

The only people putting their asses on the line are you and me. You got my back?"

"Hell yeah!" Bev nodded.

"When this is over and we get back to our ship, drinks will be on me," Berry said with a grin.

"I'm going to keep you to your word," Bev said, smiling back at him.

Berry walked over to the ladder and climbed to the exhaust conduit. As he neared the top, he paused momentarily and studied the latching mechanism. We all held our breath and listened for something inside. After a few painstaking moments, Berry tried to open the hatch. It became evident he couldn't open it with his flashlight in one hand and his weapon in the other. He tucked the flashlight into his belt, and with his free hand, he reached out and unlatched the access hatch. It swung down toward the interior bulkhead and locked in place. He pointed his weapon into the opening, moving around to gain as much of a vantage point before he climbed in. It must have looked clear, for he reached out and folded down the small platform mounted on the inside of the hatch so he could stand on it.

He looked back at Bev, and she nodded back in affirmation. He reached over to the handhold on the hatch and stepped over. I watched as he took out his flashlight and turned it on. I could only imagine his heart racing from the adrenaline that coursed through his veins because mine did the same. As Berry takes one step up, it puts him up into the conduit, which would be up to the middle of his chest. I figured he was facing where I thought there might be a breach. I waited anxiously for an answer. Deep down, I hoped I was wrong because if I was right, then I possibly just sent a crewmate to his death.

As I waited, I heard him shout, "It's confirmed. There is a breach here."

I was about to shout back to him that I wanted him to get out of there when I noticed a quick change in his stance. Although I could only see the lower half of his body, it looked like he stood straight up at attention, followed by a deep growl that made the hair on the back of my neck stand up. We watched him, wondering what he was seeing. He slowly started to turn around like a hunter, trying not to disturb their prey. It seemed like hours had passed instead of seconds. He quickly moved and fired his weapon at something in the conduit. I saw his body knocked to one side and then lifted into the conduit and disappeared, followed by another deep growl.

We watched for a sign from Bev to let us know what had just happened. She hesitated before she shouted. "Berry, what's going on up there?"

The rest of the team and I waited from the catwalk for her signal to open fire if needed. A single shot sounded, and then the silence that followed made me nervous and frightened. Bev slowly stepped forward to angle herself for a better position but stopped when she heard a low growl. When she looked up, something fell onto the deck in front of her, and she looked down to see a bloody severed arm. She gasped and looked back to the opening, then down at the severed arm again. The shock on her face quickly turned to rage. She leveled her weapon, aimed it toward the conduit, and opened fire.

The rest of the team and I followed her lead and opened fire. Soon, the pod echoed with weapons fire as we continued to shoot up the conduit. The creatures' shrill cries could be heard as they were hit by weapons fire. Bev stopped for a second and took out a grenade she must have picked up when handing out the weapons. She pulled the pin, tossed it into the opening, stepped back, reloaded, and continued to fire.

The explosion was deafening, and ringing sounds stunned my re-action time momentarily. I quickly regained my composure and took note that the creatures could no longer stay where they were. A section of conduit that held most of the weight from the creatures came crashing down to the deck along with part of the catwalk. As it came crashing to the deck, it hit an electrical junction box, knocking it off of the bulkhead, and the lights in the pod went out. A large electrical explosion, sparks, and a bright flash caused momentary blindness, and our weapons fire stopped just as the emergency lights flicked on.

I watch Bev cautiously move around, searching for what's left of the fallen exhaust conduit. As she approached the jagged opening of the fallen piece, she continued to point her weapon at the opening while taking slow side steps and staying alert. I watched as she began to dry heave from looking inside the conduit, seeing the aftermath of what was left of the creatures.

"We have the remains of four of those creatures in there, as well as what is left of Berry," she roared.

I bowed my head for losing another crew member under my command. So far, I've lost more crew members on this mission than most ships lost in years of service, except for the Discovery, the Nightingale, and the other ships with similar situations. The Nightingale and the Discovery crews were the first to encounter aliens.

I glanced down at the exhaust conduit, and from where I was standing, I could see another creature moving toward the opening.

I shouted down, "Bev! Get up here now! There's another creature coming up the conduit!"

Bev jumped up and made a run for the ladder to the catwalk. One of the creatures leaped out of the conduit and landed in front of her, tumbling until it hit the bulkhead under the catwalk. Bev stopped and turned toward the hatch that led into the ship. The other members of the team and I open fire on the creature to buy Bev time to escape. Bev reached the hatch, opened it, and ran inside.

Inside the pod, the creature finally rolled over and died. As we stopped shooting, the adrenaline rush was feeling pretty good, and I looked around to survey the rest of my team. Our arms shook slightly from the intense firefight that had just taken place. We managed to kill five creatures but sadly lost one of our own. That good feeling was short-lived as we reloaded our weapons. Something caught my eye from down below. I looked down just in time to see one of the creatures enter the ship through the open hatch.

"Oh shit. Things just got a lot more complicated." I shouted.

"Why?" asked Pops.

I pointed at the hatch and said, "Bev forgot to latch the hatch during her escape, and one has now entered the ship. I can confirm one went in."

"We have some bigger problems," stated Dawn, pointing to the conduit.

On the deck below the conduit, two more creatures emerged. From the opening of the conduit, three more were getting ready to jump down and join the others. I rolled my eyes and shook my head in disbelief. I looked down at my weapon and took an account of my ammo stock. I didn't realize that I had used more than I anticipated to kill the ones we had. There's no way we could hold off these creatures for long.

My thoughts were broken when Pops tapped me on the shoulder and then pointed to the ground.

"Just when you thought things couldn't get any worse. They're gathering down by the landing and coming out of the ground. I think we may have just pissed them off."

"Let's get out of this pod and seal off that lower deck so we can try to isolate them," I said as I glanced at Pops.

"What about Bev? She's down on the lower deck." Dawn asked.

"We're not going to leave her behind. We'll need help because we don't know how many have already gotten inside the ship," I replied.

Pops opened the hatch door from behind us, and we all left the pod. I made sure we all made it through. Dawn was the last one in, and she made sure to close and latch the hatch.

"Hatch secure," Dawn said.

"Before we go any further, I need you to do a weapons check. We need to know what we have left after that." I reached for my radio while they checked their weapons and did a stock inventory. "Lexey, this is Mike. Do you copy?"

"I'm here, Mike. What do you need?" replied Lexey.

"I need you to seal off the lower deck hatches to engineering. There are creatures loose on deck three. We lost Berry, and Bev is trapped on the deck below us. I want you and your team to meet us outside engineering on deck two."

"Do you have any idea where she might be?" asked Lexey.

"No, but I'm guessing she went to the machine shop," I replied.

"Why there?" asked Lexey.

"It's the first room she would come to and would be able to secure the doors, keeping those creatures out. Besides, it's close to the pod hatch." I replied.

"We'll meet you outside engineering," replied Lexey.

"Sam, have you been listening?" I asked.

"Yes. Lisa, Bart, Lou, and I can be there in a few to back you up," responded Sam.

"No, we need you to get this ship off this planet. Lexey should have everything ready in engineering. As soon as you get things ready up there, I want you to attempt to take off," I ordered.

"What about the port side landing gear?" asked Sam.

"Pops rigged it into the system to detonate. When you press the button to retract the port side landing struts, it will set off the explosives, and we should be able to make a clean break," I explained.

"I hope it works; even if we manage to lift off and get into space, the communications system is still down. We will have no way to tell them where we are," Sam said.

"Right now, being in space without communications is better than the one we're in. We have creatures just flowing in here. If we stay here too long, we'll be wall to wall with creatures. I don't know what we did, but it's like they suddenly decided this was the place to be, and they brought some friends."

"I was reading more of the Captain's logbook, and he had a few theories about them. I'm not sure how helpful they'll be. He figured the creatures had poor eyesight and were opposite of us. Where we need the right amount of light to see, the creatures need the right amount of darkness. Too much light or darkness, and they are blind. So if we were to hide in a bright place or an absolute dark spot, they wouldn't be able to see us. He realized it was totally dark underground, which meant they had to have another way of detecting things. He felt they could feel vibrations through the ground and how they came after his ship, but he couldn't prove it. But I think we just did."

"I don't understand. How did we prove anything?"I asked as my team made their way toward engineering. We moved slowly, checking each shadow and lighting it up with our flashlights as we went and continued to listen to Sam.

"The Captain suspected the vibration from his engines got their attention, and the normal ground settling under the landing struts told them where to dig. I believe the same thing happened to our shuttle. Then Pops set off some of his explosives at the drill site, which got their attention there. Now you had that little episode in the pod with weapons fire, and they are here. To them, it was like you were ringing the dinner bell."

"Do you have any theories on what we might do to eliminate them?" I asked.

"I do if Pops has a way to launch an explosive from here and have the explosives explode some distance from the ship," answered Sam.

I looked at Pops, and he nodded. "Pops has something in mind that will work. What's your plan?"

"Before we take off, Pops will go out of one of the topside hatches and fire off a charge or two in the direction of, I don't know, the shuttle. After they explode, we wait about ten minutes for the creatures to move away from the ship in that direction. Then we fire up the engines and get the hell out of here," explained Sam.

"Do you think this will get rid of all of them?" I asked.

"I seriously doubt it. Chances are some won't feel the vibrations of the explosion or will ignore it. I'm sure you would rather deal with a couple dozen or less rather than a hundred or more."

"I would rather not deal with them at all." I paused and then inquired, "How long do you need before we can initiate your plan?"

"We still need another half hour to an hour, and we should be ready up here. We're trying to rush the repairs. The Captain had most things complete up here except for the most important part, navigation. Can you hold them off for that long?"

"You just get us off this rock, and we'll take care of our uninvited visitors," I stated.

★★★★★★★★★★★★★★

Bev

As I hid in the shadows, I watched as one of the creatures entered through the same hatch I did. I pressed my back hard against the wall in a small opening and felt around with my right hand to get my bearings. I peeked out quietly to see what the creature was doing, and it stood at the hatch door, looking around, searching for me.

I quickly refocused my efforts on getting my bearings and finally realized that I was next to an open hatch. I quickly looked through it and then back at the creature. I continued to watch as it turned away from me and moved slowly toward engineering. I decided this was my chance and slowly inched toward the open hatch. I never took my eyes off the creature. As I was getting closer to entering, my radio caught on a conduit and fell to the deck. I froze and looked down at the radio, then up at the creature. It stopped and turned in my direction. My heart began to race as fear started to course through my veins. I ran as fast as I could through the hatch and closed it behind me. Just as I latched it shut, I heard the creature slam against it. Startled, I slowly stepped away, and on the other side, I could hear the creature scratch at the obstacle that blocked it from me and growled, trying to break through.

I examined the room, and it was almost entirely dark except for the glow from the buttons on the machines and some workstation lights. Realizing I was in the ship workshop area, I carefully moved deeper into the room. I stopped momentarily and reached around to the back of my belt for my flashlight, but it wasn't there. It must have fallen off when I was in the landing pod. I continued to one of the workstation lights and checked my weapon in the glow. I saw it was empty, so I also checked my pockets but discovered I was out of ammo. I was now feeling very alone in this room. My radio was in the corridor, leaving me no way to call for help or to let anyone know I was still alive. My weapon was empty, and I had no way to defend myself.

I heard the creature outside the room scratching at the hatch. I glanced around for a way to turn on the lights. I took a few steps forward but quickly stopped because I thought I heard something. I stilled my breathing to listen and strained my eyes to look around in the darkness. After a few seconds, I took a few more steps. I heard something and knew that I wasn't alone in this room. Knowing I had no ammo, I looked around for something to use as a weapon. I found a strut-like bar which had been cut away from some part of the ship. I quietly retrieved it from one of the workbenches, gave it a quick once over, and smiled. The weapon resembled a crude ax. I quietly walked over to a dark workstation and backed myself in between the machines to hide.

✴✴✴✴✴✴✴✴✴✴✴✴✴

Mike

My team and I checked out the crew quarters with our weapons ready. As we exited one section of the quarters, a noise from the rear of the ship caught my attention. We all turned, ready to fire, but stopped to realize it was Lexey and her team. Her team walked cautiously as they approached since everyone was a little jumpy.

"Did you run into any trouble on your way here?" I asked.

"We checked all the rooms on our way here and found nothing on this side of the ship. Have you heard anything from Bev?" Lexey asked.

"No, we haven't been able to get her on the radio, but I'm not giving up on her. She is a resourceful person. There haven't been any weapons, fire, screams, or noises from the creatures. We know there is at least one down there that followed her." I said.

From behind me, a hatch opened, and startled by the sound, everyone turned, ready to fire. A momentary pause as we all watched; my heart raced, and I felt sweat slowly bead down the side of my forehead as we all waited. Lou stepped out from behind the hatch door.

He took one step, then jumped back behind the hatch for protection and shouted, "Don't shoot! It's just Bart and me!"

He poked his head back around the door and saw everyone was lowering their weapons. I would have guessed his heart had to have been racing because mine was. I'm pretty sure he didn't expect us to be pointing our weapons at him when he came through the door. He stepped forward and approached all of us.

"Lou, what the hell are you doing down here? I told Sam all of you were to stay on the bridge." I said.

"I know. You told him we would lift off as soon as we were ready, no matter what. He sent us down to get Lexey and Pops. He felt he might need Lexey once we were ready to lift off. He also felt we needed to get Pops because if we don't get his diversion, we may never get some of the creatures off the ship and safely dock back at our own ship."

"Good thinking on his part," I said.

I motioned to Lexey and Pops to go back to the bridge with Lou and Bart. Lexey looked back, and deep down, I could tell that part of her knew this may be the last time she would see some of us. The odds were not with us getting off of the planet. I wanted to tell her we had already beaten the odds and help take the worry from her.

"Good luck, Mike," she said as she walked away.

"Don't worry, Lexey. We'll be safely back onboard our ship before you know it. One day, you will be sitting somewhere having a drink, and you'll have a story to tell that no one will ever be able to top." I said to her.

I watched her slightly smile in agreement, knowing I was trying to make her feel better about our situation. Before going through the hatch, she looked back at her friends and crewmates one last time. She was the last to go through the hatch on their way to the top deck and the bridge. I waited until she closed it to give some last-minute instructions.

"Once we go through this hatch, we will probably encounter one or more of these creatures. Some of you have already seen one, and some of you will see them for the first time. We have a crewmember who is trapped down there. This is a rescue. With the exception of Bev, all that remains of our crew is here or on the bridge. The lighting down there is not great. So what you see down there will probably be one of the creatures. These creatures are bigger than us, so do not hesitate to shoot. Keep in mind that firing our weapons may attract other creatures, so we need to move fast. Are there any questions?" I looked around at all of the faces, but no one said anything. "Good. Let's go get Bev."

We all entered through the door with our weapons ready and descended the stairs. This ship was designed with hatches at the top and bottom of each stairwell to allow them to isolate each deck from the other in case of a hull breach. At the bottom of the stairs, I looked back up to see everyone in the stairwell. My heart galloped from fear and adrenaline. I peeked inside, and as far as I could see, no creatures were in sight. I signaled for the others to proceed forward. Everyone moved along the corridor, staying close to the walls. The corridor on this level needed to be better lit, making it difficult to see.

As we approached the machine shop, I held my hand to signal the others to stop. In front of the hatch, I saw a creature trying to get in. This confirmed my thought of the location of Bev. Using hand signals so we didn't make any noise, I signaled the others to take aim at the creature. They spread out across the corridor, with some squatting down while others stood. I watched Markus squatting down to take aim; Sarah accidentally bumped him, knocking him off balance. He reached out with his left hand to catch himself, but as he fell forward, the barrel of his weapon hit the deck, making a noise like someone had just dropped a small coin onto a piece of metal.

I looked at him with shock and anger written all over my face. I looked back at the creature, which was now moving toward us.

"Fire!" I shouted.

Everyone opened fire on the creature. It fell back, screeching in pain as it hit the deck and died. I held up my hand, and they stopped firing. We approached slowly in case it wasn't dead.

✶✶✶✶✶✶✶✶✶✶✶✶✶✶

Bev

I stood there in the darkness, shaking, trying to stay quiet. My heart beat so hard inside my chest that I thought it was going to pop out any moment. I watched as the creature stopped before me, and I began to sweat as I gripped the strut tightly. At first, the creature looked away from me as if confused. Then, slowly, it turned its head back in my direction. I knew there was no way I could win if the creature saw me and decided to attack. Even though I knew it would be hopeless, I had already decided I would go down fighting.

Noise came from the corridor, distracting the beast, and I immediately recognized it as weapons fire. My crewmates had come for me; this was my chance to attack the creature. With adrenaline pumping and my heart racing, knowing help was just on the other side of that door, I lunged out of my hiding spot. I brought the sharp part of the strut down onto the creature's neck. It screamed in pain as I continued my assault, and I continued to chip away at the creature like a lumberjack chopping at a tree. It tried to defend itself, but due to the fatal injuries. It swung at me using its back paw and knocked me off balance slightly.

The creature fell to the ground, but I continued to swing until my arms finally gave out. Breathing heavily, I stepped back and stared at the decimation of the creature. I noticed the shooting stopped. Barely able to lift my arms, I dropped the strut, and after I was done staring at the dead thing I had created, I was about to head out of the machine shop. I froze dead in my tracks as I found myself staring at the face of another creature. I was only three feet away from it. I had just dropped my weapon, and I no longer had a way to defend myself.

I knew if I stood there, I was dead. I also knew that I would be dead if I squatted down to pick up the strut or tried to run. The creature growled at me. I slowly tried to crouch down to pick up my weapon while continuing to look straight at it. As I inched down, the creature decided to inch forward. I stopped, and so did it. I stood back up, and the creature backed up. I realized the creature was not going to let me pick up the strut, and out of the corner of my eye, I saw something on the workbench. I slowly inched closer to the bench to get a new weapon, and as I moved, the creature slowly moved forward, waiting to attack.

It seemed as though hours had passed, but I was soon within an arm's reach of a pipe. In one quick move, I grabbed the pipe and swung it as hard as I could, and it lunged for me at the same time. The pipe made contact, and I managed to just knock it to the side. The creature quickly lunged at me again as I was getting ready to swing again. This creature hit me with full force, knocking me into the workbench and knocking the pipe out of my hand. I bounced off of the workbench and hit the deck floor hard. I rolled over onto my back with the wind knocked out of me, trying to still fight for my life. I looked up and saw the creature swipe at me with his paw, using its claws to slice me open before I could cry out for help. The pain was like a hot knife slicing through my skin. I was fading fast from my wound, and with the little bit of life I had left within me, I watched as the creature swung its claws one more time.

✶✶✶✶✶✶✶✶✶✶✶✶✶

Mike

The others and I made our way past the dead creature and stood outside the machine shop. Markus unlocked the hatch door, and the others and I did a quick weapons check. I was finished first, so I kept watch and looked down the corridor to the hatch that Bev came through. Staring back at me was another creature, and another one entered the ship behind it.

"Markus. Get that hatch open now! " I yelled at him.

"What's going on?" Markus asked while unlocking the mechanisms.

"I think we got their attention again, and we're about to have company," I replied.

The others quickly turned to see we now had three more creatures slowly advancing toward us, and more followed them. I shot first, and the others quickly joined in, killing the first creature and then another. The other creatures walked over their dead, but they kept coming.

"We're in," stated Markus as he pushed open the hatch.

"Everyone inside now!" I shouted.

We peeled off one at a time and went through the hatch door while the remaining members continued to fire at the creatures. Two more creatures dropped dead from their sustained injuries. Soon, it is just Sarah, Dave, and me left in the corridor firing. Sarah was the first to move, and then Dave joined her in exiting the chaos. Dave suddenly stopped, and I glanced back at him. His face held a look of shock and pain; I noticed blood began to form in his mouth as he tried to breathe. Dave fell to the deck. He was dead. I saw at that moment another creature had come up from behind us. I shot a few shots at it. Weapons fire from the other side of the hatch suddenly appeared, killing the creature. I turned and fired some more at the others approaching, killing the one that was closest to me.

I jumped through the hatch, shouting, "Close it now!"

Markus, Wanda, and Sarah manage to close it and get several of the locking latches engaged before a couple of the creatures hit it from the outside. The sudden thud against it made everyone jump away from it.

Markus stepped up and examined the hatch before he turned to me and said, "We managed to get several of the locks engaged, but there is no way to engage the rest. The locks won't hold for very long if enough of them keep hitting it."

I tried to think for a moment of something we could use to help the locks keep hold.

"There are two hatches which lead into this compartment. There was one we came in, and the other was at the other end of the room.

Both led into that corridor, and we couldn't go there. Now, we came here to rescue Bev, so let's find her, and while you're looking around, be sure to look around for another way out."

I saw Cara had a puzzled look on her face as she strained to hear something. She cocked her head from side to side, trying to figure out what the sound was and where it was coming from.

"Quiet everyone. Does anyone hear that?" She said.

We all stood still and listened.

"Whatever it was, it sounded like it was coming from the back of the room. Sarah and Cara came with me. Markus, Dawn, and Wanda go around that way, and we'll work our way around to the back of the room. Take no chances. We have already lost too many."

We cautiously moved toward the back of the room where the strange noise came from. This time, we checked whatever was in front of us and behind us. Everyone was scared, and you knew it. Every sound, every echo, and every shadow made us jump and ready to fire. The room was large and dark, and we had to watch where we walked. There were too many shadows we had to light up as we went.

I thought about everything that's happened since this nightmare began. This was supposed to be a simple survey mission, just like all of the ones that I had been on before. These were my friends who were dying all around me, and everyone was looking to me to keep them safe and to figure out a way to get them out of this. I was getting frustrated at how these creatures could sneak up on us. The stress I felt was beginning to show. I began to sweat no matter how warm or cold the room was.

As we approached the back wall, I signaled for everyone to slow up so I could assess the room. I saw a row of workbenches along the back wall, and the sound we had heard seemed to be coming from the other side of a large machine. The machine blocked the other team, so they rejoined us. Since the opening in front of me was enormous, I signaled the others to alert them we would go through two at a time.

Sarah and I went first, and we would need to go all the way over to the workbench. I glanced back to see the team patterns. Markus was with Dawn, and then Wanda was with Cara. The plan was to make a line across the aisle. I scanned the area and noticed a creature was facing away from us. We quietly moved into position behind it, and at first, the creature was oblivious to us. It slowly turned its head to look back in our direction.

Small gasps came from my group as we all saw a human arm hanging from its mouth at the same time. When the creature took notice of us, it clenched its jaw shut, causing its teeth to sever it, allowing the hand and wrist to fall to the deck floor. We watched in horror as the creature began to chew and loudly heard it crunching Bev's bones with blood dripping from its chin. That was all that I could take. I opened fire on the creature, and the others joined in. I would have assumed we killed it with the first six or seven shots, but everyone continued to fire until I signaled them to stop.

It took me a moment before I was able to go up and look at the front of the creature. No one said a word as I went to investigate. They all stood there and awaited my next word of command. There were thumps, thuds, and scratching guttural sounds that came from the front of the room with the locked hatch. All of us casually looked toward it. I turned back to the dead creature and began to move closer to it. The others watched me shine my flashlight upon the front of the creature. I tried to hold my composure as I looked upon what was left of Bev. Her chest was ripped open, and most of the internal organs were gone, along with part of her right leg below the knee, and her right arm was gone, just above the elbow. Several of the team became sick at the sight of what was left of her. Others looked away at the sight of her as they must have thought that this would be their fate as well. Cara walked away from us for a moment alone, but not too far for safety. She stepped into an opening between two workbenches and put her hand on a handrail. You could hear her as she tried to fight back the urge to cry.

I finally spoke up, "It looks like the creatures haven't given up on trying to get in here to get us. Since we can't go back the way we got in, I say we set up a barricade and fight. If we are destined to die here, I'm not going down without a fight."

Everyone nodded in agreement and began to move around the room, looking for objects to use to make the barricade. Cara let go of the handrail and took two steps toward the others when she stopped suddenly. I watched as she suddenly turned back around and shined her flashlight onto the handrail she had been holding. There was another handrail mounted to the wall on the other side of the rungs. She shined her flashlight on them to see that it was a ladder mounted to the wall. Using the flashlight, she followed it up the wall to an access hatch door at the top.

"Mike! Over Here! I found something!" Cara shouted excitedly.

Everyone stopped what they were doing, curious as to what Cara had found. I almost jogged over to her in order to see what it was she found. She smiled as she shone her flashlight onto the ladder. The others gathered behind me, and everyone was shining their flashlights on the ladder and hatch. Cara had found a way out of the machine shop. I was tired of sending people to die.

"I'm going to check this out myself. The rest of you need to keep an eye out for more creatures. Once safe, I will call for the rest of you to follow." I shouldered my weapon and began the climb.

Thirteen

Ready To Fly

✶✶✶✶✶✶✶✶✶✶✶✶✶

Sam

The activity on the bridge slowed, and the thought of never making it off this forsaken planet continued to swarm through my thoughts. I overheard Kellie and Lexey discussing the pilot controls. At the same time, I watched Joan continuously check the medical supplies as though she expected someone to be seriously injured and wanted to be on the ready.

Pops, Bart, and Lou were reviewing their equipment to ensure they were ready for the part they needed to play in our plan. After they were done checking their gear, they continuously checked the schematics of the ship. Lisa and I were alone at one of the stations, and my nerves were getting the better of me. This was the first time in decades that the systems on the bridge had been up and running. The bridge was the brightest and most active place compared to any other location on the ship.

"It looks like we're ready to give it a try and see if this ship will fly," I stated.

"Shouldn't we wait for the others?" asked Lisa.

"You heard what Mike said. As soon as we're ready, no matter where they are, we are to move ahead with the plan to get off this planet," I replied.

"How will we tell them we are getting ready to lift off?" Lexey asked.

"If I know Pops, and I think I know him well enough. When he sets off the explosives, they should be able to hear the blasts no matter where their location is." I looked over at Pops, and he grinned back at me before going back to getting his gear ready. I continued, "Once Mike and the others hear the explosion, they'll know they have about ten minutes to make it up here or find something to hold on to."

"Everything was ready in engineering," Lexey said.

"Everything is ready here, and your pilot is ready to go," stated Kellie.

"Ok, Pops, it's up to you now. How many charges are you going to set off?"

Pops zipped his jacket and picked up his weapon and duffle bag, which held the explosives.

"Four. They are similar to the old military mortars, except they have more boom power. I'll aim for the ridge toward the shuttle destruction site. If we're lucky, one of the shots will hit the shuttle and make a bigger explosion. Even if I miss, the explosions together should get their attention."

"Once we hear the fourth blast, we'll start the clock. As soon as you get that fourth shot off, get back on the ship and get up to the bridge. I'm not sure if I was able to get the internal communications fixed. Still, we'll try to make some sort of announcement before firing up the engines. If you can't make it back here in time, I'll give you the same recommendation to find something to hold on to."

Pops must have been able to see the stress on my face from the pressure to ensure the ship was ready to go. He set his duffle bag down, walked over to me, and said, "Sam, I know you feel responsible for what has happened, but there was no way for you to know."

I took a deep breath and responded, "That may be true, but I'm the one who convinced the Captain to let us come down here. We should have waited until we had a backup shuttle."

"This is no time to feel guilty. We all came down here of our own free will. Nobody twisted our arm. I've been in space most of my life, and we have never encountered any alien life. There was no reason to think we were going to encounter them on this mission. You just need to hold it together for a little longer, and we'll be back home on our own ship. Do you think you can do that?"

"Thanks Pops. Why don't you go and set off your explosives, and let's go home? I don't know about everyone else, but I am ready to leave." I said.

He smiled as he patted me on the shoulder before he turned around to pick up his duffle bag and headed for his team. Bart and Lou already had the hatch cracked open while they waited patiently for him. I watched as they left the bridge and closed the hatch behind them.

"Has anyone tried to contact our ship to let them know we are alive and coming back?" Lexey asked.

"I'm afraid we can't contact them yet," I answered.

"Why? I thought you fixed the communications system?" she asked.

"Unfortunately, the system was badly damaged. I did manage to get it working, but it doesn't have a strong enough signal to get out of this planet's atmosphere. So we cannot send our ship a message until we get into orbit."

"Do you think they know we are alive down here?" Lexey asked quietly.

"The Captain is probably taking radar images of this area every time she passes over. Unfortunately, those won't give her much information, except everything is still in the same place as the previous orbit. There's no way to see into this dark crater, no way to communicate, and we have no way of knowing when she flies over us," I responded.

"That may not be true, Sam," Kellie said as she zeroed in on me.

"How so?" I asked.

"I've had a bit of time to do a little figuring. Based on the figures I came up with, she is passing over us right now. My best guess is she will be moving around to the far side of the planet when we launch."

"Well, at least that is one piece of good news," I remarked.

"How is that good news?" asked Joan.

"There are a lot of systems on this ship that we either can't fix or don't have the time to. That means we don't have to worry about colliding with them when we go into orbit. Also, the Captain won't see Pops setting off his explosives and wonder if we blew ourselves up until the next orbit," I stated while looking over at Joan. "However, she is going to get a big surprise when she comes around the next time and finds out we are gone, and fires are burning where the shuttle was."

"What's your best guess on how long you think it will be before we can dock with our ship once we get into orbit?" asked Lisa.

We all turned and looked at Kellie and waited for an answer. Silence fell over us as we waited for Kellie to fill the void.

"Hard to say because I don't know how long it will be before we lift-off. I'll be able to give you an estimate once we get into orbit," she answered.

★★★★★★★★★★★★★★

Renee

"Any word from our people on the surface?" I asked as I walked up behind George.

I could tell he was getting used to me coming over during each orbit. It was becoming such a routine that he could almost set his watch on it. Everybody was getting pretty tired, but they kept doing their job and hoping for some kind of change. Most of the crew pulled a double shift, only stopping to get something to eat. This was normal behavior when a team was down on the surface of a planet or asteroid, but this time was different. I saw the concern written on their faces as they realized this might be their crewmates' last mission. Fear and anger quickly replaced the concern as they soon realized they could do nothing to help them.

"Sorry, Captain, there is still no word from our people on the surface." He pushed a few buttons, pointed to the screen, and said,

"These are the latest radar images we made on this pass over the crater. Everything is still the same as it has been in the last few orbits."

"Why don't you get some rest and let someone else do this for a while?" I said as I tapped him on the shoulder to get his attention off the screens.

"That's alright, Captain. I'm not tired," he replied while yawning.

"You let me know if you hear anything or if there are any changes," I said.

"Do you think they are alright?" George asked as I began to walk away.

"I certainly hope so," I said over my shoulder.

"How long do you think they can survive down there?" he inquired.

"My guess is they have turned to the Discovery for shelter. They had enough rations to feed themselves for three days. I'm hoping we have the other shuttle ready before then." I said as I took a deep breath.

"What if the other shuttle isn't ready?" he asked.

"We will have to take the ship down to get them," I replied.

"What if we suffer the same fate and get stuck down there?"

There was a small silence as the others overheard our conversation. I walked back to him and waited until I could tell his racing thoughts had ceased.

"We're not going to let that happen. The plan will be the same, no matter if we use the shuttle or the ship. We will land, drop off the rescue team, and then return to orbit. We will then go back and pick them up in the next orbit. I know taking the ship there holds a bigger risk than taking a shuttle, but I have no intention of leaving them down there to die. One way or another, we will go down there and get our people back. By dropping our people off and then returning to get them, we reduce the chance of the ground giving way underneath us." I said calmly.

"If we land in the crater, won't it give way like it did on those ships down there?" he asked with a quiver in his voice.

"I don't plan to land in the crater," I stated.

"Where do you plan to land?" he asked.

"We will land on the top edge of the crater. That way, we shouldn't be there long enough to have the ground give way under us. I want you to start looking for a possible landing site where we can execute this plan." I replied.

I headed back to my seat while George continued to listen for any signals from the crew and looked through previous scans to find a landing site. I saw that in his posture; he wondered if anyone was hurt or if any other scenarios popped into his thoughts. The scans that we had recorded couldn't tell the status of the Discovery. As far as we knew, it was just one big block of ice.

★★★★★★★★★★★★★★

Pops

Lou, Bart and I made our way toward the back of the ship on the upper deck. Lou led us while I watched for creatures from the front, and Bart watched behind them for creatures. I looked around for the entrance to lab two, and this also happened to be where we planned to get access to the top of the ship. Everything was quiet on this deck, and it was such a big relief from what was going on down on the lower deck.

It wasn't long before I found lab two and stopped to open the hatch while Lou and Bart watched the corridor. I cautiously opened the hatch to find a well-lit lab. We entered and closed the hatch behind us. The lab was used to test the samples they had collected from their explorations. Most of the equipment and samples were broken on the ground as they had fallen onto the deck when the ground gave out under the ship. In the opposite corner of the room, an airlock led to the top of the ship. I made my way over toward it, opened the hatch, and set my duffle bag inside. I poked my head into the airlock and looked upward to see the emergency hatch leading to the ship's top.

I popped my head back, began putting on my safety harness, and said, "It should take me about five minutes to find a place up there to set up and about ten minutes to set up the gear. It should take me less than five minutes to launch the four charges. After the fourth explosion, Sam will begin the countdown to launch. So no matter what you hear topside, if I'm not back here in ten minutes, the two of you are to get your asses back to the bridge."

"Pops, there is no way that we are going to abandon you and leave you up there," states Bart.

"Listen, Bart," I began as I finished putting on my harness, "It's going to be slick up there, and if I slip, you aren't going to have enough time to come up there and get me before we launch. So I want you guys to stay down here and try not to make any noise that might attract those things."

They stood there quietly as they watched me enter the airlock and close the hatch. Inside the airlock, I picked up my duffle bag and climbed the ladder to the emergency hatch. I paused for a moment before I opened the hatch. I was hit with a wave of cold air as I opened the hatch. It felt like stepping into a deep freeze on a hot summer day. It was a little hard for me for the first couple of breaths that I took, but that quickly passed. I took a few more steps up the ladder and cautiously poked my head out of the top of the ship. It was very dark outside. What little light that was making it to the planet was not making it down into the shadows of the crater. I was only able to see a few feet in front of me. I decided to wait momentarily to see if his eyes could adjust to the darkness.

After a few moments of waiting for my eyes to adjust and my body acclimated to the cold temperatures, I decided it was time to move forward with my task. The first thing that I did was to tether myself to the ship. Next, I carefully set my duffle bag on top of the ship with a short tether to my belt. I pulled up my mask to protect my face from the cold before I pulled myself out of the hatch and sat on the edge of the hatch opening. I reached into my pocket and pulled out my flashlight. I examined the surface on the top of the ship. As I had suspected, ice had formed on the surface. If the ship was sitting level, this would not have been a problem, but because the ship was not sitting level, I would have to be extra careful as I moved across the top of the ship. Using my flashlight, I look for a place to set up and a way to get there.

★★★★★★★★★★★★★★

Mike

I began climbing the ladder toward the hatch that led away from the machine shop. Due to the ship's angle, it was challenging to stay on the rungs, but after the first ten feet, I found a safety cage wrapped around the ladder. The hatch was about twenty-five feet above the deck. This deck was higher from floor to ceiling because of the large cargo hold on the other side of the bulkhead. As I got closer to the top, the last three feet of the ladder cage were missing. I quickly realized this was to allow the hatch to swing downward.

With one hand still hanging onto the ladder, I used the other to unlatch the hatch and allowed it to swing down out of the way. I looked down at my remaining team, who watched me intently from below. My heart raced as I readied my weapon, slowly inched my way through the hatch opening, and searched for more creatures. I tried to comprehend the information my brain had given me about what had happened in the pod, but I needed to keep focus on the task at hand. I peeked my head up slightly, where my eyes barely looked over the edge. I looked in front of me first and then both sides to assess my new surroundings where we would enter. I looked for those glowing eyes in every corner staring back at me, ready to attack at the first chance it got. Luckily, the crawl space was empty, and I secured my weapon and exchanged it for my flashlight. With my flashlight now in hand, I stepped up the ladder and further into the space.

The beam from my flashlight shone ahead of me, and then the yellow light slowly crept back in my direction in a three-hundred-and-sixty-degree circle. I noticed paths made out of deck plating about every four feet from one side of the ship to the other. The deck plating ran from the front to the rear of the ship. This was the service crawlway where all the major needs were run for each deck. Here, in between the decks, they could run the electrical, the water, and the heat. This crawl-space was put here to allow the engineers to access all of the major lines in case repairs were needed. The sudden realization hit me that this was also most likely how the creatures were able to move freely throughout the ship. I noticed a light ahead and shut off my flashlight to see if my eyes had played a trick on me or maybe I saw a reflection. The light remained on ahead of me.

I hunkered down and stepped back down the ladder to report to everyone what I saw and planned to do.

"This is a maintenance crawl space between the mid and lower deck. There are no creatures up here, as far as I can see. I have seen a faint glow of light about twenty or thirty feet ahead in the direction of the bow of the ship that I'm going to investigate."

"Do you think we should come up there or stay down here and wait?" Dawn asked.

"Hey Mike, If it's safe up there, I think we should come up with you. That hatch won't hold those creatures out for long, and I think we would be safer up there."

I looked over at the hatch, which he spoke about for a moment, and then back down at the others and responded, "You're right. Get every-body up here. You'll have to be careful; there isn't much headroom."

I scampered back up the ladder, and from above, I watched as Markus started to help each person up the ladder. The first to go up was Cara. Like me, the first few feet were slow going due to the ship's angle. Once she reached the ladder cage, Markus tapped Sarah on the shoulder, alerting her to go next. During her climb, one of her feet slipped off one of the rungs, but she quickly regained her footing and continued up. Markus nodded to Wanda, thus leaving himself and Dawn on the deck. As Wanda started up, Sarah was getting ready to go through the maintenance crawl space hatch.

For the entirety of the time we had been in the machine shop, the creatures continuously beat themselves against the hatch that held them outside and away from us. I know that I had been consciously aware of the noise, and I assumed the others had, too, since it had never let up. I tuned it out mostly so I could focus on our safety, but I still tried to remain somewhat aware of their presence. As Wanda started to climb, there was a sudden change, and the noise stopped. Everyone froze in their spots and turned their attention toward the door. I didn't have a great view from my location, but I had hoped those on the ladder did. We used our flashlights to shine beams of light on the now quiet hatch. The silence killed me as we all waited quietly, and I wondered what the creatures were up to. A sudden, loud, ear-shattering bang hit against the hatch, followed by something metal hitting the deck.

Go! That sounded like the locking latches giving way!" Markus yelled.

I helped Cara quickly move through the hatch with Sarah close behind. Wanda continued to climb while Markus signaled for Dawn to start up the ladder. He waited for her to get up high enough so that he could start the climb. During his wait, he stood at attention with his weapon ready for action from those horrific creatures.

"Come on, Markus. Don't try to be a hero. Get on the ladder and get your ass up here." Dawn yelled down as she reached the top.

I watched as he turned and looked up with a smile while walking toward the ladder. He started up, but in his rush, he lost his footing just short of the ladder cage and swung away from the wall and then back at the wall. During the swing back, he hit his head on one of the rungs and lost grip on the ladder, falling back to the deck.

"Markus! Markus!" Dawn shouted out.

I watched as Wanda was about to go through the hatch. She looked down and saw Dawn climbing back down to the deck. She was about to say something when she held a look of confusion and started to climb back down to help Dawn. I was about to follow to ensure everybody was safe, and that's when I saw Dawn had reached the bottom, and she tried to help Markus sit up. He shook his head as though things were a little fuzzy and tried to continue clearing his vision.

"We need to get this wound taken care of," Dawn said as she examined the wound.

"You're going to have to do it up in the crawlspace. We can't stay down here. If those creatures get through that hatch, we will be in big trouble really fast."

"Do you think that you can make it up the ladder?" Dawn asked Markus.

"Maybe I might need a little help." He said, slowly nodding his head.

Dawn and Wanda helped him to his feet, and Wanda looked over and said to Dawn, "I'll follow and help him up, but you better be close behind."

Markus started up the ladder, and soon Wanda followed; she stayed close to use her body as a shield to keep him from falling again until they got to the ladder cage. From the look on Dawn's face, I could tell she would have rather gone up behind him, but Wanda was bigger and stronger than her. If Dawn had followed him instead and if he had slipped, they both would have crashed to the deck. She watched Wanda stop at the ladder cage and waited until Markus passed her before she went into the ladder cage. Dawn continued to wait on deck for Wanda to start into the ladder cage.

I saw she was getting nervous about being the last one on the deck. As soon as Wanda entered the ladder cage, she started up the ladder. Her foot had just hit the first rung when another thunderous sound hit the door, and metal hit the deck again. Another squeak of metal against metal and then something hitting the wall from the other side of the room. It was the sound of the last locking latch on the hatch breaking and hitting the deck, followed by the hatch being pushed open. The creatures had finally broken through, and I watched the color drain from Dawn's face. She knew she needed to climb the ladder as fast as possible. She was two rungs up the ladder and lost her footing. She swings out and struggles to swing back; she is able to get her feet back on the rungs securely. She was about to move forward when she looked over her shoulder and saw a couple of creatures approaching her.

Wanda looked to see that Dawn had barely started up the ladder. She peered into the room and saw several creatures advancing toward her. While still hanging on to the ladder with one hand, she drew her weapon with the other hand; hoping to buy Dawn some time, she opened fire. Markus looked down to see what was happening and did the same. Although their intentions were good, they had the wrong effect. Instead of buying her time, the noise attracted more creatures into the room. They managed to kill two of them, but they kept coming.

Dawn struggled to move up the ladder. She cried out as she tried to baby her right foot. Her shoe was immediately covered in blood as she swung away from the ladder. During the swing, she looked down to see how many creatures were below. She cried out even louder as one of the monsters swung its claw at her, and she lifted her legs, making it miss. It tied a few more times and missed. She had a look of pure terror plastered across her face because we all knew the inevitable. She still tried her hardest to stay out of the creature's reach, but soon, she realized that she would not be able to swing back to the ladder. I watched in fear, knowing I couldn't do anything to help. She tried to swing her feet back to the ladder while keeping out of the creature's reach but failed. Another swung its claws while more creatures entered the room.

"Help me, please! I don't want to die!" She said, looking me in the eyes.

Wanda and Markus looked down at her, and before they could do anything, one of the creatures managed to hit her leg hard enough that they caused her to lose her grip on the ladder, which was now hung on by one hand. As she tried to grab the ladder again, she managed to get her feet back on rungs. She was pleased that she was back on the ladder, and she reached for the rung when one of the monsters struck again, hitting her feet and knocking them back off again. This time, she had one hand on the rung, and the sudden loss of balance was too much. When she swung out, she lost her grip and fell to the deck face-first between the creatures.

"No! We have to save her!" Markus shouted.

"It's too late, Markus. You've seen what those creatures can do. Trying to save her right now would be suicide." Wanda said as she blocked his path.

"But, we have to try," he replied with tears in his eyes and agony in his voice.

I watched as one of the creatures moved on top of Dawn and started clawing and tearing at her. There were a few screams before she went silent. Wanda pointed her weapon down at them and took a couple of shots, killing the two creatures who had decimated her.

"She's dead. Now get your ass up this ladder and into that crawl space." Wanda said as she stared down at Dawn's immovable figure. "Now, Markus!" she ordered him.

Markus finally began to move up the ladder and into the crawl space. He stayed silent and found a place to sit down and weep. Everyone sat in silence as their reality sunk in of losing another member of their crew. I looked around at their faces as if it could have been any of them, including myself. At first, when we had to take refuge in this old ship, we had hoped to be able to get it to work and get it off of this planet. Now, I watched as their hope of getting off this planet slowly faltered. I know that I didn't want to watch any more of my crewmates die one at a time. I could tell some were even ready to give up.

"What happened?" I asked as I tried to get a better understanding of the situation.

Wanda looked over and answered, "We were almost all up when Markus slipped and hit his head and fell to the deck. Dawn and I went down to get him, and then I helped him up the ladder. Dawn was the last one to head up the ladder, and right after she started up, the creatures broke through the hatch. She tried to hurry up the ladder to get out of their reach but lost her footing. Markus and I started to shoot at them to give her some time, but in the end, we lost Dawn to them even after killing eight of them."

I bowed my head and thought about the crewmembers that we had lost. So far, we have lost half of the crew we had been sent down with. I knew we were far from being safe and putting this behind us. I wondered how things were going on the bridge, but I wasn't ready to use the radio, fearing the noise would attract the creatures. I looked back up at the devastated expressions on my team's faces. The only illumination was from their flashlights, giving their faces an eerie glow. I shined my light around at each of them to take in their full expressions, which only broke my heart. Except for the between-deck supports, I could see almost everything around us from being here the longest. After checking our surroundings, I decided we were the only living beings here, and these people needed some good news about going to get out of there soon. The only person who could give them that satisfaction would be Sam, who was on the bridge. I figured there was little risk of trouble at our location and decided Sam should be able to give us some good news by this time via radio.

Everyone watched as I took out my radio and turned it on. I keyed the radio and said, "Sam, this is Mike. Do you read me?"

"Yes, Mike, I do. Where are you at?" Sam replied.

"We are in a maintenance crawl space between deck two and three. We are trying to make our way back to the bridge. What is your status up there?" I asked.

"Everything is ready up here. You must return here soon or find a place to hold on to. I sent Pops to set off his charges for a distraction. He should be topside by now. You will have ten minutes from when he sets off his fourth charge to either get up here or hold on. This takeoff is going to be rough," replied Sam.

"We will do our best to get there, but don't wait for us. Start that clock after the last charge goes off, and when it reaches zero, lift off no matter what," I instructed him.

"I don't know if you're going to be able to hear the explosions from where you are. I'll try to do something to let you know when the clock starts," stated Sam.

"I don't think you'll have to worry about it. We would be able to hear Pop's explosions from orbit," I remarked.

There is a slight pause before Sam asks, "Will you make it back up here in time?"

I didn't say anything for a moment before I answered, "I don't know. Those creatures keep pouring into the ship, and so far, they are just staying on the lower deck. I'm sure it won't be long before some of them start showing up on the upper decks. We must be able to slow these creatures down or at least keep them out of certain sections until we get back to our ship. You suggested earlier this planet may have two species of creatures. One of them likes the cold and hates the heat; the other is the opposite. Is there any way that we can use that?"

"Maybe? I mean, the air temperature up top is about minus thirty, and down here, it was about zero. By all accounts, it should be colder down here, with all the shadows preventing most of the light from reaching us. Since it is warmer, I would guess there is some sort of underground heat source here. That would mean they have a pretty good tolerance for both heat and cold. My guess would be a range of maybe sixty to seventy degrees to about twenty below zero. Now remember this is only a guess, and I have nothing to support these estimates," replied Sam.

"So, your saying is we either have to make it too hot or too cold for us to be comfortable or for the equipment to work properly," I remarked.

"I'm afraid that temperature isn't an option with these creatures. The only weakness that they have that we can use is light. They appear to be vulnerable to bright light, or maybe it is just a certain spectrum of light. I'm really not sure what it is. I know this is why they can move in dim light and the beams of our flashlights. We have to hope Pop's distraction gets all or most of them out of the ship," replied Sam.

"How long before Pops launches his first charge?" I asked.

"He's been gone for a while, so I'm guessing any minute now," answered Sam.

"Just remember, don't wait for us. When the timer hits zero, launch. We will deal with the remaining creatures once we are in space."

I put my radio away, glanced at the others, and said, "Ok everybody. Time is working against us. As you heard, we could be lifting off soon. I don't want to be here when that happens. We're going to crawl toward the front of the ship for a short distance. I believe the light down there could open up into the floor of the mess hall. That should put us halfway back to the bridge. Everyone needs to stay sharp. Even though we think that most of these creatures are confined to the lower deck, there may still be some of them that might have made it to other decks. So everyone be ready and follow me."

One by one, we all began to crawl toward the front of the ship with only our flashlights to light the way. We all had reached past the point of exhaustion but somehow found the strength to go on. Most of us had been up for more than twenty-four hours and were running on pure adrenaline. The thought that this nightmare was almost over was the furthest thing on our minds. We trudged along quietly, and I was sure everyone had different thoughts on their mind. I imagined they probably thought about all those we had lost on this mission. I know I was.

I'm sure Markus still had the look of Dawn's last moments on her face before the creatures killed her. When the mission started, the two of them only fought and argued and couldn't stand each other. It wasn't long before his feelings changed, and they began their relationship. Although most of the crew didn't know about it, I did, and they were going to announce that they planned to get married after they returned to the ship. Now his best friend and other half was gone, and I'm pretty sure he felt like a piece of him died with her.

Fourteen

Let's Go Home

✳✳✳✳✳✳✳✳✳✳✳✳✳

Pops

I just finished setting up my launcher and opened the cap on top of the weapon, allowing me to load a charge. After loading it, I quickly closed the cap and carefully stepped back so I could push a button on the remote, which I clenched for dear life. A dull thump sounded as it launched, and I watched for as long as possible in the dark. I aimed toward our wrecked shuttle in hopes of hitting the remaining fuel. I wanted it to add to the explosion; the shuttle was underground, and the vibrations would be greater, drawing more of the creatures in that direction. I stood waiting and watching impatiently for the explosion. I had agreed to set off four charges but had made up five just in case. I had decided to make up an extra just in case one was a dud, but I could only afford to have one go bad.

I realized my fear had become a reality. I had just used my extra charge, and the remaining four had to go off without problems. I moved back toward the launcher to examine the remaining charges. I knew the launcher worked as it had sent the first charge on its way. My aim must have been off. I looked around for any danger and immediately sat down and picked up one of the other charges. I opened the panel on it and shivered from the effects of the cold air. I pulled out my flashlight to examine the inside of the charge. I needed to ensure everything was placed where it should be when I noticed one of the connectors was in the wrong place. It was switched with another connector; it was an amateur mistake that I normally wouldn't have made. I've been awake for thirty-seven hours straight, and I knew it was no excuse, and I needed to correct the issue and try again. I also examined the remaining charges and found the same problem in each one. After a few minutes, I fixed them and went back to try again. I got up, loaded another charge into the launcher, stepped back with the remote, and pressed the button, and there was another small thump as the charge was launched.

Again, the suspense killed me as I watched and waited for the results. I couldn't help but wonder if it would be another dud. The wait was short-lived as I saw a massive explosion followed by two quick secondary explosions. I quickly realized I had hit the shuttle and set off the first charge. I was surprised that my aim was true and actually hit my target. The thought of hitting the shuttle was a long shot. Now, there was a fireball that lit up the sky, and it brought a wide smile to my face.

The shock from the blasts of the explosion was felt from where I stood, and my grin became wider. With the night sky lit up, I glanced down to see fifty or more creatures on the ground. I lost my smile momentarily, but it quickly came back as I realized they had moved away from the ship and were moving in the direction of the explosion. I returned to the launcher to load another charge.

✳✳✳✳✳✳✳✳✳✳✳✳✳

Lou

Bart and I stood guard in the lab, waiting for Pops to return. We heard and felt the first explosion go off, and I smiled for the first time since this had all begun.

"We're going home, Bart. It is just a matter of time before we get off this frozen nightmare." I said to him.

"I don't know about you, but I'm definitely not going to miss this place," remarked Bart.

"I'm sure you won't be the only one glad to put this place behind us," I stated.

Bart nodded in acknowledgment and replied, "Let's just hope these creatures go for the explosions and leave the ship like Sam and Pops think they will."

"Well, you know Pops and how he loves his explosives. If we felt it, then I'm sure the creatures did, too. We don't need to get all of them off, just the majority. With the remainder onboard, we can just eliminate them as we find them," I said.

"You do realize we are putting all our lives in the hopes that this ship will fly. You also realize it's older than the two of us put together, and it's been decades since this ship flew?" remarked Bart.

I paused momentarily to reflect upon his words. Since we arrived upon this ship, we've been told it would fly. I couldn't remember anyone mentioning anything about how a ship this old would hold up. This ship had sat in these cold temperatures for decades, and there was no way to actually know how this ship would do under the stresses that we were about to put it through. As far as I knew, there was no one who examined the entirety of the ship from one end to the other. It brought several questions to reflect on.

✶✶✶✶✶✶✶✶✶✶✶✶✶

Sam

I heard the first explosion., and walked from one side to the other to look out of one of the windows. I was joined by Lexey, Kellie, Lisa, and Joan. We all watched in amazement as a giant plume of fire rose from over the ridge and lit the night.

"Pops is an amazing shot," I remarked.

"Why is that?" Kellie asked.

"Pops was not only able to shoot the charge over the ridge, but he managed to hit the shuttle. Now I'm out a hundred bucks." I said to her.

"What do you mean you're out a hundred bucks?" Lisa asked, confused.

"While he was getting ready, he mentioned that if he hit the shuttle, it would make for a big explosion. I bet him a hundred bucks he couldn't do it in the dark. He not only did it, but he did it on his first shot." I answered.

"Do you think it'll work and get rid of the creatures?" Joan asked.

"It should, I'm sure there will still be some onboard when we lift off. We'll just have to deal with them later." I turned to Kellie and asked, "Do you have everything ready for lift-off?"

"I've been ready for some time now. I've checked and rechecked everything I'll need to get us back to our ship. I think mentally that I've gone over every possibility and am ready for anything." Kellie said.

"Does this plan include a smooth lift-off?" I asked.

"Unfortunately, no. Every idea that I was able to come up with suggested it was going to be very rough. The real trick will be not flipping or crashing before we get up because of how we are sitting. I'm going to apply more thrust to the port engines. Once I blow the landing struts, that side of the ship is going to rise fast. It's also most likely going to throw everything toward the starboard side. Then, I'm going to increase the starboard thrust and reduce the port side thrust, which will throw everyone back to the other side of the ship. I will probably have to do this several times while we ascend. So, expect to be thrown around a bit on our way into orbit. I can't figure any way around it. These old ships just don't have the kind of stabilizers that the newer ships do." Kellie said.

"Ok then. Set the clock for ten minutes. We'll start the countdown right after we hear the fourth explosion. Everyone needs to find a place to ride this out because we're getting out of here," I stated excitedly.

Lexey, Kellie, and Joan moved to a different part of the bridge to prepare for lift-off. Lisa walked with me as we returned to the bridge's other side. I searched for something, and Lisa stopped and let me look around objects like a madman. She watched for a few minutes and then could no longer take it.

"What are you looking for?" She finally asked,

"Isn't that welder around here someplace?" I inquired.

"Yeah, I think it is over by where you worked earlier. Why?" She asked curiously.

"I was thinking about welding my chair to the deck and finding something to use as a seatbelt,' I answered.

"If you're going to weld your chair to the deck, then you had better weld mine, too. While you do that, I'll find us something to use as seat belts." She smiled and stated.

We laughed as we continued across the bridge of the ship hand in hand.

✳✳✳✳✳✳✳✳✳✳✳✳✳

Mike

The rest of my team and I were still between decks, and we arrived at the access panel into the mess hall. I was about to open the panel when we heard a loud noise and then felt the ship vibrate.

"What the hell was that?" asked Sarah.

"I think it was Pops setting off the first charge," I replied.

I opened the floor panel and peered around to make sure there were none of the creatures around us. I slide the panel all of the way open and out of our way. I squatted back down.

"I need everyone to hurry and get up into the mess hall. We are fighting the clock now." I said to them.

I climbed up into the mess hall and turned around to help each crew member to join me. We arose out of the darkness and back into the light one by one. At first, a few of them squinted as they adjusted to the change in their surroundings. As I helped them, I paused for a second at the sound of the second explosion. Markus was the last one out as the third explosion was heard. I looked around at the others as I put the floor panel back into place. They were all dirty and tired. I stood up, walked over to the cooler, took out six bottles of water, and handed them to the others.

"Listen up, everyone. I know you're tired and dirty." At that moment, the fourth explosion could be heard, and I looked at my watch before continuing, "That was the fourth charge that just went off. That means that in exactly ten minutes, no matter where we are, this ship will lift off. We can take a chance and try to get to the bridge, but if we do that, there is no telling where we will be or if we will have anything to hold on to. Our second option is to just stay right here until we make it into orbit. It will be a rough takeoff, and everything, including us, will probably get tossed around a bit. I feel that we should just stay here and wait this out. Is there anyone that objects to that suggestion?" I looked around to see if anyone objected, but no one said a word. "Ok then. Find yourself a good spot with something to hold on to."

I watched as each of the tired crewmembers found a spot to sit and something to hold on to. Markus sat quietly alone from the others. Everyone was quiet as we sat and waited for the time to pass and the engines to fire. We held our weapons in case one of the creatures found them. Each crew member bowed their head with their eyes closed as though each prayed for something. I closed my eyes and prayed for the engines to fire or our fight for survival would be over. This ship was our last hope, and if we failed to lift off, then the creatures have won.

★★★★★★★★★★★★

Pops

The cold bit into me even with my arctic gear on, and I watched the last charge explode in the distance. With a smile plastered on my face, I packed up my gear and started to make my way back to the hatch. I was looking forward to getting back inside the ship where it was warmer. My part of the plan was over, and I had to admit that I was rather proud of myself. My explosives show was louder than I had expected.

As I walked toward the hatch, I wasn't paying attention, and I stumbled and lost my footing on the slick surface of the ship. From the ship's angle, I slid toward the ship's edge and began to accelerate down the ship's side, and I reached out for anything to grab onto to stop myself. I watched as the edge drew closer and closer, and seeing there was no way for me to stop, I closed my eyes and waited. I slid off the edge like a skier jumping off a ramp. I flew about eight feet out from the ship, and when the tether I had on ran out of slack, it yanked me back toward the ship. With the sudden stop, I swung backward toward the ship and slammed into the side. I dangled from the tether and cringed in pain.

"I'm going to feel that in the morning," I said to myself.

I looked down at my watch and saw that I had nine minutes to get back into the ship before they attempted to lift off. I reached for my radio to call for help but realized I had broken it during my Olympic tryout. Dangling from the side of the ship, I looked up to see that I was just a few feet from the top edge of the ship. I struggled and tried to pull myself up.

★★★★★★★★★★★★★

Lou

Bart and I waited for Pops to return. We had our arctic gear and a harness on in case we needed to help Pops. I was beginning to get worried about Pops, and I looked over at Bart and saw the same look plastered upon his face. It had been almost two minutes since we had heard the fourth explosion. If he didn't come down soon, he would be in big trouble being out there without a pressurized space suit when we reached orbit.

"Something is wrong. Pops should have been back by now." I said impatiently.

"What can we do?" asked Bart.

"I'm not going to sit here and wait. I'm going to get my ass up there and find out what is taking him so long," I replied.

I climbed the ladder to the top side hatch and opened it. I was hit by the cold air, causing me to pull up my mask to protect my face. I took out my flashlight and shined it toward where Pops said he would go. I saw the launcher secured to the top of the ship, but there was no sign of Pops. I thought it was strange, but then again, so was the fact that we had found creatures living on this planet. I readied my weapon and used my light to look around to my left and behind me first, then moved to my right and did the same, always being on alert for the creatures. I glanced down to where Pops latched his tether, and it wasn't stretched in the direction of the launcher. It was stretched out to my right, and panic filled me. I quickly used my flashlight and followed it to the edge. I put my weapon away; I reached over to the tether and checked to see if there was any weight on it, and there was.

"Get your ass up here! Pops is in trouble!" I yelled to Bart.

I secured my tether next to Pops and quickly climbed out on top of the ship. I took a few steps and quickly realized the surface of the ship was slippery. After I got a few steps away from the hatch, Bart poked his head through the hatch.

"Get yourself secured and stay near the hatch. The surface is slippery out here, and I may need your help to get back up. There isn't much out here to get any leverage on, so if you stay near the hatch, you can use it for leverage if we need it." I paused and yelled to Bart.

"Where's Pops?" Bart yelled.

"It looks as though he might have slipped and slid off of the edge of the ship. I'm going down to see how he is. Watch the time. If we are not back before we hit the two-minute mark, I want you to get on the radio and tell them to hold the countdown," I replied.

"Just get down there and get Pops," remarked Bart.

I slowly moved down the ship, hanging on to the tether. I lost my footing a few feet down and slid down the ship on my stomach. I rolled myself over so I was sliding on my but. I felt a strong tug on my tether as Bart must have grabbed hold of it in an attempt to slow me down. Since I was sliding down the ship on a path different from Pops's, there were things I could grab onto on my way down. With Bart slowing me down, I could grab onto a handhold just short of going over the edge. I took some of the slack in the tether, tied it to the handhold, and then inched myself over to the edge.

I looked over the edge at Pops hanging there, looking bruised and banged up.

"Hey, Pops, what are you doing down there?" I asked him, laughing.

Pops looked at me and replied, "I'm just hanging around admiring the view."

"Cutting it kind of close to lift-off, we only have about four minutes to get your ass up here and get back inside the ship. Why didn't you climb back up here?" I chastised him.

"I tried but couldn't get past the edge of the ship," responded Pops.

"Give me a second, and we will pull you up." I carefully moved back up the ship to find a spot to get some leverage. After I positioned myself, I took in a big breath, preparing myself for the work ahead.

"Bart, I'm going to need your help to pull Pops up!" I yelled out.

"Let's hurry up. Time is running out." Bart said in the distance.

We both pulled on the tether attached to Pops, and he slowly began to rise back onto the top of the ship. As he came over the edge, he grabbed his tether and helped pull his way back up on top of the ship. In a few moments, he was a few feet from the edge.

"That's enough, Bart, we have him," I reported.

Breathing heavily, Pops says, "Thanks for coming for me. I thought I was going to hang there until lift-off."

I stood up, untied my tether from the handhold, helped Pops to his feet, and said, "You're welcome. You would have done the same thing if the roles were reversed." I looked at my watch and said, "We have just under two minutes left to get back into the ship."

"Then we had better get moving," remarked Pops.

We moved toward the hatch, using our tethers to help us. I looked at Pops to check on him and ensure he didn't fall.

"Take it easy, Pops. We don't want you to slip and slide off of the ship again." I said to him.

"Normally, I would be more careful, but we have less than two minutes to get back inside," replied Pops.

"Actually, we probably have a little more time than that.

"Oh?" Pops asked.

"Before I went to get you, I told Bart that if we weren't back at the hatch by the time we reached two minutes, he was to call the bridge on the radio and ask them to delay the lift-off."

"Why don't you just call them?" asked Pops as we continued to move toward the hatch.

"Well, I can't. I left my radio on the bridge by accident. We could always double-check with the bridge using your radio." I said as I took a deep breath.

"I'm sorry, Lou. Mine broke when I slammed up against the side of the ship," answered Pops.

We finally reached the hatch, where Bart eagerly awaited us. Waving his hands, he signaled us to hurry up.

"Call the bridge and let them know we are back at the hatch, and they can resume the countdown," I said to Bart.

"I can't," he replied.

Pops and I looked at him with confused expressions.

"What do you mean you can't? You did call the bridge like I asked, didn't you?"

"I tried to, I really did, but my battery was dead. I couldn't call them, but now the two of you are here, and we could use one of yours," he said with an expression of apology.

Pops looked at him and said, "Mine is broken."

"I forgot mine on the bridge," I stated.

"How much time do we have?" Pops asked.

"We have about forty seconds," Bart said as he looked at his watch.

"Awe, shit! You better move your ass, Bart, because here we come!" I stated.

Bart quickly started climbing down the ladder. I stepped through the hatch, stopping for a second to unlatch the tether before climbing down the ladder. Pops quickly followed, doing the same, and he secured the hatch. As Pops started down the ladder, we heard the engines powering up for lift-off. I can see in the expression on Pop's face that this only meant that they were seconds from lift-off, and being on a ladder was not the best place to be when this happened.

✹✹✹✹✹✹✹✹✹✹✹✹✹

Sam

Everyone was preparing themselves for lift-off. There were no orders being given or work being done. Our fate now rested on Kellie, our pilot's shoulders, and the one we watched and listened to orders now. She was oblivious to anyone else around her. I watched her as she pushed buttons, checked her monitors, and watched the clock. We all watched in anticipation, hoping we did everything right and that this ship would still fly. She pushed another button, and we could hear the engines powering up on the bridge. Although it was unusual, it was a joyous sound to listen to. Hopefully, the creatures were too far away and couldn't get back to us in time before we lifted off.

Kellie began to read off information out loud as she stared at the monitors, including the one with the countdown timer.

"Engines are warming up. The fuel flow is good. The ship is pressurized. Initiating lift-off in 5....4.....3....2....1. I am engaging the engines." The ship shook as the engines ignited. She reached for control, turned to the others, and shouted over the roar of the engines, "Hang on! There is going to be a rough jolt!"

She pushed the button to retract the port side landing struts and set off the charges to free that side of the ship. The sounds of the explosions echoed throughout the ship. Kellie must have immediately anticipated what would happen and increased power to the starboard side. She must have expected the port side to rise quickly when the landing struts were released, but the ship rocked toward the port instead of starboard. Kellie quickly compensated for the error, but she was not ready to quit.

"What's wrong, Kellie?" I asked as I noticed the error.

"The strut in the rear pod didn't completely break free. I'm going to increase the power and see if we can rip it free and get out of here," she replied.

She did as she said, and the ship shook violently and groaned under the strain. The ship was like a plane trying to fly while still anchored to the ground. The ship continued to struggle and shook to one side and then the other. I watched as everyone hung on while Kellie did everything she could to break free.

During the violent maneuvers taking place, there is a late explosion. Kellie worked hard to control the ship as it slowly rose from the surface. Everyone was jarred by the sudden release of the last strut. I watched as Kellie immediately noticed the loss of signal on one of her monitors. Still, she had her hands full, trying to keep control of the ship. Lexey tried to yell out, but her voice was lost to the noise on the bridge. She turned around where she sat because the monitor that Kellie lost was the one that monitored engineering and was controlled behind her seat. She reacted without being asked and started looking at the monitors at the station where she was stationed because it should have given her the same information Kellie would have gotten from her monitor. She was going to call out any information needed, but she discovered that her monitor was also out.

"Sam, the engineering monitors are down!" Lexey yelled louder.

I spun around in my seat and punched up the schematics. I unbuckled myself to trace the path the engineering panel took. There was a blinking red light indicating there was a disruption at that junction. I studied the schematic, tracing out different paths to bypass the problem.

"You'll need to open the panel at your feet, take the cord from plug J24, and move it over to I32. That should resolve the issue and then…." I said to Lexey.

I was interrupted as the ship made a sudden hard movement, throwing me out of my seat and tumbling across the bridge until I stopped at Lexey's feet. I looked up at her from my position and said, "On second thought, since I'm here, I will go ahead and take care of that for you."

Lexey smiled as I opened the panel to work on it. She looked across the bridge and saw Lisa just shaking her head.

✳✳✳✳✳✳✳✳✳✳✳✳✳✳

Pops

Bart reached the bottom of the ladder just as the ship began to shake as the engines fired up. Lou and I had a tighter grip on the ladder. Knowing shortly after the engines are fired up, the charges we had set in the pods would be set off.

"Hurry up and get down. It is going to get rough from here." I yelled at Lou.

Almost on cue, the explosions from the pods could be heard, and the ship shook violently from one side to the other. Lou was caught off guard and barely hung on to the ladder. As the ship shifted again, he was thrown toward the ladder and hit his head on one of the rungs. I watched as he became dazed as the ship shifted again, and this time, he didn't hold on to the ladder and fell backward. In the small, confined space, Bart couldn't move out of the way in time. Lou landed on top of him, and they hit the deck together.

As I slowly moved down the ladder, I struggled to hang on and realized something was wrong. The ship should be going up. Instead, the ship was moved like it was anchored to the ground. I wondered if it could be because one of the charges didn't go off as planned. I went over the setting of the charges in each pod in my head. I knew the first two pods were done perfectly. It was the rear pod that I wasn't sure of. I couldn't remember if we had finished setting the charges before the creatures started pouring in or if a stray shot damaged some part of the explosive, causing it not to go off. The one charge not going off had to be it. That would explain why the ship was being moved around the way it was. I figured that Kellie was trying to rip the strut out.

I continued to slowly make my way down the ladder. I was close to the bottom when I heard an explosion, and the ship pitched hard to one side, throwing me off the ladder and to the deck, where I landed on top of Lou and Bart. Lou was still dazed until I landed on him, which seemed to clear his head quickly.

Lou was the first to speak up, "Are you alright, Pops?"

"I'm fine," I replied.

"Lucky that I haven't eaten anything today. With this ship shaking, you falling on me would have probably made me puke," remarked Lou.

"I think the last jolt was a late firing charge," I remarked.

Bart spoke up from the bottom of the pile, "I know the two of you would like nothing more than to sit here and chat, but could you do me a real big favor and get the hell off of me. I can hardly breathe down here."

"Sorry about that," I replied as I rolled off of the pile and sat on the deck.

"Yeah, I'm sorry too, Bart. I wasn't thinking. Are you alright?" asked Lou as he got off Bart and sat next to me.

Bart slowly pushed himself up into a sitting position while cringing in pain. "You guys are lucky you didn't get hurt. I think I have a couple of broken ribs and a possible sprained wrist. I don't know if either of you has ever had broken ribs, but I don't think there is anything out there that can hurt worse."

"Pops, is this ride going to smooth out anytime soon?" asked Lou.

"These old ships were well known for bumpy lift-offs, but this one is bumpier than any other I have been on. Don't worry; it should smooth out once we get back into space," I answered.

✳✳✳✳✳✳✳✳✳✳✳✳✳✳

Mike

We were in the mess hall as the crew prepared for a rough lift-off. The ship shook, and we prepared for the ship to shift when the explosives went off. Soon, we heard the explosions, but the ship shifted in the opposite direction. The violent movements of the ship resulted in cabinets coming open and their contents being dumped on the heads of the crew and the deck. We had expected some sudden movements from the ship when the explosives had detonated, but what was going on now was not what we had prepared for. We watched as the supplies slid across the floor from one side to the other. First, they would go to the right, then left, and then in a completely different direction. With the way the ship moved, I felt like we were a kite flying on a stormy day, trying to break the string so it could fly away on its own.

Soon, another explosion went off, and we felt it through the ship. The sudden jolt caught most of us off guard, but we managed to grab onto something. Markus wasn't as lucky. There was nothing near him to grab onto. He was thrown across the room and tumbled toward the opposite wall. Just before he reached it, the ship shifted again, and he was tossed back in the direction from which he originated. While being tossed around like a rag doll, he was unaware that a heavy table and chair were sliding across the deck toward the same wall he was. I was about to shout out to warn him of the table and chair when he quickly snapped his attention back to normal, and he noticed the table and chair coming at him. Instinctively, he covered his face with his arms and waited for the impact of the table and chair. There was another jolt, and the angle of the deck changed again, sending the table and chair sliding away from him and the others. He uncovered his face to see he was no longer in danger. I let out a small breath I didn't realize I had been holding.

Markus had been tossed around the deck because he didn't have anything to hold on to, but now he did. It was as if the ship was trying to move him to a place that was safe as they left the planet. He sat there trying to clear his head. This was the second time in a short period of time he had hit his head. I'm sure he was beginning to think this was not his day. This day was a nightmare no one should ever have to endure. I had hoped we were almost in orbit and would be docking with our ship. It was the place that all of us had called home for the last five years. I'm worried since he no longer had the love of his life, it would just be a reminder that it was the place where he met Dawn, and now it was the place that would only be a reminder of what he had lost.

The ride slowly began to smooth out, and I decided to get a situation report. I took out my radio and said, "Sam, this is Mike. Can you give me a situation report?" I paused for a moment and waited for an answer but got nothing. I spoke into the radio again, "Sam, this is Mike;

what is our status?" Again, there was no answer. I took a quick look at my radio and quickly realized it was broken. I looked at the others and asked, "Does anyone have a working radio? Mine is broken."

Everyone takes a look at their radios. "Mine is broken too," replied Sarah.

"I'm afraid mine has a dead battery," answered Cara.

"I think I lost mine when we were trying to get out of the machine shop," remarked Wanda.

I looked at Markus and asked, "What about yours?"

"I lost it when I fell," replied Markus.

"It looks like we'll have to continue on our own. Without radios, we don't know if we have all of the creatures off or not. We suspected when we made the plan that some would not leave for one reason or another. We are on our own and have no way to call for help if we get into trouble. Now, let's stay sharp and get up to the bridge as quickly as possible," I said.

We all stood up and checked our weapons before we moved toward the bridge. Most of the remaining corridors we would need to go through were well-lit. Knowing the creatures didn't like light, this was a good sign. As we started to move, we all suddenly stopped as the lights went out, and within a couple of seconds, the emergency lights came on.

"That's not a good sign," Cara said, looking around.

She no sooner finished when red lights started to flash, and an alarm went off.

"Now, that has to be worse than just having the lights go out," commented Sarah.

Wanda stepped closer to me and asked, "Do you have any idea what is going on?"

"No, I know that it's not good. We need to get to the bridge as quickly as possible. They may need our help."

"Do you think the creatures have something to do with this?" asked Wanda.

"There's a lot about these creatures we don't know. It might be possible they could have done this, whatever this is. Decks one and two are better lit than deck three. If they wanted to move around up here, they would have to disable the lights somehow. However, this all depends on just how smart they really are." I said.

"True. There is no way for us to …..." She stopped talking because she noticed I looked around for something. First, I looked to my right, left, and back to my right again.

"What are you looking for?" she asked,

"Where did Markus go?" I asked.

She looked around briefly before she asked, "Did anyone see where Markus went?"

They shook their heads no and looked around at each other. He had slipped away quietly while no one was looking. Although nothing was ever said between them, I had a funny feeling I knew where Markus had gone and why he had left.

"Damn him! He knows we don't have enough people to search the ship for him. Of all of the stupid things he could do, this would have to be at the top of the list," I remarked.

"Where do you think he ran off to?" asked Wanda.

I looked her in the eyes and answered, "He searched for any creature that stayed on the ship, and then he planned to kill it for revenge."

"Why would he do something so damn stupid? Why would he want to get revenge? We have lost a lot of friends, but I think we need to focus on getting back alive. We can mourn our friends when this is over," stated Wanda.

I walked to the middle of the room as the alarm was silenced, I said, "I don't know where Markus ran off. The rest of us need to stick together and get to the bridge. I have a feeling they are really going to need our help. Now let's get moving."

No one said a word; they just looked at each other like war veterans and moved on. We were all tired and ready for this nightmare to end. When we left to rescue one crewmate, Bev, there were seven of us. When we return to the bridge, there will only be four. The fate of everyone will be known with the exception of one, Markus. Where had he gone, and would he return when they were ready to leave the ship?

Fifteen

Back In Space

✴✴✴✴✴✴✴✴✴✴✴✴✴
Lou

On deck one, Pops, Bart, and I were recovering from being tossed around inside the airlock. Pops had a few bumps and bruises, while I was a little worse, but I knew there was going to be some serious soreness. Bart was hurt the worst since Pops and I fell on him. The faces he made as he cringed from the pain weren't very pretty, but with the possibility of some broken ribs, I didn't dare tell him; slowly, he tried to stand. I helped him slightly by supporting his right side.

"Are you going to make it, Bart?" I asked.

"I'll make it," he said, with pain written across his face.

Pops and I helped him get out of the airlock and back toward the lab. As we exited the airlock, we paused simultaneously, and the sudden feeling as though something wasn't right was thick in the air. The main lighting was out, meaning the ship was running on battery-operated emergency lighting. It was hard to miss the red flashing light, which indicated something was wrong. I immediately looked around to scope out our surroundings and wasn't satisfied until Pops was looking back toward me. We looked around and then at each other.

"What the hell is going on?" asked Bart, wheezing.

"Whatever it is, I'm sure it's not anything good," replied Pops with some concern.

"We know for sure that we had managed to lift-off and not crash back to the surface. I'd assume we are in space and have achieved orbit. Pops, do you think we might have a hull breach somewhere?" I asked suddenly.

"That is a strong possibility. This is an old ship which has been sitting for a very long time. It's possible the vibrations could have caused a hull breach. Whatever the problem is, we better get up to the bridge and see what we can do to help. That is except for you, Bart. When we get to the bridge, you're going to stay there and rest until it's time to get off the ship. Consider yourself benched for the remainder of this mission." Pops said as he continued to look around the room.

"No argument from me," remarked Bart as he winced from the pain of breathing.

Pops led the way across the lab with his weapon in his hand. He was closely followed by Bart and me. I held my weapon in my right hand and supported Bart with my left. Bart had his right arm around me, and his other arm was on his chest. He moved slowly from his injuries but never stopped for fear of something out to get us, leaving a thick tension in the air.

We had finally reached the corridor, and Pops opened it slowly and peeked around outside. He must have determined that it was safe, for he opened the hatch fully and stepped out of the lab. I watched as he took another look in both directions and then signaled for Bart and me to follow. We were just about to go through the hatch when Pops walked farther down the corridor, and I guessed it was to assess our surroundings.

I twisted in an odd position to my right to allow Bart to go through so I could still keep a hold of him and provide support. Bart moved carefully through the opening so he didn't bump anything that could aggravate his injuries. As he was going through the hatch, the sound of ripping fabric echoed into the corridor, and I felt a pain in my arm as Bart fell to the ground. I tried to stop him from falling, but after a moment, I thought he might have tripped. He screamed out in pain as he hit the deck in the corridor, and he instinctively grabbed his left arm. Rolling over onto his back, I saw his left arm bleeding heavily. The sleeve of his jacket began to get soaked with blood as he began to pale from the pain.

"I don't know which..." he began to say as he rolled over when he suddenly quieted.

He stopped moving and didn't make another sound as he looked up and saw it. His eyes were wide with fear. I tried quickly to regain my composure, but I only tripped into the opening. It only took me a moment to regain my balance, and that was when I saw Bart's expression of fear.

He didn't trip into the hatch. Something made him fall. I turned and looked in the direction Bart stared in and saw it standing there.

"Pops!" I shouted as I pointed my weapon at the creature, which stared back at us.

It stared at Bart and me with its glowing eyes. Pops turned around, raised his weapon, and opened fire on the creature at the same time that I did. Pops charged toward the creature while he continued to fire. The creature jerked around as it was hit by the weapons fire until, finally, it just dropped dead. Both Pops and I stopped firing at the same time, and Pops glanced down at Bart, who was still on the deck.

"It's a good thing I've trained with you before at the weapons ranges, or I would have been worried you might have missed." Pop said as he continued closer to the creature.

I watched as he began to examine it. Once satisfied, he moved away from it and back down the corridor. I moved closer to Bart so I could assist him in getting off the deck while I still aimed my weapon in case any more creatures wanted to drop in on us. Pops looked around and then began to move back toward us. After I had watched Pops clear the immediate area, I turned my attention back to Bart. I ripped open the bloody sleeve where Bart was injured. I saw it was severe and needed immediate attention to stop the bleeding.

Thinking quickly, I grabbed the belt from Bart's jacket and ripped the sleeve more so I could use it as a makeshift tourniquet to stop the bleeding. Bart was paler than moments ago. He tried to stand up, but the loss of blood had made him weaker, and we needed to get him help soon, or we would lose him.

With the appearance of a creature on the deck, I knew it wasn't safe to have him in the Med Lab, so I would need to go get Joan and bring her to him. The only place that was safe would be the bridge.

I looked up at Pops and asked, "Where the hell did that creature come from? Why didn't you see it when you stepped out into the corridor? You would have had to have walked right past it."

Pops looked down at me and answered, "I didn't see it because it wasn't there yet. About ten feet down the corridor is an air vent, and that's how he got there. I think it saw that I had entered and began to stalk me when the two of you stepped out in front of it."

"It doesn't matter at this point. Bart is hurt badly, and we need to get him to Joan. Now that we know there are creatures on this deck, we can't risk bringing her to the Med Lab. I'll help get Bart to the bridge. You run into the Med Lab and grab a trauma kit and anything else that you think that she might need and bring it to the bridge."

Pops nodded in agreement and said, "You better watch your ass on the way to the bridge. There is no knowing how many creatures there are on this level."

"You do the same, and I'll see you on the bridge,"

Pops moved down the corridor to head toward the Med Lab. I helped Bart to his feet. He could hardly stand even with my help. We slowly began to make our way down the corridor toward the bridge. Bart was barely conscious and stumbled every so often, and I caught him before he fell.

"Come on, Bart. Stay with me. We're almost to the bridge. Once we get you there, Joan will fix you up and make you feel better," I said to him.

★ ★ ★ ★ ★ ★ ★ ★ ★ ★ ★ ★ ★

Renee

As I sat in my chair, I stared at the monitors and hoped for some news. I felt helpless from the beginning as there was no ship to rescue the crew. My brain began to hurt from the stress of figuring out how to get to the crew and rescue them. There was no way we could take this ship down there, for I feared it would strand the entire crew. I knew what I said to the crew earlier about my plan, but deep in my heart, it was a last resort. I contemplated the last time I had heard from the ground crew, and my headache only grew. The only radio that could reach this ship was on the shuttle, which was buried. My frustration grew as the planet became darker because when it was daylight, I could at least get detailed photos of what was happening down there. Since the night settled in, I had to rely on radar images instead of night vision and thermal pictures, all of which can be open to interpretation.

As I continued to stare at the monitors, I suddenly realized someone was standing next to me. At first, I just thought it was someone who had stopped for a moment, but I soon noticed they were still standing there. I was concentrating so hard on the information from the monitors that I didn't notice they were trying to talk to me. Maybe it was from exhaustion because I was so tired and had tuned out all the noise and chatter. I looked over and realized it was George who had been trying to get my attention.

"What is it, George?" I asked.

"I have something I think you should see," he said as he motioned to his workstation.

I got up from my chair and followed him over to his station. I yawned and stretched, trying to get the sleepiness out of my system.

"Has something changed?" I asked while he sat down and pulled up the monitors.

"Yes, at least I think so. As you ordered, every time we pass over the crater, we take pictures of what is going on down there. So far, they have been the same every pass over." He brought up pictures of the previous pass over and pointed, "There's the Discovery, and there's where the shuttle was." he said.

He paused and brought up more pictures from what I assumed was the current orbit to show me the comparison. I strained my eyes to try and see any differences within the pictures, but I couldn't.

"I don't see anything. Maybe I'm too tired to see it. What's different about them?"

"They're gone," he answered.

"What do you mean gone?" I asked, as he now had my attention.

"The Discovery should be right there. The only thing still there are three landing struts," he said as he pointed to the monitor.

"If they are not there, then where are they?" I asked.

"At first, I wasn't sure what had happened. Until I took a look at this." He pushed a few buttons, and a thermal image appeared.

I looked at the images that were displayed. Due to the cold temperatures down there, normally, a screen of different shades of blue would represent the different cold temperatures. This image had that, but it also had a lot of red, yellow, and white, which represented heat.

"What happened to them, and what happened over here?" I asked.

"Based on past experience and these hot white spots, I would have to conclude that they set off some charges and blew up the shuttle," he stated as he pointed to the spot where the shuttle's last location was.

"They blew up the shuttle?" I asked, stunned.

He nodded, and I pointed to another spot on the screen and asked, "They not only blew up the shuttle but also the Discovery?"

"No. The white spots where the shuttle was indicate the shuttle was blown up."

"I see the same white spots where the Discovery was," I pointed out.

"They are not exactly the same. The white spots where the shuttle was are hot spots of explosions. I can tell you this from the random pattern. The hot spots where the Discovery was are uniform. There are eight spots where the eight engines would have been fired for lift-off. However, by the pattern, it would appear they had trouble during lift-off. I can tell you they managed to detach the front and center strut, but the rear gave them a little bit of trouble. They managed to get themselves free."

"Where are they?" I asked.

"In orbit from the information given," he answered.

"Why haven't they contacted us?"

"I'm not sure, Captain. Based on the thermal readings we got on the last pass, I would estimate their lift-off was approximately twenty minutes before we passed over. That would put them out of our line of sight. In essence, the planet is blocking their signal."

"What is your estimate for us to rendezvous with them?" I urgently inquired.

"It depends if they made it to a low, high, or standard orbit. If they are in a low orbit, then it could take up to twelve hours or more to catch them. If we take a low orbit, and they are in standard orbit, then we would meet them in a little less than four hours. If we take a low orbit and they manage to get into a high orbit, then we will rendezvous with them in less than an hour," he explained.

"Can you give me a projection of where they might be in relation to us?"

"I already have. This is us in a standard orbit. When we originally arrived, we were in a high orbit. They don't know we changed to a standard orbit. I think when they launched, they tried to predict we would be ahead of them and not behind them. Based on our guess of the time they lifted off, I have predicted these three possible positions depending on which orbit they are in. Now we just have to figure out which orbit they are in." he said as he pushed a few buttons and then pointed to three different lines of data.

I was quiet for a moment as I contemplated the information George had given me. A sudden thought had emerged from deep within my sleep-deprived brain.

"Pilots are creatures of habit. Every time Kellie is in the pilot's chair, she puts us in a high orbit. I would say she put that ship into a high orbit. If I'm right, how long before we can communicate with them?" I said aloud.

"With the information given and not being one hundred percent accurate, I would say contact with them should be in about fifteen to twenty minutes. If we move into a lower orbit, then we might be able to catch up with them sooner." George said.

"I really need to know what happened down there. Pilot, move us into a lower orbit and increase speed." I said after I had finished looking over all of the information from the monitors.

The pilot did as he was ordered and changed the orbit of the ship. I walked across the bridge, returned to my chair, and watched as the readings on the monitors changed as we changed orbit. For hours, I sat here wondering what happened down on the planet and how to get my crew back on my ship. I was astonished they managed to get the Discovery in orbit. Pride swelled deep within me, knowing I had trained my people for anything. I was really looking forward to having my people back onboard the ship.

"I have a new projection for communication. I am transferring it to your monitor now. I estimate it will be about seventeen minutes until we can make contact." George said as he pushed the information onto my monitor.

"Keep on it, George. I want to know the minute you pick up on them so we can make contact," I stated.

✶✶✶✶✶✶✶✶✶✶✶✶✶

Sam

We all worked furiously to get some of the monitors working again. I worked on the engineering station with Lexey's help. At the same time, Lisa typed commands into the computer and checked the results on her monitors. Joan sat at the communications station and continued to try to make contact with our ship. Kellie worked from her station, trying to stabilize their orbit.

"I've finally achieved a high orbit, but I don't know how long it will last. I'm unable to locate the Star Rider. She must have changed her orbit." Kellie stated.

"How long do you think we can last in this orbit?" I asked, still working on the engineering station.

"Without the monitors, it's difficult to give an approximate answer." She paused and looked over the information she had available before she continued, "If everything held up on this ship during lift-off, we shouldn't have anything to worry about for a week."

"There was that alarm we still haven't been able to identify yet. Lisa, have you been able to get that computer to tell us anything yet?" I asked.

"I haven't found much so far. We did have some hull breaches on the port side. When they began to decompress, the emergency system kicked in and sealed the hatches in the affected areas. That could have set off the alarm, but until we can access engineering, I can't be sure the decompression was what set off the alarm. So far, it's the only problem I can find. These old computers are really unstable compared to the ones I'm used to. I'm not even sure I'm reading them right." Lisa said as she looked over toward the rest of us.

"Joan, have you been able to reach the Star Rider?" I asked.

"So far, nothing but static. They could be on the other side of the planet or just out of range. hell, I don't even know if we are transmitting a signal." Joan said.

"Keep trying. Let us know the minute that you hear something," I stated.

I turned to Lexey and said lowly, "We have to hurry up and figure out what is wrong with this station."

"Do you think there might have been something that went wrong in engineering that set off the alarm?" she asked quietly.

"I'm not sure. It could have been the decompression, but I doubt it, especially considering how our luck has been going. This is an old ship that has been sitting in the cold for decades. It's a miracle we got it to fire up and into orbit. It was a rough ride back into space, and I wouldn't be surprised if we broke something upon takeoff," I remarked.

"I can run down to engineering and check everything out," stated Lexey.

"Sorry, but I can't allow you to do that. There's no way to tell if there are still creatures on this ship, and I can't afford to send anyone with you. If we don't get this fixed by the time that the others return, we'll send a couple of them with you for protection."

We all returned to our work but were quickly interrupted by the sound of the access hatch as it was being unlatched and opened. Everyone stopped what they were doing and turned toward the hatch with weapons aimed. Immediately, Lou and Bart stepped through the opening, and we could tell Bart was very limp. Lou wrapped his arm around him and almost carried him entirely onto the bridge.

I got up from the deck and hurried over to them, helping Lou bring Bart onto the bridge fully. Joan hurried over to us and started to do a quick examination. Lisa stepped toward the open hatch in order to close it, but Pops rushed and opened it again. He held a lot of equipment, such as two duffle bags thrown over his shoulder, and hard cases tucked under each arm, and two in each of his hands.

"We need to rush Bart to the medical bay as quickly as possible," stated Joan, lost in her work.

"Sorry, but we can't. There are creatures all over the ship still, and one of them attacked us on this deck, and we killed it. I stopped by the Med Lab and grabbed everything that I thought you would need," said Pops.

Lisa shut the hatch behind Pops, and Joan took a quick look around the bridge, pointed to a spot, and then reluctantly said, "Fine, put him down on the deck over there. That way, he would be out of the way. I guess I'll make do with what's here on the bridge."

Lou and I had practically carried him to the section of the bridge that she indicated and carefully set him down. We backed up and helped Pops with the medical supplies that he carried in. We had carefully set the cases down above Bart's head and opened each one so Joan could see what was in them. Kellie walked over and began to hand Joan the medical bag that she had brought with her.

Kellie stopped suddenly and returned to her station, and Lisa did the same. Pops, Bart, and I stepped back for a moment to watch. Joan first removed Bart's jacket and folded it so that she could put it under his head and use it as a pillow. Next, she cut the sleeve of his shirt, exposed the wound to his arm, and began to treat it.

"What happened?" I snapped at Pops.

"I checked the corridor when we came out of the lab and didn't see anything, so I started out ahead of Lou and Bart. When they exited the lab, they ran right into the creature. It happened so fast," explained Pops.

"How could you miss not seeing the creature?" I questioned.

"Apparently, it came out of a ventilation duct in the wall after I entered the corridor. I think it was stalking me, and I was just as startled by Lou and Bart as they stepped out. Bart went down, and Lou was knocked back into the lab. I turned around and opened fire, and Lou opened fire from inside the lab, and we killed it. We hurried up and got Bart and got the hell out of there before any more of them showed up," Pops said.

"We knew there might still be some onboard, but I didn't realize any of them made it up to this deck. I hope there are no more of them up here," I stated.

"I'll have to agree with you. By the way, what set off the alarm? There are warning lights all over this deck," remarked Pops.

"There are warning lights all over this deck?"

"Yes?" Pops said as he nodded.

"I thought the alarm was isolated to the bridge. To tell you the truth, we're not sure. We've had some breaches on the port side of the ship, but they have been isolated and secured. We're still working on getting the engineering monitors back online, but so far, we've had no luck."

"Do you think there might be a problem in engineering?" Pops asked.

"I don't know. We checked everything else, and until we can verify there is nothing wrong back there, I am not going to rule that area out as a possible cause of the alarm."

"Let's hope the breaches were the cause," commented Pops.

"I hope the breaches are the only problem." I looked down at Joan, who was still working on Bart, and continued, "Before you showed up,

I had Joan monitoring communications trying to reach the Star Rider. Since she is occupied, do you think you can monitor communications?"

"I'll take care of that for you," Pops said.

He walked toward the communications station, and I looked back at Bart to check his status. Joan was still working on him, so I left her behind and went back to the engineering station to help Lexey. Before I made it back to the station, I paused to look around the bridge, which was an unusual situation for me. Usually, I was the one who looked for leadership and took orders. Now, I was the one to whom everyone on the bridge looked for leadership. I couldn't wait for Mike to make it to the bridge so I could turn over the strain of leadership back to him.

★ ★ ★ ★ ★ ★ ★ ★ ★ ★ ★ ★ ★ ★

Mike

As we trekked forward, we all moved quietly away from the mess hall and down to the port side corridor. As I peered ahead, something didn't seem quite right. It took me a moment because it took all of my concentration to realize the emergency lights, which were on, should have allowed us to see from one end of the corridor to the other. Up ahead, it seemed as though the light just disappeared. I motioned for everybody to stop while I tried to figure out the cause. Running on thirty-six hours of no sleep was beginning to take its toll on me. I clicked on my flashlight and tried to peer down the corridor; with the emergency lighting and the flashing red lights, it was useless. I sighed softly and peered over my shoulder to see which formation everybody had taken up. Sarah and Cara kept watch from behind, and Wanda slowly moved forward to talk to me.

"What's going on, Mike?" Wanda asked.

I pointed ahead and said, "Something's wrong. We should be able to see the other end of this corridor, but there must be something that is either blocking or knocking out the lights. We need to get to the bridge, but I don't want to take the chance and lose anyone else trying to get there. The quickest way would be to continue down this corridor. If it's blocked, we'll have to double back and head down the corridor on the other side of the ship. If that way also turns out to be blocked, the last option will be to head back to engineering."

"Do you think there are still creatures on the ship?" she asked softly.

"Yes. I just hope they are still on the lower deck and not anywhere else."

"Should we move forward or turn back?"

I didn't say anything as I wanted to reflect upon her questions, but we sat in silence for several moments while I made up my mind. I continued to stare into the darkness.

"I think we should continue to make our way to the bridge no matter what,"

"What about Markus?"

"We can't afford to look for him. Once we dock with our ship, we can get more people and search the entire ship for both him and the creatures. Until then, he is on his own," I answered sternly.

"Markus is a member of our crew and a friend. We can't just leave him to fend for himself. We should go find him," she stated.

"Remember, Markus left without telling anyone. It was a decision he made. I don't know about you, but most of us have not slept for the last twenty four hours or more. We are tired and hungry, and we just don't react as quickly as we would if we had some rest. We need fresh people and weapons before we go to look for him, and that is what we will get once we dock. You must think I am cold-hearted for letting him run around the ship alone. Well, I'm not. I'm just as worried, if not even more, than everybody else. I have an obligation to the safety of the three of you as well."

I didn't allow her to say anything else, so I motioned for Cara and Sarah to move forward. We began to slowly make our way down the corridor toward the front of the ship. Cara and Sarah continued to look behind us to make sure nothing could take advantage of us having our backs turned. The thoughts kept swarming my brain as the thought of not knowing lay ahead of us.

"Why do you think Markus left and went off on his own?" Wanda asked quietly, bringing the conversation back up.

"When I left all of you in the machine shop, he was fine. As we made our way to the mess hall, he was no longer the same person. I've seen it before; it's anger and rage."

"Why, what happened to him?" she insisted.

"I would like to ponder the thought that it was due to the lack of sleep and the loss of our crewmates, but that wasn't it. It was the loss of Dawn that pushed him over the edge," I stated.

"How did that push him over the edge?" she asked, confused.

"Markus is a good man and a good friend, but he does have a temper when pushed too far. He was in love with Dawn, and when she died, a part of him died with her. They were going to get married when we got back home. Now, all he wants is to kill all the creatures or die trying. In his mind, nothing is more important than taking revenge on the creatures that stayed onboard. That is why we will wait until we dock to search for him. He doesn't want to be found, and if we did find him, I really don't think that he would come with us willingly. He is going to have to be sedated when we find him," I answered.

"You really think we are going to have to sedate him when we find him?" she questioned.

"Yes, I know how I would feel if I were in his place. There wouldn't be a thing that you could say or do to make me stop. Maybe after we sedate him and he gets the rest he needs along with the time to cope with the loss, then maybe we might get a part of the Markus we knew back. Until then, I don't think he will be the same as we have come to know him. In fact, I don't think any of us are going to be the same after this. It's going to be a long time before any of us will walk into a dark room without our hearts racing from fear. Some might be jumpy at any little noise we hear. All of us have seen our friends brutally killed around us or attacked by alien creatures. Until we came here, alien creatures were only something we saw in the movies," I explained.

"I didn't think about it all like that. It's amazing that the rest of us haven't gone crazy by now," she stated.

"How do you know we still won't? Some of us still might when the adrenaline wears off, and we are back on our ship," I remarked.

Quiet fell between the four of us, and we had finally made it to the point where the possibility of something going wrong could happen. There was a closed hatch in front of us, and on the panel next, there was a glowing red light that shone through the darkness. I turned my flashlight on and examined the hatch to see why it had sealed. Normally, it would be open, and it bothered me that it was now closed. I pushed a button, and in return, there was a small display of information.

"Who closed the hatch?" asked Wanda.

I continued to run my hand across the hatch before I answered, "The hatch was closed automatically. There must have been a hull breach on the other side. All of the air has been sucked out of this section. The hatch is ice cold from the vacuum of space."

"What do we do now? Do we go into the crawl space above it and go over that section?"

"No, I don't think so. That area could have been compromised as well. Not to mention, I don't see any other hatches. We're going to have to double back to the mess hall and use the starboard corridor. I just hope it hasn't been compromised as well."

"What if it has? What will we do then?" she inquired.

"Like I said earlier, we only have one option left. We would have to go back into engineering and enter deck one from there. Let's just hope we don't have to go to our last option." I said, a little irritated.

"Why don't we just go to engineering in the first place?" she asked.

"I don't really want to go that route. In case you have forgotten, level three was infested with those creatures. Engineering covers all three levels on this ship, and I'm guessing they might have managed to get in from level three. It's a theory that I don't really want to test."

"Hey Mike, I think you should take a look at this," Cara called from behind me.

I began to walk toward her with Wanda close in toe. Cara and Sarah were standing next to a ventilation panel. The vent panel had been ripped open from the inside, and I bent down to examine it and confirm my fears. From looking at the damage, it was hard to determine how long ago this had been done. I was able to deduce rather quickly that this was done recently. I heard a noise deep in the ventilation duct, and I used my flashlight to peer deeper inside but saw nothing.

"They are using the ventilation ducts to move around the ship. We need to go now!" I said as I quickly stood up and backed away from the damage.

As we doubled back toward the corridor, the light was beginning to improve, and we began to move faster. We moved to the other corridor on the starboard side, and I stopped to look and see if there would be anything in our path. It didn't look like it from here, but my only concern was the steam which was being released into the corridor. We moved cautiously toward the bow of the ship and as we slowly approached the steam.

I stopped my team, and with my heart pounding in my chest, I had to take a deep breath before I was able to step into the steam. On the other hand, I was able to breathe a little more easily after seeing that there was nothing I should have worried about. Now, I was close enough to see the other end of the corridor and the hatch to the stairs, which would take us up to deck one. I turned to watch the others come through the steam one at a time before we would press on.

Cara didn't get far past the steam before she must have heard something from behind us because she broke our formation. She stopped suddenly and spun around to see the creature as it slashed out with its claws and struck her. The creature ripped her stomach open, and before she could make a sound, I watched in slow motion as she fell to the ground. She used her weapon and fired at the unseen enemy. Her shots echoed in the corridor, and she made a loud thud as she hit the deck. Wanda spun around to drag Sarah out of the way as I fired my weapon at the creature. The creature fell to the deck as I ceased firing and began to move closer to investigate.

Sarah lay on the deck gasping for air as Cara stepped forward to treat her wounds. She reached into her bag, pulled out a large bandage, and applied it. It's clear that she will need some immediate attention as the bandage was quickly soaked in blood.

"We need to get her up to medical and get Joan or we're going to lose her," stated Cara in a rush.

"I'll carry her. Wanda, take the lead, and Cara, you follow behind us." I said as I shouldered my weapon and handed Sarah's to Wanda.

I picked up Sarah and carried her in my arms as we headed toward the stairs. Wanda opened the hatch and entered, followed by me quickly behind her. Cara walked backward toward the hatch to make sure no other surprises were going to sneak up behind us. She stepped through and closed it behind her.

Sixteen

Countdown

Sam

I sat up momentarily from my spot to do a quick check on everyone. Joan had just finished stitching Bart's arm and began wrapping it up while everyone else worked on the problem. Pops continued his efforts to reach the Star Rider while Lisa ran through the computer to figure out what had set off the alarm. I lay back down by Lexey's feet and continued to work on the bottom side of the engineering panel. She sat at the engineering station and tested each item as I called it out.

"Lexey?" I called out and waited for a response. Momentarily, after no response, I called again, "Lexey, are you with me?"

"Umm…yeah, what do you need?" Lexey said, her face distracted.

"I need you to check and see if you can get anything on the monitors yet. Are you alright?"

"Yeah, I just got a little distracted." She spun around, pushed a few buttons, and looked at the monitors.

"We're all getting a little distracted thinking about what's happened to us. We have to just focus on our jobs for a little bit longer, and then this will all be over," I remarked while I continued to work on her station.

"I have something now." Data appears on the monitors and then disappears. "No, wait. It is gone again. We almost had something." she sighed quietly as though relief had just filled her body.

"That should have worked. Let me double-check some of these connections," I said as I found that one of them was loose.

"Now?" she asked.

After I fixed it, slid out from under the panel, and sat up again, I told her, "Try it now."

She tried again, and the data stayed on the screen as a program ran.

"It's working. The diagnostic program is running. I should have some information from engineering in a couple of minutes." she said, surprised.

I stood up, brushed myself off, looked at the monitors, and smiled as I turned around to look around the bridge. Everyone was still working harder than ever to do their assigned tasks. I looked over at Joan, who began to apply a bandage. Bart looked pale still from the amount of blood in which he had lost. It was evident that he wouldn't be traveling alone anytime soon and would need assistance when it was time to dock to our ship.

I began to walk across the bridge when a sudden sound erupted from the hatch that led to the bridge. Everyone else heard it as well because they drew their weapons and aimed at the hatch. It was only a few seconds, but time seemed to drag on while we all waited to see what had tried to open the hatch. We watched as it opened, and Wanda stepped in, who didn't notice all the weapons pointed at her. She turned around to ensure the hatch was wide open as Mike, who carried Sarah, entered.

"Joan! We have an emergency here! Sarah has been wounded!" He shouted as he carried Sarah's limp body.

"Bring her over here, quickly," Joan said from the other side of the engineering station.

He rushed to Joan and set her down beside Bart. Cara stepped through the hatch last and followed Mike and Sarah. The two of them started working on her, and Mike stepped back so they could do their jobs. He walked to me, and I heard another noise from the hatch. I watched as Wanda closed it behind her, and she joined us as we watched them work on Sarah.

"Where is everyone else?" I asked as I looked over both of my shoulders.

"We lost Dave outside the machine shop when one of the creatures attacked us suddenly. Bev was killed before we could get to her. We lost Dawn during our escape from the creatures in the machine shop," Wanda answered softly.

"What about Markus?" I asked.

"He didn't take Dawn's loss very well, and he went off on his own," Mike answered.

"Are we going to go look for him?" I asked Mike.

"No, we already lost two people trying to save Bev. There is no telling how many more would die if we were to go looking for him. If one of those creatures found him, then he is dead already. When we dock with our ship, we can get more people to search the ship. Until then, he is on his own." Mike said.

"We can't just leave him out there. We have to do something," I pleaded.

Mike turned to face me and said, "Look around you, Sam. We came down here with twenty-five crew members. What you see here on the bridge is all we have left. There are only twelve of us, and two are badly injured. We are bruised, battered, and exhausted. We have very little ammunition to fight off the creatures, and we don't know how many are still aboard the ship. We can't take the loss of any more people. We need everyone that is left just to get back to our ship." Mike said, almost shouting.

"I hate the idea of anyone still being out there with those creatures onboard," I said carefully to not anger Mike even more.

"I do, too," replied Mike, setting his hand on my shoulder to try to calm himself.

We all brought our attention back to Joan and Cara, and when Joan finally looked at Mike, she had a solemn look on her face. I knew from the look on her face that Sarah didn't survive from her injuries. I took a few steps forward and looked back down at Sarah, and Cara pulled a sheet over her.

"I'm sorry, Mike. There was nothing we could have done. The creature did too much damage. Most of her internal organs were damaged, and she lost too much blood. Even if we had her in our sick bay on our ship, there would have been nothing we could have done to save her." Joan said.

"Damn! What else could happen to all of us? This is going to be a mission where no one will ever believe us," Mike yelled.

"I'm afraid I have some more bad news that you won't like Mike. I found out what set off the alarm," Lexey piped up.

Everybody stopped what they were doing and put their full attention on her. She sat down at her station, and Mike and I quickly approached to see what she had discovered. Everyone thought the alarm had gone off due to hull breaches. I was utterly interested in her findings.

"Show me what you found," Mike stated.

"Until now, we thought the alarm went off because of the hull breaches. I wish that was the only problem. In fact, it may have been a factor in the alarm going off. Once we got this station working again, I could run a diagnostic on the ship." She pulled up a schematic of the ship, and several areas blinked red, and she pointed at them and continued. "The red spots on the monitor indicate sensors that have registered problems. If you notice, there are none on the starboard side, but some on the ship's port side in these areas. Do you notice where they are, Mike?"

"Yes, they are near all of the portside pods," he said as he took a closer look.

"Correct, and as you can see, the more dots correspond with the increased damage and the more tripped sensors. It appears the concussion from our charges caused the breaches by damaging the hatches," she paused.

Mike looked closer at the monitors, pointed at specific areas on the monitor, and asked, "If that's so, then what is going on back here? The last pod and engineering have a lot of dots on them."

"That is what has set off the main alarm on this ship. Do you remember when we tried to take off and were having trouble before the ship experienced a sudden jolt and was free?"

"Yes. I believe it was caused by one of the charges going off late," replied Mike.

"That was the same conclusion we came to as well. I think when we were trying to break free before that last charge went off, it moved. I'm not sure about why or how, but I think when it finally did go off, it sent shrapnel flying everywhere, and some of it penetrated the hull between the interior and the pod. That set in motion the chain of events that has set off the sensors in engineering."

"What kind of damage in one of those pods can affect engineering? The pod doesn't cover engineering." I asked, confused.

"That is true to a point. The engine coolant lines run through that wall, and I think some shrapnel ruptured them." She pointed to another monitor and said, "According to these readings, we have no coolant left to cool the engines down, and they are continuing to heat up out of control. That's what set off the main alarm."

"Then why don't we just shut them down?" Mike asks.

"We can't, I tried. The circuits to shut them down from here have shorted out. There is nothing that we can do to stop them from going critical," she answers.

"Then we will have to go to engineering and shut them down from there," stated Mike.

"We don't have enough time. Even if I knew all of the systems down there, I might be able to do it, but I don't believe it would make a difference. Without any coolant, there is nothing we can do to stop it," she stated.

"How long do you think we have before the engines go critical?" Mike asked.

"Maybe thirty minutes. Maybe we might have a little less time or a little more, but not much more. Even though we silenced the alarm, it will go off again once it gets closer to critical mass. When it does, we will only have about ten minutes left."

"What will happen when our time runs out?" asked Joan.

"The engines will overheat and ignite the fuel, causing the engines to explode," Lexey said.

Mike and I looked at our watches to note the time, simultaneously setting them for a thirty-minute countdown. I looked back at the monitors to get at least one more look at the data that it displayed.

"Have you heard anything from the Star Rider?" I asked Pops.

"There is a lot of static, but maybe I heard something. I just can't be sure this thing is working properly." Pops said.

"There may be something out there, but reading this old equipment is hard. If something is out there, it's flying in a very low orbit." Lou chimed in.

"If the Captain realized we're no longer on the surface, I might have chosen a low orbit to possibly catch up with us. That might be the Captain trying to catch us." Mike said, taking the lead.

"It could be, but we have no way to slow down, allowing them to catch us. Not to mention, can they catch us in time to save us?"

"If that's them, we need to alert them of our situation. Why don't you see if there's something you can do to improve the communications," Mike stated.

"I'm on it," I replied as I moved across the bridge.

I strutted to the communications station as though I was a man with the most important purpose on the entire ship. I pulled off the exterior panel and tossed it onto the deck. I laid down on my back and slid inside to see if there was something I could do to improve the signal. It felt like a lifetime, but it was actually just a matter of moments of me prodding around. I had found something and plugged it back in.

"Lisa, run a diagnostic on the communications and see if there is any improvement," I shouted.

"There's an improvement in sending but not receiving. Can you boost the gain some more?" Lisa shouted back.

"I'll try." I made a few more adjustments and asked, "How about now?"

"That's a big improvement," she shouted.

"Can you hear them now, Pops?" I asked as I slid back out.

It was so quiet as Pops listened intently for any sign of the Star Rider.

"It's them! It's the Star Rider!" Pops shouted excitedly.

Renee

I'd been on the bridge since we had lost contact with the crew. Several other concerned crew members checked on me and brought food so I could stay present at my position. I sat in my chair, with my head leaned back against the headrest, with my eyes closed. I tried to get a little bit of rest while I waited for word on the Discovery's location.

George, who had stayed at the communications station the entire time, had been monitoring for a signal from them. I knew what he was doing without opening my eyes. He watched for the ship to appear on his scanners. Since discovering they left the surface, he'd been broadcasting a repeated message and waited for a response. I knew he had to feel exhausted, but he also didn't want to leave, no matter how many times I excused him. I heard as he leaned back in his chair into what I hoped would be a little shut-eye while we waited.

A sudden beeping sound erupted from his station. His chair squeaked forward, and I opened my eyes and saw his posture jump to attention as he went back to work. I had slowly gotten up from my chair without even realizing it, and I watched as he zeroed his vision onto a small dot on his screen. My heart raced with the possibility of finding the Discovery. He put his headset on and looked at the dot, and for several moments, he debated before turning to my attention. I watched as he pushed several buttons and listened intently.

"There's a faint signal," George said as he pushed more buttons.

I had gotten right behind him and waited for him to continue.

"What do you hear?" I asked quietly

"It's still faint, but it has slightly improved," he said as he jumped.

"Can you make out what they are sending?" I asked.

He looked at me and replied while he pointed at one of the monitors, "We just picked up a signal on our scanner in a high orbit. Also, I'm picking up a message from the Discovery. You were right about Kellie being a creature of habit. She put the ship into a high orbit. It's our crew. They made it." He said with a toothy grin.

"Finally. Put them on speaker. I want to talk to them."

The bridge had never been so quiet as everyone listened for the sound of their fellow crew mates. George pushed a button and replied, "You're on Captain,"

"This is the Star Rider to the Discovery. This is the Captain speaking. Are you reading us?" I asked and waited nervously for an answer.

"Captain, this is Mike. You don't know how happy we are to hear your voice." Static rang through with the transmission.

"It's good to hear your voice, too. What happened down there? Is everyone alright?" I asked.

"That's sort of a long and very complicated story. I'm sorry to tell you we suffered many casualties down there," Mike answered.

"How many?" I asked, not worrying about the concern that broke through.

"I wish we had time to go over that, but we have a problem. How soon can you be here?" asked Mike hurriedly.

"What kind of problems are you having?" I asked.

"The ship was damaged during lift-off. We lost all of our engine coolant, and the engines are overheating. There's nothing we can do to stop it. Lexey estimated twenty-five minutes before going critical. Do you think you can get to us in time?" he asked through the transmission with almost a hint of fear.

"It'll be close, but we can arrive in about twelve minutes. Everybody must be ready to disembark so we have enough time to clear the blast."

"We'll be ready and waiting on the dock. You'll need to have a medical team on standby as well as a large armed detail upon our arrival,"

I was expecting to hear him ask for a medical team but was completely confused when he asked for an armed detail.

"Why do we need an armed detail at the airlock?" I asked

"Our initial scans of the planet were wrong. There were primitive creatures that dwell below the surface. They are extremely hostile and should be shot on sight. We know some made it onboard the ship before we lifted off, and we can't let them get onboard your ship. We're low on ammunition and might need help getting off this ship," explained Mike.

"We'll be ready on our end and dock with you on your port side," I answered.

"Negative, Captain. We have damage and hull breaches on that side. You'll need to dock on our starboard side," stated Mike urgently.

"Understood. Just hang in there a little longer. Help is on the way," I replied.

"You may never hear me say this again, but we'll really be glad to be back on that ship," Mike remarked.

I didn't hesitate as I barked out my next orders: "George, contact sick bay and tell Paula to get a medical team over to the port side airlock. Pilot, plot the fastest course to rendezvous with them on their starboard side."

"I've already laid in and initiated, Captain. I might even be able to shave off a few minutes on the estimated arrival time." the pilot responded.

"Excellent. We are fighting time, and every extra minute counts. Stay in constant contact with Kellie. The two of you will have to do some precision flying if we're going to do this without incident."

"Captain," another man said as he approached me.

"Good, Tom. Find out who isn't doing anything right now, put a weapon in their hands, and get them over to the port side airlock. See to that personally."

"Consider it done," Tom answered as he rushed off the bridge.

"Barbara, contact engineering and alert them that we're going to need everything they can give us from the engines to get us there as fast as possible and to get us away before the engines on the Discovery go critical and annihilate us all."

"Yes, Captain," replied Barbara.

"Walt, come over here and take over communications from George." I waited until he had stood up, and Walt sat in his spot to take over his position. "George, I want you to keep an eye on how much time we have. I want you to do a continuous scan of the Discovery and let us know the moment you see any change in her, no matter how small or unimportant it may seem."

"You can count on me, Captain. I won't take my eyes off the monitors," he said as he sat down at a station and pushed several buttons. On one of the monitors, he started a countdown clock based on the amount of time they thought they had before the engines went critical. The other monitors held information on both ships, and a thermal scan of the Discovery was also on one screen to help monitor the engines' temperature.

George paused momentarily and looked up at me with a sense of sadness like nothing I had ever seen. I stared back at him, wanting to know what thoughts were held behind those eyes.

"What's on your mind, George?" I finally asked.

"I was just thinking about the casualties. How many do you think…" he began.

I gently placed my hand on his shoulder and answered, "I don't know, George. I hope there aren't too many. We'll sort this out once we have them back onboard." I turned and walked away, leaving him there to do his work.

I returned to my chair to monitor everything going on. From my chair, I watched George and what he could see. I then focused on what the pilot saw. All of this was displayed on the monitors that hung above my chair. My heart pounded while my mind raced as I tried to think about the loss of my crew, the ship they were on about to explode, and aliens. It was a lot to take in so quickly. Knowing that I needed to stay focused. I watched the display of information on the speed and distance to the Discovery. I also watched the countdown that George started and began to wonder if we could pull this off without losing both ships.

✶✶✶✶✶✶✶✶✶✶✶✶✶✶

Mike

Kellie talked with Brian on the Star Rider to ensure constant communication continued to flow between the ships. After all, if it wasn't for them, we might not have the chance to get off this ship alive. Since Kellie no longer had control over the main engines, she decided to use the maneuvering engines to move down into a standard orbit, which would close the distance between the two ships and cut the rendezvous time in half. She informed her counterpart of her intentions before she started.

Kellie pressed the button to fire the maneuvering engines in the hope that nothing would fail. If one failed, then the ship would spin, making docking with the Star Rider impossible. She watched the readings on her display but is unsure if they are accurate. The display flickers on and off a couple of times.

"Brian, can you confirm that my engines fired and that my orbit is changing? My displays are acting up, and I don't know if I can trust what they are telling me," Kellie said.

"Everything looks good from here. Your orbit is changing, and the ship is level," he replied.

"Good. Let me know when to fire them again to achieve a standard orbit."

"Ok, Kellie. Prepare to fire the engines on my mark," stated Brian.

Kellie held her hand on the button as she waited for his command. There was a pause that seemed to drag on forever.

"Fire the engines now," Brian said.

As Brian had instructed, she fired the engines briefly before she asked. "I think I should be in a standard orbit. Can you confirm?"

"I confirm you are now in a standard orbit. I estimate we should rendezvous with you in six minutes. I am now adjusting our course to your new orbit."

"Mike, I managed to change orbit. We will now rendezvous with the Star Rider in six minutes instead of twelve." Kellie shouted over her shoulder.

"Good job, Kellie. The sooner we can get off this ship, the sooner we can end this nightmare." I replied.

Joan had quietly walked toward me without saying a word.

"Will Bart be able to move on his own, or will we have to find a way to carry him?" I asked her.

"He'll be able to walk. He's still pretty weak, so he will need some help," Joan answered.

"Alright, I want Cara and you to help him," I told her. I turned to the rest of the crew and continued, "Kellie, Lisa, and Lexey, once we dock, you're going to need to secure your stations and get ready to move with us. Kellie, I need you to set the autopilot to move this ship away once we are back on our own ship."

"I'll do my best, but I'm not sure if that system is working," stated Kellie.

"Well, do what you can. When we leave this bridge, we'll need to stay close together. Sam and I will take the lead. Lou, I want you, Pops, and Wanda to stay close to Joan and Cara. They will have their hands full with Bart, so you protect them. Kellie, Lisa, and Lexey will bring up the rear, so watch your backs. Are there any questions?"

"I have a question. What are we going to do about Markus? We can't leave him behind. We need to let him know to get to the airlock so he can get off the ship with us." Cara asked.

"I'm not sure there is any way that we can reach him. He doesn't have a radio," I stated.

"There might be a way." Sam interrupted.

"What do you have in mind?" I asked.

"This ship has an internal communications system. I think I may have fixed it. I'm unsure if it will work or how much of the ship it will cover."

"I can even put messages up on all of the computer displays. If he doesn't hear the message and passes a display somewhere that is on, he can read it there." Lisa added.

"Ok, Sam. You make the announcement, and Lisa gets to display your message. At least we'll have tried to get him off the ship." I motioned for Lou to join me.

"What's on your mind, Mike?" Lou asked.

"You're going to be the most vulnerable on our way to the airlock. I want you to carry Bart's weapon as a backup. Keep an eye on everything, especially the air vents," I said.

"I'm not going to let anything happen this close to getting off this ship," responded Lou.

"Is everything alright, Joan?" I asked from the nagging face that she made.

"I'm just nervous about going out where the creatures are," she replied.

"I wouldn't worry too much, Joan. Wanda, Pops, and I will cover you from the front, and Kellie, Lisa, and Lexey will cover you from behind. With all that protection, we should be able to keep you from being injured."

"Speaking of injuries. There is something that I have been meaning to ask you about Bart. When I examined him, I found out that he had several broken ribs. Do you want to tell me how that happened?"

"Well, we kind of fell on him," Lou said as his face flushed from embarrassment.

"What do you mean by we?" I pipped in.

"Yeah, and how do you kind of fall on someone?" laughed Joan.

"Well, Pops slipped on the top side, trying to get back to the hatch. Bart and I had to go up there and help him. As we reentered into the airlock, the launch started at the same time. Bart made it to the bottom of the ladder. I lost my grip on the ladder and fell on him first from about halfway down the ladder. Pops had finished securing the hatch and was still close to the top when he lost his grip and fell on both of us. When things settled down, we discovered he had a few broken ribs. It was just a freak accident."

Joan and I laughed at what he told us. Of all the injuries they had seen so far from this mission, this was the first that was not caused by the creatures. Normally, I wouldn't have laughed at someone getting injured, but it was kind of funny to see Lou stumble through telling them what happened.

I stopped laughing, but the smile still echoed in my voice. I replied, "I'm sorry, Lou. I know that it isn't funny, but after everything that we have been through, I just get this funny image of the two of you lying there on top of Bart."

"I'll bet he was a little mad at the two of you," Joan added.

"Yeah, he was a little mad at the two of us. All that room in that airlock, and we both managed to fall on him and come out without an injury. I'm sure once he feels better, we will never hear the end of it." Lou said, smiling.

"I made the announcement. I just hope that Markus heard it." Sam said.

"The message is now displayed on any active terminal for him to read," Lisa said as she spun around in her chair.

"Good job, guys. Where is the Star Rider at?" I asked.

"She is maneuvering up along our starboard side right now. I'm getting ready to extend the docking sleeve as soon as she is in position." Kellie said.

Renee

I watched as Brian carefully maneuvered the ship alongside the Discovery. He had his headset on to hear what Kellie was telling him from the Discovery while keeping an eye on the monitors in front of him, which continuously fed him information. On one monitor, the computer's targeting display showed whether he was lined up. The marks on the display turned green when he was lined up and red when he wasn't. Two of the monitors showed camera images. One was from the right side of the airlock, and the other was from the left. Everyone on the bridge sat silently as they watched and waited for them to dock.

"What is our status, Brian?" I asked.

"Kellie's extending the docking sleeve, which will allow for us to dock. It's tricky docking with such an old ship. Back then, they didn't have any of the sensor points that the modern docking sleeves have. I had to maneuver using both cameras and computer sensors. It's been a long time since I had to dock this way. It will take us a little longer, but I'll get us there," Brian said with confidence.

"Take your time, Brian. I know you will do it," I reassured him.

I pressed a few buttons to bring up the same displays he saw. I watched and sat quietly as he made small maneuvers to get into position. Images of the docking sleeve slowly moved closer toward my ship. The screen showing the computer's targeting display had a little red light, and Brian made a slight adjustment and corrected it, thus changing it back to green. I listened intently as I heard only a one-way conversation he held with Kellie.

"Alright, Kellie, hold her steady. We're lined up and almost there. We have twenty feet to go, and everything is looking good." He continued to make minor adjustments while he checked each of the monitors. "We are now at ten feet; stand-by to lock on." He paused before continuing, "We are now at five feet." There was another pause before he said, "And we are docked; lock it down."

I breathed a sigh of relief as I said, "Good job Brian."

"Thanks, Captain. It was just a walk in the park," he replied as he slouched in his chair.

"Captain, this is Tom," a voice said over the intercom.

"Go ahead, Tom," I said as I pushed a button to reply.

"I have the armed and medical detail here at the airlock. We're waiting for the sleeve to pressurize," Tom said.

"How many people did you get for the armed detail?" I asked.

"I managed to round up thirty crewmembers and armed each of them," he replied.

"Good; as soon as the sleeve is pressurized, I want you to take half of the crewmembers across to the Discovery. By no means are you to go any farther than just outside of the airlock. You are ordered not to search for them. They must come to you. Keep the medical team on this side, and the remaining armed crewmembers are to stand guard on our side in case something gets past you. Remember, there are hostile alien creatures onboard that ship. Don't put anyone at any unnecessary risk. Your time over there is limited. They only have about fifteen minutes to get to the airlock and get off the ship. If they haven't shown up by then, I will give the order to return regardless of whether we have them all or not. I cannot risk this ship and the people on it to save only one person. When I give the word about to pack it up and leave, then it's time to go. Do you understand?"

"Yes, Captain. I understand," he replied.

"Good luck, and bring our people home," I said as I sat back in my chair and once again waited.

I switched the cameras so I could watch them. By the airlock, Tom already picked the fifteen crew members who were about to cross with him. The rest were positioned in a semicircle around the entrance to the airlock with the medical team behind them. Tom stood and watched the gauge to the docking sleeve as it continued to rise. They all waited for the light to change from red to green before anyone would be able to open the hatch. He looked through the window and then back at the gauges.

Finally, the light turned green, and he opened the hatch. They proceeded into the docking sleeve and moved quickly across it to the outer hatch of the airlock on the Discovery.

"Bridge, this is Tom. We are onboard the Discovery and waiting for the crew members to join us." Tom said through the radio.

"Understood. Let us know when you have them and when you are on your way back."

Seventeen

The Rescue

Mike

We were gathering our gear and were getting ready to move to the airlock. Bart sat up but was in a lot of pain and still slightly groggy. Joan and Cara gathered their medical supplies before they moved to help Bart. Kellie entered some instructions for the main computer to activate its autopilot navigation function. Lexey made some last minute calculations to figure out approximately how much time was left before the engines went critical. The rest of the crew checked their weapons and signaled that they were ready to leave the bridge.

"Ok, is everyone ready to get off this ship," I asked.

"We have a successful dock, and the sleeve has been pressurized. The outer hatch has been opened, so some more of our crewmates must be onboard and waiting for us there," Kellie said.

"I took a moment and downloaded the entire database they had here. That includes everything they collected on their mission, personal logs, pictures, and navigation logs." Lisa said.

I was surprised because I had never thought about downloading the database. I thought the Captain's written log, which Sam had, would be enough. With all we had been through, my only concern was returning to our ship alive.

"That's impressive, Lisa," I stated.

"I figured when we get back home, most people aren't going to believe us about what happened here. I just figured that after their investigation, they will probably think we have all gone crazy, and none of us here will ever be able to get a job in space again. The database included pictures and videos of the creatures on this planet. Since no one has ever seen an alien, we need the proof to show we aren't crazy."

"Good thinking. I don't think any of us will ever be able to look at space the same again," I remarked.

"I've done some new calculations, and we have about nineteen minutes before the engines go critical," Lexey said.

"I have set the autopilot to fire its thrusters in twenty minutes to begin its descent back down to the planet. I just hope that it works." Kellie said.

"Pops, let the Captain know about Lexey's estimated nineteen minutes and Kellie's plan about setting the autopilot. Also, let her know that as soon as you end the transmission, we will leave the bridge and head for the airlock," I stated.

Pops complied, and then we were ready to leave the bridge. Joan and Cara helped Bart to his feet and began to move toward the hatch. Everyone positioned themselves to move out, with Sam and I taking the lead, followed by Pops, Lou, and Wanda. I took one final look at each person, and they nodded in agreement because we were all ready to leave this ship.

Sam was about to unlatch the hatch when Cara pulled back.

"What about Sarah? Are we going to leave her body here?" she asked.

I looked at her and then at the lifeless body of Sarah, which lay on the deck covered with a sheet.

"I'm afraid we don't have anyone to spare to carry her back so we can give her a proper burial. I'm sorry, but we're going to have to leave her body behind." I said with sadness in my voice.

Everybody took one last look at her, and each paid their silent respects in their own way. After everybody was comfortable, I looked at Sam and nodded for him to unlatch the hatch. We made our way off the bridge and into the corridor, and carefully, we moved to the stairs and down to the second deck. We watched the shadows for any sign of the creatures. I knew we should not move too fast ahead of Joan and Cara, or they would be left unprotected.

We paused at the end of the corridor on deck two and waited for everyone to get off the stairs. I looked down the corridor at the wall of steam that I had come through earlier. This was where I had run into one of the creatures once before, and that encounter was still vivid in my mind.

"Is something wrong, Mike?" Wanda asked.

I turned to look at Wanda and motioned with my head toward what was ahead of us.

"Up ahead is where that creature attacked us and got Sarah," I told everybody.

"I remember. I also remember we killed it." Wanda said.

"True, it was just in front of that wall of steam," I stated.

"So what's the problem? We'll have to be extra careful when we go past that vent," replied Wanda.

"When we killed that creature, we left it in the corridor," I said.

"I still don't see the problem," stated Wanda.

"Ask yourself, where is the creature we killed? It's not there now." I asked.

She looked down the corridor and saw the same thing I did, nothing but steam.

"Your point is received. I'll pass word to the rest of the team." Wanda muttered.

"Is that where it got Sarah?" Sam asked as he stepped closer to me.

"Yeah. It came out of the vent on this side of the wall of steam, but the part that worries me the most is that the creature either didn't die or another one collected the corpse," I answered.

"We better be careful when we pass it. I wouldn't want to die this close to getting off this ship," remarked. Sam.

I looked at him briefly, laughed slightly, and then signaled everyone to move forward. As we approached the wall of steam, I slowly moved to one side of the corridor. Sam looked back and saw the rest of the crew was doing the same. He realized within moments that we had approached the vent we all just talked about. Slowly, we moved past the vent, and I was the first to go through the wall of steam. Sam and Wanda followed behind me, and as Lou entered, we continued to move our formation forward. The corridor was poorly lit, and I knew that help was just a few hundred yards away. We saw an area ahead of us where the mess hall was, and just beyond that was the airlock where they waited for us.

★★★★★★★★★★★★★

Tom

The crewmembers of the Star Rider continued to wait at the airlock. The knowledge of this ship's engines wasn't a secret, and the fact that we were protecting an airlock from hostile creatures that we had never seen before made everyone stand on edge.

"Tom, I know this may sound like a silly question, but does anyone here know what these hostile aliens look like?" one of the crewmembers asked as he stepped closer to me.

"I'm sorry, they didn't have time to send us pictures. If you see something coming at you and it doesn't look human, then it is a hostile alien, so shoot it." I said.

"What if the crew is already dead?" he asked.

"If they don't get here soon, we will have to assume they are dead and leave," I replied with a heavy heart.

"I think there is movement down the corridor." another crew member said.

Everybody faced the direction of the movement and readied their weapons. I stepped behind a crouched crewmember and strained to see down the corridor. I thought I saw the same movement but was unsure if it was them. I shook my head to clear my vision.

"I can't verify what you saw. Do you think it's them?" I asked.

"I'm not positive from this distance. It could have been a shadow. I think it was about a hundred yards down the corridor, but I can't be sure with the emergency lighting and flashing red lights," he replied.

"Check with the thermal image. That should give us a better idea," I stated

He pulled out a hand-held thermal image device they used to help find lost people in emergency situations. He pointed it down the corridor, and we looked at the display screen. A few other heat sources showed, but we continued to watch. After a few seconds, we were able to make out a person walking toward us. At first, there was only one, then another appeared in formation, and then there was another behind them. I quickly realized it was them and stood up in relief.

I stared in their direction as they approached, and soon, they came into view. I looked down at my watch and was pleased to see they were there with time to spare. As they approached, I lowered my weapon and extended my hand to shake Mike's outstretched hand.

"Welcome back," I said.

"Thanks. You have no idea how happy we are to see all of you again," he said.

"Is this all that made it?" I asked in shock.

"I'm afraid so. It's just the eleven of us. Markus ran off on his own, and we have no idea if he's dead or alive. I wish we had time to search for him. If it wasn't for the engine issue, I would organize a search party for him." Mike said as he nodded his head in sorrow.

"You said that there were eleven of you, but I only counted eight," I said, confused.

Mike quickly turned around to see who was missing. Sam had already begun to walk toward the airlock.

"Sam!" Mike shouted.

Sam must have heard him shout his name as he turned around and quickly walked back. He must have done a headcount of his own.

"I know who's missing," Sam said.

"It's Lisa, Kellie, and Lexey," Mike stated as he looked down the corridor to see if they were just lagging behind.

"I have to go back for her!" Sam shouted as they realized nobody was behind them.

Before Mike could respond, Sam confronted another crewmember, took his weapon, and ran toward the corridor.

"Sam, wait up!" Mike shouted.

Sam kept going down the corridor.

"Damn him!" Mike cursed. He turned to another crewmember and said, "Give me your weapon now!"

After receiving the weapon, he turned to those who had come with him and shouted. "Pops and Lou come with me."

As the three of them trotted down the corridor, I shouted, "You have six minutes, and then we will have to leave!" I looked back at my armed detail and saw they were wondering what to do.

"The four of you, go help them," I said as I waved my hand.

I watched as four of the crew members whom I had ordered to help ran down the corridor to catch up with them. I turned to look back at the others. The ones that watched the other directions looked over their shoulders at him with a skeptical look. Wanda and the others stood there staring down the exit path they had just taken. The two crewmembers that no longer had weapons also stared at me.

"What do we do now?" one of the disarmed crewmembers asked.

"I want the two of you to help Cara and Joan get Bart to the sick bay and tell the Captain what's going on over. The rest of us need to spread out to cover for the missing crew members."

Cara and Joan left the ship to go to the sick bay. Wanda decided to stay and took up a position next to me. I looked at her and saw that she had a rough time since she had gone to the planet. I could tell she hadn't slept while they were away. I really couldn't blame her. If I had been down there with hostile aliens, there would be no way that I would have been able to sleep either. She was dirty, bloody, and bruised as well.

"You don't need to be here. Take yourself to sick bay and get yourself fixed up." I said to her.

"We went through a lot down there. I wouldn't abandon them down there, and I'm not going to abandon them here either," she replied.

"Was it really bad down there?" I asked.

"You have no idea just how bad it really was," she answered.

★★★★★★★★★★★★★

Sam

I stopped at the wall of steam and glanced over my shoulder to see Mike, Pops, Lou, and four other crew members behind me. I know the only place we could have lost Kellie, Lisa, and Lexey was on the other side of this wall of steam. I also knew there were only four hatches between where I stood and the hatch to the stairs I had taken to come down. I tried to listen for any noises, but the sound of the ship and the steam being released seemed to muffle any other sound.

"Damn you, Sam. You know what these creatures can do to someone. I know how you feel about Lisa, but you should have waited a second before charging off to her rescue. We have about five minutes before the Captain orders them to return to the ship and leave." Mike said as he caught up to me, a little breathless. "All three of them were armed, and we never heard them fire a shot. We may go through that wall of steam and find nothing. You may have to face the fact that one or more of those creatures may have surprised them and killed them."

"No! I don't believe that," I replied with a little bit of anger in my voice. "If they were dead, then I would feel it. They are alive. I know it. There are four hatches leading to four rooms on the other side, and I will check all of them."

I turned and stepped through the steam, followed by the rest of the rescue team. On the other side, I stopped while looking straight ahead. When Mike came through, he aimed at the vent where he had encountered a creature before. He walked forward while he watched the vent until he bumped into me. He turned to look at me and then down to where I was looking. That's when he saw it. Three of the creatures were clawing at one of the hatches.

Mike whispered to one of the crewmembers to watch the vent for other creatures. He motioned for the others to make a line and prepare to fire. For Mike, Lou, Pops, and me, this was no surprise. For the four other crew members with us, I could see the same fear in their eyes as it once was for the rest of us down on the planet when we first saw these creatures. Luckily for us, the creatures didn't notice our arrival, but we were about to change that.

We readied our weapons, and then Mike signaled to open fire. The first shot got all three creatures' attention. They turned and quickly began to move toward us. Mike, Lou, Pops, and I held our ground and continued to shoot. The other crew members began to slowly step backward. Finally, one of the creatures dropped dead, and then another. The last one was a bit stronger than the others, but with the other two creatures dead, the shots were now concentrated on it. The last one was a bit stronger than the others, but with the other two creatures dead, the shots were now concentrated on it. The last creature made a last-ditch effort to reach us but dropped to the deck dead, only two feet short of reaching us. Mike, Lou, Pops, and I checked our weapons, oblivious to the creature at our feet. The other crew members just stared at the creature in disbelief.

"I think you're right. My guess is they are behind hatch number one." Mike said as he finished checking his weapon.

"I accept your apology and agree we should check hatch number one first," I said.

We hurried toward hatch number one, and the other four were still staring at the dead creature when they realized we had moved on. They quickly joined us as they realized it was in their best interest to stay close to us if they wanted to stay alive. I quickly looked at the damage the creatures made to the outside of the hatch before I unlocked and opened it. I saw Lisa lying on the deck with Kellie kneeling on one side and Lexey kneeling on the other. I felt like my heart skipped a beat. I noticed blood on all three women, and my first thought was that

Lisa was dead. Kellie and Lexey both just stared back blankly. I slowly stepped in, expecting the bad news as I approached her body.

"What happened here?" Mike asked as he stepped in after me.

"It happened so fast. Joan, Cara, and Bart had just stepped through the steam wall when one of the creatures came out of the vent. We stopped as another one came out." Lexie said.

"Why didn't you shoot at them?" Mike asked.

"We tried to fire, but my weapon jammed, and Lisa and Lexey's weapons malfunctioned, too. We began to back up, but the clicks from our weapons got their attention."

"We ran. I opened the first hatch I could. Kellie went in after me, and Lisa entered last. As you can see, the hatch opened out into the corridor toward the creatures. When they charged the hatch, they hit it so hard that it knocked Lisa flying across the room, knocking Kellie and me down. We got up quickly and secured the hatch."

"Once the hatch was secured, Lexey and I turned around to see Lisa lying on the deck unconscious." Kellie looked at Lexey and then back at Mike, saying, "We figured you would have thought we were dead and left us behind."

"We don't want to leave anyone behind. Now we better get going, or they are going to really leave." Mike said.

I stepped forward and handed one of my weapons to Kellie and the other to Lexey. Then kneeled down and picked up Lisa. As we were getting ready to leave, Lexey watched Kellie suspiciously.

We proceeded back into the corridor, and no sooner had we entered than a couple of the creatures stepped out of a vent. I thought momentarily and ordered one of the crewmembers to open the hatch to the stairs.

"Everybody gets to the stairs!" I yelled as I carried Lisa through the hatch.

Everybody else fired their weapons at the creatures as they backed into the hatch. Two more creatures were killed as more appeared out of the vent. The last person through the hatch closed and secured the hatch. Everyone was scared by the sudden appearance of more creatures.

"I think we miscalculated things," Mike said as he breathed heavily.

"What do you mean?" I asked.

"There sure are a hell of a lot more of those creatures that stayed aboard this ship than we thought," Mike said.

Everyone chuckled except the four new crew members who had just joined us.

"How will we get down that corridor with all those creatures out there? If we don't get out of here, they are going to leave us here to die. You heard the Captain's orders." one crew member stated.

"We'll find a way," stated Mike.

"What's to stop those creatures from going down the corridor and cutting us off or, worse, getting on our ship?" asked another crew-member.

The wall of steam will stop them. These creatures like the cold and hate the heat. From their point of view, walking through a wall of fire would be like," Mike said.

"Do we have a plan about how we will get back?" asked another.

"How long do we have Mike?" I asked

"We have about four minutes left," Mike said as he looked at his watch.

"Alright, this is what we're going to do. We're going to go up these stairs to deck one, run to the rear of the ship, and enter engineering. Then we will go down one deck and enter deck two from engineering," I explained.

"I don't want to sound like the pessimist of the group, but there is a lot of noise down in engineering, and I'm sure it will be a hotspot for these creatures. If memory serves me right, these creatures are attracted to noise," stated Lou.

"Actually, I don't think we will have to worry about that once we get there. If you recall, engineering is essentially one big three deck room with catwalks around the edge on decks two and three. There are stairs that will take us down from deck one to deck two, but there are only ladders that will take us from deck two down to deck three. Now, unless I am mistaken, these creatures haven't learned how to climb ladders," I stated.

"Sounds like a great idea to me," stated Pops as he pushed his way to take the lead up the stairs.

Lou turned and headed up the stairs to join him with Mike and me close behind. The rest of the crew quickly made their way up behind us, just as anxious to get off the ship. Once we were all at the top of the stairs, we paused for a brief moment before moving out into the corridor. Lou and Pops kept a lookout for any creatures. Once in the corridor, we jogged toward the rear of the ship and engineering. We stayed close together and everybody made sure that I stayed in the middle of the group since I carried Lisa. Lexey and Kellie were both hurting from their head wounds but were determined not to stop until they got off the ship. I noticed that Lexey had made sure there was some space between Kellie and me and Kellie and her. I couldn't think of that now, but I made a mental note of it.

We raced to get back to the airlock, and the ship seemed so much bigger than it was when we were just walking around it and back on the surface. The question of whether or not we would have enough time to get back was running through everyone's mind.

"Does anyone have a radio with them?" Mike yelled.

"I have one." one of the crewmembers responded while he took out his radio.

He caught up to Mike and handed it to him. Deep down, I could tell Mike knew that they wouldn't make it back to the airlock in time. They might only have a chance if he calls ahead to tell them that they are on their way back.

Wanda

Tom, several other crewmembers, and I stood ready to defend the airlock. We heard the weapons fire down the corridor, and everyone was ready and waiting for something to happen. Growling noises, which I was familiar with, came from where the search team was located. I thought about running down to them for more help but realized it could be fatal. If we went there, we would be stepping into the line of fire and possibly right into the path of one of those creatures. I felt so helpless, just waiting and wondering what had happened. As quick as the weapons fire started it stopped. I still heard some growling noises, and it made me fear the worst.

"What the hell was that?" Tom asked.

"They were attacked by one or more of those creatures," I replied as I surveyed the area around us.

"What's wrong, Wanda?" Tom asked as he noticed something was wrong.

He started to look around to see if he could figure out what I was looking for.

"Does anyone see a large air vent anywhere close by?" I asked.

"There is an air vent right over here." one crewmember said as he pointed at the bulkhead almost across from the airlock.

"Don't get too close, but shine a light into it," I said as I moved into position.

The crewmember slowly moved closer to the vent and stooped down to shine his light inside. As soon as he turned his light on, the face of one of the creatures stared back.

"What the hell is that?" he shouted as he fell on his butt as he scrambled away.

I opened fire at the vent. Tom, the startled crewmember, and a few others join in. Pieces of the vent cover exploded as the weapons fire hit it throwing pieces of it in all directions. I signaled for everyone to stop firing. I stooped down to pick up the dropped flashlight and shine it into the vent. I saw a dead creature on the other side.

"I want you to run across to our ship and get some bright work lights," I said to one of the crewmembers.

He turned and ran across to get the lights, and I stepped up, pulled off what was left of the vent cover, and set it aside. I shone the light further down the vent to see if more creatures were coming. Tom stooped down and looked over my shoulder at the creature just a couple of feet inside the vent.

"Do you think more of those creatures will come?" Tom asked.

"If we light up the area out here, we might get lucky, and no other creature will come this way. If we don't, then I am positive more will come. One thing I do know for sure is they are attracted by loud noises, and we just make a lot of noise. We may be able to stop them from coming this way, but they are going to come," I explained.

Eighteen

Get Off Or Be Left Behind

Wanda

I had them set up one of the lights facing downward into the vent. The other three were set up to light the three corridors that merged around the airlock. As the crew members worked around the creature, they couldn't help but stop and stare.

"I want you to keep an eye on that vent and shoot anything you see coming toward us," Tom ordered one of the crew members as he looked at his watch.

"Hopefully, the lights will keep them away. If not, we will at least be able to see them coming," I said to him.

We sat silently and waited for the others to return. Tom looked at his watch again to see how much was left before we needed to pack up and leave. He looked back at the airlock and thrummed his fingers on his weapon. His nerves were getting the best of him, and he continued to watch the airlock as though he was expecting someone to come across and tell him it was time to leave. He turned back to me and was about to say something when he was startled by a voice that came across his radio.

"Tom, this is Mike. Are you there?" Mike said over the radio.

"Go ahead, Mike. Where are you at?" Tom said as he pulled out his radio.

"We were cut off by some of those creatures and had to get back by a different route. We're on deck one, making our way back to engineering. We'll get back down to deck two from there, but I don't think we are going to make it back there in time. We need you to give us a couple of more minutes." Mike said breathlessly.

"I don't know how much longer the Captain will let us stay. I'll try to delay her as long as I can, so hurry," replied Tom.

"We need the doctor and a stretcher standing by when we get there. Lisa was hurt and is unconscious," Mike said.

"Understood, Mike. You need to hurry. We're running out of time."

"According to the Captain, I'm supposed to pull everyone back in a minute," Tom said to me as he looked at his watch again.

"If we leave now, then we are leaving twelve of our friends here to die. I don't know about you, but I couldn't live with that." I said to him in a huff.

"Neither could I. If we stall things just a little bit, we could save eleven of them. There's no way to know if Markus is still alive."

"I know. I'm still hoping he will show up before we leave. What can we do to stall?" I asked.

"I could wait until the Captain sends someone and that might buy a minute or two. I could send them back a couple at a time, and we do have to recover these lights. That might give the team three to four minutes, but I think that's the best we can do. We can only hope that the estimate on the engines was wrong."

"Let's hope they can get back here in time," I remarked.

We sat quietly, waiting for the team to return. Tom and I switched positions and now watched for them in the direction of engineering. Tom rechecked his watch and looked disapprovingly at me.

I heard someone running across the docking sleeve.

Another crew member appeared and moved directly to him, saying, "The Captain sent me to tell you to get back to the ship now. I would do as she says because she didn't sound very happy. She told me to drag you back by your hair if I have to."

"Here we go," Tom said to me.

"Show time," I whispered.

He turned to the rest of the crew and said, "Ok everybody, it's time to pack it up and get back to the ship. We need to grab the lights as well. Keep a look out for any of those creatures as we pull back."

He began the plan of ordering us back to the ship a few at a time in order to give Mike and his team a little bit more time. I noticed they weren't moving very fast and realized they must have heard us talking about the plan. I concluded that they must not have wanted Tom to take all of the blame. Tom looked over at me and smiled.

★★★★★★★★★★★★★★

Mike

My team and I opened the hatch to engineering. After Pops took a quick peek in both directions on the catwalk, he signaled for the rest of us to follow him.

"Hey, Mike. I think you were right. There's a lot more of those creatures onboard than we thought."

I looked down, and in the dim light, I saw about a dozen creatures walking around.

"It's amazing we got off the ground with that many creatures still onboard," I said as we moved quickly toward the stairs to the catwalk on deck two.

"You have to admit these creatures are pretty damn smart. Down on the surface, they couldn't get to the ship, so they made the ship come down to them," Sam stated.

"Let's hope their learning curve stopped there, and they haven't figured out how to climb ladders. If they have, then we are so screwed," I replied.

We made it to the stairs and descended to the next catwalk. Below, the creatures could hear us and began to growl. I watched as Lou glanced down toward the engines, and I noticed the numerous pairs of glowing eyes staring back. Lexey looked down and completely ignored the creatures to check on how bad the engines were. Steam came out in many different areas of the engines, and I noticed that the creatures had stayed away from those areas. An alarm went off, but we didn't stop moving as we approached the hatch and headed to the second deck.

"Lexey, what's that alarm trying to tell us?" I asked.

"The engines have reached the red zone. The core temperature has reached critical, and catastrophic failure is imminent!" she shouted over the noise.

"How long before the engines will explode?" I questioned.

"No more than eight minutes, maybe less! How much time do we have before the Star Rider leaves us here?" Lexey said, shrieking.

I looked at my watch and replied, "They should have left us two minutes ago. I can only hope Tom managed to stall them."

✳✳✳✳✳✳✳✳✳✳✳✳✳✳

Wanda

Everybody had returned to the ship except for Tom and me. We stood at the airlock and hoped the others would get here soon. We waited without backup, standing close to the hatch as we looked all around us to ensure no creature could sneak up on us. We kept one of the work lights and made sure the area we were in was lit up as best we could. We wanted to keep an eye on the vent.

From behind us, I heard someone approaching. Neither Tom nor I dared to look behind us, as we already knew who it was. We looked at each other, knowing we were in big trouble with the Captain for stalling. I glanced over my shoulder to see that the Captain had approached us. She carried a weapon and had a very angry look on her face.

"I don't think we can stall any longer," I said to Tom.

"Does she look mad?" asked Tom.

"More pissed off. I think we should expect to get all the crappy jobs the rest of the way home," I stated.

"Do you think there is any way we can talk our way out of this?" asked Tom.

"I don't think she is in the talking mood," I said, shaking my head no.

"What the hell are the two of you still doing over here? You were supposed to be back onboard the ship with the others! You're lucky I don't leave the two of you here. I've already lost enough people coming to this frozen planet!" The Captain shouted.

"Sorry, Captain. They got cut off from coming back the same way because of those alien creatures. They had to take the long way back. They radioed us and said they were on their way. I just wanted to give them a few more minutes. I didn't want to leave them here to be blown up." Tom explained.

"Neither do I. I can't base my decisions on personal feelings. I have eighty other crew members to think about. Sometimes sacrifices must be made to ensure the safety of others."

"He stayed because of me, Captain," I said as she looked at me directly. "After all we went through down there and on this ship, I just didn't think it was fair to go through all that and be so close to going home only to be left behind. That's why they went after Kellie, Lisa, and Lexey. They didn't want them to get this close and fail."

The Captain was about to say something else when an alarm went off inside the Discovery. The Captain paused briefly before she looked at her watch.

"What's that?" asked Tom.

"It's telling us we are out of time. We have to get back across right now. If you are not with me when I get back to our ship, then I am going to have no choice but to leave you behind," explained the Captain as she turned to return to her ship.

Tom inhaled a deep breath in defeat, and I watched as he decided to take one last look before returning to the ship. He shined his light down the corridor toward engineering. All of the hope that he had just left his entire body as he strained to search for anybody. He was about to turn around when his posture changed, as though something caught his eye. He took a second look, and the light that had just extinguished inside of him was relit.

"Captain, wait! Here they come!" Tom shouted to the Captain.

The Captain stopped and turned around. I saw in her posture that she hoped he was right and not just trying to stall for time. She hurried back to us and looked. The feeling of relief washed over her as we all saw them running toward us. Deep down, I don't think she really wanted to leave us here to die. Leaving someone behind to save the lives of the rest of the crew was a decision that no Captain ever wanted to make, and thankfully, it was now one she wouldn't have to make. She smiled as they approached the airlock. She took another look at her watch and realized they would be cutting it short on time.

Pops and Lou walked past Tom and the Captain without a word being spoken. The rest of the crew grouped up around them. They were all breathing heavily from the running as fast and safely as possible to get here.

"Captain, thanks for waiting for us," Mike said as he stepped up to the Captain, still breathing heavily.

"You should be thanking Tom and Wanda. If they hadn't stalled us, we would already be gone. Now let's get out of here." The Captain replied with a sad look.

He was about to speak to Tom and me, but something caught his eye. He turned to see what it was but didn't get to say anything before it happened. Out of the shadows, a creature swiped its claw at Sam, who dodged slightly, but the creature took a second and third swipe at him and sliced Sam on the back of his calf with the tip of its claw. Sam hit the deck, fell backward, and clung to Lisa. Tom turned the work light toward the attacking creature, and it squealed in pain. Everyone opened fire on it. The creature fell over, dead.

As the last shot fired, I watched the Captain stare at the creature. I looked at the Captain and saw the same expression every other survivor had when we first encountered the creatures. Knowing the effect wouldn't last long, we needed to get back to Star Rider.

"We need to get off of this ship. Tom and Wanda watch for any more creatures. Pops and Lou, I need you to help Sam back to the ship. I'll carry Lisa. The rest of you need to get back across. Last one out, close the hatch," ordered Mike without regard to the Captain.

Tom and I complied with the order as Mike picked up Lisa and followed us. Lou and Pops helped Sam to his feet and put their arms around him to support him as they followed the others. The Captain started toward the ship but paused momentarily to take one last look at the creature before stepping off the Discovery. Tom grabbed the light while I shut the airlock hatch. As Mike was about to step back onto the Star Rider, he took one last look back. Pops, Lou, and Sam did the same just before they set foot back on their ship.

Medical teams waited for them on the ship as they arrived. They set the injured down on the deck to be treated before they are moved to the sick bay. Each crewmember returning from the surface was cut, bruised, battered, and exhausted. I could only imagine their thoughts as they had survived the alien attacks.

The Captain stepped up to an intercom, pressed a button, and said, "Bridge, this is the Captain. Release the docking clamps, and let's get out of here. As soon as we clear the Discovery, take us full speed away from it."

"We have a problem, Captain. The docking clamps won't release." Brian said with a pause.

"Help me up and help me get to that panel by the airlock," Sam said.

Mike and Pops helped him up and almost carried him over to the airlock, with the medic objecting to every step they took. The Captain and most of the others stood there and watched him. The medic working on Sam had only applied a temporary bandage to his leg and was now watching, just like the others.

Sam opened the panel and began to inspect the circuitry quickly. He did a quick inspection of the wiring but looked dissatisfied. Next, he pulled out several small circuit boards and gave them a quick look before putting them back. As he pulled out the fourth circuit board, he paused. There was a large burnt spot on this board.

"We don't have enough time to fix this," Sam said.

"How long would it take you to fix it?" the Captain asked as she took a deep breath.

"It will take at least an hour to fix, and we don't have that much time. The only way to release the clamps is to release them from the other side," answered Sam.

"Captain, I'll go. I was responsible for those who lost their lives on that mission, stated Mike.

The Captain is about to say something when the sound of escaping air and some mechanical sounds on the hull can be heard. We all looked around momentarily before realizing it was the docking sleeve. The Captain, Mike, and Sam struggled to look through a small window. I quickly followed suit and looked through another one to see what was going on. At the other end, looking back at us from the Discovery, was Markus. We could only watch as we slowly moved away from the sleeve and the Discovery.

"I don't believe it. He survived and saved all of us. I wonder why he didn't come back with us. He knew where to go," remarked Sam.

"Dawn died on that ship, and so did a big part of him. I guess he couldn't bring himself to be that far from where she died," replied Mike.

We all continued to watch as we moved farther and farther away from the Discovery. Others, including the survivors of this mission, gathered at other windows to watch. Soon, the Discovery was just a small dot against the planet.

"You know Mike, I never thought I would see the day that I would be grateful for a malfunction," stated Sam.

"Why is that?" asked Mike.

"Before we left the bridge, Kellie set the autopilot to engage the thrusters. That should have happened when we were in engineering," Sam replied.

A bright flash from the planet lit up a part of the darkness in space. We all watched as the light disappeared, and I began to think about those who hadn't made it back. The doctor stepped up behind the Captain, and she turned to face her.

"That makes fifteen dead and six wounded. This is not what I would call a successful mission."

"There was no way for you to know there would be any hostile alien creatures down there. From what we could tell from here, there were two ships down there and nothing else," explained Sam.

"I should have known something was wrong when two ships landed and neither one left. I had a bad feeling about this place the moment we found those ships," the Captain stated.

"On the bright side, we solved the mystery of what happened to the Discovery and the Nightingale," Mike chirped in.

"It would have really been something if we could have brought back the Discovery with us," Sam said sadly.

"You know, I thought Markus had gone crazy when he went off on his own. It turns out that he was the hero that saved us from destruction. I think someone should note what happened on this mission in the report," Mike stated.

"I will note that in my report," The Captain said as she looked around at all of us. While pointing at Sam, Mike, Lou, and Pops, she said, "Right now, I think you guys need to get to sick bay and get checked out. I don't want to see any one of you for at least twenty-four hours. Now get out of here and get some medical attention, food, and rest."

Sam looked over at her, nodded, and smiled. Pops and Lou help him make his way to the sick bay. Mike handed off his weapons to one of the crewmembers and followed. The Captain handed off her weapon and left.

Sam

Three days had passed since we returned from the Discovery, and life aboard the Star Rider had slowly returned to normal. I entered the sick bay on a pair of crutches with my injured leg wrapped. I made my way to the bed that Lisa lay in. She was lying in bed with her eyes closed and her head bandaged. I pulled my usual chair to the bedside to sit beside her. As I moved the chair, she opened her eyes and turned to look at me.

"Hi there. How are you feeling today?" I said suddenly.

"Not bad, I guess. How long have I been out?" she said hoarsely.

"Three days. It's good to see you awake." I leaned forward and kissed her gently, then sat down and placed my crutches on the deck.

"What happened to you?" she asked as she pointed at the crutches.

"I almost got out with nothing but cuts, scratches, and bruises. While I carried you out, a creature attacked. It injured my leg before we killed it. I had to get forty-five stitches and will have to do some major rehab. Per Doc Paula, she's not sure if I'll have a permanent limp,"

"How many did we lose?" she asked.

"We lost fifteen. Everyone else had been bandaged and returned to duty. I'm going to be on light duty for a while. Bart's going to be laid up for at least a week, and we'll have to ask the doctor about you," I stated.

Paula, Mike, and the Captain walked up to Lisa's bed as if on cue. I looked at the Captain and saw she looked a little more stressed than normal. Mike had a bandage on his head and his wrist wrapped.

"It's good to see you're finally awake. How are you feeling today?" asked Paula as she checked Lisa's chart.

"I'm feeling pretty good for a person who's been unconscious for three days. How long do you think I'll be here?"

"I'd like to keep you here at least one more day, then I'll release you for light duty," replied Paula.

Sam looked up at the Captain and asked, "How did Command respond to your report on this mission?"

"They are understandably concerned about what happened. I have been communicating with them ever since you got back. I think some don't believe that we encountered an alien creature. They are, however, interested in what we found on the Discovery and the Nightingale."

"We have a lot of information for them to look at. I brought back the Captain's written log, and Lisa downloaded the database from the Discovery." I turned to Lisa, "Wanda told me she recovered the storage module from the Nightingale for you to look at when you get out of here." I said.

"If you bring it here, I can start working on it right away," Lisa said excitedly.

"There's no rush, Lisa. You'll have plenty of time to work on it on your way home," The Captain said.

Paula continued to examine Lisa as everybody continued to talk. She documented this in her chart, and as soon as the examination was over, she excused herself and left. I held Lisa's hand while the conversation drifted from one subject to the next. I noticed Mike had been quiet and looked like he wanted to say something but didn't. I also noticed he was standing very close to the Captain.

"Did you send out a letter to the families of those that didn't make it?" I asked the Captain.

"I sent them with the reports I sent to Command," she answered.

"I can't imagine how hard it was for you to write fifteen. Is Command going to do anything to honor those that died?"

"They told me they would be flying in the families and going to host a memorial service for them in a couple of days. I decided that we will hold one of our own here tomorrow. If there's anything you need during your recovery, don't hesitate to ask." the Captain said.

"There's something I have been meaning to ask you, Captain. I've noticed you seem to have a close relationship with Sam. You let Sam get away with things most others would never tolerate. I've asked Sam, but he always seems to avoid the question. So I'm going to ask you. What is your relationship with Sam? The only conclusion I can come up with is that the two of you are related somehow." Lisa asked as she changed the subject.

"Do you remember how I told you I was adopted?" I said as I quickly glanced at the Captain, but held my attention to Lisa.

"Yeah, I remember," answered Lisa.

"When I was old enough, I went searching for my relatives, and I found several. That's how I got so wrapped up in my family history.

You're right when you said you think we're related. In fact, she is my biological mother," I stated, pointing at the Captain.

"That explains a lot. Now I see why she defended you when others complained about you for things such as your music. Did you ever manage to find your father?" Lisa asked with wide eyes.

"Unfortunately, no," I answered.

"Actually, Sam, you've met your father," Mike said.

"Who?" Sam questioned.

"I am your biological father. My real name before I had it changed was Hauzer. Captain Hauzer was my grandfather." Mike said.

I turned my head and gawked at Mike. I have wanted to find my father for years, and now I find out he has been here all along. I realized now that this is why Mike seemed to be protecting me down on the surface. This would be the longest ride home, but it would give me the chance to get to know the real him.

"You need to get some rest and heal before returning to work. On our way home, you have a lot of data to compile and organize," Mike said to Lisa.

The Captain handed her a tablet, which I hadn't noticed her holding before. Lisa took it slowly, slightly confused.

"We've had a chance to skim through the data brought back. I read your report, and you had a lot of questions about Captain Hauzer. I know you got some of your answers from the log books. Well, we found a video file from Captain Hauzer in the data you brought back. We've seen it, and I think you need to as well. We took the liberty of loading it on the tablet," The Captain said.

I turned to Lisa, and she turned the tablet on. I positioned myself closer to her so that we could watch it together. She tapped on the file, and the video started.

The camera was pointed to an empty chair, and someone walked around and sat in it. He looked at the monitor to ensure he was in the right spot to be seen on camera. His uniform was dirty and torn, and he now had an unkept full beard and mustache, a bandage on his head to cover some type of wound, and his overall appearance was tired and very dirty. He looked like a homeless person, and from his general appearance, it seemed as though stress had taken rampant upon this person simply from the wear and tear on his body.

He looked at the camera, cleared his throat, and began with his hands resting on the desk, "To whoever sees this. This is a record and a warning of what happened here. I am Captain Hauzer. Captain of the Discovery." He paused and looked around his surroundings before he continued, "Or at least I used to be. We were on the homeward leg of our journey when we found this frozen hell. I gave the order to land here. My crew just followed my orders. We were to be the first crew to go out this far, and when we found this frozen planet with one spot that had no ice, we just couldn't pass it up. This would have been the crown jewel of our trip out here. Instead, landing here sealed our fate. I hope you weren't drawn in by this mystery like we were. If you were, leave now or suffer the same fate we did. You are not alone here! We found out too late. Those alien bastards dug a tunnel under our port landing gear. The weight of the ship was too much, and the ground collapsed under the strain. At first, we thought it was just bad luck. We soon discovered it was alien creatures, and they lived underground in the dark. When the light went away, that's when we saw them."

He paused and coughed, then took a drink before he continued to talk with a raspy voice like someone telling a horror story around a campfire. "Half of my crew was gone. Six members were either taken by those bastards or were buried when the ground gave way outside the ship. The sudden shift by the ship caused bumps and bruises and even some broken bones." He looked down at his desk at his log book, ran a hand across the cover like a magic wand, then looked back up and continued, "We even lost a few on the ship. The rest of us banded together, determined to repair the ship and get back home. These alien creatures had other plans. We were all armed and on edge the first night we saw them. We soon learned they would hide by day and come out at night. We tried to rest during the day and did some repair work. When they came out at night, you heard the clicking noises from their claws on the deck, screeches from them clawing at the bulkheads, and their bone-chilling growls, which they constantly liked to make."

He stopped, took another drink, lit up a cigarette, and continued, "We managed to keep them out for a couple of days. They found a way in. I don't know if it was instinct or if they were just smart. We managed to kill one and stored it in the cargo hold to show everyone back home. Slowly, they managed to take out the rest of my crew." He pointed at the camera and stated, "I want the record to reflect that I had the best damn crew out here. They are all heroes in my book. They all died doing what they loved." In a lower voice, he remarked, "They all died because of me." He leaned back in his chair, took a deep breath, puffed on the cigarette, and said, "Once the crew was gone, I just locked myself in my cabin. I didn't know what to do. You see, this ship required five people to fly. I was the only one left. Did I think about killing myself? I sure the hell did! There was no way I would let those things have me for a meal. I almost did when suddenly I had a thought. If I died, then I would dishonor the memory of my crew. I wondered if I could reroute controls so I only needed one person to fly this ship? After all, many newer ships only needed one person to fly them. I'd have all day to work on it. First, I would need a good place to hide during the night. I made a panic room in my cabin out of anything I could find. I stocked it with food, water, and lots of light. I discovered these things hated the light. Now, I had everything I would need to survive. The next thing was to figure out where to make the changes so I could fly out of here. I worked for days and got into a routine. I would get up. Watch the aliens move back underground, work on the ship, and return here until they come out at night."

He stopped again and took another sip of his drink. "I kept this up for…. umm…several weeks. One morning, I was having my morning drink and looked out the window, watching those things go back underground like I always did. I glanced up, and I saw them. It was a rescue party. They found me. Before I could react, those bastards saw them and attacked. All I could do was watch while those things tore them apart." He stopped for a moment with tears rolling down his face.

He took another puff of his cigarette. He slammed his fist down on the desk. His voice began to tremble as he mumbled, "More blood on my hands. One decision has caused so much loss of life." He wiped away the tears and cleared his throat. "The image of them being ripped apart was burned into my mind. I had trouble concentrating on work, so I came back to my quarters early. I stared out the window as the light started to fade away that day. I had to look twice, but there were more people approaching the ship with flashlights. There was no way I was going to watch this happen again. I grabbed my weapons, lights, and jacket and ran out of the ship. The attack had already begun before I got there. This group was armed and fighting back. I got there and joined in. I managed to get three of them and started back to this ship. By the time we got to this ship, two more were dead, and the remaining one was wounded."

At times, it seemed like his mind wandered off, but he continued. "It was good to have someone to talk to. Over the next week or so, I got to know her. It turned out she was the Captain of the Nightingale. I heard of that ship. Further repairs and modifications on my ship were no longer needed. We planned to run up the crater to her ship and get off this frozen hell." In the background of the video, the howling and scratching was starting. "Well, it is late, and those things are beginning to arrive, and we plan to run up the crater in the morning. I have the blood of two crews on my hands. If you are watching this, leave this place. Get off this planet while you still can." He walked away, and the video stopped.

I looked at the Captain, and Lisa turned the video up. I thought momentarily and therized, "That would explain how he got up there. I am guessing since he made it up there wounded, she must have been killed along the way."

"That's the same conclusion we came to," answered Mike.

"I'm going to need your report of what happened down there as soon as you feel up to it. I know there may be some gaps in your memory due to the head injury, but do the best you can. In the meantime, get some rest. We miss you on the bridge," stated the Captain with a smile.

We continued to chat about the wedding when we got back home. For the first time in my life I was happy. I had both my mother and father and wife to be here like one happy family.

✳✳✳✳✳✳✳✳✳✳✳✳✳✳

Kellie

Lexey walked up behind me, standing at the door watching Sam and Lisa. Lexey looked in to see that I continued to watch Sam.

"I know what you tried to do to Lisa on the Discovery," Lexey said.

"What are you talking about?" I asked.

"You tried to kill Lisa and make it look like the creatures did it," replied Lexey.

"I don't know what you're talking about," I said nonchalantly

"You tried to get rid of Lisa to get Sam back," remarked Lexey.

"I would never do anything like that," I said as I looked into her eyes.

"When we went into that room to get away from those creatures, Lisa was right behind me. Yet somehow, you got in there before her. She was the last one in and got hurt," stated Lexey

"I guess she was just slower than me," I remarked without any feeling.

"You just wanted her out of the picture so you could have Sam," Lexey theorized.

"Maybe you want him, and you are making this up. I've seen how you look at him. He will never want to be with you. Besides, it's a long trip home, and a lot can happen."

"Consider yourself warned. I'd advise you to find a new ship when we get home. I'm going to keep an eye on you." Lexey stated in a stern voice before she left.

"Yes, it's going to be a long trip home," I said as I looked back at Sam, smiled, and walked away.

Daniel has lived in Ohio all of his life and worked as a computer field technician. When he was younger, he was asked to write for his High School paper a year earlier than those in his class. He entered a writing contest for a local weekly newspaper. He won first prize, thus becoming a stringer reporter for that newspaper for the next three years. The passion for writing began with short stories turning into full manuscripts. He enjoys writing and finds it relaxing to immerse in the stories his mind has created.

Printed in the USA
CPSIA information can be obtained
at www.ICGtesting.com
JSHW051928040524
62238JS00001B/1

9 798869 280060